"An in...

You will not want to put this down"
LAINI TAYLOR

"Keeps you on
tenterhooks
as the action unfolds"
ELLE

"Carey writes with
compassion and fire"
LAUREN BEUKES

"Enigmatic and
utterly gripping"
HARPER'S BAZAAR

"Heartfelt, remorseless
and painfully human ... a jewel"
JOSS WHEDON

"If you only read one novel this
year, make sure it's this one"
MARTINA COLE

By M. R. Carey

The Girl With All the Gifts
The Boy on the Bridge

Fellside

Someone Like Me

By Mike Carey

Felix Castor
The Devil You Know
Vicious Circle
Dead Men's Boots
Thicker Than Water
The Naming of the Beasts

M. R. CAREY

SOMEONE
LIKE ME

www.orbitbooks.net

First published in Great Britain in 2018 by Orbit

1 3 5 7 9 10 8 6 4 2

Copyright © 2018 by M. R. Carey

Extract from *A Boy and his Dog at the End of the World* by C. A. Fletcher
Copyright © 2019 by Charlie Fletcher

The moral right of the author has been asserted.

Bellows, "For Rock Dove" (lyrics © Oliver Kalb), from the album *Blue Breath*

A CIP catalogue record for this book is
available from the British Library.

ISBN 978-0-356-50949-5

Typeset in Bembo 11.25/15 pt by Palimpsest Book Production Limited,
Falkirk, Stirlingshire
Printed and bound in Great Britain by Clays Ltd, Elcograf S.p.A.

Papers used by Orbit are from well-managed forests
and other responsible sources.

Orbit
An imprint of
Little, Brown Book Group
Carmelite House
50 Victoria Embankment
London EC4Y 0DZ

An Hachette UK Company
www.hachette.co.uk

www.orbitbooks.net

To Ted and Pel, Mammoth and Vole, Billy, Silly and Lily and Mival —
our other selves

a prayer for a life not lived
to dignify screaming till you can't anymore
so ashamed of the love you carry
the crowded rooms where you speak the dark side of
    your heart

what if like geese we could migrate, migrate
to a place no one follows?

                    Oliver Kalb, from Bellows' "For Rock Dove"

Maybe this is on me, Liz Kendall thought as she tried in vain to breathe. A little bit, anyway. For sure, it was mostly the fault of her ex-husband, Marc, and his terrifying temper, but she could see where there might be a corner of it left that she could claim for herself. Taking responsibility for your own mistakes was important.

It was Marc's weekend with the kids, and he had brought them back late. Except he hadn't really brought them back at all. He had left them outside, in his car, and had come inside to tell Liz that they were going to grab some dinner. You know, since it was already so late and all.

Hell, no.

Liz had surprised herself, speaking up for her rights and the kids' routine, reminding Marc (which he knew damn well) that tomorrow was a school day. She had been overconfident, was what it was. She had lost the habit of victimhood somewhere, or at least temporarily mislaid it. Forthright words had spilled out of her mouth, to her own astonishment as much as Marc's.

But Marc had some words of his own once he got over the surprise, and the argument had moved through its inevitable phases: recrimination, rage, ultimatum. Then when there was nowhere left for it to go in words alone, it had moved into actions, which speak louder. Marc had grabbed Liz by the throat and slammed her backward into the counter, sending the bags of groceries she had laid in for the kids' return cascading down onto the tiles.

"I'm going to fix you once and for all, you fucking bitch!" he roared into her dazed face.

Now she was down on the floor among the spilled foodstuffs and Marc was kneeling astride her, his teeth bared, his face flushed with effort, his wild eyes overflowing with hate. As Liz twisted in his grip, trying to open a passage from her windpipe to her lungs, she glimpsed a box of Lucky Charms on her left-hand side and a bottle of Heinz malt vinegar on her right.

Egyptian pharaohs sailed into the afterlife in reed boats piled with all the treasures they'd amassed in their lives. Gold. Jewels. Precious metals. In heaven, Liz would have condiments and breakfast cereal. Great, she thought. Wonderful.

Darkness welled up like tears in her eyes.

And that was when the iceberg hit.

Hard.

It hit her from the inside out, a bitter cold that expanded from the core of her body all the way to her skin, where it burned and stung.

She saw her hand, like a glove on someone else's hand, groping across the floor. Finding the vinegar bottle's curved side. Turning it with her fingertips until she could take hold of it.

Her arm jerked spasmodically, lifting from the ground only to fall back down. Then it repeated the motion. Why? What was she doing? No, what was this rogue part of her doing on its own behalf? Now that it had a weapon, why wasn't it even trying to use it?

A wave of glee and fierce amusement and anticipation flooded Liz's mind as though her brain had sprung a catastrophic leak and someone else's thoughts were pouring in. Stupid. Stupid question. She was *making* a weapon.

Three times is the charm. With the third impact, the bottle smashed on the hard tiles. The vinegar seeping into her lacerated skin made Liz's dulled nerves twitch and dance, but it was a dance with no real meaning to it, like that strange event she had seen once when she picked Zac up from his school's summer bop: a silent disco.

She drove what was left of the bottle into the side of Marc's face as hard as she could.

Marc gave a hoarse, startled grunt, flicking his head aside as though a fly or a moth had flown into his eye. Then he screamed out loud, reeling backward as he realized he was cut. His hands flew up to clutch his damaged cheek. Pieces of broken glass rained down onto the floor like melting icicles after a sudden thaw.

Some of them had blood on them. Liz's stomach turned over when she saw that, but it was as though some part of her had missed the memo: satisfaction and triumph rose, tingling like bubbles, through her nausea and panic.

That surge of alien emotion was terrifyingly intense, but in other ways normal service was being resumed. Liz's arms dropped to the floor on either side of her as though whatever had just taken her over had flung them down when it was done. The prickling cold folded in on itself and receded back into some hidden gulf whose existence she had never suspected.

Liz sucked in an agonizing sliver of breath, and then another. Her chest heaved and spasmed, but the sickness of realization filled her quicker than the urgent oxygen, quicker even than the over-powering smell and taste of vinegar.

What she had just done.

But it was more like what *someone else* had done, slipping inside her body and her mind and moving her like a puppet. She hadn't willed this; she had only watched it, her nervous system dragged along in the wake of decisions made (instantly, enthusiastically) elsewhere.

Liz tried to sit up. For a moment she couldn't move at all. It felt as if she had to fumble around inside herself to find where all her nerves attached. Her body was strange to her, too solid and too slow, like a massive automaton controlled by levers and pulleys.

Finally she was able to roll over on one elbow, her damaged hand pressed hard against her chest. She watched a ragged red halo form on the white cotton of her T-shirt as the blood soaked through, conforming sloppily and approximately to the outline of her fingers. A year-old memory surfaced: the time when Molly had painted around her hand for art homework with much more exuberance than accuracy.

Marc lunged at her again with a screamed obscenity, one hand groping for her throat while the other was still clamped to his own cheek. But he didn't touch her. Didn't get close. Pete and Parvesh Sethi from the apartment upstairs were suddenly there on either side of him, coming out of nowhere to grab him and haul him back. For a few seconds, the three men were a threshing tangle of too many limbs in too many places, a puzzle picture. Then Pete and Parvesh put Marc down hard.

Pete knelt across Marc's shoulders to pin his upper body to the ground, facedown, while Parvesh, sitting on his legs, took his phone out of his pocket to request—with astonishing calm—both a police visit and an ambulance. Marc was raving, calling them a couple of queer bastards and promising that when he came back to finish what he'd started with Liz he'd spend some time with them too.

"Lizzie," Parvesh shouted to her across the room. "Are you all right? Talk to me!" From the concern in his voice, she thought maybe he had asked her once already and she had missed it somehow in the general confusion.

"I'm fine," she said. Her voice was a little slurred, her mouth as sluggish and unwilling as the rest of her. "Just . . . cut my hand."

But there was a lot more wrong with her than that.

"Pete," Parvesh said, "have you got this?"

"I've got it," Pete grunted. "If he tries to get up, I'll dislocate his shoulder."

Parvesh stood and walked across to Liz. Marc struggled a little when he felt that his legs were free, but Pete tightened his grip and he subsided again.

"Fucking queer bastard," Marc repeated, his voice muffled

because his mouth was right up against the tiles. "I'll fucking fix you."

"Well, you could fix your trash talk," Pete said. "Right now, it doesn't sound like you're even trying."

"Let me see," Parvesh said to Liz. He knelt down beside her and took her hand in both of his, unfolding it gently like an origami flower. There was a big gash across her palm, a smaller one at the base of her thumb. Parvesh winced when he saw the two deep cuts. "Well, I guess they're probably disinfected already," he said. "Vinegar's an acid. But we'd better make sure there's no glass in them. Have you got a first aid kit?"

Did she? For a second or two the answer wouldn't come. The room made no sense to her, though she'd lived in this house for the best part of two years. She had to force herself to focus, drag up the information in a clumsy swipe like someone groping in the dark for a ringing phone.

"Corner cupboard," she mumbled. "Next to the range, on the right."

It was still hard to make all her moving parts cooperate—hard even to talk without her tongue catching between her teeth. She thought she might be drooling a little, but when she tried to bring her good hand up to her mouth to wipe the spittle away her body refused to cooperate. The hand just drew a sketchy circle in the air.

When your own body doesn't do what you tell it to, Liz thought in sick dismay, that has to mean you're losing your mind.

Parvesh got her up on her feet, the muscles in her legs twanging like guitar strings, and led her across to the sink. He ran cold water across the cuts before probing them with a Q-tip soaked in Doctor's Choice. They were starting to hurt now. Hurt like hell, with no fuzz or interference. Liz welcomed the pain. At least it was something that was hers alone: nobody else was laying claim to it.

Marc was still cursing from the floor and Pete was still giving him soft answers while leaning down on him hard and not letting him move a muscle.

5

"The kids!" Liz mumbled. "Vesh, I've got to go get the kids."

"Zac and Moll? Where are they?"

"In Marc's car. Out on the driveway." Or more likely on the street, parked for a quick getaway. Marc wouldn't have had any expectation that he was going to lose this argument.

"Okay. But not bleeding like a pig, Lizzie. You'll scare them shitless."

Parvesh was right, she knew. She also knew that Zac must be getting desperate by now, only too aware that the long hiatus with both of his parents inside the house meant they were having a shouting match at the very least. But she had made him promise never to intervene, and she had made the promise stick. She hadn't wanted either of her children to come between her and Marc's temper. In the years leading up to the divorce, protecting them from that had been the rock bottom rationale for Liz's entire existence.

Whatever happens between him and me, Zac, you just stay with your sister. Keep her safe. Let it blow over.

Only this didn't seem like something that was going to blow over. Liz could hear sirens whooping a few streets away, getting louder: repercussions, arriving way before she was ready for them. When she still didn't even understand how any of this had happened.

The iceberg. The alien emotions. The puppet dance.

The room yawed and rolled a little. Liz went away and came back again, without moving from the spot where she stood. One of the places she went to—just for half a heartbeat or so—was the Perry Friendly Motel. A suspect mattress bounced under her ass as Marc bounced on top of her and she thrust from the hips with joyous abandon to meet him halfway.

Okay, that was weird. That was nearly twenty years ago. What was she going to hallucinate next? A guitar solo?

The next thing she was aware of was Parvesh applying a dressing to her hand, bending the pad carefully around her open wounds. "What did he do to you?" he asked her, keeping his voice low so the conversation was just between the two of them.

Liz shook her head. She didn't want to talk about it because that meant having to think about it.

"You've got bruises on your throat. Lizzie, did he attack you?"

"I've got to go out to the kids," she said. Had she already said that? How much time had passed? Could she make it to the street without fainting or falling over?

Parvesh tilted her head back very gently with one hand and leaned in close to examine her neck.

"He did. He tried to throttle you. Oh Lizzie, you poor thing!"

Liz flinched away from his pity as if it were contempt. She had tried hard not to let anyone see this. To be someone else, a little bit stronger and more self-sufficient than her current self. And since she had moved into the duplex, she had felt like it was working, like she had sloughed off an old skin and been reborn. But here she was again, where she had been so many times before (although something strong had moved through her briefly, like the ripples from a distant tidal wave).

"How did it happen?"

"It's his weekend. I was just . . . unhappy because he brought the kids back so late. I told him not to." The kids. She needed to make sure they were okay: everything else could wait. Liz headed for the door.

But she still wasn't as much in command of her own movements as she thought she was. She stumbled and almost fell. Parvesh caught her and sat her down on one of the chairs. She noticed that there was a dark streak of blood across the blue and yellow polka dots on its tie-on cushion.

The back of her head was throbbing. Putting a hand up to feel back there she found a lump like a boulder, its surface hot and tender. When Marc knocked her down she must have hit the tiles a lot harder than she thought. Another wave of nausea went through her but she fought against it and managed not to heave.

More talking. More moving around. The kitchen floor was still rising and falling like the deck of a ship. Liz lost track of events again, feeling around inside herself for any lingering traces of that presence. Her interior puppetmaster.

The outside world came back loudly and suddenly with the kitchen door banging open and then with Marc bellowing from the floor for someone to let him up because he was being assaulted and illegally restrained.

"So what happened here?" another voice asked. A female voice, calm and matter-of-fact. Liz looked up to find two uniformed cops in the kitchen, a woman and a man. She closed her eyes immediately, finding that the light and movement were making the nausea return.

Marc was talking again, or yelling rather, swearing that he was going to sue the Sethis for every penny they had. Pete told him to make sure he spelled their names right. "It's Mr. Queer Bastard and Dr. Queer Bastard. We don't hyphenate."

"Her husband attacked her," Parvesh said. "That guy over there. Him."

"Ex-husband," Liz muttered automatically. She opened her eyes again, as wide as she dared. "The kids. My kids are . . ."

"We've got an officer with them right now, ma'am," the lady cop said. "They're fine. Is it okay if we bring them around by the front of the house? We don't think it's a good idea for them to see this." She nodded her head to indicate the smears and spatters of blood all over the kitchen floor, on the side of the counter, on Liz and on Marc.

Marc was sitting up now, his back against the fridge. The Sethis had retired to the opposite corner of the room but the man cop, whose badge identified him as Lowenthal, was standing over Marc and a paramedic was kneeling beside him, holding a dressing pad to his face. Blood was oozing out from under the pad, running along its lower edge to a corner where it dripped down onto Marc's shirt. It didn't make much difference to the shirt: you couldn't even tell where the drops were landing on the blood-drenched fabric.

The lady cop talked on her radio for a few seconds. "Yeah. Bring them through the front door and find someplace where they can sit. Tell them their mom and dad are okay and someone's going to be with them soon." She slipped the radio back into the pouch on her belt and looked at everyone in turn. "Suppose we run through this from the beginning," she said. "What exactly happened here?"

"She ripped my face open with a bottle!" Marc snarled.

"A vinegar bottle," Liz added unnecessarily. The lady cop turned to Liz and gave her a hard, appraising look. Her badge read Brophy. A nice Irish name. She didn't look Irish. She was blonde and wide-faced like a Viking, with flint-gray eyes. Maybe cops got Irish surnames along with their badges. Except for Lowenthal.

"Are you saying this is true, ma'am?" Officer Brophy asked. "You assaulted him with a bottle?"

"Yes," Liz said.

"Okay, you want to tell me why?"

I can't, Liz thought bleakly. I don't even understand it myself.

"He was on top of me," she said. "Choking me." It was absolutely true. It was also irrelevant. That wasn't *why* she'd done what she did; it was only *when*.

"Can anyone corroborate that?"

"Yes, ma'am," Parvesh said. "We saw the whole thing. We live upstairs. We heard the noise through the floor and ran down. The kitchen door was open, so we let ourselves in, and we saw Lizzie on the floor with this man—" He nodded his head in Marc's direction. "—on top of her. She's Elizabeth Kendall and he's her ex-husband, Marc. Marc with a *c*. He had his hands around her throat. We were so amazed that for a moment we couldn't think of what to do. We just shouted at him to get off of her. But he didn't stop. He didn't even seem to hear us. Then Lizzie grabbed the bottle up off the floor and swung it, and that was when we stepped in. Am I missing anything, Pete?"

"That's how it went down," Pete agreed.

"Look at her neck," Parvesh told Officer Brophy, "if you don't believe us."

"I didn't touch her," Marc yelled. "They're lying. She just went for me!"

Officer Brophy ignored Marc while she took up Parvesh's invitation. She walked across to Liz and leaned in close to look at her bare throat. "Could you tilt your chin up a little, ma'am?" she asked politely. "If it doesn't hurt too much."

Liz obeyed. Officer Lowenthal whistled, short and low. "Nasty," he murmured.

"How's the gentleman looking?" Brophy asked the paramedic. She shot Marc a very brief glance.

"He'll need stitches," the paramedic said. "They both will."

"You just got the one ambulance?"

"Yeah. The other one is out in Wilkinsburg."

"Okay, then you take him. Officer Lowenthal will accompany you, and I'll follow on with Mrs. Kendall. Len, you ought to cuff him to a gurney in case he gets argumentative."

"I'll do that," Lowenthal said.

"This is insane!" Marc raged. "Look at me! I'm the one who's injured. I'm the one who was attacked." He swatted away the paramedic's hands and pulled the dressing pad away to display his wounds. The eye looked fine, if a little red. The semi-circular gouge made by the bottle ringed it quite neatly, but there was a strip of loose flesh hanging down from his cheek as though Liz had tried to peel him.

"That does look pretty bad," Officer Lowenthal allowed. "You just hit him the once, ma'am?"

"Once," Liz agreed. "Yes." And hey, she thought but didn't say, that's a one in my column and a couple of hundred in his, so he'll probably still win the match on points even if he doesn't get a knockout.

She shook her head to clear it. It didn't clear. "Please," she tried again. "My children. I can't leave them on their own. I haven't even seen them yet. They don't know what's happening."

The two cops got into a murmured conversation that Liz couldn't catch.

"Well, you go on in and talk to them," Brophy said eventually. "While we get your husband's statement." *Ex-husband*, Liz amended in her mind. *Took the best part of two years to get that ex nailed on the front, and nobody ever uses it.* "They can ride with you to the hospital, if you want. Or if you've got friends who can look after them . . ."

"We'd be happy to do that," Parvesh said.

". . . then they can stay here until you get back. Up to you. You go ahead and talk to them now while we finish up in here."

"I'm making a lasagna," Pete said to Liz, touching her arm as she went by. "If they haven't had supper, they can eat with us."

Liz gave him a weak smile, grateful but almost too far out of herself to show it. "Thanks, Pete."

"I was attacked with a bottle!" Marc said again, holding fast to this elemental truth. "She shoved a bottle in my face!"

"You told us that," Officer Lowenthal said. "But she missed the eye. You got lucky there."

"I'm filing charges. For criminal assault!"

"Okay," Brophy said. "We're listening, sir. Tell us what happened."

Liz got out of there. She didn't want to hear a version of the story where she was the monster and Marc was just in the wrong place at the wrong time.

The trouble was, if she told the truth she had to admit that there *had* been a monster in that kitchen. She had no idea where it had come from, or where it had gone when it left her.

If.

If it had left her.

Zac and Molly were sitting on the sofa next to an impassive police officer with a Burt Reynolds moustache. They jumped up when Liz came into the room and ran to her, hugging her high and low at the same time. The cop gave her a nod of acknowledgment, or else he was giving them permission to embrace.

Zac's arms reached around Liz's shoulders, his head bending down to touch the top of hers. As soon as he hit puberty, Zac had started to grow like he'd drunk a magic potion, but he had yet to fill out horizontally even a little bit. Now, at age sixteen, he was a willow twig, where his father—shorter and broader and a whole lot harder—was more like the stump of an oak. He had his father's red-blond hair, though, where Molly's was jet-black and—just like her mom's—had less tendency to curl than a steel bar.

Molly had been born tiny, her five-pounds-and-one-ounce birth weight landing her right on the third percentile line, and she had stayed resolutely tiny ever since. Some of that was probably medical: severe bronchiectasis had played hell with her ability to latch onto the breast and feed, leading to a lot of broken nights and baby hysterics and a short-term failure to thrive that left a long-term legacy. At Moll's sixth birthday party, only a few weeks before, Liz had served up the cake on a set of bunting-draped kitchen steps instead of the dining room table so Molly wouldn't need to stand on a chair to blow her candles out.

But Molly was tenacious, and she had a way of being where she needed to be. Right now, she squeezed her way past her big brother to get a better purchase on her mommy. Her stubby arms closed around Liz's leg, where she held on like a limpet.

God, Liz loved them so much. They were the counterbalance for everything else, for the years of abuse at Marc's hands and the slow extinguishing of all her other dreams. Because of the kids, her life made sense and had a shape. A meaning. Because of them, she had never forgotten how to be happy, however bad things got.

"Are you okay?" Zac asked her.

"Mommy is okay," Molly mumbled into the back of Liz's thigh. "Mommy is fine." Molly seldom asked questions about the things that really mattered. Generally, she made categorical statements and dared the universe to contradict her.

"Mommy is," Liz agreed, giving them an arm each. Taking as much reassurance as she gave. In actual fact, her head was throbbing and it hurt her to breathe. Her mind kept rushing away at reckless speed and then lurching to a halt, again and again. Even if you ignored the fact that she'd just had some kind of psychotic episode, there were lots of ways in which the word *okay* was a loose fit on her right then. But she very much wanted Zac and Moll to not be afraid anymore, to believe the crisis was over.

"We had a kind of an . . . an accident in the kitchen," she said, trying to keep her tone light, "but everything's okay now."

Zac gave her a searching stare, reading in everything she wasn't saying. "Then what's the matter with your voice?" he asked. His gaze went down to the bruises on her neck and his eyes opened wide. "Oh, Jeez! Mom . . ."

"Everything's fine," Liz repeated firmly, with a meaningful glance down at the top of his sister's head. Molly's dark, spiky hair was quivering slightly, a reliable emotional antenna. "And don't curse, okay? I've just got to go to the hospital to get my hand looked at." She held up the bandage for them both to see—a much safer topic than the bruises. "I cut myself on a vinegar bottle, which is why I smell like a half-made salad. Zac, can you take Molly upstairs to Pete and Vesh's? They've said you can stay with them until I get back."

"I'll go with you."

"No, buddy, it's best if you stay here. You've both got school tomorrow and there's no telling how long I'll be gone. Plus I'll just be happier if I know the two of you are here. Together. This doesn't have to wreck your day."

Zac gave her a very intense look, indicative of all the things he wanted to say but couldn't because Molly the limpet was right there listening.

Finally, reluctantly, he nodded. "Call us when you're coming back," he insisted.

"I will. I promise."

Liz bent to pick Molly up, but the instant rush of wooziness told her that was a bad idea. Instead, she delivered a fleeting kiss to the top of her daughter's head and straightened again quickly. She led Molly over to the sofa and sat her down, the cop scooching out of the way to make room.

Molly's breathing problems, diagnosed before she was even born, made others—especially Liz—a little overprotective of her, but she was fiercely stoical on her own account when it came to physical hurt, picking herself up with a shrug after every fall. It was emotional upheaval that wrecked her, turning her into a tiny incendiary device packed with anxiety and woe. Liz wanted to give her five minutes of normality before she headed for the hospital. Zac knew what she was doing and played along, prompting Molly when Liz asked what they'd done with their day.

"You made a tower, didn't you, Moll?"

"I made a Lego tower. For Harry Potter and Ron and Hermione and some dragons from the dragon lands. And the roof lifts off so the dragons can come out."

"That sounds cool."

"It's very cool. I brought it back in the car so you can see it."

"And Jamie did your nails," Zac reminded her.

"Yes. Jamie did my nails." Molly held out her hand with the fingers extended. Her nails had been painted in five Day-Glo colors—the colors of the rainbow with indigo and violet missed out. Jamie was Marc's new partner, who had taken him in after he and Liz separated—soon enough and casually enough that Liz felt sure they must already have been having an affair. She'd done a good job with the nails, neat and even, and if nail varnish looked a little bit weird on a six-year-old it was still apparent that Molly was enormously proud and pleased.

"Lovely!" Liz exclaimed.

"It's like Princess Peacock Feather," Molly said. "She has all the colors. Yellow and pink and green and blue."

"Red and orange and purple too," Liz finished the rhyme. "Only you don't have pink or purple."

"Yes, I do!" Molly exclaimed. She held up her other hand, which had the rest of the spectrum and then some. Liz shielded her eyes, pretending to be dazzled. Molly giggled in delight.

"Did you read a chapter of your book?" Liz asked.

"Not yet."

"Do one now with Zac, okay? And take a puff on your nebulizer before you go to bed. I'll see you both in a little while. Be good."

"We're always good," Molly said with incontrovertible certainty.

"Molly is," Zac amended. "I'm chaotic neutral."

It was a roleplaying game joke, and Liz just about got it. "So long as you don't crit-fail on your SATs," she said. "Finish that test paper, okay?"

"Trust me," Zac told her. And Liz did, a hundred percent, so she didn't nag him any further. She kissed them both and withdrew.

Zac took over from her seamlessly. He kept Molly busy getting her reading scheme book, *Little Witch's Big Night*, out of her school bag and finding her place in it. When Liz got to the doorway and looked back at them, he mimed "call us" with his thumb and his pinkie finger. She nodded that she would.

15

She went back into the kitchen. She just about made it there on her own two feet. Then she had to lean against the wall for a few seconds while her gyroscope rocked and rolled and readjusted. The dizziness ought to have gone by now, surely? Maybe she had a concussion.

Could a concussion dislocate your brain from your body? Turn you into a passenger inside your own skin?

The crowd in the kitchen had thinned out. Marc and the guy cop, Lowenthal, and one of the two paramedics had left together in the ambulance. Parvesh had also gone, presumably upstairs to check on the lasagna. Officer Brophy was taking a statement from Pete, who was courteous but categorical. "Yes, I would totally say it was self-defense. He had his hands on her throat. He was trying to kill her."

Brophy asked Pete a couple more questions about where he was standing when he saw all this stuff and where Marc and Liz had been when he first came into the kitchen. Then she let him go, put her notebook away and turned to Liz. "We should go on over to the hospital," she said as Pete waved goodbye and made his exit. "Get your injuries looked at. Get them photographed too. This is most likely going to court."

"I have to get treated at the Carroll Way Medical Center," Liz said.

The cop looked doubtful. "Will Carroll Way even be open outside of office hours? I know for sure it doesn't have an emergency room. I'd better drive you over to West Penn."

Liz demurred. "Maybe I'll just leave it," she said. "I mean . . . I probably don't need the hospital anyway. I'll be okay. You could take the photos here, right?"

Officer Brophy had no time for that idea at all. "Look, Ms. Kendall, you need stitches in your cuts and you need to be checked for a concussion. Plus, to be honest with you, you'll weaken your position if you don't do this properly. Your husband's lawyer will say your injuries were trivial or maybe even invented. Take my advice and cover your ass."

16

But that was the point. Liz's ass was far from covered. "I've got a terrible insurance policy," she told the cop. "It's from my previous job. There's a co-pay unless I use that one place. I don't have the ready cash right now, and I can't afford to get into any more debt."

"Well, you're between a rock and a hard place, Ms. Kendall," Brophy said after a moment. "I can take the photos, sure, but I can't give expert testimony on your injuries. Your husband might walk on account of the evidence looking less robust than it should. Plus, you know, you really should get looked at. Suppose you've got internal bleeding or something? I mean, how much is the co-pay likely to be?"

"A couple of hundred, maybe," Liz hazarded. But it could be anything. The last time she'd used the policy was when Zac got a wisdom tooth removed, and the billing had been unfathomably complex. One damn form after another after another until she wanted to scream and rip the damn things up and turn the small print into smaller and smaller print until there was nothing left.

But there was no gainsaying Officer Brophy's point about the evidence trail. If there was something she could do to keep this from happening again, she had to try—and kick the financial fallout into the middle distance. "Okay," she said. "You're right. Let's go."

The cop drove her to the hospital in her city-issued Taurus, keeping up a breezy conversation throughout as though she thought Liz needed to be distracted from what had just happened. After the fourth or fifth time Liz called her "Officer Brophy," she told Liz firmly that her name was Bernadette. Beebee. She had been an officer for seven years, but had only been in Larimer for two of them. Before that her beat was Lincoln-Lemington, on the other side of Negley Run, which she said she missed a lot. "Nicer people there," she said, "which is not to denigrate, but you know. Sometimes if you live in a shithole the shit sinks into you a little bit."

At any other time, Liz would have jumped to Larimer's defense. She liked it here. Liked the urban farm, the shops on Bakery Square, the zoo. Liked walking over the bridge on a Monday evening to the Cineplex where they would pick up the staff discount and then, if she was feeling flush, she'd treat the kids to supper at the Burgatory (*best milkshakes in the US!*) or Plum Pan.

They had moved here way back when Liz got pregnant for the first time. Marc had hated the new house and the new neighborhood, a serious step down from South Oakland where they had been renting before. "How the hell do you bring a kid up in a place like this?" he had demanded rhetorically, throwing up his hands to indicate the house, the street, the whole damn shooting match.

"You make a home," Liz told him, with the *duh* strongly implied. And that was what she had done. Happily, even joyously, one day and one brick at a time.

The police car took a right onto Liberty without slowing down much. "Like rush hour," Officer Brophy growled. "Where the hell is everyone going at this time of night?"

It felt to Liz like a very fair question.

Her thoughts dipped into the past again, but it was the more recent past this time: the moment when she picked up the bottle and hit it against the kitchen floor. Three times. The violent exhilaration when she pushed it into Marc's cheek was disturbing enough, but that cold calculation was terrifying. She had smashed the bottle because if she had just swung it against Marc's face it would have hit with a dull clunk and he would have gone right on throttling her. So she had used the tiled floor to make the bottle fit for purpose. Whatever had been inside her, moving her, had read the situation, found the tools and executed a plan while Liz had been thinking about pharaohs and icebergs and imminent death.

The puppeteer had saved her. But she hoped more than anything in the world that it would never happen again.

A brief, hiccuping whoop from the police car's siren scattered her thoughts. A car mooching along in front of them pulled quickly to the right, out of their way.

"Sometimes they pretend they don't see you," Beebee said. "Can't make like they didn't hear."

18

Fran Watts clawed her way up out of a shallow, sweating sleep. Quickly, in a panic, as if she were scaling a ladder and something nasty was right behind her.

She came up fighting, scrambling backward, twisting to bring her legs up and kick her attacker right off the bed onto the floor before he could get a proper grip on her.

It took her a few seconds after that to realize there was no attacker. What she'd kicked was her pillow, on which her laptop had been propped when she fell asleep over her homework. The laptop had landed on top of the pillow, thank God. There would have been seven kinds of hell to pay if she'd broken it after her dad worked two months' overtime to buy it for her.

A siren. A siren had woken her. Fran blinked sleep-sticky eyes and tried to bring herself into the present, out of a miasma of broken images. In her nightmare she'd been back in the Perry Friendly. Bruno Picota was there too, which wasn't much of a surprise, but this time he'd shown up as a big, lurching mass of shadow with a knife in every hand. Which was a lot more than two hands.

The mood of the dream was still with her, sliming up the inside of her head. She looked over at the clock, which was a cat with big cartoon eyes that rolled back and forth. It was barely nine o'clock, and she wasn't due any more meds until eleven. After that, the night yawned, wide and pathless. She had had a nightmare before she had even officially gone to bed, which was a crummy omen for the next eight hours.

In the absence of chemicals, she went for the next best thing. She called out for Jinx, speaking her name in a whisper. Sometimes Jinx sneaked off to her secret den at night, but she always came as soon as Fran called her. Fran didn't even need to whisper: Jinx heard her just fine if she talked inside her head.

The little fox arrived at once, unfolding from the bottom of the bed as though she had been there all along. She looked immaculate, her fur sleek and groomed, and she was instantly alert. That was just one of the many advantages of being imaginary, Fran thought with a slight twinge of envy.

Jinx had two forms. Mostly she was a regular fox, slightly stylized and childlike but more or less realistic. But when she chose, she could put on her armor, stand up on her hind legs and be Lady Jinx, knight errant and champion of the queen. Seeing Fran distressed, she transformed at once, the armor enveloping her in a swarm of shiny motes before coalescing into its proper shape.

Fran! Jinx clapped a hand to the hilt of her sword and drew it halfway out of its scabbard. *What's the matter? Tell me!* The sword was called Oathkeeper, but in Jinx's high, slightly lisping voice it came out as Oatkipper. It was an enchanted sword. Fran couldn't remember what it did exactly, and she felt bad asking because it was something she ought to remember, but it was definitely magic.

She also didn't want to admit that she was yelling for Lady J just on account of another bad dream, so she made something up. "There was a siren out on the street, Jinx. Is everything okay?"

Without hesitation, Jinx sheathed her sword. Sword and armor disappeared again with the same sparkly effect that reminded Fran of a *Star Trek* teleporter (original series). The fox exited through the open window in a single graceful bound, her huge white-tipped brush whipping from side to side behind her.

Fran rubbed her eyes with the heel of her hand. She sat up, still fuzzed with sleep and with the nightmare-hangover. God, why now? Why did it have to be *now*? With pre-SATs looming behind a ton of homework and the Indian summer all hot and sticky and Tricia Lopez freezing her all the way down to zero about Scott Tam who she didn't even like.

Her laptop had moved. It wasn't in the mess on the floor anymore: it was over on her Ikea desk, propped open with her *Attack on Titan* screensaver playing. Not a good start. Fran stiffened and braced herself for worse.

Lady J climbed back in through the window.

It was a police car, Jinx said. *It went up Penn Avenue.*

Fran had known that already, of course. She could tell a police car from an ambulance siren, and either of them from a fire truck. You didn't grow up in Larimer without getting extensive lessons in siren taxonomy. But it was nice to pretend that Jinx could see things she couldn't, and go places all on her own. That she was real, in other words. If Jinx was real, then it didn't matter so much if Bruno Picota was real too. Oathkeeper's touch was like a burning brand to evil (or something). Jinx could take him.

Even though she was alone in the room, Fran rolled her eyes at her own embarrassing lameness. She had turned sixteen exactly one month earlier and she hadn't watched *Knights of the Woodland Table* in almost a decade. She knew it was crazy—the kind of crazy that was not okay—to be clinging to this kiddie stuff in the way she did. But then the nightmares weren't okay either. Especially if they were going to start coming out again when she was awake. She shot a sideways glance at the desk. The laptop was being all nonchalant and pretending it had never moved at all, but there was no point in pretending.

Very reluctantly, Fran reached up onto the shelf behind the bed and got down her journal. She eyed its anonymous navy-blue cover with disfavor. You again, she thought.

I can take care of that for you, Jinx offered, once more dropping a paw to Oathkeeper's jeweled grip.

Fran smiled in spite of herself. It was an appealing thought. "I wish, Lady J," she said. "But I need it in one piece."

She opened the notebook and grabbed a pen. *Had another nightmare,* she wrote. *About him. He was sort of a spider thing this time, with lots of arms. It was in the evening. I dozed off when I was doing my homework. First time that's happened in ages. Also, maybe I had a bit of a hallucination right after. Nothing too wild, just I thought my laptop was in one place and then it was somewhere else, but I'm supposed to write everything down so there you go. I was definitely freaking out for a while after I woke up.*

Dr. Southern insisted on the journal. He said the meds were all very well in their way, and certainly you couldn't argue with them if all you were looking for was a symptom-suppressant. But he also said you didn't get well by suppressing symptoms. You got well by understanding what made you sick in the first place. Hence the journal, which was where Fran was meant to write down all the things that came into her head with a view to panning them with Dr. Southern the next time they met up.

"Panning?" she'd repeated when he used the word the first time. "Like what movie critics do?"

"No, like what gold miners do—or used to do, back in the day. They had a pan with a sort of wire mesh in the bottom, like a sieve. They got handfuls of wet mud from river beds, put it in the pan and shook it out again through the mesh, hoping to find little nuggets of gold in there."

When Fran pointed out that they weren't looking for gold, Dr. Southern said they were. He said their gold was the truth. Then he apologized for how corny that was and Fran said yeah, he'd better be sorry.

She closed the journal and put it back on the shelf. She stayed where she was on the bed for a long time, picking at balls of fluff on the crocheted coverlet. Jinx stood guard, respecting her silence and trying not to break it.

22

The coverlet had nine big squares in nine different colors. It had taken Fran's mom two years to make it, and she hadn't quite finished it before she got too sick to sit up. After she died, Fran's dad, Gil, tied off the loose threads as best he could, but the unfinished corner looked like someone had taken a bite out of it. Fran always put that corner at top left so she would be facing it as she fell asleep. Somehow it made her feel a little bit closer to her mom, as though she might come back some day, pick up her crochet hook and her balls of wool and just take up again where she left off.

Fran's mom hadn't had much time for Dr. Southern. "You take what you can get, I suppose," had been Elsa Watts' sour verdict on that subject. Meaning that the psychiatric care Fran was receiving came from the legal liability part of Bruno Picota's medical insurance—a cheap-ass provision written into the small print of a cheap-ass policy. It was part of the settlement after Picota was found guilty of kidnapping and attempted homicide, but it came with strings attached. If Fran wanted to keep getting treated, she had to go to Carroll Way, which was a big walk-in clinic ten blocks south. Dr. Southern came in there twice a week and handled every psychiatric referral they got. There was an actual therapy unit at West Penn Hospital, but the Watts family couldn't get a piece of that action unless they paid for it themselves. That had been impossible even when Fran's mom was still alive. It was doubly impossible now that it was only Gil who was earning.

Fran could just cut loose, of course, and wing it with no chemical safety net at all. But her hallucinations came back hard and strong if she went off her meds, and in any case it was a requirement of her staying within the state school system that her condition should be "actively managed"—a typical piece of mental health doubletalk that Gil had duly translated for her.

"Means they've got to look as though they're doing something whether there's something to do or not."

"Like they even know what my condition is!" Fran had grumbled. That had been four years ago, when she transferred from

23

Worth Harbor Elementary to Julian C. Barry, and the monthly pilgrimage out to the clinic had started to feel like a heavy injustice.

"It will get better," her dad had promised her, and it had. She wasn't on Ritalin anymore and her risperidone prescription was down to a maintenance dose—only half what it had been back in what Dr. Southern called her acute phase. "And given how big you're growing, that means it's really about a quarter dose," Gil had pointed out. "Half the dose spread over twice the body mass. Or maybe three times the body mass, what would you say?" Which of course meant the discussion ended in a pillow fight because every time her dad hinted that she was fat it was Fran's part to pretend to be furious. In fact, she was skinny and getting skinnier, as though her fervid brain was a wick burning up her body's fat, but there wasn't much you could do with that that was funny.

Her dad had been right about things being better. And in a lot of ways, she knew, she was really lucky. She got all her care for free as part of the settlement, and all her meds likewise. That counted for a lot, since Gil's income was just enough to push him over the Medicaid threshold and his workplace policy didn't cover mental health. But she had been right too, when she said that Dr. Southern, along with all the other smiley white-coated men she'd had to talk to over the years, hadn't known what was wrong with her to start with and still didn't know now. For ten years, the diagnoses had wobbled all over the place. Dr. Southern had read them aloud to her once and more or less admitted that his predecessors had been throwing darts at a medical textbook and writing down every word they hit. Juvenile incipient schizophrenia. Schizoaffective disorder. Early onset paraphrenia. His own approach was to deal with each crisis as it came and hope they were just aftershocks from the big earthquake that had happened all those years before.

The earthquake named Bruno Picota.

Right now, though, Fran realized with a feeling of helpless

misery, the tremors were starting up all over again. Without even looking around her, she could feel it happening. The little glitches, the pockets of turbulence in the way things looked and sounded and even smelled.

She couldn't hide from it. Hiding from it wouldn't help. She raised her head and stared around the room.

Yeah, there it was. The middle square of the coverlet, which had always been bright red, was gray. Her little statue of a Chinese guy playing a flute, an unlikely souvenir from a vacation trip to New York, had turned into a lady with a fan. The chess position set up on her chest of drawers had gone from an endgame to a starting lineup.

The smell of honeysuckle coming up from next door's garden was suddenly a smell of roses.

The traffic sounds had faded, as though Lincoln Avenue had backed away from her house in a hurry when it noticed she was listening in.

Worst of all, when she saw her own reflection in the mirror, her thick black hair was standing up in a glorious, untamed Afro instead of the tight braids she had gone to bed with.

It was a lot, especially coming all at once. Fran, who had closed her teeth on her lower lip at some point, tasted blood in her mouth and realized that she had bitten down harder than she had meant to.

Jinx read her anxiety and jumped up on the bed beside her, instantly solicitous. *Fran, tell me what to do. Let me help.*

"Sorry, Jinx," Fran muttered. "I'm on my own on this one."

But that wasn't strictly true, was it?

Fran had an uncompromisingly realistic sense of her own abilities. She disliked letting other people do things for her that she could do herself, having found out the hard way that people would do everything if she let them. But by the same token, she didn't kid herself when the odds were against her.

She went downstairs. Jinx tactfully stayed behind. It fazed Fran a little to have her imaginary friend standing around in the background when she was talking to other people. The times when she needed Jinx the most were the times when she was alone.

She found her dad watching a Steelers game on the TV. Gil Watts had his own way of watching football, which was a kind of radically engaged stillness, leaning forward on the couch with a frown of concentration on his face and his bald head shining with sweat as though he was making all those runs and passes himself. Gil loved the Steelers more than almost anything else in the world. He had a ball signed by James Farrior in the living room cabinet next to the photo of Fran's mom whose frame was also an urn and contained her ashes. He felt that Farrior deserved to be considered the Steelers' best linebacker of all time, and part of the passion he brought to that argument came from the fact that Farrior, like him, was an African American man born in Chesterfield County, Virginia.

But the sight of his only daughter with blood trickling down her chin like a vampire disturbed in the middle of a meal made the game instantly irrelevant. Gil hit the remote, jumped up and crossed the room to meet her at a stride that was halfway to a run.

He put his hands on her shoulders and leaned in to inspect the damage. "What happened, Frog?" he asked.

"Changes," Fran told him, lisping a little because her chewed up lip was starting to swell.

Gil winced visibly at the word.

"When? Just now? Up in your room?"

Fran nodded. "And a nightmare too. I fell asleep over my homework and had a real stinker."

Gil pursed his lips, and the breath he'd been holding came out in a series of barely voiced pops—a habit he had when he was thinking something through and not committing himself to words until he'd found some.

"You want to go over to the clinic?" he asked Fran at last.

Another nod.

"Tomorrow?"

"Wednesday will do. There won't be anyone there tomorrow."

26

There would be plenty of people, of course, but Dr. Southern wouldn't be there and nobody else would be able to help her. Wednesday was one of the doc's two days at Carroll Way, the other one being Friday: if Fran was lucky she would be able to tack herself onto the end of his appointments for the day.

"So anyway, do you want to hang out for a while?" her father asked her. "Since you're here."

"Sure." Fran tried for an off-hand tone and missed it by a long, long way.

"Play cards."

"You think you can afford it?"

Gil laughed out loud. "Oh, that's fighting talk!"

He washed her face first, wiping the sticky blood away very carefully and tenderly as though she was a little kid again. He also painted the cut with a styptic pencil, a weird thing that looked like a stick of chalk and tasted of mint and raw bleach. It was meant to close and disinfect shaving cuts, but Fran had never met anyone other than her dad who used or had even heard of one.

That done, they got down to some serious gin rummy—with *Songs of Leonard Cohen*, Gil's favorite album, playing in the background. Fran had the run of the cards, which was far from unusual. In the space of an hour, the burden of Gil's debt to her rose from thirteen million dollars to seventeen million and a few odd thousands. They always played for reckless stakes.

"You want to go back on the higher dose?" he asked her at one point as he shuffled the deck for the next hand. His tone was carefully neutral. "You're sure?"

"I think so," Fran said. "I'll see what Dr. Southern has got to say."

Gil remembered the bad old days, presumably better than Fran did since she had been a smiling dingbat for most of them. He believed Dr. Southern was just waiting for the right moment to dose his daughter all the way back to placid imbecility. Fran let him put the blame on Dr. S because she was ashamed of how scared she was of the nightmares and the hallucinations. Ashamed

27

to still have Picota in her head after all this time—a huge, clotted mass of darkness like the gungy stuff in a blocked drain. So much of it, and so concentrated, that it spilled out of her mind and silted up the world with tiny impossibilities.

If the changes were coming back, then she had to inoculate herself against them. She needed to keep things real, even if that meant packing her head with shit and cotton wool. Even if it meant saying goodbye to Jinx for a while. She couldn't go back to mistrusting the whole world, watching everything out of the corner of her eye in case it became an enemy. If that happened, she was pretty sure she wouldn't survive.

Risperidone was a lesser evil. The chemical intervention was something she knew and understood. She didn't remember any too clearly what it had felt like from the inside to be smiling dingbat Fran. But she would go there if she had to.

As soon as they got to West Penn, before any actual treatment started to happen, Liz's wounds and the bump on the back of her head were photographed from every angle as evidence in an ongoing case. That was a lot less exciting and TV-movie-forensic than it sounded. Beebee just took the photos with her phone, having activated the time-stamp functions. Then a nurse put seven stitches in the bigger cut and taped a Steroplast strip over the smaller one.

Liz thought they might let her go home after that, but it turned out they were only getting started. They had to X-ray her chest to make sure she didn't have a pulmonary edema, and they had to take a soft-tissue X-ray of her throat. Then they wheeled her over to another department for an MRI scan. Literally wheeled her: they weren't going to let her walk anywhere until they'd ruled out concussion and something else called a TBI—an acronym they refused to unpick for her.

"You're doing okay," one of the doctors reassured Liz after she asked this question for the third time—as if all she wanted was reassurance as opposed to, say, actual information. "Most of the damage to your throat is just swelling and bruising. Your hyoid, which is a little bone that sits right here under your chin, isn't broken, and there's no vertebral fracturing."

"Lucky me," Liz said. Her voice came out as a croak. Her throat had started to ache badly in the car and it hurt to talk. The doctor was younger than she was, and she didn't want to give him a hard time. She did want an answer, though, so she gave it another try. "Look, what's this TBI? Please. Inquiring minds want to know." She smiled to take the edge off the insistence.

"It's a complication we see sometimes in cases like this," the doctor said. "Brain-related. It's not common, though. It would depend on how long your husband was actually applying pressure to your throat."

"Ex-husband."

"Ex-husband, sorry. Anyway, with strangulation there are a whole lot of collateral conditions we have to test for. I mean, even if we're pretty certain that everything's okay. There was a case last year where a man was discharged from hospital after a manual strangulation attack and he died a week later. That was because he got a heart attack, but the brain damage from the throttling brought it on." The doctor seemed to regret sharing this little anecdote as soon as it was out of his mouth. "Not that that's going to happen to you," he added hastily. "The odds are way, way long."

Never play the odds, a friend had told Liz once. Go into everything expecting the worst. Owning it like you already bought it. That way you had no beef and no regrets.

"So I'm guessing the B in TBI stands for brain."

"Yes, it does," the doctor admitted.

"And the T? Terrible? Traumatic? Tangerine-flavored? Just give me a clue."

"Traumatic, yes. Traumatic brain injury. But again, Ms. Kendall, you're not at risk. That guy I mentioned was in his sixties. You're clear on the MRI scan. Nothing weird in your tissue densities, no edematous masses. So unless you've got any reason to think you might have a brain injury . . ."

Liz hesitated. She didn't want to say it. She could imagine how it would sound if a lawyer stood up in court and read it aloud. But maybe what she had experienced was an obvious symptom of a known condition. Maybe if she didn't speak up it would happen again. Keep on happening. Get worse. Maybe she'd lose her mind and never get it back.

"There was one thing," she said in the same ridiculous croak. "I mean, there might have been something."

She did her best to describe how she had felt when her hand picked up the vinegar bottle and hit out with it. As though she was watching it happen rather than deciding on it and controlling it.

She had been in a band once. Briefly, in her early twenties. If anything, it had felt just a little bit like that: like the displacement you got when you were playing and everything flowed so seamlessly you kind of became a machine, the movement of your fingers on the strings like something flowing into you instead of out. Like you were a receiver, picking up whatever was out there. This had been like that, only without the euphoria.

The doctor heard her out, nodding from time to time to show he got it. He was professionally interested, but not alarmed.

"That doesn't sound like any kind of brain damage I ever heard of," he assured her. "Well, some kinds of right-hemisphere lesion maybe, but nothing you could get from choking or concussion. Has it recurred since?"

"No."

"There you go then. Trauma artifact, for sure."

The doctor asked her a few more questions. Had she ever experienced anything like this before? Did she have any sense right now that her feelings or her thoughts were not her own? Was there any residual tingling or numbness or paralysis of any part of her body? No, no and no, Liz told him.

"I think you're fine in that case. But I'll mark it up on your file. If the condition recurs, you should come in and maybe have a psych evaluation."

"Sure," Liz said, slightly reassured. "I will." That sounded like a good thing to do, if it didn't turn out to be an exclusion on her insurance. If Carroll Way did psych screenings. And if the bill for tonight turned out to be less than an arm and a leg. Which meant she definitely wouldn't be doing it because who was she kidding? The only treatment she could afford was crossing her fingers and hoping for the best.

They still weren't done. A male nurse took her on another wheelchair outing to yet another department where she was given a laryngoscopy. This was probably the most physically uncomfortable procedure out of all of them: in spite of the topical anesthetic they sprayed down her throat, she could still feel the optical filament scratching down there and the sensation gave her an unexpected surge of panic. She almost jumped up off the table, but a hand grabbed hold of hers and squeezed at just the right moment and she was able to keep it together.

The hand turned out to belong to Beebee. Liz was amazed to discover that the policewoman was still around. "Don't you have crimes to solve?" she wheezed. "I'm grateful, but I don't want to get you in trouble."

Beebee shrugged. "I wanted to make sure you were okay," she said. "Plus I didn't take your statement yet, and I didn't want to do it while you still sounded like Darth Vader choking on a peanut. But we can totally book another time, if you're not up to it."

"I can talk," Liz said.

"Okay." Beebee got out a tiny device that looked like a BIC lighter but turned out to be a voice recorder. She clicked it on. "Let's start with tonight and work backward. What time did your ex-husband roll up?"

Liz described the whole encounter concisely but fully. There wasn't all that much to tell. The only hard question was what specifically she had said to make Marc lose it. She found to her embarrassment that she couldn't remember. "When he's in that mood, it seems to make him mad that I'm talking at all. Like, I should just say, 'Yes, Marc,' and leave it at that. When we lived together, I'd sometimes go hours and hours without saying a thing."

"Candidly," Beebee said, "that sounds fucked up."

"Yeah," Liz agreed. "Hence, you know, *ex*-husband."

"But it took you a while to get to that point?"

Liz sighed. The breath caught painfully in her bruised throat. "It took me sixteen years. That's how long we were married."

"And he was like that the whole time?"

"No, it happened gradually. He was different when we were . . . you know. Courting. He could be an asshole at times, but everyone has their moments, right? And the rest of the time he was really sweet and attentive. Maybe a little controlling, but to be honest I had a hard time telling that from the attentiveness. The one thing kind of merged into the other. Like, he was interested in everything I did, which was nice, but he also had an opinion on everything I did, and sometimes it was that I should stop. I gave in too easily. I always do, I guess. And by the time I realized it was a pattern, it was hard to break out of it."

There was so much buried in that bald summary. When she first met Marc, she had still been the guitarist in a band called the Sideways Smile. They were only starting out, working bars and student venues, and music was much more of a hobby for her than a career, but still it had been a really important part of her life. Guernica, the band's lead singer, had been Liz's first and only girlfriend, an experiment that hadn't worked out at all but had still been earthshaking at the time. She was also the friend who had given Liz that piece of wisdom about owning the odds.

Marc didn't get punk rock, and he didn't like the rest of the band. Guernica, Villette and Jo hadn't liked him much either, and somehow between their strong antagonisms Liz had lost track of what she herself wanted and settled for what seemed to be the lesser evil. She had stopped doing gigs.

It wasn't the first surrender, or the last, but somehow it was the one that stood out. It was the first time Liz gave up something that turned out to have been a part of her own identity. A lot of surprising things faded away along with that punk rock persona: her self-confidence, her sense of humor, even part of her sex drive. The aggressive, unruly part.

On the other hand . . . the day she hocked her Fender American Standard with its customized V-shaped headstock so she could buy a crib and a playpen for her soon-to-be-incoming son, she realized that her center of gravity had shifted in any case. She hoped she would play again someday: she had kept her battered amp (nobody would have bought it anyway), her crappy little electronic tuner and the embroidered strap Guernica had made for her. But her attention for the time being was with the little jelly bean growing inside her. The jelly bean needed her in a way that rock and roll probably didn't.

"So your husband was psychologically abusive," Beebee summed up. "Did that ever turn physical?"

"Not then," Liz said. "But when we'd been together about five years—after I had Zac—he lost his job at Westinghouse. That was when the rot set in, I guess. He had this idea about setting up his own business. Kind of a courier thing, with bikes. Only you could also rent the bikes, so even if he wasn't carrying a lot of messages he could still make money. But he never managed to get a start-up loan. He'd spend weeks and weeks doing a business plan, then take it into a bank without an appointment and just sit there all day, asking if one of the managers would talk to him. Then he'd bring all the papers home again, burn them in the back yard and start over. It all . . . everything . . . just made him madder and madder."

It wasn't even close to being an adequate explanation. But even if she had a million words, Liz knew she still wouldn't be able to fill in the blanks. In the end there was no explanation. No way to build a bridge between the good times and the bad.

In the good times, they had sat curled up together on a second-hand sofa, watching old movies and inventing new dialogue for them, giggling like kids. Before that, when he was still a secret from Liz's parents, they met up at cheap motels (the cheapest they could find) for sex that felt thrillingly illicit rather than grubbily compromised. God, she had been so horny that first year—and before it, come to that. But never after.

Later on, it was Marc who cut Zac's cord, at the midwife's invitation, and laid his newborn son reverently on Liz's chest to take his first meal.

After Molly was born, all four of them would spend Sunday mornings at their tiny garden plot next to the urban farm. Until she could walk, Molly sat in a papoose strapped to Marc's back, good as gold while they worked. When she could walk and talk, she joined them, singing "I help you!" as she waddled around the tiny plot of ground with a tablespoon to use as a trowel.

The change was probably gradual, but it seemed in retrospect to have hit as suddenly as a traffic accident. Marc stopped playing with the kids. Embargoed the garden plot. Had no time for movie nights. He would spend his evenings sitting and staring at nothing, his head tilted back as though all his failures were piled up in front of him so high he couldn't see over the top of them. Liz couldn't bear to see him like that. She had tried to help, to comfort him, and that had been the wrong move. So, so wrong. It gave him something closer to concentrate his bitterness on: something he could actually reach out and touch.

He had reached out and touched her in ways she had not seen coming.

In their last months together, things had got to the point where just seeing her, just having her be in the same room with him, was a trigger. There was enough anger there to keep him filled up constantly: every outburst emptied him, exhausted him, but only for a little while. He'd cry and say he was sorry, and Liz would cry and forgive him. And then he'd start building up to the next one.

And at the same time, Liz had been reaching a point where all her arguments for staying with him failed her, one by one.

He'll come out on the other side of this. But he never would. Once you give yourself permission to treat the person you're supposed to love like shit on your shoe, you don't ever rescind that permission.

The more you do it, the more momentum you seem to get from having done it before. The benchmark keeps moving further and further, and there isn't any end point except the obvious one.

If you love him, you've got to see him through the bad times. But the bad times were bad for both of them, and part of Marc's sickness was claiming all the grievance for himself. That didn't leave a role for her except as one of the things that were turning out bad.

We've got to stay together for the children's sake. That one was the last to go, but it went at last on the night when he dragged Molly upstairs by her arm and shut her in her room because she was playing too loud and he couldn't think straight. Liz could have borne anything if the kids were okay, but the kids needed to be saved from Marc too. Zac in particular needed to be saved from his influence, from having that poisonous macho pantomime in his line of sight every day of his life until it sank into his soul and curdled him like milk.

"Did you file for full custody?" Beebee asked. She was sticking to the procedural stuff, steering clear of the barbed wire entanglements of old feelings.

"I did," Liz said. "Yeah. And there was sort of a history. Hospital visits. Times when neighbors called 911. Times when he'd left marks on me. There was an evidence trail, you know? But Marc is . . . He's plausible. Likeable, even. And his sister paid for him to get a decent lawyer whereas I had court-appointed counsel and he didn't read up on anything before the day. A lot of the statements and evidence I'd collected got disallowed, and the judge decided that the kids needed a dad as well as a mom. So . . ."

"So you've lived with this bullshit ever since."

"Exactly. Well, no, it's mostly been okay. He gets Zac and Molly two weekends a month, and he seems to try his best to give them a good time when they're with him. And he met someone, a woman named Jamie Langdon. I think she's been good for him. She makes jewelry. And she's studying web development at CCAC. She's in her second year."

"That's great," said Beebee noncommittally. Liz realized she had gone without a break from talking about her own life to talking about Marc's. When they were together she had done that all the time, as though she was the starting act and he was the main event. This wasn't something she could blame Marc for, it was a fault line in her—an instinct for surrendering to a more powerful personality that was probably part of what had drawn her to him in the first place.

And yet, with other boyfriends, she had been confident. Had taken control and shown them what she wanted. And punk rock Liz, Sideways Smile Liz . . . well, she hadn't taken any shit from anyone. Where had that gone? It was as though Liz had had the potential to be someone else entirely. Then Marc had come along and locked into place in her life, in her mind, as if he belonged there. But in so many ways he was a piece from out of the wrong jigsaw.

"I think I wore you out," Beebee said into the lengthening silence. "I'm gonna leave it there for now, and maybe come back to you with another round of questions after I've put your statement up next to your ex-husband's and measured the gaps. Not that I think his story will make a difference to the legal situation, but you know. We have to talk to all sides."

"I understand."

"I'm happy to stick around a while longer if you want me to. I mean, if it would make you feel safer."

"No," Liz said. "I'm fine, Officer Brophy. Thank you for everything."

Beebee tore off a sheet of paper from somewhere, wrote a number on it and handed it to Liz. "It's Beebee," she reminded her. "The first number there is my personal cell and the other one is the number for the precinct. If your husband comes back around, just give us a call. If you even see him in the neighborhood, call me or call the department—either way works. He'll make bail, I have no doubt, but that doesn't mean you've got to be scared the whole time in case he turns up for round two."

"Thanks," Liz said, meaning it. "Thank you, Beebee."

37

Officer Brophy took her leave. Liz was hoping to get away herself now, but there was another long hiatus while the hospital's pharmacy rustled up the meds she had been prescribed, which were mostly painkillers and anti-inflammatories plus a foil pack of temazepam in case either physical discomfort or stress gave her insomnia. She took the opportunity to call Zac, with a pang of guilt because she'd left it so late.

He was fine, he told her, and so was Molly. They had spent the evening upstairs, first of all having dinner with Vesh and Pete and then watching what Zac called "a really, really super-old movie" with them. It turned out to be *Strike Up the Band*.

"Well, you know, gay guys and Judy Garland . . ." Liz commented.

"Who's Judy Garland?"

"I never felt like I neglected you until now, Zachary. We'll have a Judy Garland season next week. *Wizard of Oz. Babes on Broadway. Meet Me in St. Louis.* We can eat dinner in front of the TV for a few nights for the sake of culture. Is Molly still awake?"

"No. I put her to bed at ten. That's way late for her. She's gonna be wiped in the morning."

"I know. If she's too tired to get out of bed, I'll take her into school a little later. I'm not starting my shift until noon. What about you?"

"I'm fine." A pause. "Mom, we can't keep doing this. Dad's an asshole and I don't want to stay with him anymore."

Liz hesitated, somewhat conflicted. She had tried hard never to criticize Marc in front of the kids, separately or together. But it felt like that ship had finally sailed. "I don't want that either, Zac," she said. "Whenever you're over there I count the minutes until you're back with me. I'm worried the whole time in case he . . ." She tried to find a way of saying it that didn't sound melodramatic.

"He never touches us. It's just the things he says. The way he is. Even Jamie sees it. She spends half the time apologizing for him and the other half telling him to shut up."

Liz contemplated that sentence, amazed and chagrined. Her own conversations with Marc had never gotten close to such a frank exchange of views. Jamie must have something she didn't. Balls, maybe. Or self-respect.

"We'll have to see what happens in court," she said. "Maybe you'll see less of him now."

Especially if he does time for assault.

"Can I talk? In court, I mean? Can I say what I think of him?"

Her instincts recoiled from that proposition. Even if Marc's rights of access were curtailed, there was no way of cutting him out of their lives altogether. And *say what I think of him* sounded kind of irrevocable.

"I don't know," she temporized. "I'll ask. But most likely it will just be about what happened tonight."

"It should be about everything. It should be about us as a family."

She could tell by Zac's tone that the *us* in that sentence took in himself, his sister and her and left Marc and Jamie off somewhere else. She was a little ashamed of how happy that made her. Whatever Marc had done to her, Jamie seemed to be a sweet girl and it sounded like she was fighting the kids' corner when it needed to be fought. She didn't deserve to be landed in the middle of all this.

"We'll be a family no matter what happens," she promised. "I love you, Zac."

"Love you, Mom."

"I'll be home soon. But don't stay up."

"I am definitely staying up," he told her.

But when she finally got in at around 11:30—having taken two buses, because it turned out they only let you ride in an ambulance if you actually needed one and not having the cab fare didn't count as a reason—he was asleep on the sofa in the family room. She tiptoed past without waking him, then tiptoed back to put a blanket over him and woke him anyway.

"Hey, Mom," he murmured, rubbing the sleep out of his eyes in a way that made him look much younger than his sixteen years.

"Hey. You look like mice made a nest in your hair then moved to a better neighborhood."

Zac grinned reluctantly. He had never been able to resist the challenge of a *yo mama* contest with his actual mom. "You look like someone scooped out your face with an ice cream scoop, turned it upside down and put it back in," he riposted. Then he said, "I want to know what happened. All of it."

So she told him, speaking very low so as not to wake Molly. He held her hand while she talked, and after she'd finished they hugged for a long time, their foreheads touching.

"You remember that story you told us?" he asked her. "About when you were in the band, and you bought that crazy effects unit?"

Liz had to think for a moment. More recent memories loomed large enough to blot out everything else. She laughed when she remembered. "The Strange Device," she said. "Sure."

What made that a story was that the Strange Device had been given to her by a devoted fan who said it would revolutionize her playing. It was suitcase-sized and opened like a cupboard. Inside it were four foot-pedals that could be locked down by stepping on them once and released again with another tap of the foot. There were also lights around the edge of the case that pulsed rhythmically whenever the damn thing was turned on. The effects were awful, but Liz had carted the stupid thing from venue to venue and displayed it prominently onstage because the guy who gave it to her was sure to come and see the Sideways Smile play at least one gig in three. She just couldn't bear to break his heart.

"You said you nearly got a hernia carrying that box around," Zac reminded her.

"It's true. It weighed a ton. Are you drawing an analogy here, Zac?"

"I guess I am."

"About the overuse of electronic effects in rock music?"

"About ditching something if it's doing you no good and even hurting you."

He was staring at her very hard and very seriously. She leaned in and kissed him on the forehead. "Your dad's not going to hurt

40

me again," she told him. "I won't let him. You've got my word on that."

"Okay."

"Okay then. Go. Sleep. You'll be a zombie in the morning."

"I love you, Mom."

"And I love you," Liz said. "You and Moll are my whole world." It was the simple truth. There was nothing she wouldn't do to keep them safe and to keep them together.

Zac went off to bed at last, visibly staggering, and Liz went into the kitchen to clear up the mess there. Zac had picked up all the fallen groceries, but he was deathly squeamish and hadn't even attempted to tackle the bloodstains on the floor or the furniture. Seeing them again now brought the whole experience back to Liz with terrifying clarity. The feeling of being a passive observer of her own body, forced into the passenger seat as it moved of its own accord.

Was she going mad? Or just trying to duck the responsibility for what she'd done? But that made no sense because she didn't regret it. She was absolutely certain she would be dead now if she hadn't hit back at Marc when she did. She couldn't conceive which part of her had found the strength to resist him, but she wasn't trying to get any distance from it. God, she wished it had shown itself sooner. A whole lot of bad shit might never have happened.

But then again, neither would Zac and Molly. Whatever she thought of the choices she made, they were the counterbalance that kept her from wishing for what might have been. Any world that didn't have them in it wasn't worth living in.

The second time was different.

Liz had been afraid at first, and very much on her guard, but three weeks of business as usual had disarmed her fears. Her cuts had healed nicely. Beebee had called to say that the police were pressing charges of assault against Marc. He was remanded on a bail bond of twenty thousand dollars, the money having been posted by one J. Langdon.

Jamie. Standing by her man.

The next day, Liz had gone down to the precinct building to review her statement with a lawyer named Jeremy Naylor, who worked in the county attorney's office. She was amazed at how young Naylor looked: he had peach fuzz hair and the baby face of an innocent untouched by the world. But his questions showed a keen mind applying itself with complete concentration to a congenial task. When they were done, he said he would have a court date arranged by the end of the week.

That was the good news. He proceeded to give her the bad. "There's no way we'll be on the docket before October, Ms. Kendall, and that's optimistic. I don't like the thought of your ex-husband having ready access to you all that time. I think we should apply for a TRO—that's kind of an interim restraint order, issued on the basis of perceived risk. It's a long shot. The defense will argue that it's prejudicial, which, you know, they will have a valid point. But I'd like to give it a try all the same. For the sake of your peace of mind, and mine. Can you be free at short notice this week or next week? This will be a motion in judge's chambers, and it will mostly be based on the police paperwork, but you might still have to go in and talk about your past history with Marc if the judge asks for specifics."

Liz said yes, she could get the time off work. She would take it unpaid if she had to.

She went home feeling like her life was getting back on the rails. The doctor at West Penn had been right after all: everything that had happened had been a side effect of the assault she had suffered. A trauma artifact, as he put it. So long as she avoided being throttled and slammed into tiled floors, there was no reason it should ever happen to her again.

Everything was looking up. The weather had stayed fine. Molly had gone four whole weeks without an asthma attack. All three of them had watched *The Wizard of Oz* and the kids had been enthralled. True, Liz had had to work fourteen hours' worth of overtime to pay what she owed for her medical bills, but in her upbeat mood that had mostly been enjoyable. "I don't understand how you can smile like that when you're working the concessions stand," her colleague Bella had marveled. "You know you're gonna smell like burgers and fries all day, right?"

"Absolutely," Liz shot back. "And guys go crazy for that smell. I'll be getting more action than I can handle." She picked up a lettuce leaf from the fixings tray and rubbed it behind her ears. "There. That should bring the vegetarians to the yard too."

Bella guffawed and lowered the bar still further with a joke about why vegans give the best head. When Nora DoSanto, their supervisor, came by a few minutes later, she had to tell them to dial down the smut out of respect for the Pixar movie that was showing in screen three.

"Sorry, Nora," Liz said, still giggling.

"Sorry, boss," Bella echoed.

Liz felt like she was waking up after a long, troubled sleep. She even went back to doing the occasional volunteer shift at Serve the Homeless, which she'd stopped the previous spring when money and time were too tight and somehow never started again. She was back in the world, and the world made sense.

Then, like lightning out of a clear sky, she had another attack— and it was worse than the first.

It was a weekday morning, so Liz was dropping Zac and Molly off at school. Zac hit the ground running, taking off with a hurried "Bye, Mom!" as soon as she pulled up outside Julian C. Barry. No hugs or kisses. Public displays of affection with parents were kryptonite for teens, as Liz well knew.

At Worth Harbor, though, she took her time like always. She got to use one of the two disabled spaces right next to the front gate on account of Molly's chest. The alternative was to park round the back of the school, which was a long trek for Moll at the start of the day.

She walked Molly to the steps and knelt to give her a hug which was enthusiastically returned.

"You be good," she told Molly.

"I'll be very good," Molly said with her usual banner headline emphasis, "and get a star."

"Well, that would be great," Liz said. "But regular good is also fine. Nobody gets a star every day, kiddo."

"Bye, Mommy."

"Bye, baby."

Molly jog-trotted into the school. In spite of her condition, she never seemed to be content with just walking. Wherever she was going, she made sure she got there fast.

When Liz got back to her car, she found herself boxed in. Someone had parked a big black SUV side-on in front of both disabled spots. Liz waited a while, then finally went off in search of the driver, trying to repress a feeling of exasperation. Her shift at the cinema didn't start for another three hours, but she had a ton of stuff to do before then, including the week's grocery shopping.

Mrs. Hannah at reception did everything she could, which was basically to give a shout-out over the PA system to the car's owner, asking for them to come back and move it. Liz thanked her and went back outside.

The car was still there. Two women were standing next to it, talking in a very relaxed way as though they were there for the long haul. Liz walked up to them.

"Hi," she said. "Is this your car?"

The nearer of the two women turned and looked her over. Liz felt a little bit intimidated by that cool glance. The woman was a head taller than her, broad-built and statuesque. Her blonde hair had a sheen to it, as did the blue satin jumpsuit she was wearing. In fact, she was all-over glossy, as was her car.

"Yeah," she said. "What of it?"

"You've kind of blocked me in. Could you please roll forward a few feet so I can get my car out?"

The woman looked from Liz to Liz's very unglossy Kia Rio, and then back to Liz. "What," she said, "so I'm meant to believe you're disabled?"

Liz kept her tone neutral, suppressing her irritation. "My daughter is disabled. She's got a respiratory condition."

Jumpsuit lady looked at her friend, who fanned herself theatrically as though this was dramatic, late-breaking news. She was blonde too, but less emphatically so. There was a pecking order, clearly. "Okay," she said. "But it's not on your license plate, is it? So I guess you've got one of those placard things from the DMV. Show me."

"I'm sorry?"

"I said show me. Show me you've got the right to use that space."

Liz felt herself blush furiously, not with embarrassment but with anger. She didn't have time for this. But a shouting match would only waste more time, even if she had the stomach for it. Better to be the grown-up and let it pass.

At the same time, she didn't want to condone such shitty behavior or make it seem like she accepted it. As she took out her keys, she said, "I'm going to make a note of your registration and report this to the school. Just so you know."

The two women exchanged another glance, clearly not thrilled with this pronouncement. "So now you're threatening us," the jumpsuit lady said flatly.

"I'm not threatening you. I'm just saying. There are rules here."

"Sounds like a threat to me," not-so-blonde said. "This is a free country, you know."

"Yeah," jumpsuit lady agreed. "I'm within my rights to park here unless you got a placard. Which you didn't prove it, so here I stay until you do."

"You can't intimidate us," added not-so-blonde. "Anyone gets reported, sweetheart, it's gonna be you."

Liz turned and walked toward her car.

"Yeah," jumpsuit lady said. "That's right, bitch. Put up or shut up."

Liz's hand was raised to click the key and open the door. The blue DMV placard, stamped and up to date, was sitting right there on the dash.

But the thing inside her was quicker. It broke over her all at once, ice-cold, freezing her volition, taking her limbs away from her like a pickpocket.

Taking control.

Wait, Liz protested. *No.*

Her lips didn't move. Her breath didn't stir.

She turned around slowly to face the two women.

"Would you mind running that by me again?" she said with brittle courtesy. Only it wasn't her saying it. She just felt her lips move, heard the words coming out of her mouth.

"What, are you deaf?" jumpsuit lady demanded.

Her friend shook her head in a more-in-sorrow-than-in-anger kind of way.

"No placard, no can do," jumpsuit lady said. "Just the way it is. If you're kosher, it's all good. But if you're abusing the system, then you're gonna find out you picked the wrong—"

Liz was up in her face before she finished the sentence. "You know," she said, "I'm finding a little of you goes a really long way. So here's a thought. How about you shut the hell up right now before I shove my hand down your throat, drag out that little dangly thing at the back, the uvula or whatever it's called, and tie it round your neck tight enough to tourniquet the sucking wound you call a mouth?"

Jumpsuit lady's eyes went wide. "Hey!" she said, "you are way out of line. You can't talk to me like that. That's a threat. You threatened me!"

She tried to push Liz away, two-handed, but Liz leaned hard into the push and didn't budge. As before, she was watching all this happen, feeling it happen, but someone else was running the show and making all the decisions. Either that or her body was acting by itself.

Her hand came up as fast as a whip, pressing her car keys against the blonde woman's cheek just underneath her eye.

"Monocular vision is okay for most things," Liz said, "but it's for shit when it comes to depth perception. If I poke your eye out right now, the fist fight is going to be hilarious."

Jumpsuit lady gasped. Her friend reached out to grab the keys. Liz intercepted her without even looking. She took hold of the woman's thumb, left-handed, and bent it back. A surprisingly little pressure made the woman shriek with pain and drop to her knees. Liz's right hand, holding the keys, didn't waver by so much as a millimeter.

"Really?" she said. "You want to do this? I mean, look at little me and look at the two of you. I could scar you both for life and call it self-defense." Liz felt her lips curve into a grin, and she felt the intent behind it as a prickling rush across her own nerve endings. The thing that was moving her meant the grin as intimidation, but at the same time just . . . meant it. It was genuinely happy, genuinely enjoying this. Being in the driver's seat, making the decisions, was pleasurable. And the confrontation was pleasurable, for its own sweet sake. Laying down the law to these two sizeable adversaries. Being better than them, and knowing it, and proving it.

The woman whose thumb Liz was twisting whimpered, bowed down almost all the way to the ground.

"Oh, now that's a sweet sound," Liz said. "I want some more of that." Her wrist flexed. The woman on the ground gave a short, bleating squeal.

The thing inside Liz stared the jumpsuit lady down with cold joy. Liz wanted to take her own gaze out of that equation but she couldn't. Her eyes weren't her own.

"You're crazy!" jumpsuit lady protested.

"Not impossible," Liz said. "That's probably what I'll go with, anyway. I mean, if you decide to hide your ass behind a lawsuit, because that's the kind of pussy move a pussy bitch like you falls back on when she can't loudmouth her way out of trouble."

The blonde woman backed away. The key had left a bright red mark on her cheek. She got the door of her car open and scrambled inside. "Let Eileen go," she said. "We'll leave. We don't want to fight with you!"

"Then go ahead and roll your cunt-mobile the hell out of my way," Liz countered. "Eileen and me, we're bonding over an intense experience. She'll join you when we're done."

Jumpsuit lady started the SUV and moved forward about twelve feet in a series of bunny hops, too scared to keep her foot straight on the pedal.

"Eileen what?" Liz said in a mild, almost gentle tone.

"Garaldi," the kneeling woman gasped. "Oh God! Eileen Garaldi."

Liz cupped both of her hands around Eileen's one hand—a gesture that in other circumstances might have been a benediction. "Well, it's really nice to meet you, Eileen Garaldi. But just this once. If I ever see you again, my boot is going straight up your ass, okay?"

The woman whimpered again.

"Okay?" Liz prompted, squeezing just a little bit harder.

"Yes! Yes! Yes! Oh God, please! Let me go!"

There was a moment when it could have gone either way. The thing inside Liz, the puppeteer, was seriously considering breaking the woman's thumb. It was reluctant to let her—to let the both of them—just walk away with no real souvenir of the occasion.

No! Liz found some purchase at last. The ruthless, sadistic calculation gave her something to push off from. She flailed inside her own flesh, uselessly truncated, unable to find the point where her nerve endings connected to her floating, futile point of view.

But futile or not, it had an effect. The feeling of disconnection strobed quickly, off and on, her fingers twitching as they responded intermittently to her will. Liz fought to maintain that control, to push it further as the other part of her, the puppetmaster part, retreated. Its triumphant self-assurance was shot through now with doubt and anger. It hadn't expected this counterattack.

Liz flexed her fingers, surprised and overjoyed when they responded. She went for broke, dropping her arms to her sides so that the woman's hand slid out of her grip. Eileen Garaldi found her feet and scrambled away, her eyes full of tears and her cheeks red. "I'm calling the police," she yelled. "I'll sue you."

The puppetmaster wanted to lunge at her but Liz was pulling in the opposite direction. Caught between the two impulses, her body swayed a little on the spot.

"I seriously doubt it," Liz said. Liz's *mouth* said. "But go ahead if you want to. I'll see you in court. And in some other places that aren't so well lit."

The woman broke and fled for the passenger side of the SUV, which drove away with a melodramatic squeal of stressed rubber.

Liz staggered back to her own car, so weak at the knees she felt as though she was about to go sprawling full length on the asphalt. She got inside and just sat there for a while, eyes closed, until the last frigid remnants of that alien presence melted out of her.

I'm going mad, she thought. Or already there maybe, her will and consciousness broken into separate pieces that were at war with each other, that took turns to come out and play.

As before, she came back to herself by tiny increments. She didn't try to drive for around half an hour. There was no dizziness this time, no loss of balance, but the sense of dislocation was if anything even stronger than before. She needed to be absolutely sure her body would do what she told it to. She tried it out, one muscle at a time, putting it through its paces. Fortunately, there was nobody left in the parking lot to watch her. The school bell had rung long before and the other parents had all departed.

By the time Liz finally started up the car and eased it out into the street, there was no sign of the SUV. No sign of the police either, to her huge relief. For all she knew, though, there could be a general alert out for her by this time. She might get pulled over at any moment. She might get tasered and cuffed right there in front of her daughter's school.

Under the circumstances, she didn't feel up to driving around the block to the SuperFresh and getting in the week's groceries. She went home instead, and sat in the parked car for a while longer wondering what the hell she should do next.

She couldn't live like this. Nobody could.

Maybe hitting back against Marc and coming out of it in one piece was a gift horse she didn't want to examine too closely. But she had just picked a fight with two complete strangers. Assaulted them. Turned a pointless wrangle about a parking space into an armed standoff.

And even now, some small part of her—or maybe it wasn't small at all, but only (for the moment) far away—was thinking that she should have taken it further. Should have done some real damage to make absolutely sure those two impeccably shiny ladies got the point.

No, no, no. It had to stop. Had to. That voice had to be not just silenced but dug out of her brain and safely disposed of.

Liz went into the house at last and called the Carroll Way

Medical Center. She gave her name and her policy number and asked if she was covered for a psychiatric evaluation.

"Has it been recommended by a medical professional?" the receptionist asked.

"Not exactly," Liz admitted. "But I had . . . kind of . . . an accident last month. I went to West Penn. They probably sent along a summary of treatment or something?"

"They sure did, Ms. Kendall. It's right here on your file. But it's just a note, not an actual referral."

"So I'm not covered?"

"Well, let me talk to West Penn and have them clarify. I'll get back to you shortly."

After Liz put the phone down, she took stock. Her body was doing what it was told to again, but there was a kind of static fizzing along her nerves, as though they were still thrumming from that alien touch.

She locked herself in the bathroom and took a bath. The water was hot enough to be uncomfortable, but she deliberately topped it off every time it threatened to cool. She wanted to feel something, and to have the reassurance that it was her—really, undeniably her—that was feeling it. On an impulse, she dropped in a scented bath bomb that Zac had bought her for her last birthday. It turned out to smell of pretty much everything in the world in about equal quantities, but the sensory overload was exactly what she needed.

Half an hour later she emerged, dried and dressed and trailing clouds of intense floral fragrance. She went through into the kitchen to see what she had in the fridge and the cupboards that could conceivably lie on a slice of bread and pass for a sandwich. The food court was an expense she didn't need right now. While she was debating between peanut butter and Cheez Whiz, the phone rang again.

It was the receptionist at Carroll Way. "West Penn confirmed a case for treatment, Ms. Kendall," she said. "They just faxed over the paperwork and it all seems to be in order. You can see Dr. Southern.

All of our psychiatric referrals go to him. He comes in on Wednesdays and Fridays, and I think I can fit you in on Wednesday."

"Great," Liz said. "Thank you. Um . . . I hate to be a broken record, but what's the situation with my policy?"

"As this is arising out of a physical trauma that was covered, you get six sessions covered too. If you carry on after that you have to pay."

Thank you, nonexistent God! "That's great," Liz said. "Yes, please. Sign me up." She ran through her week's schedule in her mind. She had been intending to do a shift at Serve the Homeless on Wednesday, the only day when she finished early at the Cineplex, but she hadn't been back there long enough yet for Father Connor to build her into the duty roster. She wouldn't be letting anyone down. "You think I could get an appointment at the middle of the afternoon?"

There were a few seconds of silence, apart from the tap of an occasional key. "6:20 p.m. is the only slot I've got left."

Liz didn't hesitate. "6:20 p.m. it is, then. Thank you."

She finished making up her lunch and headed out for the Cineplex. Wednesday afternoon seemed like it was a long way away. The best thing to do until then was to put aside all thoughts of this and bury herself in the ordinary and the everyday. She felt a certain amount of trepidation—even dread—at the thought of describing what had just happened to a stranger. But mostly it would come as a relief. Saying it out loud would turn it into someone else's problem. Dr. Southern would tell her how to make it go away.

Gil Watts' hours at the fire department were meant to be nine to five, but he worked a lot of weekends and more than a few evenings. He was a systems inspector, which meant that he went wherever he was sent and stayed as late as he had to. The upside of this was that when he needed to borrow a couple of hours in the middle of the week he could usually swing it.

He was there waiting for Fran when she came out of school, leaning against the passenger side of the car so he could open the door for her and give her a heel-clicking bow as if he was her butler.

"Okay, Frog?" he asked her as she shoved her school bag down between her feet and strapped in. She waited a couple of seconds before closing the door so that Jinx could jump in and clamber over into the back of the car.

"Yeah," Fran said. "Fine."

Gil wasn't making small talk, and neither was she. He meant: did it come on again during the day? Had she had any hallucinations? And she was telling him that she had stayed within spitting distance of normal the whole day through, so yay!

Jinx curled up on the back seat. It occurred to Fran to wonder, just for a moment, why Jinx insisted on using doors and windows as though she was real but was content to ignore gravity and acceleration if they became a nuisance. Just because, she assumed. All of Lady J's rules had exceptions, and she herself was the exception to almost everything. She was a secret Fran shared with nobody, not even Gil. The cherished symptom that she needed just in order to function, so she cheated and didn't think of her as a symptom at all—even though Jinx came and went as she pleased and was only ever nominally under Fran's conscious control.

Maybe you're my symptom, Lady J said prissily.

"Pretty sure I'm not a fox dreaming I'm a little girl," Fran whispered, too low for her dad to hear. The thought made her smile in spite of herself.

Jinx snorted and curled up on the seat, pretending to be asleep. She was just being cranky because she didn't like Dr. Southern and hated when Fran had a session with him. Fran thought Dr. S was a good guy, pretty much, and did a tough job as well as he could. Jinx saw him as the enemy, which was only natural when you thought about it. He prescribed Fran medication that sometimes made Jinx not be there anymore. They were never going to be friends.

Gil had booked her a 5:30 p.m. appointment—her usual time, which she had agreed with Dr. Southern a long time ago. Dr. S put a lot of store by the healing effects of routine, as though sanity was something that could rub off on you. Fran was well positioned to see the flaw in this argument: she didn't spend a whole lot of time with the sane people at her school, or even with the other weirdos. She was the cat who walked by herself. But she appreciated not having to miss lessons and then play the enervating game of catch-up.

"Do you want me to sit in?" Gil asked her as he eased out of Negley Run into the heavier traffic on Washington. He made it sound like he didn't mind either way, although Fran knew how much he agonized about this stuff. He had been with her through the worst times, right after her abduction, and then again when she fell to pieces after her mom died. He had suffered along with her, hating that he couldn't protect her against all the horses that had already bolted and the stable doors that had hit her in the face. He often joked that he was a pencil pusher at the fire department, not a hero with a sooty face and a fire ax. "I'm not in the rescue business," he would say. But it killed him that it was always already too late for him to rescue his little girl. He would have died to do it, Fran knew.

But since he couldn't, it did no good to either of them to make him sit through her sessions. "Nah," she said as casually as she could. "It's just same old, same old. I guess he'll bump up my meds a little bit, and we'll be out of there."

"Yeah," Gil said, watching the road. "I guess." The corners of his mouth tugged down a little.

The waiting room at the clinic had exactly the same magazines it had had on their last visit, and the one before that. Gil picked up the May 2015 issue of *Car and Driver*, not for the first time, and read an article about a big, gleaming object called the Lambo Centenario. It probably cost more than he'd earned in Fran's whole lifetime.

Everyone sat together at Carroll Way in the one big waiting space, so there was nothing to indicate to anyone else that Fran was there to see a psychiatrist. Even so, she felt exposed and anxious, as she always did. She leaned back as far as she could in her chair so her dad and her dad's magazine shielded her from the outside world.

That usually worked okay, but today the outside world got a little pushy. Sitting right across from Fran was a boy she knew from school. Skinny. Sandy-haired. Paler than the average white dude by about three or four color swatches. He wasn't in any of the same classes as her but she had seen him around the playground and they had once been in the semi-finals of a citywide public speaking competition together. Neither of them had made it through to the final.

Zac. Zachary Kendall.

With the name came a few more memories. A Clock Reads T-shirt that he wore for a while after everyone else had stopped, which probably meant that he actually liked their music. A stupid joke he told in her hearing once. "You see all those 'Keep off the grass' signs, right? How do you suppose they got there?" His ride, which was a beat-up old thing that looked as though it would fall apart if you farted too loud. Only it was his mother's ride, of course, because he'd only just started driver's ed. And that was his mother sitting next to him.

Fran stared at her hard. Then she stared a lot harder.

There was nothing that remarkable about Zachary Kendall's mom. She was a short, slight woman with close-cropped black hair that looked pretty good on her. Her eyes were vivid green, with a little blue in one of them which was freaky but also quite cool. She wore a gray sweatshirt, faded jeans and brown leather ankle boots that were either meant to be vintage or had just gone bald in places. On her wrist there was a bracelet that flashed every now and then when it caught the light. None of which mattered at all.

What mattered was that Zac Kendall's mom was *changing*. Nothing else was. The rest of the room looked fine. The rest of the people in it looked fine. It was just this one woman who was acting up.

As Fran's hallucinations went, though, this was a fresh twist. Normally when she was seeing changes in the world around her, it would be a specific detail that was altered: red into blue, metal into plastic, old into new. If the woman's hair had grown longer or her brown leather boots had turned into high heels, that would have felt like familiar ground.

With Zac Kendall's mom, though, something different was happening. It was like there were two of her at the same time, overlapping each other and holding the exact same pose, but not quite in sync when they moved so you caught the lag if you were looking at the right moment.

Fran tried hard not to stare but her gaze kept being dragged back. She couldn't help herself.

It's a monster, Lady Jinx said. *But it hasn't seen you yet. Run away!*

Fran shook her head, keeping the movement as small and subtle as she could. *It's okay, Lady J,* she said inside her mind. Lying. Actually it was another assault on the normal world, bubbling up out of her rucked and twisted brain. Another reminder that nothing about her life was ever going to get back to being okay.

Zac Kendall was looking at her now. He had seen her staring. Resolutely, Fran looked away. It was bad enough that he'd noticed her at all. If he noticed her acting crazy, the story would go all around the school. She had had way more than enough of that stuff already. Having accidentally caught Kendall's eye once, she made sure not to do it again.

Then the receptionist called her name and told her to go to consulting room 14. She had to walk past Kendall and his mom on the way. Kendall pretended she didn't exist, and she extended the same courtesy to him. Jinx, though, gave both the boy and the woman a piercing glare as she followed Fran out of the room, baring her teeth in a very convincing threat display.

Fran made her way down the corridor and knocked on door 14, then went on inside.

Dr. Southern was sitting in a plastic chair that was inadequate for his bulk, but he stood up as Fran came into the room. "Frankie!" he boomed. "Long time no see. Sit, sit."

He ushered her into the ancient floral-patterned armchair that sat in the corner of the room. Like Southern himself, it was too big for this tiny space. It was also too soft, the deep cushion sucking your butt in and down so you had to choose between perching on the edge of it like a trapeze artist on a swing or sitting right back and getting half swallowed into its innards.

Fran always took the first option. Perching made it easier to look down at the paisley-patterned carpet if she got uncomfortable under Dr. Southern's unblinking stare.

Jinx ignored the chair and went and sat on the window ledge. Fran was surprised that the fox had come into the consulting room with her, given her strong feelings about Dr. Southern. Maybe it was because of Zac Kendall's two-in-one mom. Maybe Jinx thought Fran needed a bodyguard. Whatever it was, Jinx had put on her armor and her sword belt.

"How's the chess?" the doctor asked Fran, pulling her back to reality.

Fran nodded. "Pretty good, yeah. We've got tryouts for regionals next week and I'm playing lots of games against the computer."

"Winning?"

"Losing two out of three. But I shoved the difficulty setting right up to the top, so that's not a bad average."

"Still into the Hedgehog Open?"

"Of course. On account of it's still awesome."

"How's your dad?"

"He's fine."

"I bet he was surprised to see Juju make that catch."

"Nope. He won a bet on that."

Dr. Southern guffawed. He was a Steelers fan too, but Fran was pretty sure that if he wasn't he would have found some other thing to hang his small talk on. He always started their sessions with the same two topics, and with that box ticked he always got right down to business.

Like he did now. "So we've got some kind of a relapse going on," he said. "Is that right?" He sat back down again, the plastic chair creaking a little under his weight.

There's a Krispy Kreme box on the desk there, Lady Jinx said in a voice that dripped with contempt. *Look! Right next to your file folder. He's been pigging out on donuts. A whole box of them. Piggy piggy piggy! I bet he doesn't give one to you.*

Fran nodded, answering both of them. She'd seen the donut carton, and it didn't bother her. She figured Dr. Southern had as much right to eat donuts as anyone else did. Being fat didn't mean you had to live on lettuce. And Jinx only got all judgy like this when it was him she was judging. She didn't notice other overweight people at all.

"Okay," the doctor said. "Talk me through it. When and where and how much?"

"Stuff moving," Fran said. "Stuff changing. I dozed off over my homework last night—"

"In your own room, the living room, what? Paint the picture for me."

Like that makes any difference, Jinx scoffed. *He wants to show you he's listening, that's all.*

"In my bedroom. And I had a bad dream. I woke up feeling like someone was coming after me. Trying to grab hold of me."

"Someone?" Dr. Southern tapped the point of his pencil on the desk, on a corner of it, close to his hand, where there was a little patch of bare wood probably made by years of this kind of impact. "Call it, Frankie. We're talking the *obvious* someone, right?"

Fran handed over her journal. She didn't want to say it out loud. Picota as a giant spider had felt terrifying but would sound lame, like a childish nightmare based on a childish fear. Even so, the words were forced out of her as Southern scanned the recent pages.

"Yeah, it was him. Well, it was a big spider-thing, kind of, and I don't think it had a face, but it was still him. I mean, it was that memory and that place, so it didn't really matter what the monster looked like."

"The monster," Southern repeated, still reading. "That's how you were thinking of him?"

"He had, like, a dozen arms, Dr. Southern."

"And by 'that place,' you mean the motel? Where he took you?"

"Yes."

Duh, Jinx muttered.

"Okay." Southern set the book down on the desk and turned his frank gaze on Fran again. "So you were reliving your abduction. I just wanted to make sure that was the context here."

Fran didn't say anything to this. From where she was sitting, it was a question that answered itself. Whenever her brain reached for nightmare imagery, it infallibly dipped into that same well.

59

"And the bad dream woke you. And then the changes kicked in after that?"

"I think a siren woke me. An ambulance out in the street. Or maybe it was the sound that made me have the nightmare, I don't know. But yeah, I guess I was still thinking about Picota after I woke up. And then the weird stuff kicked in."

She flicked her hand to indicate the same old, same old. Little bits of the world sliding in and out and round about like the squares on a Rubik's Cube, which was a cool puzzle her dad had given her for Christmas once that had taken her more than half a day to figure out.

At the mention of Picota's name, Jinx had drawn her sword and was thoughtfully testing its edge against the ball of her thumb. Now she took out a whetstone from the little pocket-purse-thing on her belt that Fran didn't know the right name for and began to sharpen the blade.

"What weird stuff?" Dr. Southern prompted.

"Changes. Like, the colors of things changing. Where they were in the room. Or one thing turning into a different thing. You know."

Like you told him all the other times. Stupid man!

Southern put the journal down, picked up his pencil again and did some more tapping with it.

"This was a one-off?" he mused.

"I suppose."

"Well, it was or it wasn't. Was this something that just happened all by itself, or was it part of a sequence you didn't tell me about yet?"

"It was a one-off."

"And it was right after a triggering incident. The nightmare."

"Yeah."

Now tell me how that made you feel, Jinx muttered, mimicking the doctor's deep voice in her piping treble.

"Okay, give me some background," Southern said. "Before it happened—I mean, in the days leading up to this, or even earlier on that same day—did you feel any increase in tension or unhappiness? What was your mood?"

Fran interrogated her memory as well as she could. It wasn't an easy question. What was anyone's mood? It went up or down depending on what was happening. You could wake up happy and then bang your head on the bedpost and hate the world. But there wasn't anything that came looming out of the recent past like the great big shadow of a great big wrecking ball to shatter her ever-fragile buzz. There was just the usual run of ups and downs.

Your mood was fine, Jinx said. *Everything was going fine.*

"My mood was okay," Fran said.

"Nothing stressing you or freaking you out?"

"Nothing more than usual."

Dr. Southern scratched his beard.

"Well, then I'm inclined to sit this out," he said. "For now."

"No," Fran said quickly. And then, as he looked at her in mild surprise: "I mean, I'd like you to increase my meds. I want to go back to a full dose of risperidone. Please."

"Why?" Southern asked her. He shrugged his shoulders, just a little, making the single word mean more—like he didn't see the need. Like she had to justify the request somehow, when the reason was right there in front of them both, gruesomely obvious.

"Because I don't want it to start happening again." Fran didn't bother to mention that it *had* happened again, right outside in the waiting room. She just wanted to collect her prescription and get out of there, not get into another round of discussion. "I don't want to go back to all the . . . you know, to the hallucinations and the panic attacks. I want to be normal."

"Normal," Dr. Southern said flatly. "Right. But there are different flavors of normal, Frankie. We're all trying to be normal in our own way."

"What does that mean?" Fran asked him. She was trying not to sound angry, but she hadn't come here for the kind of platitudes she could have got at a school assembly.

The doctor gestured vaguely, shaping something in the air with his fingers. "Well, it means we've got an idea in our minds when we say the word, but there's probably no definition we can all agree on. Look, here's the thing." He held up Fran's journal, like a preacher waving a Bible around to prove he was on good terms with God. "This is, what, the fifth or sixth notebook you've gone through? There's year after year of you telling me about everything in your life that isn't normal."

"So?" That one word, all by itself, sounded really belligerent, but Fran couldn't help it. She felt as though she was being talked into something. Something she wasn't going to like.

"So I'm wondering if talking about your symptoms has become a symptom in itself. You see, I don't know what we're doing now, exactly. There are two possibilities here. The first—" He put the journal down again so he could hold up his index finger. "—is that your condition is entirely post-traumatic. Your mind responding to extreme stress. But if that's what it is, then after nine years I would expect to see some change. Recovery, in a perfect world, but definitely change. Systems under stress aren't stable. They either pull back toward stability or else they fall apart. You're not doing either."

Fran wasn't so sure about that. There were times when *falling apart* described her interior landscape pretty well. Dr. Southern only had her words to go by. He didn't know what it felt like to live in a world where all the objects that surrounded you might start spinning like the reels of a slot machine and come up different. Cherries into oranges. Red quilt into gray. A flute player into a fan lady.

Dr. Southern held up a second finger. "Option two is that the trauma just exacerbated a problem that was already there. That you've got what we call an endogenous syndrome. But in that case it ought to be possible to find a drug and a dosage that would switch off your symptoms once and for all. They shouldn't come and go in the way they do. We ought to be able to do better than a standoff."

He stopped talking and just looked at Fran, as though it was her turn to speak. As though he was expecting her to have an answer.

She threw the question back at him instead. "So which is it?" she demanded.

"I don't know," Southern said. "I really don't. That's why I'm not happy just loading you up with some more meds and saying goodnight and good luck. Frankie, these drugs have serious side effects. You don't seem to be getting the weight gain, but even without that there are plenty of things to worry about. Headaches. Nausea. Loss of balance. You know, it's even possible that the drug is causing your anxiety and your nightmares. We could be making the situation worse by treating it."

"But it's my choice," Fran said.

This was the ace of trumps, and she played it with a flourish. Dr. Southern had told her once that he would let her make her own decisions when it came to treatment—that he would lay out the choices but not make them for her. If that meant anything, it meant she walked away today with a prescription rather than a sermon.

Dr. Southern looked unhappy. "Absolutely," he said. "If that's what you want, I'll write you up and send you on your way."

"That is what I want," Fran confirmed. It was obvious he wasn't even halfway done, but if she heard him out it would be a lot harder to stick to her guns. "Please, Dr. Southern."

There was a long moment when he just looked at her. Lady Jinx came up behind him. Oathkeeper rested on her shoulder, newly whetted, as she held it in a firm, two-handed grip. Even though Dr. Southern was sitting down, she didn't quite come up to his shoulder. She measured the angles with a speculative eye.

"Okay," Dr. Southern said at last. "You got it, Frankie."

Lady J relaxed her stance and sheathed her sword.

The doctor took his prescription pad out of the desk drawer. He closed the drawer again right after, but while it was open Fran saw the name of his next client written on the cover of a manila file, identical to her own, that was sitting on top of a short stack.

Zac Kendall's two-in-one mom.

The doctor wrote out the prescription. He folded it in half, and Fran held out her hand to take it. She felt a little ashamed of how she had beaten him down even though she hadn't really had any choice.

"Do one thing for me," Southern said.

"Okay," Fran agreed. "What?"

"Don't up your dose just yet."

She did look at him then. It was a low blow. "What's the point in giving me the meds if I'm not allowed to use them?"

"Use them if you need to is all I'm saying. Stick to your current dose unless you have another episode. I think we should have a follow-up meeting in a week or two to see where we're at. If the weird stuff starts up again before that, and if you feel like you can't cope, then you go ahead and up your dosage. But to my mind that would be a backward step when we ought to be trying to walk forward. I'd much rather we came up with a different approach."

"There isn't anything."

"Maybe there is and we just haven't thought of it yet." He sighed heavily. "Frankie, I'm not trying to make things any harder for you. Swear to God. It's my job to make you better. It would be easier to dose you up to your eyeballs, believe me. It would be easier to say risperidone isn't working so let's try a different pill. A stronger one. You're old enough now that nobody would raise an eyebrow at that. But I don't know if it's the right thing to do. And I don't like the idea of you coming to depend on the pills any more than you do already."

Fran got to her feet, with difficulty because of the damn armchair and the damn cushion. "It's my choice," she said again. "I know what I'm doing, Dr. Southern."

It was true, she thought defiantly. She reached over and took the prescription out of the doctor's hand.

"Okay," he said. "Well, then let's leave it there for now. I'll see you again week after next and we can review. If you do have another attack in the meantime, use your journal to get it all down—in as much detail as you can."

"Of course," Fran said. "Continued in next episode."

She hated that he thought she was a coward. To her embarrassment, she felt the stinging in her eyes that meant she was about to cry. She wasn't miserable, just ashamed and angry at being judged.

By a big, fat, donut-eating fat man! Jinx chimed in.

Fran got out of the room as quick as she could. Dr. Southern was still saying goodbye to her when she slammed the door shut behind her.

He's just a dick, Lady Jinx growled.

"No, he isn't," Fran said, her voice thick. "He's trying his best. But he doesn't get it."

She had to pull herself together before she went out to her dad. She took a side corridor that led to the bathrooms. There was a water fountain there too, so she pretended to be taking a drink, letting the water run while she bent over it and gulped back tears. They kept coming, though. Because if Dr. Southern didn't get it, who would? And if he was going to block her off from doing the one thing that would make all the craziness go away, then there was no way out of this at all.

A rustle of movement from somewhere close by made her freeze. She wasn't alone anymore. She waited for whoever it was to go away.

"Are you okay, Watts?" It was Zac Kendall's voice. And he was right behind her.

"I'm fine," Fran mumbled.

"Can I get you anything? Or call someone? If you're—"

She spun round to face him. "I said I'm fine, Kendall!" she yelled. "Are you deaf or something?"

Kendall looked stunned. Too bad. He should have minded his own business.

Fran took to her heels and ran, out the side door and into the parking lot. She texted her dad from there, saying she was all done and waiting by the car.

By the time he arrived, her cheeks were dry and her face was composed.

"All good?" Gil asked.

"Yeah. All good." Fran forced a smile, holding up the pink prescription slip. "Can we swing by Walgreens on the way home?"

Wednesday seemed to be taking its own sweet time to come around. Liz had been living in fear of another psychotic episode, and the constant tension made her start at shadows. Any time she got angry or even a little irritated, she stopped dead and probed the feeling to make sure it was hers. And since it was impossible to be completely certain, she tried to steer away from feeling anything at all. She was queasily conscious of holding the world at arm's length. Even her fellow volunteers at the homeless shelter, who were glad to see her back. Even the kids, which she flat-out hated.

That was the main reason why she had asked Zac to drive her to Carroll Way. Learning to drive was still enough of a novelty for him that he relished getting behind the wheel of a car, even if the car in question was a tired old wreck, steered like a boat despite being the size of a roller skate and wore the dust and sap of a Pittsburgh summer like an extra coat of paint.

The sitter, Christine Keithley, arrived at 4:30 on the dot. She was a classmate of Zac's who mostly sat at the weekends but was prepared to do a couple of hours midweek as an occasional one-off. Word had gone around among the Worth Harbor mothers that Christine was capable and reliable.

"I already cooked Molly's supper," Liz told the sixteen-year-old. "All you've got to do is warm it up."

"Okay," Christine said happily. She was a stocky teen with fiery red hair who played in Julian C. Barry's junior volleyball team as a wing spiker. Zac said a lot of the boys were scared of her because of something unspecified that she had done to a boy who had gotten too fresh with her at a school dance. Liz felt an instinctive warmth for her on account of that story. She also liked that Christine had brought some schoolwork with her: it showed a serious mind.

"I'll be back in time to put her to bed," Liz added.

"So there's really nothing I have to do except make sure she doesn't set the house on fire?"

"Well, you'll probably be drafted in for Lego duty."

"Excuse me?"

"Through there. You'll see."

Christine went through to the family room, where the Lego table was out and Molly's latest work-in-progress was . . . well, everywhere. By the time Liz had got her coat on and found her car keys, Christine had been recruited to build a dungeon for a dragon who had been naughty. Offenses unspecified. "I sort of feel like your daughter is running an authoritarian state, Ms. Kendall," she told Liz.

"Every kid is born a fascist," Liz said. "You have to pound democracy into them a little at a time."

"Fair."

"Don't let her bully you, though. If you need to do your school-work . . ."

"I'll get to it. Right after we build the dragon utopia."

In spite of Liz's good intentions, she and Zac were silent when they first got into the car. Mostly that was because driving still required his full attention, but she sensed that he was also a little bit freaked out at the thought that his mom was going to a psychiatrist. Liz didn't blame him. She felt the same way about it, truth be told.

"So Nora wanted to add a new clause to my work contract,"

she said at last. "So she can fire me if I turn out to be of unsound mind."

Zac shot her a sidelong glance, scandalized. "She what? She can't do that, can she?"

"She said she could, yeah. Said it was standard practice. It's called the sanity clause. I told her she wasn't gonna fool me with that one. My daddy told me there ain't no sanity clause."

Seconds went by. Zac shook his head. "That was terrible," he said. "On a scale of one to ten, it's . . . wow. It's on a different scale. I can't find it on the scale, Mom."

"Pretty bad, right? And it's not even original."

"No, I'm relieved. If you made it up, I'd have to go get myself DNA-tested in case I'm related to you."

"Only by birth, sweetheart."

"Well, thank God."

They sat in the waiting room for twenty minutes, which for Carroll Way was on the low side of average. Zac saw a girl he knew from school sitting over on the other side of the room with a man who was presumably her father. "Go ahead and talk to her," Liz urged. "I'm fine just sitting here."

"I don't know her that well," Zac hedged. Liz wondered if she was seeing a budding crush until he added, "Francine is really weird. Most people think she's crazy."

"And here's your mom going to see a shrink," Liz reminded him.

"Ha ha," Zac mumbled. "Very funny."

The girl got called in ahead of her, and Liz got a good look at her as she passed. She was a petite African American teen with a metallic blue streak down one side of her tightly curled hair. That was the only flamboyant touch in her appearance: she dressed right down toward camouflaged blandness in a white T-shirt with no logo, a pair of black jeans and unbranded sneakers. There was nothing strange about her that Liz could see, except that her slim build maybe shaded over a little too much toward actual gauntness. There was a solemnity about her that was unusual in a kid that age. Liz thought it might be the face you ended up wearing if everyone at your school thought you were crazy.

"She seems nice," Liz said.

Zac only shrugged.

Liz's name got called fifteen minutes later, when the girl was still fresh in her mind. She registered the fact that they had both been sent to the same consulting room—to Dr. Southern. This Francine must have genuine mental health problems over and above what the school's whisper line said about her. Poor kid.

Liz's first impression of Dr. Southern was that he was an affable idiot. He tried to make her relax by making a few bland observations about the weather and asking her about her taste in movies—which since she worked in a movie theater was pretty low-hanging fruit.

He was just trying to put her at her ease, Liz knew. But there wasn't much hope of that considering what she was here for, and the doctor gave it up when he saw she wasn't going for it. After that, things went a little better. He invited her to tell him about the two incidents and he unpacked the details with terse, focused questions.

He was particularly interested in the second incident. He asked Liz how she had been feeling when it all went down. Was she angry at the two women? Did she enjoy hitting out at them? Was it cathartic?

Liz tried to be honest. "Mostly I was scared. Really scared. Not of them, but of what I might do to them. I know it sounds like the classic payback fantasy, but it didn't feel that way from the inside. I was trying to hold back, but I couldn't, and that was . . . well, it was terrifying."

Southern nodded like he understood. "Okay," he said, "but still. I'm guessing there must have been some satisfaction to be had in retrospect, no? Thinking about how you sent them running?"

"No," Liz said. "Really not. The loss of control was too frightening. And so was the thought of what might happen next. You know, if they called the cops or something."

Southern switched tack. "You said your husband had hit you before? That he had a history?"

Liz licked her lips, which were feeling a little dry. She found she didn't want to admit to it—to having stayed so long in a relationship that was so badly messed up. To having been a victim. "Sometimes," she said, feeling as dirty and ashamed as if she was confessing to some sick sexual turn-on.

"Often?"

Liz gestured helplessly. "How do you measure that?"

"Once a year? Once a month?"

"Once every few months. And, I guess, you know, getting so it was more rather than less."

"But you never hit back, on any of these other occasions? You didn't retaliate?"

"No."

"Did you want to?"

Liz found it hard to answer that question. She turned it over in her mind. What had she done when Marc cut loose? What had she thought about?

Surviving. Not doing anything to make his mood any worse. Keeping quiet so the kids wouldn't come down and see what was happening. Not once had she ever thought about fighting back.

"I just shut down," she said. Beyond that, it was too hard to explain. "I didn't let myself want anything."

Southern nodded again, as though that answer confirmed something he was already thinking.

"What?" Liz asked him. "Do you know what's wrong with me?"

The doctor sat back in the plastic chair, making its legs splay out in a way that looked frankly dangerous. "Snap diagnoses are for fools and phonies, Ms. Kendall. We've only just met. But I can tell you what ballpark we seem to be in. Thing is, though, it's going to sound worse than it is."

"Tell me," Liz said. "Please."

"Very well. I'd say that this has all the classic hallmarks of a dissociative episode."

71

The words didn't mean anything to Liz. And then suddenly they did. She'd seen some far-fetched thriller by Shyamalan or someone—in disjointed pieces, out of sequence, as she saw most movies—and a few TV specials that did the same thing on a lower budget. "Wait," she protested. "You mean like in dissociative identity disorder? The multiple personality thing?"

"Exactly."

Liz threw up her hands. "No. No way."

Dr. Southern didn't seem perturbed by the emphatic response. "Okay, so you've heard of it."

Yes, she had. In tawdry, implausible stories about people with a dozen or a hundred different identities to choose from, one of which was inevitably a serial killer. She was vaguely aware of a less dramatic reality underlying the movies and TV shows, but she still rebelled against the idea. That wasn't her. It couldn't be. "I don't have a menagerie inside me, Dr. Southern," she said, hearing the hostility in her own clipped tone.

"Of course not," Southern said. "Dissociation comes in many, many forms, and most of them are far less extreme than the popular conception. It doesn't have to mean that you have alternate personalities. At rock bottom, it just means being shut off from parts of yourself. From thoughts and feelings you don't want to cope with. Be honest now. When your husband hit you all those times, and you didn't fight back, wasn't there some anger there? Some very strong resentment and even rage at being treated in that way by someone who was supposed to love you?"

It was the wrong question, so Liz didn't answer it. "I already told you, I wasn't angry when I hit out at Marc. I wasn't anything but scared. Scared for my life."

"And you acted to save yourself." The chair creaked again as Southern leaned forward. His voice was annoyingly gentle and coaxing, as if she had to be nudged into seeing what was obvious. "But you didn't want to be the one who did that. The one who picked up the bottle and used it. So maybe—I'm just saying maybe—you made someone else do it."

Someone else, Liz thought, her mind running with the idea even though she tried to pull it back. Someone with more of an appetite for mayhem. She thought she knew who that might be— what name she might give to the parts of herself she had buried in order to go on with the thankless task of being Marc's wife.

Punk rock Liz. Axewoman Liz. Sideways Smile Liz.

"No," she protested.

"Why not? Tell me."

She groped for an answer. *Because I don't want to admit I'm that sick. That out of control. Because if I'm breaking in pieces like that, I belong in a mental hospital, not out in the world. Because I might be a danger to my own kids.* "Because if this was just me acting out what I wanted to do," she said instead, "I would have enjoyed it while I was doing it. I didn't. I keep telling you, I was scared out of my mind!"

And that was true. But the second time, with Eileen Garaldi and her nameless friend . . . She *had* hated those big, braying women. Their coarseness and their casual superiority. She had wished them ill. And maybe that wish had been a kind of summoning.

"Scared out of your mind," Southern repeated. "So what was it that came into your mind when you went out of it, Liz? It wasn't a ghost or an alien or a hypnotist. It was still you. But it was a part of you that was capable of doing what needed to be done."

Liz opened her mouth to refute that argument too, but she was fighting a losing battle because it all made perfect sense. That was, objectively, what had happened—if you could be objective about something that had only happened inside your head. Marc was killing her. She wanted to live, wanted that very much, but she hadn't been doing anything to make that happen.

So she stepped aside and let someone else come up to the plate. A designated hitter.

"But . . . the second time," she protested. "There wasn't any need for it."

"Need?" Southern repeated with careful emphasis. "In the sense of . . .?"

"I wasn't in any danger. It was nothing. Just an argument about a parking space."

"And yet you gave yourself the same permission. This other part of you that you'd only just discovered, that you'd only just empowered, came out again. And why wouldn't it? It had worked so well the first time. It had saved your life. Why wouldn't you go there again when you were suddenly in a stressful situation and probably still not entirely recovered from that earlier trauma? It makes perfect sense to me that the threshold for your other self showing herself would get a lot lower in the wake of that first time. Because the first time was a slam dunk. It was mission accomplished."

Liz sat in silence for a long time. The sense of it was slowly sinking into her. That she had called out for a savior and now the savior was sitting inside her mind like a cuckoo in a nest. Screwing up everything.

"I can't live like this," she said to Dr. Southern. "Seriously, I can't."

"And you don't have to." The doctor was tapping a pencil on the desk as he spoke, adding emphasis to each word. "I said this was classic dissociation, but actually it's different in a couple of significant respects. Most people who present with the full dissociative syndrome—and we're talking a tiny number in the first place—they've got a history of severe childhood trauma. You don't. You're a grown woman, and your personality is fully formed."

"So?"

"So there's every reason to believe that this was a one-off response to an extraordinary crisis—literally, a life or death situation. In which case it will almost certainly just go away by itself."

"I can't take that chance."

"I'm not suggesting you should."

The doctor reached for the bookshelf and took something down. A battered paperback with a lime-green cover. "I've got your prescription right here," he assured Liz in the teeth of all the evidence.

"Mindfulness," Liz said, reading the title upside down. "What's that?"

"A treatment with no side effects," Dr. Southern said. "And a good place to start."

When Liz and Zac got home, it was to find Molly asleep on the sofa. There was Lego all around the living room like the aftermath of a gas main explosion, and Christine was shamefaced.

"I tried to keep her awake, honest to God," she said as the three of them collected up the building bricks and stacked them in the drawers of the plastic worktable. "She was hyper for an hour and a half and then she flaked out all at once, like her batteries had just run out. I did manage to make her sit still long enough to eat her dinner, though."

"You did great," Liz said, handing over a twenty. "Thanks again for taking her at such short notice."

The sound of the door closing behind the babysitter roused Molly from her deep doze. She was briefly disoriented, and then immediately launched into a plaintive story about how Christine had made her eat broccoli.

"Oh, you poor baby. How you must have suffered."

"Yes. And it was green!"

"Green broccoli! The worst broccoli there is!"

"She let me have a hippo-yogurt-mousse, though. A strawberry one."

"So you survived. That's the main thing."

Since Molly was back in the waking world, Liz got her to read aloud from *Little Witch* while Zac played the latest instalment of some military-themed console game in his room with his headset on. Every so often he'd say something to one of the other players, almost always a monosyllable.

"Right!"

"Go!"

"Now!"

"Hey!"

"Whoaaaa!"

"Do you want to watch a *Thomas the Tank Engine*?" Liz asked Molly when they were done with *Little Witch*. "Or should we play Lucky Ducks?"

"Can we do both?" Molly asked.

It turned out they could. After having a nap earlier in the evening, Moll was a live wire. She didn't crash until after nine o'clock, by which time Liz was failing too. She looked in on Zac, who was still playing, and waved to him from the doorway. With both hands on the controller of the PlayStation and a live mike at his lips, all he could do was give her a grin and a nod in return. On another night she would have tasked him about homework assignments, but if his routine was broken it was down to her more than him. She decided to let sleeping dogs of war lie.

In her own room at last, she took out the book that Dr. Southern had loaned her. *Mindfulness: Think Your Way to Health* by Peter Bateman. It sounded like snake oil, but Southern had assured her it wasn't. "It's kind of an offshoot of cognitive therapy. The idea is that most bad attitudes and behaviors start off as bad thoughts. Bad habits that your mind gets into. Mindfulness puts you in the moment, makes you experience things more directly and intensely so you can see those bad thoughts coming and avoid them. If what you suffered was a sort of mental short circuit, this ought to help you mend your wiring."

Liz read the first chapter, which promised no amazing revelations but did suggest (with a few provisos and cautions) that new ways of thinking could often bring unexpected benefits. It ended with the instruction to *Play meditation one.*

Liz had already unearthed her old CD player from the back of the closet and set it up on the bedside table with fresh batteries in it. There was a photo of the family that sat there, and in repositioning it she looked at it properly for the first time in years. It showed Liz seated, with Molly in her arms and Zac kneeling next to her. Marc stood behind them all, his hands on Liz's shoulders in a way that had once seemed affectionate but now looked like a statement of ownership. Time for a new photo, she thought. Way past time, actually.

She plugged an old pair of gaming headphones—Zac's, long ago outgrown as both tech and fashions had advanced—into the back of the player and inserted the CD that had come with the mindfulness book. With the headphones on, she pressed PLAY and lay back on the bed.

"Meditation one," a rich male voice said in sonorous tones. "Finding the stillness inside yourself." Liz didn't know for sure if that was something she had ever been issued with.

The meditation made her concentrate on each part of her body in turn, tense it and then relax it, shift her awareness to it and then away from it. She felt slightly ridiculous lying on her bed fully clothed, trying to commune with her own physical extremities. But there was definitely an effect. At the end of the meditation, she felt both really relaxed and strangely self-aware. She held herself on the brink of sleep for a little while, floating on the surface of an interior ocean until, ever so slowly, she let herself sink.

In the last moment before she dozed off, she became aware of something else. There was an inflection to the silence inside her mind, as though something else was being silent along with her; holding itself absolutely still so it wouldn't betray its presence there.

Her designated hitter. The thought came quickly, with absolute conviction. She just knew. That disowned but undissolved fragment was still with her, not advancing or retreating, communing with itself on the unmapped margins of Liz's consciousness. Ready to step back in again the moment Liz dropped her guard.

Ready to take over.

Fran had gone to bed on Wednesday night with a head full of foreboding. She had dropped a risperidone a half hour before she turned out the light, but the memory of Zac Kendall's mom at the clinic, changing without changing, two things at once, was very vivid. She was afraid of what the night might bring.

Feeling alone and vulnerable, she whistled softly for Jinx—and was hugely relieved when her friend came padding out of the darkness in the corner of the room. She had been afraid that the increased dosage would hold Jinx at bay, as it sometimes had in the past.

"Where do you go when you're not with me?" she murmured as Jinx curled up on the duvet beside her.

You know where I go. My secret den.

"Where is that?"

It wouldn't be a secret if I told you.

"Okay. But how do you get there?"

It's magic. First you step, then you slide. Back to front and side to side.

"Don't tell me then."

I did tell you. Someday I'll take you there.

They dozed off together, Jinx's soft breathing lulling Fran quickly over the threshold of sleep.

In the event, the night didn't bring much of anything at all. Fran didn't have any nightmares, and when she woke her room looked one hundred percent normal. But the mood of queasy dread wouldn't lift. She went into school on Thursday morning so tense and wired she felt like she was a human version of the ball of elastic bands her homeroom teacher, Miss Sutherland, kept on her desk.

She just about held it together through first period, but the pressure was building inside her. She had the risperidone in her school bag. During morning recess, she took it with her into the bathroom and sat on a toilet seat staring at it for the full ten minutes. When the bell rang, she popped a pill quickly, trying not to think about it too much but feeling obscurely ashamed just the same. Thanks a million, Dr. Southern, she thought glumly. Now I've got guilt as an extra side effect.

There's nothing to be guilty about.

"I know that, Jinx," Fran muttered. "Doesn't help. Good that you're still here though."

I'm always here. I will never, ever leave you.

Fran threw the little blister pack back into her bag with distaste and went to her next lesson, which was math with Mr. Van Nuys.

That was when the changes started.

Nothing big. Nothing flashy. The first thing she noticed was the graffiti on the top of her desk. The names of the desk's previous owners, scraped into the wood with the point of a classroom compass, rewrote themselves and slid into new configurations. They didn't even wait until she wasn't looking. They did it right in front of her eyes.

When Fran scanned the room, looking for more bad news, some of the posters on the wall had changed too. The one about Shakespeare's tragedies, her favorite, was now about someone named Theodore Roethke, who found his fate in what he didn't fear and learned by going where he had to go. All right for some, Fran thought bleakly.

That was all. The classroom stayed stable for the rest of the period. But the damage was well and truly done. Fran couldn't do anything but sit there and wait for the avalanche that these first few pebbles threatened to set off. She exhausted herself with watching, and didn't hear more than six words Mr. Van Nuys said. The quadratic formula? Variables? Differentiation? Factorizing? Variables she knew about, for sure, but the rest slid off her like water.

At lunch she sat with Maisie Gillis and Sarah Hatch, both of them chess club nerds like Fran herself, and she didn't hear them either. They were talking about the regionals and who was most likely to get chosen, and then about Rob Carpenter who was at the top of that list and also coincidentally extremely hot—the thinking girl's eye candy.

Fran nodded along and said almost nothing. Ate almost nothing too, until she realized that she must be looking kind of weird when what she wanted was for nobody to notice her or ask her a direct question.

She cut a corner off her meat loaf. Or tried to, rather, because nothing much happened when she sawed the knife across it.

The knife was a spoon.

"Shit!" Fran yelled at the top of her voice. She threw the thing down so hard that it bounced and hit the underside of the next table. She stood there shaking, first at the creepy horror of having a change take place right in her goddamned hand, and then at the enormity of what she had done.

She heard someone say, "Wow!" A girl's voice, but not anybody Fran knew. And then someone laughed, and someone else joined in. On the next table, a group of boys started up a slow handclap.

"Freaky Frankie does it again!" said Lucas Millard. "Outstanding!"

"Francine Watts!" John Dean Clark whooped, fist-bumping with Lucas Millard. "The woman, the legend, the retard."

"Don't take it out on the poor spoon, Francine!"

"Hey. Why don't you leave her alone?"

That last voice wasn't anyone in Lucas's posse, but it was very familiar. Fran looked around in dismay and disbelief.

And there he was. Zac Kendall. Walking over from wherever the hell he'd been sitting. Kneeling down. Fishing the spoon out from under the table. Bringing it across to her.

Holding it out.

"Get lost," Fran told him in a strangled voice. But getting lost wasn't an option now. Lucas was up on his feet too. He wasn't walking over here yet, but his face was stiff with affront. He pushed his chair back, which was total melodrama but also a serious warning.

"Now what you say?" he demanded.

Zac flushed a little. "She just dropped a spoon, man. Let it go."

"Let it go?" Lucas looked around the room, most of which was watching. "The man is telling me to let it go. What, you want to get into her pants, Kendall? You pulling this white savior shit so you can grab some ass-time with Freaky Frank? She's my cousin, man."

"Then look out for her," Zac suggested. He held the spoon out for a second longer, then when it was clear Fran wasn't going to take it he lowered his hand again, his face suddenly, belatedly, full of doubt.

Now Lucas came across to join them. Three other boys, John D. C. and Nathan and Will Buckell, trailed along in his wake and fanned out around him. "Well, thanks for the advice, Kendall," Lucas said. "I never know how to behave unless I'm told. You want to tell me some more? You got my attention, man."

Zac's eyes flicked left and then they flicked right. He looked trapped. He was going to say something, Fran thought in despair. He'd already made this into a drama for the whole student body to enjoy, and now he was going to lecture Lucas to his face and get his stupid head punched. Which would lead to Lucas being on a one-week suspension at the very least, and probably the repercussions from that would go every which way including hers.

She had to stop it. And in the heat of the moment she could only think of one way to do that.

"Hey," she said to Zac, who was still holding the spoon. "You want some of my lunch? You only had to ask." She grabbed a little scoop of mashed potato and flicked it at him. It hit him on the front of his shirt and stayed there.

Hilarity broke out on all sides. There were no abstainers. Zac Kendall, like Fran herself, was a marginal enough figure in the high school universe that nobody really had his back at a time like this. They might have felt differently if Lucas had thrown a punch at him, but this kind of nonviolent comeuppance ticked every box.

Lucas shook his head in admiration at Fran's classy move and pity—probably insincere—for Zac's humiliation. "Okay," he said. "I guess you got your answer. Go save someone else, Superman."

He went back to his seat triumphant, his posse at his back. Zac stayed where he was for a moment longer. He put the spoon down in front of Fran's plate. His knuckles, which she got to see right up close, were white. "Probably shouldn't use it again," he muttered. "Five-second rule."

He walked out of the cafeteria, pursued by chuckles and catcalls.

"Well, that was brutal," Maisie observed.

"Thus perish all creeps and shitheads," said Sarah.

Fran bent over her meal and tucked into it with totally fake enthusiasm. She kept her head down so nobody could see her face.

There was a homework club that ran in the library from 3:30 to 5:00 every afternoon. Fran had seen Zac Kendall there a few times but had no idea what his deal was or which days he turned up. Most times attendance at homework club had nothing to do with homework. It was all about waiting for your ride or about not being able to go home until someone was there to open the door.

Her luck was in. She found Zac in one of the study bays at the back of the room with nobody else in sight. She sat down opposite him and he lowered the book he was reading. *The Great Gatsby* by F. Scott Fitzgerald. The margins of the book were full of dense notes that spilled over into the text, pencil lines and printed lines all interwoven. Fran disapproved. Notes were for notebooks. She hated picking up a book and finding someone else's scrawl all over it—or worse, the gray fog and crumple left by a careless sweep with an eraser.

Kendall wasn't holding a pencil though, so maybe they were someone else's notes. He got the benefit of the doubt.

He was looking at Fran in silence, waiting for her to speak.

"I saved you from getting your ass kicked, Kendall," she said. "I don't owe you an apology."

Still nothing. The boy just raised his eyebrows and then lowered them again, which didn't mean all that much.

"But thanks," Fran said, "for trying to help. Not that I needed it or anything. I'm used to people thinking I'm weird, so none of that mattered as much as it probably looked like it did. But it was nice of you. Hella stupid, but nice."

"Why was it stupid?" Kendall asked.

"Big audience. Big stakes." Those were the two most obvious things. Fran didn't bother to say: bad optics. Standing up for a black girl against black boys. Putting them in a corner where they would pretty much have to come out fighting.

"It's Zac, by the way," Kendall said.

"Francine."

"I know."

"Not Frankie. Some people call me that, but only because they forgot to ask me if it's okay. My name doesn't shorten to a boy's name."

"So what does it shorten to?"

"I'll tell you if you ever need to know."

You shouldn't talk to him. Lady Jinx stuck her head out from under the table and bared her long, white teeth. *His mom is a monster.*

Fran shot Jinx a stern glance. She knew better than to interrupt in public, especially if that was all she had to offer.

Jinx withdrew, growling in her throat.

"So are we done?" Zac asked. "I've got three chapters of this word salad to read for tomorrow."

"*Gatsby*'s not word salad," Fran scolded him. "It's poetry, you goon."

"Yeah, looks like it's written in prose."

"That's just to fool you."

"It worked."

There was a silence. It had definite edges, like they'd come as far as they could with this everyday stuff, and now they had to put up or shut up. Were they friends, or on the way there, or would they just back off into their corners?

"How's your mom?" Fran asked, since Jinx had already raised the subject. Zac did that same thing with his eyebrows again, the noncommittal up-and-down. Quite right, Fran thought. It was a lot more than a question. It was an acknowledgment. *I'm not just a general purpose weirdo; I'm a mental case. And your mom is too.* Like they might turn out to be friends because they already had a secret that was just theirs. Goosebumps.

"She's okay," Zac said. "She's going through some stuff."

I bet. "Did she tell you how Dr. Southern has this huge ass but he sits in a really tiny chair?"

Zac grinned, then laughed. "No, she didn't mention that. She just said he eats Krispy Kremes by the box and leaves the evidence in plain sight."

Fran laughed too. "Hey, you don't know. Someone could have had a birthday."

"Or maybe he's working two jobs."

"Exactly. Delivering donuts when the supply of crazies dries up."

Something crossed Zac's face. Concern maybe, or a trace of pain. "My bad," Fran said quickly. "I'm not saying your mom is crazy."

"It's okay," Zac said. But she could see that it wasn't and she felt bad for him. Maybe his feelings for his mom were like her dad's feelings for her—wanting to make things better and not having any idea how that could be done.

"You go home up Lenora?" she asked him.

"Of course."

"I'll show you a better way."

Every Larimer kid was taught in the third grade and at frequent intervals thereafter that the eponymous William Larimer, local boy made good, had made his fortune as a railroad baron before moving into land speculation. Even so, Larimer wasn't well served by trains. A loop of the Amtrak came through, but the light rail didn't get any closer than Steel Plaza.

There was a plan though, or maybe a pipe dream. All of Pittsburgh was going to be linked up to a fully integrated urban transport system by 2050 so a future generation would be able to get into town without having to take the bus, which was so slow you could grow old and have kids and die before you got to Three Rivers. Mostly this amazing new transport network only existed on paper— blueprints on file at the town hall, puff pieces in the lifestyle supplements of local papers—but a little piece of it existed north of Lenora Street behind the Negley Run, tucked in among moth-balled factories and rusting corrugated outhouse buildings that could have been anything before they were locked up and abandoned.

Fran led Zac through the gap in the fence at the Orphan Street end of Lenora. She felt a tiny thrill of proprietorial pride when she saw his jaw drop.

"Whoa!" Zac said eloquently.

"Yeah. It's cool, isn't it?"

Westward, the tracks stretched out ahead of them as far as the eye could see, which to be fair was only about a mile. To the east, they stopped dead after a hundred yards. A barricade of sumac, poison oak and brambles with wrist-thick stems shut them off from Washington Boulevard so thoroughly they couldn't even hear the traffic. Dragonflies looped in the still, fragrant air, crickets droned and dust motes hung like a curtain.

"How did I not know about this?" Zac demanded, awed.

"The city doesn't keep any secrets from me," Fran said. "She's got tells, and I can read them every time she sits down at the table." Zac shot her a frankly suspicious glance, and although she tried hard to keep up her deadpan it broke into a grin. "John Constantine, Hellblazer."

"Whoever that is."

"Goon."

They walked west, finding a little shade in the lee of a gray brick rampart shoring up the south side of the tracks. After five minutes, Zac got another surprise. Two broad stretches of immaculate white concrete rose ahead of them, bracketing the tracks—platforms about two feet high, twelve feet wide and forty feet long. This was going to be a station eventually, when all the lines got joined up and the trains started to run, but the only infrastructure they'd bothered to put up in the meantime were these two wannabe platforms and a pair of welded uprights supporting a steel and plastic notice board. No notices yet though, except for JAZ SUCKS BALLS and INTERURBAN CREW.

Fran sat down on the edge of the platform, her legs dangling. Zac wandered around, looking in all directions, probably trying to figure out which real-world location might be the closest to this little pocket wilderness.

Finally he came and joined her.

"This is amazing," he said.

"I know, right?"

They sat in silence for a while. It was a good silence. They were both on the same wavelength, drinking in the inexplicable peace.

It was Zac who broke it. "My dad beat my mom up a few weeks back," he said. "Almost killed her."

"You are shitting me!"

"Seriously. The cops had to come and arrest him. It shook her up."

"Like you'd expect," Fran interjected.

"Like you would totally expect. Anyway, she had some kind of a moment at my kid sister's school. She lost it and got into a fight with someone. That's why she's seeing Dr. Southern. For the stress. She wants him to help her keep it together."

The silence fell again. My turn, thought Fran with resignation. His confession had created a vacuum and her mind was nudging her to fill it whether she wanted to or not.

"I don't need to know what you were there for," Zac said right as she opened her mouth. "That's your business. I guess I wanted to explain why I jumped up like an idiot and almost started a fist fight in the cafeteria."

"You weren't an idiot," Fran told him.

"I thought you said it was hella stupid."

"What you *did* was hella stupid. Wanting to help isn't ever stupid." She looked at his face. There was a conversation going on behind it, she thought, and it was chasing its own tail somewhat. There weren't many people in Fran's experience who were easier to read than she was herself, but Zac was one of them. He'd pretty much just told her that his stepping in to help her was a kind of fallout from not being able to help his mom when she needed him. That was simultaneously a sign of him being a real human being and a thing that ninety-nine guys out of a hundred wouldn't have been able to say out loud except under torture.

"Your mom's lucky to have you," she said. "And your dad's a huge dick and he should die. Apologies if that's controversial."

"It's not."

"Good. Anyway, you shouldn't feel bad. If you promise to

cheer up, I'll promise not to pelt you with mashed potato anymore."

"You've got a deal, Watts."

"Fran."

"What?"

"Me. My name. It shortens to Fran." She took a deep breath, and let it out. "Look, my thing with Dr. Southern goes back ages and ages. To when I was a kid."

"I said you didn't have to—"

"I know, and I'm not. Not the whole of it, anyway. But there's part of it you probably already know. It happened right around here, and it was a whole big deal. I can tell you that part in just one word. Get it over with. And then maybe we'll fill in the gaps another time."

"Only if you want to," Zac said. And then, "What's the word?"

Don't, Lady Jinx said, her sharp little face suddenly right there in front of Fran's, tawny eyes with no whites blazing into hers. *You shouldn't tell him. We never tell people.*

"Shadowman," Fran said.

With a final bark of scandalized disapproval, Jinx faded out.

"It felt like something we needed to protect you from," Liz told Zac. "That's why we didn't discuss it at the time. And then later, you know, it would just have been . . . There wouldn't have been any point."

Talking about the Shadowman still made her anxious, she discovered. Even now, the best part of ten years after the fact. She walked to the door and glanced through into the living room. Molly was sitting on the floor with two other six-year-olds from her class at school, Hayley Brake and Rhian Molyneux, all of them watching a Netflix show in which an animated tyrannosaurus was rapping about his eating habits to some dayglo-colored robots. This was nominally a play date, but no actual playing had happened yet. Liz was going to have to initiate some if it didn't happen soon—that was part of the implicit contract when you invited other people's kids over—but right now she was happy to find that Moll was fully absorbed and not listening in.

She rejoined Zac at the kitchen's tiny, narrow breakfast bar. They were sharing rocky road ice cream right out of the tub. The court hearing was very much on Liz's mind, and this was a ritual between her and her son whenever one or both of them was feeling hassled or emotionally bruised. Zac fished out and devoured the marshmallows and almonds; Liz then polished off the interstitial ice cream, laying open a new layer for excavation. It was conducive to intimacy, and to a kind of generalized sentimentality. Seven-year-old Zac rose up very vividly in Liz's mind. He seemed to be sitting right there at the table with them.

"It was such a horrible thing," she told present-day Zac, a touch defensively. "And the little girl was almost the same age as you. I hated that you even had to live in a world where stuff like that could happen. I didn't want you to have to *know* it was there."

"You gave me the stranger-danger talk, Mom," Zac pointed out reasonably. "I think that was when I was five."

"Right, but I gave you the general one. Not 'there's a psycho who's been living a few blocks over.' It would have been different if he was still on the loose, you know? We would have talked you through it. We would have had to. But since they caught him . . ."

Zac continued his deep drilling operations in the ice cream tub, but he looked alert and thoughtful. There was nothing casual about his bringing up this topic. "Did he? Live just a few blocks away? None of the articles I found online were that specific."

"He lived on Paulson Avenue, between Mayflower Street and Polk Way. And we were in the old house back then, obviously. On Stoebner. It felt close enough. Zac, why are you interested in this? It's ancient history now."

He looked up at her, his gray eyes—which were Marc's gray eyes—candid and troubled. "She goes to my school."

Liz was lost for a moment. "Who's this now?"

"Fran Watts. The girl the Shadowman abducted. I was hanging out with her today."

"Seriously?" Liz was amazed. She had always assumed the family had moved away. Why wouldn't you, after something like that happened to your kid? Why would you make them grow up in a place that had such horrible memories attached to it?

"Seriously," Zac assured her.

"How is she?"

"She's . . . well, I guess she's okay."

"I mean, a trauma like that would have to . . ." Liz stopped, making the connection. "She was the girl at the clinic. In the waiting room. She went in right before me." To the same room. To Dr. Southern.

She drew the obvious conclusion, and Zac watched her do it with equally obvious alarm. All these years later, and the kid was still suffering! Of course she was. You might come away from something like that alive, but that didn't mean you came out intact.

"She didn't say it was okay for me to tell you any of that," Zac said. "We were talking about it in confidence, Mom. We've got to respect her privacy."

"Of course we have." Liz put a hand on his. "I wouldn't say a word, Zachary. I'm not an idiot. Plus, she's got the goods on me too, right? We'll keep each other's secrets." She thought for a second. "Assuming I get to meet her. Will I?"

Zac got up, not exactly hastily but abruptly. "Maybe," he said. "Some time."

"Well, she's welcome to come over for dinner any time you want to invite her."

"Thanks, Mom. I've got to go. Andrew is expecting me at six."

He had been paired with his classmate Andrew Abramson on a physics assignment and tonight they were working together over at Andrew's house. Mrs. Abramson had offered to sweeten the deal by calling out for pizza. But Zac's sudden sense of urgency probably had less to do with the pizza and more with Liz having taken too much and too visible an interest in his having a friend who was a girl.

"Don't stay out too late," she said, giving him the lightest and most forbearing of hugs.

"I won't," Zac promised.

After he left, Liz found herself mulling over what he had just said. There really wasn't anything surprising at all about the news that Fran Watts was at Julian C. Barry. There were any number of reasons why the family might have stayed in Larimer. But Liz couldn't think about it even now without experiencing the same shiver of unhappiness she'd felt when Zac first told her.

When she said the Shadowman thing was ancient history, it was because that was how she wanted to see it. She had experienced that huge surge and plummet of relief when the man was caught, and a smaller one when he was sentenced, and then she'd barely thought about it since. But the news that Fran Watts was at Zac's school—and even more, the fact that she was getting psychiatric therapy—made her painfully aware that the past is never really as dead as you want it to be.

Liz tried hard to shift her thoughts onto a more positive track. If it had been a little later in the evening, she would have gone up to her bedroom and done one of the meditations from the mindfulness book. As it was, she had three six-year-olds to entertain and she had been goofing off. She turned off the TV and herded them into the kitchen. Since the program had been about dinosaurs, she got them to make dinosaur masks for themselves, and then tails. While they worked, she told them how some dinosaurs had sneakily avoided going extinct by evolving into birds, which the kids thought was very cool.

"Which kind of birds?" Hayley Brake asked.

"How did they get so small if they started out as dinosaurs?" Molly added.

Liz tried to explain the theory of evolution in six-year-old terms, hampered both by the need to simplify and by her own ignorance of the fine details. She did the best she could, then when she ran out of road she put some music on. *In the Hall of the Mountain King*, in the Magnetic Melodies edition. "Dinosaur dance!" she announced.

The tiny dinosaurs went on a syncopated rampage. After which two of them got picked up by their parents while the third, who was wheezing a little, had to have a session with her inhaler and nebulizer sleeve.

Then there was dinner to make, and the clearing up, and the fractal business of putting Molly to bed and putting her back there a few times when she wandered. The Shadowman went right out of Liz's mind.

But he came back again as soon as she ran out of distractions.

Probing the sore place, she did what Zac had done earlier in the evening. She googled all the articles from ten years before and read through them, awakening a ton of old, unwelcome memories.

Fran Watts, aged six, had failed to come home from school one Friday night, and her parents had called the cops straight out. They might have been fobbed off with a wait-and-see except that somebody had already seen. Fran had been grabbed off the street in broad daylight, and there was a witness. The man who took her was driving a white pick-up, maybe a Dodge, with a bolt-on camper sitting up on top of the flatbed. The man was wearing bib overalls, and he was short and overweight. Also bald, or balding, although the witness said he didn't look that old.

The cops went from door to door around the neighborhood, showing Fran's picture but also asking about the fat man in the overalls. There were road blocks at all the big intersections and a police copter in the air coordinating a search. Fran's mom and dad popped up on the news appealing to Fran's abductor not to hurt her but to bring her home safe to her family, who loved her and were missing her sorely.

There was some vigilante stuff too, Liz remembered. Small groups of serious-looking men, some white and some black but no mixed groups, walking up and down the cross streets off Negley Run with their hands inside their jackets to hide whatever it was they were packing.

And in spite of all this, twenty-four hours went by with no news. Not a thing. Liz remembered thinking—when that Saturday afternoon drained away into a pallid, rain-drenched evening—that the little girl had to be dead by now. She had wanted not to believe about the fat man and the pick-up, but now she couldn't keep up the argument against her own fatalism. If a child just lost her way or got into some scrape on her own account, she surfaced again quickly. Kids didn't stay lost, not in a city of two million people.

A night and then another day meant Fran Watts had indeed been taken.

Liz had put Zac to bed. Moll hadn't even been born back then. Liz read her son a Dr. Seuss book, *I Had Trouble in Getting to Solla Sollew*, and teared up ridiculously when she got to the part where the little creature who narrates the story gets stuck in a horrible tunnel full of garbage. It made her think too vividly of where Fran Watts might be, and what she might be going through.

Then on Sunday the police caught a break. They'd been running down all the white pick-ups they could find that were registered to addresses in or near Larimer, which was needle-and-haystack territory but better than doing nothing. One of the trucks belonged to a man named Antony Picota. The address was right out at the edge of their search, on the south side of Homewood, but they went there anyway. No truck to be found, and Antony Picota was a gaunt man in his late fifties with a shock of white hair, so the two cops who went to his place were sure as soon as they saw him that they'd struck out.

Until Picota asked them if they'd found his son.

When they cross-checked, they discovered that he'd placed a missing person call the night before. The missing person was Picota's adult son, Bruno, who lived in a basement apartment on Paulson Avenue and was the other registered driver of Picota Senior's white Dodge 200. He had borrowed the car earlier in the week and was meant to have brought it back the previous evening. "You got a camper on that?" one of the cops asked, oh so casual. And Mr. Picota said that yes, he had a 1976 TravelMate that was still in perfect condition. He and his son took the car down to Ohiopyle State Park twice a year where they fished the banks of the Youghiogheny and lived on what they caught there.

"What does your son do?" the cop inquired, feeling like he was on a roll now.

"He's unemployed," Mr. Picota said. "He used to clean and do odd jobs at the Perry Friendly Motel over by the veterans center, but they let him go."

It was something to go on, at last. They went on it. They called in an all-points alert on Bruno Picota, and while that percolated they swung by the Perry Friendly Motel just to see what they might see.

What they saw was a Dodge 200 with an eight-foot TravelMate parked in the service area at the back of the lot. They parked right behind it and walked on through to reception. At the first mention of Bruno Picota, the desk clerk rolled his eyes. Sure, he said, Picota used to work there. He'd been a strange one, kept himself to himself and was hardly ever seen. Spent most of his time in room 22, which was the furthest away from reception on the ground floor. Room 22 had been turned into a storage space some years before, and now contained only cleaning materials.

When the SWAT team kicked the door in less than three minutes later, they found that room 22 also contained Bruno Picota and Fran Watts. He hadn't touched the girl, not sexually or in any other way, but he had a knife in his hand—an eight-inch folding hunter, probably part of the kit he and his father toted down to Ohiopyle for their fishing trips. He was waving it in front of the six-year-old's face, one officer said in testimony later. Like a teacher with a pointer, but he was pointing at her eyes and who the hell knew what he was seeing in them? He didn't try to hurt her, even then—just kept babbling incoherent explanations for why he was the good guy here and they should all help him to kill the kid because he wasn't sure he could do it on his own. The cops put him down fast and hard, and it was all over.

That part was, anyway.

Liz was reading the articles out of sequence, just opening them as they came up on the search list. The early ones referred to Picota by his actual name. The later ones called him the Shadowman, picking up on something he said in the course of the trial. They didn't explain the nickname though, and Liz couldn't remember what it referred to—just the word itself, full of grim and slightly supernatural threat. It was an unlikely word to describe the lumpen, round-shouldered figure who stared out of some of the photos; a man who even when he was standing in place looked like he was shambling. That was one pretty solid shadow, right there.

The Perry was just a shell now. It had shut up shop eight months after that raid, bowing to the inevitable. And Bruno Picota was in a secure mental facility in Grove City, where he would most likely die.

Enough. Liz closed the search window in a mood of sour melancholy. Her own memories of the Perry Friendly sat very queasily with what she had just read. She had forgotten until now that Picota had chosen to take his intended victim to the place where she and Marc had first flicked the switch of their relationship from flirtatious to full-on carnal.

They hadn't used the Perry Friendly for very long, though. On one of those nights of unbridled passion—the last, as it turned out—Liz had awakened in the night to hear a vicious altercation going on in the next room. A single voice, talking low and hard. It could have been a man or a deep-voiced woman. "If you get it wrong, I'm going to cut you," it said. And then, "You dumb little bitch." And finally something like, "I'll kill you first." The person who was being spoken to didn't answer at all, or if they did Liz didn't hear. She roused Marc, who said he couldn't hear a thing. By that time, Liz couldn't either.

She got dressed and went to the front desk, over his protests. It was none of their business, surely, and they didn't need the hassle. But the desk clerk said the next-door room wasn't rented out, and when he finally opened it with his master key there was nobody there.

Liz wished she could remember the number on the door of that empty room. She was seeing a 22 in her mind's eye, but that didn't prove anything except that she was pretty damn suggestible, which wasn't news at all.

Zac still wasn't home, and Molly had finally settled. This seemed like a really good time to find the stillness inside herself. Liz went into her bedroom, closed the door and put the headphones on. She chose meditation two: *Know That You're Here, and This Is Now.*

Lying full length on the bed, arms limp at her sides, she let the words wash over her and sink into her.

Surrendering to them was a luxury. The voice murmuring in her ear felt simultaneously very close and far away. Liz's sense of spatial relationships was dislocated, the world becoming a tide that ebbed and flowed with her breath. The paradoxical message of relaxation and awareness came in on the same tide, and took her out with it.

It was just like the last time. She became a single point of consciousness in a space that had no measure.

And just like last time, she wasn't alone.

Maybe it was because she had spent so much of the evening thinking about Fran Watts' abduction, or maybe it was because she wasn't drifting off to sleep this time, but the sense of proximity was much stronger. So was the sense of threat.

Her other self was there. Outside? Inside?

Circling.

Very close already, and getting closer with each breath.

With a violent shudder, Liz brought herself up out of the shallow trance, opening her eyes and sitting bolt upright.

Molly was sitting beside her on the bed, knees drawn up to her chest and lower lip thrust out in a belligerent pout. Liz took off the headphones. Peter Bateman was still talking, but with the headphones discarded on the bed he sounded like an erudite mosquito.

"Mommy," Molly said. "I was talking to you and you weren't answering me."

"I'm sorry, Moll," Liz mumbled. She opened her arms. Molly held out for half a second, still indignant, then folded herself into her mother's embrace with a small grunt of acquiescence.

They dozed comfortably together. Molly often ended up in Liz's bed at some point in the night so this was business as usual. Except.

"Mommy," Molly whispered after a while.

"Yes, babe?"

"Who was that?"

Suddenly wide awake, Liz propped herself up on one elbow to look down into her daughter's face.

"Who was what, babe?" she asked. Trying to make the question sound normal. Trying not to let her surging panic unstring her voice so it spooked her little girl.

Eyes closed, drifting away, Molly frowned with the effort of remembering. "The other lady."

Under REASON FOR ABSENCE, Liz wrote "family illness." But she told her supervisor what the real deal was.

"My ex-husband is up on an assault charge. He beat me up, and the cops arrested him. So now I'm applying for a temporary restraining order so he can't come near me and the kids until the trial date."

"Roast the bastard alive," Nora DoSanto said. She picked up the APPROVED stamp and slammed it down on Liz's application for leave with a lot more force than was really needed. Nora had been divorced twice and consequently had a low opinion of men in general and ex-husbands in particular.

Liz was grateful that there would be no fuss made about her missing her shift. It was bad enough that she was losing the day's wages. The shortfall would play out in duller meals, fewer treats, harder choices. All of which would be feathers in the scale if she could finally get herself and her kids free from Marc.

Mr. Naylor had told her to be at the courthouse by ten. Liz drove the kids to school as usual, then came home and changed into a sober two-piece that made her look like an Amish housewife on a day trip. She drove over to Lincoln, parked her car on the street and took the P17 bus into town.

Naylor had promised to meet her at the courthouse, but Liz got there too early. She killed some time by walking around the block, stopping under the bridge on Ross Street that connected the courthouse to another building—maybe a jail, although it looked like a fairy tale castle with both round and square towers. She was ninety-nine percent certain that she had seen both the bridge and the castle in a movie some time, but she couldn't dredge up the memory. She felt obscurely ashamed to have such big pockets of ignorance about the city where she'd lived her entire life.

When she got back around to the front of the courthouse, Naylor was waiting for her on the steps. They walked inside and went through security together, the young attorney telling Liz what to expect even though he'd already gone over it with her on the phone. "This is a meeting in chambers, not a hearing. The other side will be there, but there won't be any formal arguments. It will mostly just be me and my opposite number, Mr. Quaid, talking to Judge Giffen about the situation you find yourself in. He'll make a decision on the basis of our presentations and the police statements. It's possible, though, that he'll want to talk to you or your husband to fill in some of the fine detail."

Liz had very mixed feelings about that. The thought of talking on the record about everything that had passed between her and Marc in the course of their mess of a marriage was daunting, but she really wanted to get that restraining order. She was tired of sleeping with one eye open.

"It's this way," Naylor said, leading the way up the broad stone steps to the upper level.

Everything was a lot more crowded and noisy up here, with clusters of people in front of the courtroom doors waiting to go inside. Liz made to keep on going, but Naylor put a hand on her arm to make her hold back. "Your husband is going to be there already," he said. "I saw him and Quaid heading up a few minutes ago. And we've still got ten minutes to go even if Giffen is running on time. That's fine if you're fine with it, but there's no reason at all why you've got to see him. We'll both be cooling our heels outside until we're called, after all."

Liz was tempted, but she shook her head. "I'll be okay," she said. Thinking that if she couldn't look Marc in the eye out here then how was she supposed to face him down in court and tell the truth about the things he'd done to her? Let him hide from her if he wanted to. She couldn't—mustn't—hide from him.

So they walked along to the judges' chambers, which were at the far end of the corridor. And there he was, sitting with Jamie Langdon on one of the benches right opposite the door. He gave Liz a sulfurous stare as she came into view. She met his gaze levelly. *Yeah*, she thought, *maybe you can do me some damage with your hands, honey, but I'm not flinching from your naked eyeballs. Not anymore.* She chose a spot a little way away and leaned against the wall in full sight of him.

Jamie looked back and forth between them, frankly curious. Liz wondered whether it had dented her feelings for Marc to see him up on an assault charge. Surely at the very least you'd be thinking *there but for the grace of God*. Unless standing by your man meant not believing a single word anyone said against him.

"You want a cup of water?" Naylor asked.

Liz shook her head. "I'm good. Thanks."

"Well, I'll take a little. I never drink any when I'm in front of the judge. Don't like to break eye contact in case it looks like I'm being evasive."

He walked back the way they'd come.

Liz found her gaze being drawn back repeatedly to Marc. He seemed to know it too. Every time she looked, he was being physically attentive to Jamie: stroking the back of her neck, putting his hand on her shoulder or his arm around her waist. Maybe it was meant to remind Liz of what she was missing, but it did the exact opposite. He thinks he owns her, she thought, disgusted. Just like he thought he owned me. Like he thinks he *still* owns me, even though we're not even married anymore.

A rage rose in her, one slow inch at a time. It wasn't a blinding rage at first, but when it reached her eyes they filled with unbidden visions. It wasn't just moments of violence she was remembering; it was other things too. She saw Marc belittling and demeaning and blaming her, sniping and questioning and undermining, picking away at her self-esteem with every tool he could get his hands on as though demolishing her was a long-term craft project.

The fury was like bile in her throat now, like a bitter taste, something she had to spit out before it poisoned her. Her mind reeled and retreated, seeming to travel backward without moving. The world was dropping away.

In its place, and in force, came her designated hitter. Her other self. But Liz saw it coming, and braced for the impact.

They met right behind her eyes, which didn't blink. The other tried a straightforward takeover like before: slipped its limbs into Liz's limbs and tugged, trying to shrug her on like a garment.

Liz stood her ground. The moment passed, and she was still herself.

The other made a second attempt, but Liz had the measure of it now and it never even got over the threshold. The trick, Liz realized, was to let her mind go blank. Her own thoughts were the carrier wave that her alter ego rode in on. It was hard at first, but it got easier each time.

The silent invasion came and went, came and went, receded and was over within the space of a minute. The designated hitter was gone as suddenly as it had arrived. Liz had beaten it back.

Amazed, incredulous, she braced herself at first for a renewed attack. Then when it didn't come she examined the corners of her mind, alert for some sense of a residual presence. There was none. She'd won. She had actually won. She was alone on the field. She had to fight to keep from laughing aloud in triumph and relief.

"You're on," Naylor said at her elbow. She hadn't heard him approach.

She followed him into Judge Giffen's chambers, where she talked—calmly, clearly—about what she had been through at Marc's hands. The things she had just recalled in a near-frenzy of rage and resentment she reviewed now with cold dispassion. Defeating her other self had drawn all that fury out of her like snake venom from a wound.

Had Marc verbally abused her? Yes, he had. Liz provided examples.

"Would this be in the course of an argument, Ms. Kendall?"

"Sometimes. Not always. Not often, even. I was afraid of arguing with him, because he never argued just with words."

"You mean he was violent with you?"

"Aggressive, first. Then violent."

"Can you explain the distinction?"

"Whenever we argued, he felt like he had to touch me to get his point across. Like he'd grab me by the arm if he was explaining something to me, or if he thought I didn't hear him. He hated having to repeat himself. Or he'd jab me in the chest for emphasis, or just press his hands against my shoulders. Pin me up against a wall so I couldn't walk away until he was done with me."

And so on, moving in a natural progression to the application of fists, and feet, and ambient objects. Something about the whole process reminded Liz of the earnest overexplicitness of pornography. Zoom in on the details; don't leave anything to the imagination. But she did what she had to do, and she did it with a self-possession she didn't know she had in her.

She came away with an injunction, to be renewed by a fresh application every two weeks between now and the date of her trial.

"Which is October 13," Naylor told her as they walked away. "Nice job in there, by the way. You were articulate, convincing and sympathetic, which is three lemons in a row. I can't wait to get you in front of a jury."

Evening. Then night. Liz had the talk with Molly, and Molly listened with fidgety impatience. It was awkward stuff, and Moll didn't do awkward.

"So we're not going to see Daddy for a long while. He can write to you but he won't be able to see you."

"He'll see me on my birthday."

"No, Moll," Liz said. "Probably not even then."

"He'll take me to the Pizza Wheel and we'll get ice cream with refills."

"I can take you there."

"And Daddy will come and be with us later."

Liz considered a lot of possible answers. In the end, she decided that later was open-ended enough that it could mean almost anything—like, for example, Molly choosing to seek Marc out when she was an adult and making her own decisions. "Later," she repeated. "Maybe, sweetheart. We'll see."

There was no point in pushing it. Molly had been in one of her hyper-hyper moods for most of the evening. Now she was freefalling toward sleep so fast you could measure the droop of her eyelids in real time. Her bedtime story was three sentences.

Zac was wide awake though, and eager to share the moment now that Molly was tucked up in bed and it was safe to talk. They split a bottle of beer. He was almost seventeen and Liz was sure, without having asked him, that he must have experimented with alcohol. She didn't feel like she was tarnishing his innocence.

"We're almost free, Mom," he said, raising the bottle in a solemn toast. "We're going to be free of him. And then we can just be us."

He took a swig, and passed her the bottle. Liz drank too, accepting the toast. "There's still a long way to go," she said. "This was the first battle; it wasn't the whole war."

She interrogated that metaphor while the beer was still going down. "It's not that, though," she told Zac. "A war. It's just . . . you know what it is. It's something that's happening now, it's not for ever. There's going to come a time when he wants to see you again. Be in your life again, and Molly's life. You'll make up your own mind then, and . . . it's fine. It's fine with me, whatever you decide. You don't have to shut him out because he hurt me one time."

"He hurt you lots of times," Zac said forcefully. "And he can go to hell for all I care. I never want to see him again."

"What about Jamie?" Liz hadn't meant to say it, but it slipped out anyway. The woman's stare had stayed with her. The way she had kept looking from Liz to Marc and back again, as if she was trying to reconcile Liz's version of Marc with the man she knew.

"What about her?" Zac asked. He didn't say it belligerently. He just seemed surprised to hear her name mentioned at all.

"You've gotten to know her pretty well over the last year or so. And she's been good to you both."

Zac stroked the side of the bottle with his thumb, making patterns in its foggy sheath of condensation. "Yeah," he said. "She has. I guess Moll might want to see her again. I just . . . I can't help thinking of her as the other half of Dad. It would be weird."

"But if she wanted to?" Liz pressed.

Zac looked up and met her gaze, absolutely candid. Liz thought:

he doesn't have it in him to be cruel. To be his father. It was only then she realized that was what she had been scared of.

"If she wanted to, then I'd see her," Zac said. "Obviously. I'm not going to shut her out because of him."

"No. Of course you won't."

They talked about other things. School, and the part-time job he'd just applied for at Game On in Bakery Square. If he got it, they'd be able to walk to work together sometimes—and Zac could start saving for the second-hand dirt bike he wanted to buy. Liz asked after Fran Watts, and Zac said he'd been hanging out with her a lot. Currently she was teaching him chess.

"Wow!" Liz marveled. "This girl has superpowers. I could never even get you to play checkers!"

"Because checkers is lame. Chess is . . . strangely awesome. There are a million different ways you can play. Strategies that people have worked out. Like battle plans. Fran likes the Hedgehog Open."

"Which is what?" Liz asked, taking another swig of Dos Equis.

"You build up a wall of pawns and keep your big pieces behind it."

"And that's a hedgehog because . . .?"

"Because it's like you've got spikes. The other player attacks, they get skewered on your pawns and they don't hurt you at all."

Liz thought of some valid reasons why Fran Watts might take that approach to life in general, but quickly decided not to go there. She gave Zac the bottle and told him to finish it. Which he did in one appreciative swallow.

"Does this mean it's okay for me to have a beer with dinner now?" he asked Liz.

"What do you think?"

"I think I'll have to wait until we beat the crap out of Dad in court."

"And then I'll introduce you to champagne," Liz promised.

She kissed him goodnight and got a big, open-hearted hug in return. "I'm so happy for you, Mom. Happy for all three of us."

She went into her room. The mindfulness book was lying on

the bedside table, the headphones right beside it. It was in the corner of her eye as she got ready for bed, but very much front and center in her mind.

Her rogue personality had tried to come out at the courthouse, and Liz had faced it down. She was almost certain the meditations had helped with that. They had given her a keener sense of her other self, which meant both that she could see it coming and that she wasn't completely helpless when it arrived. The balance of power had shifted.

Maybe it was time for the two of them to finally meet for real. Or as real as this inherently surreal situation could get.

She closed the door, and after a moment's hesitation locked it. Whatever happened next, it felt as though she would need to be alone for it. Okay, the word *alone* came with provisos too, but she wanted to contain the fallout. She wasn't scared for Zac and Molly, exactly. The designated hitter only swung at things that were threatening Liz, not at things she loved. Her rage was on Liz's behalf. What frightened her—deeply—was the thought of her kids, and especially Molly, seeing her when that other version of her was in control.

But if things worked out right that wouldn't ever happen again. If she could bring the two halves of herself together, and hold them there, wouldn't they just heal up again into one normal person?

It had to be worth trying.

Liz sat down on the bed and put the headphones on. She selected the same meditation she had used the last time. *Know That You're Here, and This Is Now.* This time the title seemed like a warning: the moment of truth.

She pressed PLAY, and lay back. The rich, measured voice started up, telling her to hold the world in her awareness and then to let it go.

She couldn't at first. She was too tense, and too aware of her immediate agenda. The whole point of the meditation was not to *have* an agenda—to be in the now without projecting into the future or tunneling into the past. But Liz had had enough practice by this point to be aware of what she was doing wrong. Little by little she let go of her intentions and made her wandering thoughts sit still.

The words flowed over her, and found their level.

The ocean arrived.

Liz waited, not perfectly passive but as close as she could get. The blankness in her mind was like the blankness of a radar screen when no vessels were in range. There was only her, lying on her own bed and yet paradoxically cut loose from everything.

Almost everything.

Her other self was out there, at the limits of her perception. It seemed to be standing still, but it was possible that the two of them were both moving in synchrony through some unresisting space. They were motionless in relation to each other.

Let's talk, Liz said. *Flag of truce.* She didn't speak the words aloud; she just let them form in her mind and held them there. There was no need to shout, even if shouting was an option. The closeness between her and her other self, more intimate than any marriage, was a given. It couldn't be very hard for this wayward fragment of her own mind to pick up the words from where they lay at the threshold of Liz's awareness, since that was presumably where it lived.

The other consciousness, the misplaced and metastasized part of her, drew closer. Loomed larger. It came right up beside Liz and then was all around her, leaning in from every direction at once. It was putting on a show of force. See what I could do, if I wanted to.

Please, Liz thought again. *Let's just talk.*

The other pushed at her, tentatively at first and then much harder. The strangeness of that disembodied pressure made Liz afraid for her sanity all over again, but there was no denying that she felt it. She let go of her doubts. For now, all they could do was distract her, when she needed all her concentration to resist.

There was nothing for her to anchor herself to here, in the

111

interior void of her own tranced mind, except the certainty that she couldn't be moved. Liz dug her nonexistent heels into that, and braced. The push and her resistance met in the same plane, and canceled each other out. Waves of pressure spread out from the place where they touched.

Waves of sound, and throbbing vibration, and finally of light, or something enough like light that Liz could see.

She was suspended in a space that seemed to move outward from her in all directions as she stared into its depths. It had happened quite gradually, but her awareness of it was sudden and all at once. She had been nowhere, and now she was somewhere. Somewhere that had no color, no scenery, no shape: a huge void dimly lit with a sourceless, hueless glow, like the mildewed underarm of the sun.

The designated hitter floated in front of her: a blanked-out silhouette standing on nothing, human-sized and human-shaped.

We need to talk, Liz thought for the third time. *We have to stop fighting each other. We're just two halves of the same thing.*

No, the other spat back. Just that single word, quick and hard and flat.

Liz knew the voice, of course. It was the one she was expecting to hear. And when the other's outline filled in slowly, the details drawing themselves on the air, she was prepared for what she would see and was not surprised. Except, perhaps, by the implacable hostility on the other Liz's face, the twist of raw contempt on her lips.

You don't know me. The words were thick with challenge, with an anger that crackled like electricity. *You don't know me at all.*

If there's a way to say this that doesn't sound like a big teetering tower of bullshit, I don't know what it is.

The other spoke without moving her lips. And Liz was aware that what she was hearing wasn't really sound. It was a voice identical to the voice of her own interior monologue, as though someone was thinking her thoughts for her rather than speaking to her.

But this stranger both was and wasn't her. She wore Liz's face and spoke with Liz's inner voice, but her hair was longer and there was metallic green eyeshadow on the lids of her eyes. She wore a jacket with a snakeskin pattern. She looked the way Liz herself would have looked around now if she had pressed on with her rock star career and made it work.

You think? the other grinned without the slightest trace of amusement. *You don't know a thing. But I'll tell you, since we're here. I want you to know. Nobody deserves to be as ignorant as you are.*

Liz tried to answer, but she didn't have the trick of that soundless thought-speech yet. No words came. She felt a twinge of foreboding, almost of panic. She had thought this was a cure, a ballsy therapeutic strategy, but it seemed that all she had done was to fit the meditation CD into the pattern of her delusions.

Either way, she was afraid. Even in the absence of any direct threat from her alter ego, the space in which they faced each other was unsettling. Its drab uniformity and silence seemed somehow aggressive, or at least projective. As if it swallowed light and shouted silence. Liz wondered how far it extended. The answer might be forever, and she found that thought terrifying.

It's you, you idiot, the other told her coldly. *The inside of your brain. There's nowhere else we can talk, unfortunately. I would love to meet you out in the real world and smack some sense into you, but that's not a practical proposition.*

Liz tried to speak again, with no more success than the first time.

Yeah, you've got nothing to say here, the other said—somehow conveying a sneer even in a voice that had no tone. *Just listen. I'm trying to tell you something. Something you need to know.*

Liz raised her hands in a gesture of surrender. She had come here because she wanted to put her fractured mind back together. That wasn't going to happen if she suppressed the other piece of her, or ran away from it. She had to start by understanding it.

Well, isn't that big of you? the other said with a sour smile. *Okay, then let's keep it simple, so you've got a sporting chance. My name is Elizabeth Healey. Healey, not Kendall. I married a man named Marc Kendall, the same way you did, but I didn't take his name. Because, you know, not a doormat. No offense. I don't go by Liz, either. Not since high school. My friends call me Beth.* The other's hands twitched—a movement of quick irritation. *Called me. Called me Beth, back when they called me anything. Doesn't matter. The point is I'm you. A different you. I was going to say better, but we're not in a competition. Are you getting any of this? Is it going in? Shit, don't try to talk. Life's too short. Just nod.*

Liz nodded. Nothing that she was hearing made any sense just yet, but she reminded herself that she was listening to her own subconscious. Its logic and perspective were unlikely to coincide with hers.

The other's face twisted into a snarl. *Jesus! I said to listen. Don't try to fucking explain me. You don't have the equipment.*

114

Or maybe you do. Make an effort, at least. My life equals your life, okay? Give or take. I hooked up with Marc, and we raised a family. Two great kids. I don't need to tell you what their names were, do I? Zac was like his dad, strong but never much for thinking things through. Molly took after me more. Heart on her sleeve, head up in outer space somewhere. Didn't make any difference, though. Marc didn't play favorites. When he was in the mood, he beat the shit out of whichever of us was within range.

Liz felt a chill of shock at the words, but they gave her a handle on what she was hearing. Her other self was articulating her own fears—the ones she had tried to suppress when she and Marc had been together, even while she tutored Zac in how to avoid antagonizing him and made sure to be right in between them whenever his mood seemed to have an edge to it.

She's my Cassandra, Liz thought. My canary in the coal mine. The thought filled her both with sadness and with queasy disgust. Marc had been every kind of bastard except for that one. He had never once harmed their children, and she didn't need to concoct horror movie fantasies to justify her fear of him. It was grounded in solid fact.

Facts aren't solid, Liz Kendall. They're just smoke blown in your face, is all. So your Marc didn't start in on the kids yet. Lucky you. But he will, sooner or later. Trust me, I speak from experience. More experience than you can possibly imagine.

I like to think I didn't ask for it the way you seem to. But I took it when it came, and I kept him away from the kids as far as I could. Only he got worse, in that regard, as time went on. I think maybe that's just the way that particular sickness works. It's not that a violent man isn't capable of love; it's more like his love turns inside out sometimes, so everything he loves most he just suddenly hates and wants to hurt.

I never did get the truth of how Molly died.

Liz's mouth opened. No sound came out. Somewhere far off, a shudder of horror ran through her physical body. Here in this colorless nowhere, she felt that tremor the way you might feel the aftershock from a distant earthquake.

Stop it, she thought, and she was talking to herself. Her real self, not this funhouse mirror self. Stop doing this. Find some way to turn it off.

The other shook her head, slowly, sternly. *Oh, pace yourself, Liz Kendall, we've got a long way to go yet.*

It was a Saturday and I was at work, pulling overtime over at the zoo shop because Marc was working on one of his stupid fucking schemes and I was the only one bringing money into the house.

Anyway, I wasn't there when it happened. Marc said Molly was riding her bike out on the street in front of the house, and then he heard this big crash and he came running. He saw Molly on the ground and a car, a big electric blue Hummer, pulling away.

He called an ambulance. They declared Molly dead at the scene. The coroner accepted Marc's version and said it was death by misadventure. An accident, more or less, even if the hit-and-run turned it into a crime.

They put out an APB on the car, but without much hope because Marc's whole description was just those two words: electric blue. Nothing about the driver, the condition, the number plate or any damn thing else.

I sat there and listened to this bullshit and I felt like my heart had turned to stone. There was never any car, never any accident. You know anyone in Larimer who drives a Hummer? I don't. And if Molly died out there on the street, why was there a smear of her blood on the living room carpet? Tracked in on his shoes, Marc said, when he came inside to call 911. Sure.

He is a plausible bastard, my husband, I'll give him that. The kind of bastard that will have you wracking your brains, after he hits you, about what awful thing you might have done to bring that on.

I was stupid with grief for a while. I couldn't think of anything to do or say. I let my job go, because how can you work with kids at a petting zoo when the very sight of a kid makes you go into hysterics?

Marc didn't like that I wasn't working. That I wasn't making meals, or keeping the house up. He wanted me to heal up around Molly's absence as easily as he did. What he didn't realize was that I was only holding myself together at all for Zac's sake. Zac was close to a breakdown too. He couldn't believe his little sister was gone, couldn't cope with it, and Marc was as impatient with Zac's grieving as he was with mine. What was wrong with the two of us? People get run down all the time, and life goes on.

That's easy for you to say, I snapped back at him one night. You fucking killed her.

And that was the end of me.

Not right then. I don't mean he jumped up and stove my head in. You'd have to be lost to the world to do that, and he wasn't.

That was the worst of it, when I think back. He killed my kid, but he wasn't so crazy-rabid out of his mind that he couldn't think things through. Like when he scraped up a half-assed story that Molly was killed by a car, and made it work. Like that. Yes.

It probably didn't feel like a decision: I'd be lying if I said I ever got to the bottom of how his mind worked. But I think I died right then, when I accused him, and it was only a question of how and when I was going to get the follow-through.

Oh, and where.

It was in the lounge, turns out. This lounge you've got here, or my version of it. The lounge of the new apartment, anyway. You came here just with the kids; I still had his high and mightiness in tow. Lucky me. I told you I wasn't a doormat, and I don't think I was. The only reason I was staying with him was because of Zac, like I said. Because I couldn't think of a way to get him out of there and I wasn't going to leave him alone with his father. Stupid. There were lots of ways if I'd only had the balls and the imagination.

Anyway. Sunday. Real quiet. Zac out at the movies with his friends; Marc and me alone in the place and—you would think—nothing much to hang a quarrel on. But I'm skittish around him and he sees this. He sees it, and he dislikes it very much. What, is a man going to be judged in his own house? Is he going to walk on tiptoe to the fridge to get himself a beer so he can have something to sip on while he watches the game? Has he always got to be watching out of the corner of his eye in case something he does somehow fails to come up to scratch?

Motherfucker.

Motherfucker, I shouted in his face, you killed your own fucking kid. My kid. MY kid. You killed her and you took her tiny little body in your

117

hands and you faked a fucking crime scene with her so I didn't even get to say goodbye. So the police got to her before I did, you

fucking

motherfucking

waste of

I died with my own blood in my mouth, but only because I didn't get a chance to spit it out at him. It wasn't a good way to go, but I think I'd been waiting for it.

I think, in some ways, it was a relief to get it over with.

Beth bowed her head, eyes closed, and shook herself like a dog. She was done, that shake said. She had got it all out of her, and having nothing left to say she took her leave.

It happened quickly. Between one heartbeat and the next she receded, not like someone backing away of their own accord but like someone falling headlong into a chasm. The direction wasn't *down* exactly, but she was falling just the same.

The recoil hit a moment later. Liz fell too, in the opposite direction.

Through nothing.

And more nothing.

And still *more* nothing.

Out of the colorless void and back into her flesh, her bed, her right mind.

Her chest was heaving, not just for breath but for the unutterable sadness of it. The loss and the longing, as though they were hers; as though that whole wasted life had been hers.

As though it had been real.

Oh God, it had *felt* real. Less like a hallucination than like a memento mori. Liz had imagined an entire life, both like and unlike her own, and another version of herself to live it. It was almost as though she had wished that whole hideous chain of events into existence.

"I'm sorry," she whispered to Beth, for all that she knew there was no Beth, and never—never!—had been. "I'm so, so sorry."

When the tears came, they came in a violent flood. Afterward she felt as though she had purged herself of something. She must have been incubating this nightmare for years, since before her divorce even, and one way or another it had had to come out into the world.

Then when Marc had put his hands around her throat and she needed someone to save her from the terminal mess she had made of her life, she had dreamed up Beth and thrown her right into the line of fire. Her savior and her fall guy all rolled into one.

But it must be over now, surely. Now that she knew. Now that she had looked in the mirror and seen that twisted caricature staring back. Beth had passed through her the way a fever does, and now she was gone. Recognizing the nightmare, naming it . . . that was how you robbed it of its power to hurt you.

Please, Liz thought. Please let her be gone. Let me never go to that place again. She couldn't pray to God because she didn't believe. She could only release the prayer into the void inside her and then wait, in hushed fear, for the echo.

When Fran asked her dad—midway through breakfast—if she could bring a school friend home, and when further conversation obliged her to use male pronouns for the friend in question, she knew very well that Gil would make a real performance out of it. He didn't disappoint her.

"Wow, they grow up so fast!" he marveled, shaking his head. "I mean, in front of your very eyes. One minute you're saying boys have cooties . . ."

"He's not my boyfriend, Dad. It's a study date."

". . . the next you're going steady, wearing some guy's letter . . ."

"That hasn't been a thing since we got ourselves a new millennium."

". . . changing your Facebook status to 'he totally noticed me.'"

Fran embedded her spoon in her cooling oatmeal and folded her arms in a mock-truculent display, joining in the game by seeming not to. "Okay, I'll tell him no."

"What," Gil said, "I don't even get to meet your fiancé? He can't marry you without my permission, you know."

"Gross! He's just a friend. You'll stop joking when you see him."

"Why, is he a hunchback?"

"No! And why would that matter?"

"A Republican?"

"I didn't ask."

"Oh God, just tell me he's not a Ravens fan."

Fran looked at her watch. "Oh look," she said. "Sarcasm hour is over."

"Yeah, but we're still right in the middle of wise-ass month. I'm running with this."

"Then I'm going to school."

"Flying to the arms of your beloved. That's really romantic, Frog."

"Uck! I hate you."

Fran pushed the bowl away and flounced into the hall to collect her jacket and school bag. She looked over her shoulder. Gil had followed her and was leaning against the kitchen door frame, grinning broadly.

"I look forward to meeting him," he said. "How about if I make spaghetti?"

"That'd be cool, Dad. Thanks."

"But the Ravens thing . . . that's a deal-breaker. He needs to know."

"It's okay. I don't think Zac knows what a football looks like."

"So long as he doesn't think Alex Lewis looks like a football player."

Fran texted Zac from the bus, riding in to school. IT'S ON, SHERLOCK.

A few moments later he responded. A GAME IS THE FOOT.

Literary puns. She had to admit, she did find that pretty hot.

They had a really good evening, all things considered. Fran's dad did everything he could to make Zac feel welcome, and only mentioned the Steelers once. Primed by Fran, Zac gave the right answer, which was to say that they'd had a strong start to the season, but they really needed to improve their red-zone scoring and round out their receiving corps just a little.

"Do you have any idea what any of that stuff means, son?" Gil asked.

"No, sir," Zac admitted. "Not the slightest clue."

"Well, you said it with real conviction. Good job."

"Thank you, sir."

Fran made their excuses and hauled Zac off to her room—leaving the door open as part of a pre-arranged deal. Her dad trusted her implicitly, Fran knew, but as always he was trying to protect her, in a generalized and mostly undefined way, from life. The same way, she now knew for certain, Zac was trying to protect his mom. It was funny how something like that could go in either direction and still make perfect sense.

Zac took his books out of his bag, along with a bag of sour worm candies. He opened the bag and solemnly offered Fran first pick. She went for a blue one, and raised the candy in a salute, as though it was a shot glass, before dropping it into her mouth. "The good stuff," she said, chewing with her mouth open. "Thanks, slick. I never did have much use for tooth enamel."

"Look," Zac said. "If you twist two of them together, like this, you get an Ouroboros."

"You get a what now?"

"Ouroboros. The snake who eats his own tail. It's a symbol of eternal recurrence. Life ends in death, but then gets reborn."

"Oh, *that* Ouroboros. Bad idea, Kendall."

"How come?"

"If you eat symbols of eternal recurrence, they always repeat on you."

Zac made the *ba dum dum cha* noise and its accompanying gesture. Fran bowed to an imaginary audience, accepting the accolade.

She sat on the bed, with Zac taking the desk, and they pretended to work for most of the first half hour. Mostly, though, they showed each other YouTube clips: sketches from *The Whitest Kids U'Know* and *Monty Python*, songs by Bo Burnham and the Lonely Island.

And at a certain point, *Knights of the Woodland Table*.

"Why this?" Zac asked, mystified.

"I loved it as a kid," Fran said. "Especially this episode."

It was the one where Lady Jinx found her magic sword and got herself knighted by Queen Yuleia. As the two of them watched it, Lady J herself came out from wherever she had been and crept silently up to sit beside Fran. Fran felt a glow of pleasure and relief. Jinx had been sulking with her since she told Zac about the Shadowman, and hadn't shown her face. It was really good to have her back.

"I don't think I ever watched this," Zac confessed. "It felt like girls' stuff. No offense."

"None taken. Girls' stuff is the best stuff, Zachary, and don't you forget it. I was kind of obsessed. From kindergarten through to . . ." She tailed off. She had stopped after Picota. Fantasy hadn't meant much in the face of that terrible reality.

"I was more of a *Batman Beyond* sort of guy," Zac said.

"Like," Fran pursued, "I used to talk to the characters. I played games where I was one of the knights, and our back garden was Fandamir Forest. We had a shed back then. That stood in for the Woodland Keep."

"Which one were you?" Zac asked. "Lancea, right?"

"No."

"The badger with the white cape?"

"Pelerin. No."

He was looking at her with interest, waiting for her to answer. Fran hesitated. It wasn't something she ever thought about, or talked about, maybe because the game had never really stopped. Jinx was looking at her too, her eyes wide and her mouth hanging open a little to reveal her long, pink tongue.

"I was Lady Jinx," she said.

"The sly little fox!" Zac grinned. "Is that how you see yourself?"

It was hard to read Jinx's expression, for all its intensity.

"Jinx isn't sly," Fran objected. "She hates it when people say that. She never breaks a promise, or tells a lie. She wants to prove that foxes can be honorable too. That's why her sword is called Oathkeeper."

Zac laughed. "I stand corrected."

You pretended to be me? Jinx whispered.

I did, Fran said to her, moving her lips but only a very little. *You were always my favorite.*

Jinx sat up, and a shiver went through her fur. She stared with avid fascination at the laptop's screen, where a duel was going on between Lady Jinx and Lady Subtle. *I think . . .* she murmured.

"Are we going to get back to some homework?" Zac asked.

"What?" Fran prompted. She was talking to Jinx, whose rigid posture and raised hackles alarmed her a little. Maybe she should have asked before showing the cartoon to anyone else. Except that that would have been completely crazy, because who would she have been asking?

"Quadratic equations. Are we going to work through some of the examples?"

I think I played pretend games too, Jinx said a little wistfully. *It feels like a long time ago now.* She made a small, sad sound in her throat and slunk away, dropping from the bed to the floor and out of sight.

Fran moved the mouse pointer over to the little x on the browser tab, to close the YouTube window. But something made her hesitate. Something on the soundtrack, that she must have heard wrong. Instead of turning off the video she clicked on the time bar to replay the last twenty seconds.

"You did say you used to be obsessed, past tense?" Zac remarked, nudging her elbow.

"Just a sec," Fran muttered. "I want to . . ."

There. When Jinx drew her sword, and shouted defiance against that week's bad guy, Lord Thule. "You face Oathkeeper, traitor. No evil can stand against her magic blade."

"Solve the following for all possible values of x," Zac read aloud. "$7x^2 + 8x - 3 = 0$."

What was weird? What had struck her ear, or her mind, as somehow not quite right?

"So do we just feed it into the formula? I don't get where A, B and C come in."

"A is the quadratic," Fran said automatically. "B is the straight multiplier. C is the solo variable."

It was . . .

"Solo, like Han? It's a heroic space-bum variable?"

Oathkeeper.

Jinx in the cartoon said Oathkeeper. Not Oatkipper. Her voice was high and fluting but there was nothing wrong with her pronunciation.

So how had Fran come up with that misspeaking?

A low growl from under the bed warned her not to go there.

Liz's volunteering with Serve the Homeless was done at House of the Covenant Presbyterian Church on Frankstown Avenue.

"I'm not a Presbyterian," she had told Father Connor the first time she turned up there. "Is that okay?"

"Beggars can't be choosers," the young priest told her. "To be honest, we'll take actual cannibals at this point."

Liz didn't even know for sure what a Presbyterian was. But she fitted in well with the crowd who cooked up the dinners in the massive kitchen and doled them out to Larimer's homeless community. Most of the other volunteers fell into one of two categories: they were either in late middle age or else they were college kids taking their social conscience out for its first walk. But regardless of age, they were all good people and good company. They had their own in-jokes and their own secret language, which Liz picked up quickly. *Mud* was any meal that was basically a sauce thrown over rice or pasta; *the pay-off* was dessert; a *twinset* was someone who tried to get into both sittings by using two different names, and so on.

An absence of almost a year and a half ought to have left her feeling like an outsider again, but Liz picked up where she'd left off and was welcomed back without comment.

There were some new faces, both among the volunteers and in the docile, uncomplaining line that started to form outside the church a good twenty minutes before the door opened. But there were also lots of people Liz remembered from before.

There was one face in particular she kept on looking for, and not finding. He was in his late fifties, a tall, gaunt man in a long, shapeless coat. He had an unfeasible volume of snow-white hair and a very tenuous grip on reality, and he went by the name of Sergeant Bob.

The sergeant was sort of the reason why Liz had started volunteering in the first place. This was back when they were in the old house on Stoebner Way and the little garden plot at the urban farm had fallen into their lap without them even having to pay for it. Their neighbor, Mr. Newhart, had given them his key before he moved out of the area, and had written down for them (on the back of a Bed, Bath and Beyond voucher) the number of his tiny plot. "It came with the house. I'm paid up for the remainder of the leasehold, which is fifty-three years. It's meant to lapse when the plot changes hands, and the next guy will pay plenty, but if you don't tell them, I won't."

The garden plot had been a wonderful addition to their lives. But in taking it up they had had to evict Sergeant Bob, who had been sleeping in the tiny shed. Liz had felt guilty and dismayed about that. Marc said yeah, it was a shame, but who else in Pittsburgh got to live rent-free? "And it's a goddamn shed, Lizzie. He's way better off finding himself a proper bed in a shelter somewhere."

So Liz had found him one. And in the process she had found the Pittsburgh Cares website, which had led her to House of the Covenant. It had worked out pretty well, really. The only thing Liz could afford to donate was time, and precious little of that, but time was what the Serve the Homeless mission needed.

So since her return, she had looked out for Bob, hoping to catch up on his news and reassure herself he was still okay. But for the first few weeks, he was a no-show.

"You could ask the other veterans,"Violet Shoen suggested. This actually made Liz laugh. Bob wasn't a vet. The vets mostly stuck together and looked out for each other, and they had a certain way of holding themselves when they came to the front of the line, like charity was something they endured in the same way as they had endured combat. Bob was a loner, belonging to a regiment of one. His rank was self-awarded.

Three nights after her face-to-face encounter with her imaginary alter ego, Liz finally caught up with him. He had come along to the hall but hadn't joined the line. Just sat down in a corner, almost out of sight behind some stacked up boxes.

Liz brought him a bowl of stew and sat down beside him. She slid the bowl in front of his face, the spoon already in it so he could just help himself. But he didn't. He looked at the bowl as though he wasn't quite sure what it was he was seeing.

"How are you doing, Bob?" she asked him gently. "Everything okay with you?"

Bob blinked a few times and shook his head as if to clear it.

"Weather's going to turn soon," Liz tried again. "Are you sleeping over at Clancy House these days, or are you on the street?"

Bob cleared his throat. It took a while. "Had a room," he said at last. "Had to move out."

"Was that at Clancy House? On Allemania?"

"No."

"Well, was it somewhere in Garfield, or East Liberty? If there's a new shelter you should tell Father Connor, in case he doesn't know about it yet. He can add it to the bulletin board."

Bob looked at Liz for the first time. He frowned. It didn't seem like he remembered her, but that had happened before. Bob's mileage varied from day to day. From hour to hour, even.

"Not a shelter," he said.

"No?"

"No. It was a motel, kind of a place. Shut down, way back. But there was too many people there. All hours of the night. Talking. Shouting."

129

Liz felt a cold fizz of unwelcome surprise. It couldn't be. Could it? Coincidences didn't follow you around like that.

"Was it the Perry Friendly?" she asked. Hoping hard for the answer *no*.

"Was a motel," Bob repeated. "Over to Homewood. Closed down, boarded up, yeah. People should all've gone." He stared at Liz with myopic intensity. "You were there," he said. "Couple of times. I think maybe you was on fire. Or mebbe it was the girl was on fire and you lit her up. Thought better of you than that, to be honest."

He discovered his stew at last, dug his spoon into it and took a half-hearted mouthful. He didn't eat it, though. Just kept it on his tongue like he was waiting for Liz to leave before he did anything so intimate as swallow.

Liz left him to it. She was more than happy to let the conversation lie. In her current mood, with her personality split down the middle and the other half committing hate crimes, she couldn't shrug it off as she normally would. Bob was a substance abuser who lived rough: his mind was inside out most of the time. But still, she wished his delusions hadn't crept so close to the edge of her comfort zone.

And the night wasn't over yet. The rest of her shift went by without incident, but when she walked out to her car, chatting with Violet and a couple of the other volunteers, she found it comprehensively vandalized. Someone had spray-painted the word WHORE all along the driver's side, SLUT down the passenger side and BITCH across the trunk.

"Oh my God," Liz said blankly.

The volunteers rallied round her, and so did Father Connor. He was mortified that something like this should happen when Liz's car was parked right out in front of the church. He insisted on helping her scrub the car clean, and Violet stayed to help.

It was hard work. The paint seemed to be some kind of acrylic, and only lifted off with a hell of a lot of scrubbing. Even then, if you stood at a certain angle the swearwords were still there. They had left ghosts of themselves on the car's blue paintwork, which Liz had to hope would fade with time.

"I'm going to preach a sermon about this," Father Connor promised. "If it was local kids, Liz, I'll get you an apology at the very least."

Liz assured him that it was fine, that it didn't matter, but her brave face kept slipping. All that hate and spite out of nowhere made her feel like she'd been kicked in the stomach. She got away as quickly as she could, finding that the priest's well-meaning sympathy only made her feel worse.

"I just felt so exposed," she told Zac after she got home. "I know it's only a car, but it was like someone was taking it out on the car because they couldn't get to me and they still wanted me to feel it."

"Assholes are everywhere," Zac said, hugging her. "It's nothing, Mom. You have to not let it get to you. People who pull this shit are cowards, and they're not worth you losing any sleep over."

He was half-right, and Liz clung to that half. The rest of it was knowing that whoever painted that shit on her car knew the driver was a woman. Had maybe watched her as she walked into the church; had bided their time until the doors were closed and everyone was busy inside.

She told Zac she wasn't sweating it. That was a half-truth too. It had shaken her badly, but it wasn't anywhere near the top of the stack when it came to her big worries. The impending trial trumped this sleazy little stunt, and so did Beth.

Beth trumped everything.

Liz hadn't realized until afterward, but using the meditation tape as a way of making contact with her other self had largely sabotaged her therapy. The mindfulness stuff had seemed to be working, calming her and making her feel more in control of her own emotions. But since that imaginary conversation with her imaginary alter ego, she was afraid to use the tape again.

That vision of another possible life had left her devastated and terrified. It was as if her unconscious mind had decided she wasn't scared enough of Marc already; that the full experience required more paranoia and more violent imagery. Afterward she had been too wrung out even to move. She had ached all over, inside and out, as though she had caught herself a dose of the flu.

The next night, and the night after that, Beth was silent. No sign of her during the days either, though Liz was hyper-alert for any sign of her presence. She hoped that meant the confrontation had healed her—that the broken-off piece of her own mind to which she'd given a name and a history had now been reabsorbed into the totality that was *Liz*. But what if using the meditation tape set Beth loose again? What if she came back in Liz's dreams or—God forbid—into her waking life?

Dr. Southern had called it right. Living with Marc had meant shrinking herself down into a narrower and narrower space—jettisoning in the process whatever didn't seem to fit. Year after year, until finally the parts of herself she had hidden away, denied or just ignored had reared up and demanded to be heard.

Well, Liz had heard them, and once had been enough. She missed the peace and calm the meditations had brought her, but if the price of having that was meeting Beth again then she would just have to do without it.

She tried to tire herself out with unnecessary chores, washing and drying the dinner dishes by hand, tidying the kitchen cupboards, reorganizing the endless boxes of superannuated junk in the garage. But in spite of everything, she went to bed wired and she slept in fitful snatches.

She didn't meet Beth, or dream about her, but she had the feeling, each time she woke, that someone had just left the room. She was alone, but if she had opened her eyes a moment earlier . . .

In the morning her head was heavy, as though she was working off a hangover. The light hit her eyes from the wrong angle and every sound had a jagged edge to it. Reading her mind, or more likely her face, Zac took some of the strain and got Molly ready for school. They were late heading out, despite his best efforts.

They were even later arriving. Someone had let the air out of the car's two back tires, leaving spent matchsticks in the valves to hold them open.

So now it was Fran's turn to be the guest. It was nice, mostly, but also a little weird.

The nice stuff came out on top. Zac and his family lived on the ground floor of a split-level duplex on Mayflower Street that was a little on the small side for a family of three but had its own little apron of garden. There was even a gas barbecue out there, with a spherical canopy about the size of a soup bowl. Zac's mom got it going and cooked burgers and corncobs for them all, which gave the potluck supper out on the patio something of a festive atmosphere in spite of the heavy traffic going by right on the other side of the fence.

Afterward they played Lego with Zac's kid sister Molly, who was as cute as a button but only half the size. Molly had a crazy imagination. She mixed up all her Lego sets so the Harry Potter characters got to hang out with dragons and cowboys and big, Frankenstein-like Duplo guys. Fran found one of the Ghostbusters and Penny from *The Big Bang Theory* in there too.

"Blue pieces are magic," Molly told Fran confidentially.

"Just the blue pieces?"

"Yes. Just the blue ones. So if you want to make something

that's magic, it's got to have some blue in it. That's the rule."

"Well, rules are rules."

Zac caught Fran's gaze and they both smiled. She could see how much he loved Molly, and how much he liked that Fran was prepared to kneel down on the carpet and play games with her. But the truth was, Fran was enjoying herself. Having no brothers or sisters of her own, the only time she ever got to do this little kid stuff was when her younger cousins came over, which was about once every ice age.

Jinx liked it too. She couldn't play with the Lego, of course, but she sat beside them and watched them avidly, her triangular snout turning this way and then that way as though she was watching a tennis match.

So that was all great. The weirdness came from Ms. Kendall, Zac's mom. Liz, as she invited Fran to call her. It wasn't that she wasn't nice; she really was. She definitely had something or other on her mind, so even during dinner when she was trying hard to be welcoming and to take an interest she had kept drifting off into her own thoughts. But Fran didn't think that was something she could help, and she didn't blame her for it.

No, what rattled her was that there were still *two* of Liz, overlapping but not quite in phase. One Liz's movements lagged behind the other's as though she was a very short chorus line that hadn't rehearsed its routines properly. Viewed from this close up, the effect was even freakier and more unsettling. It had a rhythm to it that was almost hypnotic.

Normally, Fran was painfully aware, something like this would be the first pebble in an avalanche. When the changes started, they escalated fast. But what was happening with Liz seemed to be different. She didn't bring on other changes. In fact, she didn't really change herself: there were just—inexplicably, but unmistakably—two of her.

Fran tried hard not to stare, but she couldn't help herself. When Zac's mom noticed, Fran scrambled hastily for an excuse. "I really like your bracelet, Ms. Kendall," she blurted. It was true, at least.

The bracelet was the same one Liz had been wearing at Carroll Way. It was white gold, with several small stones bracketing one large pink tourmaline, and Fran thought it was very cool. "I got it when I was about your age," Liz said, seeming pleased but also surprised that Fran had noticed it. "It was the first gift my ex-husband—Zac and Molly's dad—ever gave me. *The shiftless bastard*."

Fran gaped. The unexpected curse-word took her by surprise. But Zac didn't even seem to notice it, and Molly kept right on playing.

"The . . . the two of you don't get along anymore?" Fran stammered.

Liz seemed to be surprised in her turn by this blunt question. "Actually, Fran, it's not something I really feel comfortable talking about," she said. And Zac shot Fran a slightly anguished glance.

Fran mumbled an apology and went back to the game, her cheeks burning.

"Why would you want to ask her that?" Zac whispered to her, the next time his mom went out of the room.

"Yes, Francine," Molly chimed in primly. "Why would you want to?"

Fran and Zac both burst out laughing, and the little bubble of tension popped. But Fran was left with a sinking feeling just the same. Was she hearing voices now as well as seeing things? Because that would be great!

And either way, she had just torpedoed whatever first impression she'd been making and left both Zac and his mom thinking she was rude and graceless. She already knew how protective he was of Liz: she couldn't have chosen a worse thing to screw up on.

She wondered if she should tell Zac about what she was seeing, but she couldn't imagine how that conversation would even start. "Hey, Zachary, why are there two of your mom? Is that a thing in your family?"

She's a monster, Lady Jinx said, as if this settled everything.

But it didn't. Not really.

Ms. Kendall came back into the living room to announce the

imminence of bedtime. "No," Molly pleaded, aghast. "Noooooo. Francine wants to finish the game."

"Francine will have to live with the disappointment," Ms. Kendall said. "Sorry, kiddo." They stowed the Lego back in the plastic worktable. At least, Zac and Fran did. Molly was kept busy making sure that all the Lego characters from all the different franchises got a goodnight kiss.

Zac got a kiss too.

And finally, so did Fran.

"Thank you for coming to play," Molly said. "You can come back tomorrow for another episode."

"Maybe not tomorrow," Fran said, "but I'd love to come back soon."

"Then you can. Zac will bring you."

Ms. Kendall picked Molly up and carried her off down the hall with Hermione Granger in one hand and Stormbringer, the Lightning Dragon in the other. She was still talking as she receded out of their sight. "Francine says she wants to come back soon. Zac will bring her for dinner. We'll have hamburgers again, and corn on the cob, and ice cream. And Fran will make a ship with dragon wings, and I will help her. Then the ice princess will dance, and we'll— "

"Wow!" Fran marveled.

"She's just like that. It's like she's six kids crammed into one tiny body."

Fran shied away from the metaphor, but it was a good way to describe the tiny, hyperactive rubber bullet she had just met.

"So," Zac said, "I told Mom this was a study date. What do you want to study?"

"The depths of your big blue eyes," Fran said.

"They're gray," Zac said with a grin.

"So you can see I need to study."

But actually she had brought her school bag and actually she did have a history test coming up the next day. Zac didn't, but he was a day past deadline on his English homework. "It's for Mrs.

Foyle, though. She always gives me an extra day if I ask for one. I think she heard about the court case and wants to give me a break."

"No," Fran said. "She's just a pushover. You could get three days if you played hardball."

They worked side by side on the sofa in the family room for a while. It was nice, even if they didn't talk much. Jinx lay curled up at Fran's feet, bored and disgruntled because Fran couldn't pay any attention to her. Eventually she fell asleep.

Either Zac had forgotten Fran's indiscreet brain-fart, or else he'd decided not to mention it. It was nothing in any case, she told herself: she must have misheard something Zac's mom had said that was totally ordinary and not weird at all. And the other stuff, the way there were two of her and they were a little bit out of sync with each other, was just one more symptom of Fran's . . . condition. It would go away as soon as she got steady on the risperidone.

That thought took the edge off her good humor instantly. It reminded her of what Dr. Southern had said, about her meds being part of the problem rather than a solution to it. If that was true then she was in dead trouble, because the problem was getting worse.

He had talked about coming up with a different approach. Fran had no idea what that would even look like.

Zac had noticed the change in her mood. "Are you okay?" he asked.

"Right now," Fran said, "or in general?"

"I meant right now. But, you know, either."

"No," Fran admitted. She hadn't consciously decided to go for total honesty: the word just slipped out.

"Is it anything I can help with?"

She shook her head.

A different approach . . .

"Although actually . . ." she said, "I don't know. Maybe. Possibly. Yes."

"Hashtag mixed signals."

"Only signals I've got, Zachary. Love them or leave them." She gave him a smile to show she was joking. It wasn't much of a smile, but it was the best she could do. Zac smiled back, perplexed but interested. Waiting to hear what she was going to say.

"I'd like to take you somewhere," Fran told him. Weirdly excited at the thought, even though a terrible weight of shame and fear stirred in her belly. "Show you something. A place that . . . well, it's hard to explain it, really. You'd have to see."

Lady Jinx had awakened and come bolt upright. Suddenly she was armored, and her hand was on the hilt of her sword.

You wouldn't dare! she yelped. And then, *Fran, we can't. It's too dangerous!*

"I'd like that," Zac said. Really quietly. With no winks or innuendo, not trying to make it be something it wasn't. "I'd like to go with you."

After that dramatic opening volley, the psychological warfare intensified very gradually—gradually enough that Liz was able to persuade herself for a while that all the things that were happening were random and unconnected.

The third strike in particular felt like a de-escalation. It was a bag of dogshit left on the front doorstep. The bag wasn't set on fire or anything; it was just thrown down there like a gauntlet. Kids' stuff, Liz thought. But there was a message on the side of the bag, and that freaked her out a little.

Hope you like the taste, it said. *More coming.*

Then there was nothing for five days, which got her hopes up. Malice takes a lot of effort even when you're highly motivated, and most people can only keep it up for so long.

On the morning of the sixth day, the car tires were flat again— all four of them this time, so it took Liz and Zac fifteen minutes to pump them up with the tiny BellAire inflater Parvesh kept in the garage. The same thing happened the morning after, but this time the vandal had squirted superglue into the valve heads. There was no way to pump the tires up again without installing new valves, and no time to call Triple-A. Liz had to abandon the car and take Molly to school by bus while Zac walked in on his own.

He really didn't mind, he said. For one thing, it meant he'd be walking right past the front door of Francine Watts, his new best friend, and the two of them could walk on to school together. Liz wondered (again) if it was more than a friendship. On the whole, she hoped it was. At seventeen, Zac was well overdue for his first big romantic crush, and Francine seemed like a sweet kid in spite of all the awful things she'd been through.

They had touched on that subject, very lightly, on the night when Fran had come over. There was a moment when Liz was putting away the barbecue utensils and Fran had been helping. Liz said something about how every hour you spent enjoying yourself got you two hours of cleaning and tidying.

"Yeah," Fran said. "But that's . . . you know, it's worthwhile. Important."

"You mean the treats?" Liz asked. "Yeah, I agree. You've got to build some pleasure into your life."

"You do," Fran agreed. "But I meant the tidying. It's good to be able to find things when you need them." She folded her hands across her chest, rubbing her elbows as if she were cold, although it was a mild evening. "I freak out if I'm looking for something and it's not where I left it. It makes me feel sort of helpless."

"Helpless?"

"Because . . ." She seemed to become aware, suddenly, of what her hands were doing. She dropped them to her sides. "If there was a zombie apocalypse and you couldn't find your chain saw, you know . . ."

"You could rig up a flamethrower out of a hairspray," Liz pointed out.

"Yeah, there's that."

They had conspired to turn it into a joke, but for a second it hadn't been. Fran had meant every word, at least up to the zombie apocalypse, and Liz had known that helpless feeling too. The feeling you got when the whole world wasn't where you needed it to be, and everything went into freefall. Fran was terribly young to have had that feeling, but she seemed to be coping with it pretty well, all things considered. She was tougher and braver than she looked.

The thought of her and Zac maybe being sweet on each other made Liz happy, and put the whole business with the dirty tricks campaign right out of her mind.

Until she got back from taking Molly to school and found a dead pigeon lying on the front stoop. It had been caught in a wire snare, the wire still looped around its throat and beads of black blood congealed in the feathers on its breast. Liz had a good look around. There was no clue to how the bird had got there, but a thin smear of red on the door frame at chest height suggested it might have been thrown, say from the window of a passing car.

She disposed of the remains and scrubbed the porch with disinfectant. Practical and sensible. But there was a panic welling up inside her—exactly the kind of panic Fran Watts had described—and once she'd finished with the busy-work she couldn't hide from it anymore. She slumped on the living room sofa and sat there for a while in a paralysis of worry, and the only things she could reach for to pull herself out of it were other worries. She had to get to work. She couldn't afford to be late or miss a shift right now. She needed the job too much.

The bus took its time in coming, and she only just made it to Bakery Square for ten o'clock. Since she was the last to clock in, Nora put her on cleaning, which sucked a little but was absolutely fair because she applied the same rule to everyone. Vacuuming up stale popcorn, steam-washing the toilet stalls and freeze-blasting wads of gum out of the carpets wasn't fun, but it was something you got used to. Unfortunately, it occupied Liz's body but left her mind free to obsess. By the end of the day she was exhausted, not with the physical labor but with thinking about what she was going home to.

Nothing, as it turned out, but her nerves were still on edge and she was jumping at every random sound. She went through the evening routine like an automaton, barely aware of what the kids were saying to her. Over dinner Molly told a complicated anecdote about what happened when Gina Pasko tripped Elena Casablanca over with her jump rope and said it was an accident but then laughed like it was funny. Liz heard one word in ten, and had to copy Zac's facial expressions because she wasn't clear enough on the through-line to react on her own behalf.

After Molly was in bed, she told Zac about the dead bird, and showed him its corpse in the trashcan. She felt like he needed to know, but she regretted it when she saw how rattled he was. "Mom, you should call the cops," he pleaded. "Call Beebee at least. Someone needs to do something about this."

"I'm not sure what they can do, Zac."

"Me neither. But let's at least ask them!"

"If it happens again, I will. Maybe, you know, it will just stop by itself."

"Why would it stop. If he's trying to scare you . . ."

"He?"

Zac shrugged. "Someone." But they both knew who he meant by *he*, and Liz had thought it too. She just hadn't admitted it to herself until then.

If you walked down to Lincoln Avenue and headed west across the bridge, you found yourself in Homewood. There were actually two bridges, two broad double spans of red-brown stone butting up together in kind of a V shape, with a little half-wild hinterland spreading out under and all around them.

Zac and Fran stopped halfway across, with the traffic on Washington Boulevard roaring past underneath them. In the slanting late afternoon light, their bodies were dots at the end of the long exclamation points of their shadows.

"Where does the other bridge go to?" Zac asked.

"It's part of the Pennsylvania Railroad," Fran told him. "It's called the Brilliant Cutoff Viaduct, and it's a historical landmark. You see the trees? They grow all along the top. You're not meant to walk up there but you can climb up the cutting from Silver Lake Drive and go right across."

"I think I'll pass," Zac said.

Fran shook her head pityingly, but she didn't mean it. She did it to make him laugh. "Chicken. Come on."

She led the way and he followed, looking more and more uneasy as they came off the far end of the bridge and struck off from the main drag into the side streets. But Zac's nerves were nothing compared to Jinx's. Every now and again Fran caught sight of her, tailing them from a hundred yards back, sneaking from one thin patch of shadow to the next, peeping out from under cars and behind dumpsters. Panic showed in her wide eyes and in her posture, her forelegs bent and her front end scraping the ground.

She had been incandescently furious with Fran ever since Fran first suggested this expedition. She hadn't said a word as she and Fran were walking home, and she had forsaken the foot of Fran's bed when it got to bedtime. She went off to her den, a purely hypothetical place where Fran couldn't join her. This seemed to Fran to be a good indicator of her own mixed feelings: the part of her that manifested as Jinx telling the rest of her that she had shit for brains.

Today at school, Jinx had made a point of letting Fran glimpse her again and again so she could stalk away each time with her tail and snout high, showing her intense disapproval in the only way she could. But now, as they got closer and closer to their destination, she was there. She had to be on guard when Fran was doing something dangerous, however much she disapproved.

"How much further?" Zac asked, trying to make the question sound casual.

"Almost there," Fran told him, although she had nothing to go on beyond an address and a quick reconnaissance on Google Maps. She was doing all this on a kind of autopilot, trying not to think about it too much in case she realized how crazy it was and finally talked herself out of it.

The neighborhood had delaminated around them. Every block here had at least a couple of houses that were still lived in, but they got further and further apart. Mostly the buildings were boarded up and silent, the overgrown yards silted up with ancient garbage.

"Are you sure this is the right way?" Zac asked, visibly anxious. "Homewood is supposed to be dangerous."

"So is Larimer," Fran shot back.

"Fair."

"Just means it's poor, Zac. And mostly black. You know that, right?"

She led him across the old freight yard and into a kind of broken no-man's-land of shut-down warehouses, vacant lots and the occasional dead office block. Sometimes these tumble-down derelicts had FOR SALE signs out in front of them, as though their current state of disrepair was just a temporary thing, but it was hard to believe they were fooling anybody.

At the end of a long stretch of nothing, between two boarded-up buildings with the freeway overpass as a distant backdrop, Fran found what she was looking for. A wrought-iron arch, its elaborate scrollwork red with rust, curved over two brick gateposts that stood about twelve feet high. Beside them, a mildewed lightbox sign advertised WEEKDAY SPECIALS, CABLE TV AND POOL.

"This is it," Fran said unnecessarily.

"Let's not go in the pool," Zac said.

"But I brought my swimsuit!" she protested, and they both laughed like idiots. It wasn't that funny a joke, but laughing burned off some of the tension that seemed to have been growing in both of them since they crossed the bridge.

Fran led the way up a broad driveway whose concrete was all in pieces like a slab of toffee that had been hit with a hammer. It was pretty well furnished for a driveway. They passed a rotting sofa, a couple of office chairs and an ancient roll-top desk. Butterfly weed and goldenrod grew between these out-of-place items, the flowers dazzlingly bright as though someone had set them on fire and then hit the PAUSE button.

Fran was suddenly aware that it was just the two of them standing in the driveway. She looked back. Jinx was sitting on the sidewalk where they'd just walked in, staring forlornly after them.

I can't, she said. There was something bleak and broken in the way she said it.

I'm sorry, Jinx, Fran said inside her mind. *I think I have to.*

With a pang of guilt that made no sense at all, she turned away.

Jinx's responses were her own responses, of course, so she must be getting some kind of emotional comfort out of having one small part of her say *no no no!* while the rest of her took a boy she barely knew into the frozen, fucked-up heart of her psychic landscape.

They had come to the motel's parking lot, where they had to pick their way carefully because there were concrete dividers hidden in the speargrass that came almost up to their waists. There was a heavy dirge of flies and crickets, cut through with sharp, sweet skeins of birdsong. At one end of the Perry Friendly's decayed frontage, there was a second scrollwork arch that led through into a rear courtyard. Fran headed in that direction.

The courtyard was secluded and eerily quiet, surrounded on three sides by the motel's two stories of rooms. The fourth side was the back of an advertising hoarding, leaning at a slight angle now because two of its supports were gone. Ragged strips of paper, bleached yellow-white by the sun, hung down from it like stalactites—all that remained of the last ad it had held.

All the windows had been boarded up, and even the graffiti on the boards had a historical flavor. It referenced the Wu-Tang Clan, Ludacris and the 41-0 margin by which the Steelers had once, in times gone by, beaten the Browns in Cleveland.

The weeds here were thicker still. They came all the way up to the building as if they were trying to push against it and knock it down. There was even a tree growing up through the stairs at one end of the arcade, its upper branches thrusting between the concrete risers and the wrought iron of the rails. Fran thought of the hands of a prisoner, shoved up through steel bars.

It was completely still. The crickets and the birds all seemed to have stayed in the parking lot out front. Fran had the ridiculous sense that the building was aware of her. Had maybe been aware of her all this time, even when she had been elsewhere, doing other things. Nonetheless, she made herself move.

Some of the doors had lost their numbers (presumably they were lying in the weeds under their feet), but the door to room

22 was still hanging in there. It was right at the end of the arcade, on the ground floor. Like all the other doors they'd passed, it had a steel L-beam with a dozen big rivets in it all the way up its right-hand edge, sealing the door to the jamb. It looked formidable, but when Fran put her hand against the door and pushed, she felt it give. The rotten wood didn't cleave to the rivets at all. They both put their shoulders to it and it opened with a soggy sigh.

The room was dark and empty. Now that they had come to the threshold, Fran was afraid to step over it. The atmosphere of her dreams rose smotheringly, gluing her feet to the ground. It was Zac who broke the spell. He ambled in as though it was nothing, fanning the air in front of his face.

"Wow," he marveled. "This place reeks."

He wasn't exaggerating. A hot stink of earth and damp and mildew welcomed Fran as she stepped inside. It was strangely reassuring. Nobody had disturbed the Perry Friendly's decade-long sleep before them.

The room was completely empty. The carpet had been torn up, revealing warped and discolored boards with a whole lot more weeds growing up between them. The curtains over the boarded-up window were like the ghosts of curtains, faded almost to invisibility, their pattern persisting only as random blotches here and there on the leprous white. A doorway off to one side led through to what must once have been a bathroom, the white tiles on the walls the only remaining clue. Holes in the floor marked the places where the sink and toilet must have stood, and where pipes had gone through. The bathroom door lay on its side against the wall.

Fran stood just inside the door, struck to silence. She was seeing the past through the holes in the present. She knew the word for this: it was a palimpsest. Something that had been written on, imperfectly erased and then written on again. That was her whole life, right there, in that one word.

"Fran . . ." Zac sounded uneasy. Probably the look on her face right now was something to see.

"I was over here." She made herself move, to prove to herself that she could. Away from the door, from the outside world and safety, all the way to the back of the room. She pointed down. "You see the chalk?"

Zac didn't at first. She had to make him kneel down on the rotted, nearly colorless linoleum. The line was barely there at all now, but Fran traced out with her fingertip the segments that still showed so he could see it for what it was, or at least what it had been. A circle.

"He put me down and then he drew all around me. He told me not to step across the line. When I got tired, I was allowed to sit down but not to lie down—because if I lay down some of me would be outside the circle. When I dozed off, he slapped me to make me wake up."

"How did you go to the bathroom?" Zac asked, and then immediately he went red and shook his head. "I'm sorry, that was a really stupid question."

"Actually, it was a problem," Fran said. "I kept asking him and he kept saying to hold it in. But it got to where I couldn't. You can only cross your legs for so long, you know? He shouted at me not to pee on the floor. I think he was scared that I'd wash away the chalk. He ran into the bathroom over there, and then back again, two or three times. Like he was trying to figure out a way to bring me to the toilet, or the toilet to me. In the end, he rummaged on the shelves—they were on that wall, right there—and found an old paint tin. I peed in that."

"Jesus," Zac said weakly.

Fran walked back to the boarded-up window. She tried to make it casual, but her heart was bang-bang-banging in her chest and her legs were shaking. It was a relief to be moving back toward the door. She sketched out a space with her hands. "There was a kind of a chest of drawers here. From before they made it be a storeroom, I guess. Look, it was screwed into the wall here. You can see where all the plaster came off when they took it out.

"He had this big metal box. Green. Like, army green. It was a tackle box, for fishing, but I'd never seen one so I just thought it was a toolbox like my dad has. He put it up on the chest of drawers, and that's when I found out what his name was. It said Bruno on the front of it. Not Bruno Picota. Just Bruno.

"He took a knife out of the box. I never saw what else was in there. Just that knife."

Zac looked at the broken plaster, and then at Fran's face. "You don't have to talk about any of this," he told her.

Fran shrugged. So chilled and indifferent. Such a liar. "I'm okay with talking about it."

"Really? If it was me I'd be freaking out. I mean, what you went through here . . ."

"It was a long time ago. Anyway, that's what I came for. I wanted to see it again. Sort of . . . test myself against it." Out of sheer bravado, Fran sat down on the rolled-up carpet. After a moment, Zac came over and joined her there.

"I get nightmares," she told him. "About Picota, and what happened here. Not everything, just little bits of it. Details. Or not even that. The way it felt, not the way it happened. There are only a few real things that make it into the dreams. Like the knife. The knife he had. That turns up a lot. He didn't . . ." Oh boy. Oh boy! She clenched her fists tight. "He didn't cut me with it but he kept it in his hand the whole time, and it seemed like . . . you know, sooner or later it was going to happen. But then the police came through that door." She pointed. "And through the window, right here. Like a kind of explosion, there were so many of them. They got Picota down on the ground and hit him and kicked him a whole lot of times. I mean, they really beat the shit out of him. That part I remember. Then someone—a cop, it must have been— carried me out of the room on his shoulder. I looked back, and they were still laying into Picota. I could barely even see him. Just the nightsticks going up and down."

"Good," Zac said.

Yeah. Good enough, if that was all there was. She wanted to tell him the rest, but it was hard because words were all she had and words wouldn't really carry it.

150

"In the nightmares, though, there are never any police here. It's always about the time before. When it's just me and him. Or sometimes it's me on my own, but I know he's coming. Or he's already here, maybe, but I can't see him. There was a really bad one where he kind of was the whole place. The room was talking to me in his voice."

Fran plucked a weed up from the floorboards, a single green stem with a froth of pale yellow at the top, and twirled it in her fingers. "In case you didn't notice," she said, "I'm a little bit crazy."

"No." Zac shook his head with absolute finality. "You're not."

"That's nice of you to say, Zac, but the evidence is on my side. I'm on anti-psychotics. And I'm seeing a psychiatrist, you know? They don't waste their time hanging out with sane people."

"The same psychiatrist my mom is seeing," Zac said. "She's not crazy and neither are you."

"Okay, here's the thing." Fran heard the edge in her voice, and tried hard to soften it. "The thing I'm afraid of, since you asked."

She folded the stem of the weed in two, and then in four, and finally in eight—because she knew her hands would start shaking if she didn't give them something to do, but mostly so she could carry on talking to Zac without looking at him.

"I said he didn't cut me. But I only know that from being told. And from not having any scars, obviously. I don't remember it."

"What?"

"When I think about what happened to me here, it's kind of just a soup." She was having to work hard now to get the words out. It was as though something didn't want them to be spoken. She didn't know if that something was inside her or in the room. "I was in this place for a day and two nights and it feels like it was just minutes. There are these . . . holes. Most of it, really, is holes. And they . . . they've got bigger, as I got older. As though it's a disease I caught here, and it keeps getting worse. Sometimes I'll reach for a memory of something I absolutely know I saw or heard or felt, and it's gone. Just not there at all."

She swallowed hard. "I don't even remember my mom dying. I

151

was eight. I was old enough, you know, to understand . . . But it's just gone."

"Sometimes we've got these defense mechanisms," Zac offered. "You know, if it's something bad that we don't really want to remember. We shut it out."

"Yeah, but then sometimes I remember things that didn't happen at all. Falling off a bike I never owned and breaking my arm. It was a *pink* bike! Like I'd be seen dead on a pink bike! Fighting with a bigger kid at Worth Harbor when she split my lip and I bit her arm. Except that the kid I remember fighting was Justin Dipper's sister, and he doesn't have one."

She took another deep gulping breath. "And I remember Picota putting the knife right up against my side—like he was finally going to use it. I could feel the point of it, going in a little way. The pressure, and then the pain. High up . . . on my left side. Where my . . ."

Heart is. Not that you know where your heart is, exactly, but . . . The sense of that intrusion. Something cold and sharp and stinging that had no right to be there. The shock of it, like *no, no, no, this isn't something that can happen*. Which it didn't, because when the police took her away there wasn't a mark on her.

There was a sound that came with that memory. The sound of her feet thumping a ragged tattoo against the floor as she tried to run. Only Picota was holding her and she couldn't. Couldn't get moving. Couldn't get away.

But she did anyway, somehow, and she was gone for the longest time. Days? Weeks? Until she woke up in a bed on the children's ward at West Penn Hospital, surrounded by more toys than she'd ever seen in her life. Thinking *well, this can't be right*.

But what did that mean, exactly? How did you get back to *right*, when you'd forgotten what it even looked like?

"Do you know what homeopathy is?" she asked Zac softly.

"No."

"It's kind of a theory about how medicine works. The idea is if you want to get better you take a little bit of the thing that's making you sick. Like, you drink poison, but in really tiny doses. That's what I thought might happen, if I came here. That I might stop being afraid of it."

"Is it working?" Zac asked her.

"No," Fran admitted with a slightly crazed laugh. "Not yet."

She stood, and dropped the broken stem. It fell across a part of the faded chalk line that was still visible, its ragged roots within the circle and its flowering tip outside. "This was really stupid," she said, her voice sounding eerily hollow in her own ears. The sense of being listened to was even stronger now. Fear was welling up in her as though she was sucking it out of the ground. "Let's get out of here."

She walked back out into the courtyard.

But the courtyard had changed into a pristine stretch of paving stones, rose-pink and white. Two big gas barbecues stood at one end of it, under a sign that said SUMMER GRILL SHACK. The billboard was gone, or at least hidden behind a towering conifer hedge. The air smelled of roses, pine resin and someone's garden fire.

Fran simply wasn't ready for a change on this massive scale. With a yelp of dismay, she sank down on her knees among the weeds that were there to the touch although she couldn't see them anymore. She crouched on all fours, head bowed onto her chest.

Zac was beside her at once, his hand on her forearm as gingerly as if she might explode. "Fran, what's wrong? Tell me what's wrong!"

She had shut her eyes, but the scents were still there. Sounds, too. Faint music with no bass, maybe from a car radio. A man and a woman talking in desultory tones in one of the rooms right behind her, their voices clear enough that they must have left the window open.

"When are you going to tell your folks about us?"

"Soon. Or maybe never."

"Oh, is that how it is?"

"My mom will freak. She doesn't like the thought of anyone having fun when she's not there."

"Nobody," Fran whispered. "There's nobody here."

"There's me," Zac said. "I'm here. I'll get someone."

"No!" She grabbed his hand with her own and held it tight. It felt like a lifeline right then because he belonged to the real world and he was still there. He was a weak-ass anchor, but he would have to do.

"Tell me what you can see," she muttered between her teeth.

"What?"

"Shit! What's there, Kendall? Just look around and tell me!" She was panicking now. It was as though the Perry Friendly had done this to her on purpose, as a show of force. You think the little changes are bad? What if you couldn't see the real world at all? What if all you could see was me?

There was just Zac's breathing, for a moment or two, and hers. And the music in the background, a song she vaguely knew but couldn't place.

"I see . . . the motel," Zac said. "The arch we came in through is over on the right. A sign on the side of the arch says reception, and another one says ice machine. They've both got arrows, pointing. And there's weeds everywhere, obviously. An old billboard that's more or less falling apart. Flies. Lots of flies around. Clouds in the sky, but not that many of them. It's still real bright."

He went on and on for a long time, naming things. The sounds and the smells came right again one by one as he was talking. Finally, Fran opened her eyes, and found that the world had reset. The changes had stopped.

She let go of Zac's hand and stood up on legs that shook.

"Thanks," she muttered.

"You're welcome," Zac said. "Can I . . .?" He paused for long enough that she turned to look at him. "Can I ask what that was?"

"That?" Fran let out a long, uneven breath. "I told you I was crazy, Zachary."

The look he was giving her was troubled. Uncertain. But it wasn't disgusted or amused, so that was something. "What were you seeing, then? If it wasn't this?"

"It *was* this. Just a different this. That's the way my craziness works. If the amnesia and the false memories weren't crazy enough. I see the world changing its mind."

This got the same look from Zac. Except that maybe his forehead creased up a little bit more as he tried to think his way around that one. "Could you maybe give me an example?"

"I saw the motel as if it had never closed down. As if it was still going strong."

"Like, an alternate universe?"

"Like a hallucination." She looked at her watch. "We'd better get going. It's almost seven."

She walked toward the archway. She was aware that Zac had fallen into step beside her, although she was looking at the ground rather than at him. "So this homeo thing."

"Homeopathy."

"Maybe if it didn't work, it was because you didn't get the dose right."

"I think once was enough."

"I don't mean you should come back here," Zac said. "There are other things you could do." He was so serious that Fran almost laughed in spite of how threadbare and raw her brain still was from the changes. He was trying to compensate for how badly her big experiment had worked out by being more on her side than she was. It was kind of sweet.

"Share your thoughts, Mr. Holmes," she said, but she needed to put on a voice to make the line sound funny, and she couldn't bring herself to do that yet.

"You've got gaps in your memory. And the memories you do have don't fit together the way they should. That's your problem, right? And maybe your mind reacts to that by making other things not match up—like what happened to you just now. But everything that happened to you here is written down somewhere. It's got to be. There would have been a thousand news articles about Picota, and you, and the whole thing." Zac held up his phone by way of a prop for his oratory. "You don't have to come back here; you only have to go online. Get the facts. Nail it down."

Fran gave him a curious look. It was actually a pretty good idea, and she was kind of amazed that it had never occurred to her. "When you read the news, you don't always get the facts," she said, but she was just being a dick. You could triangulate. If two sources disagreed, you went back to *their* sources. She knew how to research.

Beyond that, though, Zac had just thrown in—as casually as if it were obvious—a possible explanation for the changes. And it made really good sense. Trauma had bent her memory out of shape, just about that one terrifying day she spent with Picota and his knife. So her mind rebelled by bending everything else.

Maybe the truth really would set her free.

Jinx was still waiting where they had left her, lying at the end of the driveway with her head resting on her forepaws. She jumped up when she saw them coming and trotted quickly back and forth until they joined her.

You're all right! What happened? I'm so glad you're all right! Tell me what happened!

Later, Fran mouthed. And she gave Jinx a quick smile to show her that everything was okay.

Or at least, that it might be.

What finally tipped the scales for Liz was something a lot smaller and more trivial than the dead pigeon. Coming home from work a couple of days later, she found that someone had poured molasses into her mailbox. There wasn't any real mail in there: just a *Reader's Digest* mailout telling her that she might already have won a million dollars and a couple of bills which would reliably come back around. But enough was enough.

Liz called Beebee on her cell rather than on the department's number. "I've got a stalker," she said. "I think maybe I need some help."

"I'm there," Beebee said.

She came right on over, and she brought another cop with her to make it clear that this was official. It was Lowenthal, the officer who had been with her when she responded on the night Marc was arrested. They took Liz's statement on the sofa in the family room. Zac sat in, or to be more accurate he prowled around. He picked up the story whenever Liz flagged, with more hand gestures and heavier emphasis.

Beebee scribbled in her notebook the whole time, getting the details down. When they were finished, she looked up at

Lowenthal, who nodded his head to indicate she should speak first.

"Quick question," Beebee said. "Did you keep the bag? The one that had the message on it?"

"No! It had dogshit all over it. It went right in the trash." Liz only realized as she said it what a stupid move that was.

"And the trash has been taken out since then?"

Liz nodded. "Sorry."

Beebee shrugged it off. "Never mind. I was just thinking aloud, you know . . . the guy's handwriting, maybe a fingerprint or two. Would have been nice to have that if it was there to be had. But anyway, there's more than enough here to prove you're being deliberately targeted. Stalking laws apply, if we catch the son of a bitch. Pardon my French."

"I've called him worse inside my head, believe me," Liz said. "So is there anything we can do about this?"

"Well, the first thing is you fit locks on the windows. He's stayed outside up to now, but you shouldn't assume he'll stick to that."

"The windows have all got cockspur handles. But we're still getting the last of the hot days and we don't have any AC. I need to let the bedrooms cool down so Moll can sleep."

"Lockable window screens," Lowenthal said. "You need the solid ones that sit in a frame." Which would cost hundreds of dollars, Liz knew. She'd have to use the credit card, which she was trying really hard not to do.

"Plus you should fit a chain on the door," the cop went on. "Or better yet a security bar. And some outside lights if you don't have any. Good and bright. Cameras are really useful too, especially at the back of the building."

Liz shook her head. They were straying into fantasy fiction now. "I definitely can't afford to fit cameras."

"Maybe you can," Beebee said. "There's got to be a neighborhood watch around here. Join it, and ask if they've got a bulk-buy scheme. They can get you a discount on most of this stuff, and probably fit it for you so you don't have to pay for someone to install them."

Lowenthal's turn. "Get into the habit of checking every door and window before you go out. Never leave anything unlocked."

Then Beebee again. They had a great little double act going, which made Liz uncomfortably aware that they must have done this a lot of times. Was the world full of bird-killing, dogshit-hurling creeps? "Park the car on the drive, not the street. Might be whoever it is will think twice before coming over your property line, especially if the lights are on."

"Which you should leave one on all the time, even at night," Lowenthal chipped in. "You'd be amazed how well that works as a deterrent."

"So that's you," Beebee said. "The other half of the equation is what we can do. There's a car on flexible patrol most nights. I'll see if we can shift it to this side of Lincoln for the next week or so, so if anything does happen and you have to dial 911 you'll get a quicker response."

That was comforting. "Thanks, Beebee."

"You're welcome. Okay, I'm thinking aloud here. There are some CCTV cameras up on Meadow Street. I'm going to pull the footage and take a look. If your perp isn't local, he most likely came in along that route. We've got the dates and times of the incidents to go on. We might get lucky. If the same face keeps popping up, we can feed it into the face recognition program and see what falls out."

"Thanks," Liz said again. "Thank you."

"If there's another incident, let us know right away," Beebee said. "Or if you see someone hanging around, or especially if you get another written message." Her tone had become brisk. She shifted her weight, preparing to stand. "We're right on the end of the phone, okay?"

Zac looked from one cop to the other, and then to Liz. He seemed surprised that things were wrapping up so fast. "What about my dad?" he demanded.

Beebee and Lowenthal both looked at him, wearing identical deadpans.

"How do you mean, Zac?" Beebee asked.

"Well, shouldn't you haul him in and question him?"

Liz had been thinking the same thing, but had fought shy of saying it. A part of her just found it too hard to go there. In spite of the violence and the verbal take-downs, the years of intimidation and grinding down, she couldn't make herself believe that the man she'd loved and lived beside and made a family with could put so much thought and effort into making her unhappy.

"It's reasonable to raise the question," Beebee said, but her hands were raised with the palms out. *Hold your horses.* "I don't think interviewing Marc would be a good idea. That is, unless there's something that points to his being involved. Is there anything?"

"The message on the bag of shit," Zac said with an incredulous laugh like it was obvious. "That was a threat. Like, this isn't just someone playing stupid tricks, it's an attack. A . . . a campaign. And the bird, you know. It was killed with a wire snare. My dad taught me how to make one of those when I was ten and he was trying to get me to try out for wilderness scouts. You should look to see if he's got wire and garden stakes in his house."

"Lots of people do, son," Lowenthal said. "Wouldn't actually prove anything now, would it?"

Beebee closed her notebook and put it away as if to show that she was going off the record. "Here's the thing," she said—to Liz, not to Zac. "We haven't gone to trial yet. When we do, your ex-husband's lawyer will be looking to poke some nice big holes in the police evidence, because it's strong and it's damning. If we go and brace Marc about this without anything to show by way of due cause, well, we're just strengthening his hand. We're actually giving him ammunition to prove a prejudicial process, and he could use that to get an acquittal. You could have him all up in your lives again."

"So you can't go after the most likely suspect because that would mean admitting he's a suspect," Liz summed up.

"It sounds stupid, but yeah. That's it exactly. You're always tempted to join the dots when something like this happens. Why wouldn't you? But you've got to wait until you've got enough dots to make a shape."

"Get those cameras," Lowenthal said. "If you possibly can."

"Yeah," Beebee said, nodding. "If you were to catch Marc on your property, breaching his restraining order, then we'd be off to the races." The two officers stood up. "Call me if you just want to talk," Beebee said. "Any time."

Liz promised she would. She was doing sums in her head, trying to see if there was any way of buying a security camera. Maybe one of the pawnshops down from the church on Frankstown Avenue would sell her a second-hand one, but it didn't seem all that likely.

Lowenthal examined the door jamb on the way out. "You could fit a nice, thick slide bar on here, see?" he said.

"Yeah," Liz said, trying to sound enthusiastic. "Good idea."

She closed the door behind the two cops. The visit had done little to reassure her, despite Beebee's kindness and very evident wish to help.

Zac was even more unhappy, not to mention frustrated and angry. "Okay," he said, "maybe they can't talk to him, but we can. We can let him know we're onto him."

Liz went back to the door and turned the key in the lock. "If it is him, Zac, I'd rather leave him to make his own mistakes, rather than telling him what we're thinking. Whoever it is, our best chance is if they screw up." After a few moments, she said, "I don't know how, but I'm getting those cameras."

She did her best to lift the mood, offering to take her son on at *Sonic the Hedgehog*—a Neolithic console game that Liz had played in her youth and had introduced to her kids courtesy of a *Greatest Hits of the Nineties* compilation for Zac's console. Zac agreed, but they only got halfway through the Green Hill Zone before they folded. Sonic was a feel-good game, and they just couldn't get there.

"I guess I'll turn in," Liz said, kissing Zac on the cheek.

"I guess I'll play some *Mass Effect*," Zac said.

Neither of them stuck to those plans. When Liz passed Zac's door on her way back from the bathroom, she saw him talking to Francine Watts on Skype.

And in her own room she sat awake, listening to the house and to the occasional gusts of wind hitting the side wall. Everything at night sounds like a home invasion, if you're in the right mood. She wearied herself with the strain of constant attention and constant reading in.

Liz's cell rang twice. The same unfamiliar number both times. She didn't bother to answer. Cold call or wrong number, she didn't want to have to deal with either. She was still thinking about the cameras, and the security bar for the door. She had the money her mom had left her, almost three thousand dollars. It was sitting in a savings account where she'd hoped it would become the core of a little nest egg for Zac and Moll. She'd never been able to add so much as a dime to it. Maybe now was the time to smash that piggy bank, however much she hated the thought of her mom telling her *I told you so* from beyond the grave.

When she finally dozed off, around about 2:30 in the morning, Beth was waiting for her.

Fran lay on her bed, fully clothed and with her laptop propped up on her knees. Lady Jinx was curled up beside her, lightly asleep or else pretending to be. It was well after midnight, but someone down the street who was learning guitar was still playing languid chords, just about in tune. The sound came in through her open window like a reminder that the city never sleeps.

Her dad did, though, and tonight he'd crashed out early after three hours' overtime at the firehouse and their first Chinese takeout in absolutely ages. Chinese food and a DVD screening of *Who Framed Roger Rabbit* had been Fran's ultimate treat through most of her childhood. It reliably cheered her up, which of course was why Gil had suggested it. He could see that his little girl was preoccupied, and he must have assumed that meant she was sad. If anything, though, the opposite was true. The quest Fran had embarked on with Zac Kendall filled her with a tense, prickly excitement.

She had tried to medicate her fear away, and that hadn't worked out so well. Her visit to the Perry Friendly had been another kind of medication, trying to domesticate the fear into something she could cope with. That hadn't worked either.

Now she was hunting it. She had equipped an expedition. A small one, admittedly, but every quest has to start somewhere. Even the Fellowship of the Ring had just been a bag of random hobbits until Frodo got Elrond to handle the crowdfunding.

That skinny little white boy is not Elrond, Jinx growled without opening her eyes.

Maybe he's Samwise, Fran said, inside her mind so Zac wouldn't hear.

His mom is a ring-wraith!

Zac's face loomed and lurched on the screen in front of Fran, her laptop's crappy video card chopping up his movements into jerky stop-motion. She could see glimpses of his bedroom behind him, teasingly revealed and hidden as he moved. It was the first boy's room Fran had ever visited, even virtually. The superhero figurines, the drum kit, the iPod dock whose speaker was in the shape of the little robot beachball from *Star Wars* . . . it was all kind of thrilling and exotic. Like everything in the room was made out of Y chromosomes.

"So shall we, like, do a mission briefing before we start?" Zac asked her. "Because I got a ton of stuff here, but I fell down a little bit on the quality control. A lot of it is tabloid crap. Bruno Picota, portrait of a psycho, kind of thing." He held up a thin sheaf of papers in front of the webcam so she could see he'd done his homework.

"Mission is to accumulate facts," Fran said. "Nothing is irrelevant. The more I know, the more I understand, the better."

"Do we need to know where the gaps in your memories are? Like, make a list, or something, so we can tick them off as we go?"

"It's hard to see a gap, Zachary. If you don't know what's meant to be there, you don't notice it when it's not. Ditto with stuff you remember wrong. I vote we throw our net real wide to start with, and narrow in as we go."

"Cool," Zac said. "Well, I found out why the TV news started calling Picota the Shadowman."

The name brought a soft, rumbling growl from Lady Jinx.

"I know that one," Fran said.

"Of course you do. You were there. See, you've got an unfair advantage on all this stuff."

Fran stuck her tongue out at him. "I don't know it from when I was six, goon. I told you, after the cops pulled me out of that room my brain was scrambled eggs. And my mom and dad kept me away from all the trial coverage. I was the one kid in Pittsburgh who didn't know one thing about Bruno Picota.

"But then when I was eleven there was a TV special. My dad made sure I was nowhere near the TV when it came on, but he forgot about the magic of the internet. I was round at Maisie's house one afternoon—Maisie from chess club—and she downloaded it from some pirate site she found. She thought it was cool, and she was pissed with me when I wouldn't watch it with her. She ended up watching it by herself, and then she told me some of the best parts. She thought I had to be interested. Until I started crying and wouldn't stop. That showed her."

Zac was staring at her with a troubled look on his face. "Hey," Fran said. "I'm not eleven anymore. No tears, look." She drew trickle-lines down her dry cheeks, which made him laugh and stop being freaked out. Freaked out was no good to either of them.

"Shadowman," she said. "Go."

"Picota said there was something wrong with your shadow. That was how he knew there was something wrong with you. He also said you might actually *be* a shadow in disguise." Zac took a quick glance at his crib notes, but he seemed to have it pretty much by heart. "Shadows kept on being a key theme all through the trial. His lawyers read out a whole bunch of stuff he'd said to the psychiatrists who were examining him, and most of that was about shadows too. It seems weird that it all got said out loud in court, because it's nine miles north of nuts. But I guess the defense was based on his being insane, so yeah. Probably didn't do him any harm."

"Probably not," Fran agreed. "You think that's what he was doing? Trying for the fruit bat defense?"

"Personally? I think he was a for-real lunatic, so it's moot."

"Yeah, that's what I think too. He had this whole touched-by-Jesus thing going on, didn't he? Like, he believed there were all these people walking around Pittsburgh who were really devils or had a bit of the devil inside of them. But if you were on God's team, you could tell them by their shadows so you knew who you had to fight."

Zac consulted his notes again. "He didn't mention devils," he said.

"Yeah, he did." That was one of the things Fran remembered from Maisie's summary.

"Not according to the newspaper reports. He said something else. Something out of Native American mythology that I can't pronounce. Skank-God-Munch, or something like that. It was some kind of monster."

"Devil, monster. Comes down to the same thing, right?"

"Not if you're a Native American, would be my guess."

"I thought Picota's family was Italian."

"On his dad's side they were Italian. His mom had an ancestor who was First Nations. A long way back, though. Maybe he heard the stories when he was a kid and they stayed in the back of his mind."

"Okay. Something that's like the devil only different. Picota grabbed me because I was one of the people he thought had been . . ."

"Touched."

"Corrupted."

"Affected."

"Poisoned. Come on, Zac, he was gonna cut the evil right out of me. There's no point in trying to find a polite word for it."

Stand down, Lady J, she added inside her mind. *Don't sweat this.*

I wouldn't have let him cut you! The little fox had come out of her curl and was showing her blindingly white teeth in a battle snarl.

I didn't even know you then, Fran said. *You didn't come along until afterward.*

Jinx didn't answer. Fran looked down to see that she had retreated further under the bed and turned to face the other way.

"Okay, poisoned it is," Zac said, oblivious to all this drama. "He was on a crusade. Trying to stop all these Skank–God shenanigans before shit got real. It turned out he'd attacked a man in the street a few days before he took you. Hit him with a wrench about a million times, and then ran away thinking he'd killed him. The police were already investigating that assault when the word came in about you. But the MO was different, so nobody made the connection."

"Because Bruno grabbed me and took me somewhere instead of attacking me on the spot."

"Right."

"And I'm very grateful for it, believe me. Profoundly fucked up, but not dead. I will take that to the bank."

"By the way, the guy who Picota attacked—Jeffrey Mallen—confirms all this shadow stuff. He said Picota was going on about his shadow, yelling and freaking out about it, right before he started hitting him."

Zac flicked through his stack of printouts until he found the one he was looking for, and read aloud. "He said, 'Where did you get that?' I thought he was pointing at something I was wearing, so I said, 'What? Where did I get what?'

"He said, 'The shadow! The shadow! Where did you get it? You better tell me.' He was getting angry, and I tried to calm him down. I made a joke out of it, saying I'd always had it. 'We're born with them. Haven't you got one?' The next thing I knew he had this wrench in his hand and he hit me in the face with it. I went down, trying to protect my head. He kept on hitting me, then walking away, then coming back and hitting me again. He was shouting the whole time, and I think he was crying.

"Finally he hit me a good one and I lost consciousness. I only found out about the rest afterward. If that couple hadn't come running up I would have been dead. He was clearly insane. There was no way he was going to stop until he'd killed me."

Zac had read Jeffrey Mallen's testimony in a flat, inflectionless voice. Fran thought that she would have put some drama into it, but she could understand why he hadn't wanted to do that. It might have felt like he was turning it into a joke.

"Anyway," he said. "That's all I got."

"It's a great start," Fran told him. "Thanks. If we use some of these words as search terms, maybe we can dig up some more." She toggled to her browser and typed *Picota, shadows, delusions, psychotic* into the search engine. Two million hits in under a second! But the first three items she clicked on were wiki articles about Picota that just regurgitated the same things Zac had already found out. And after that, everything the search engine gave her had ~~Picota~~ next to it in the margin.

Skimming some of these non-Picota articles, she discovered that shadow people were in the top ten of reported hallucinations, even if the people who were doing the hallucinating didn't have a mental illness. You could see shadows doing things they weren't supposed to when you were very tired, or when you were going under the anesthetic before an operation.

Zac was obviously looking at a very similar set of results. He voiced her thoughts. "This isn't what we're looking for, Fran."

"No. It isn't."

"Bruno didn't see you as a shadow. He saw something in your shadow, or something about it, that shouldn't have been there."

"Could be the same psychosis, though," she offered. "Showing itself in a different way."

"Could be, yeah. But the best way to understand Picota is to look at what he actually said. The whole shebang, not just the tease-y little bits that ended up in the media reports."

Fran toggled back to the Skype screen so she could see Zac again. "You mean his psych evaluations? We're not gonna get that."

Zac looked a little bit smug, like he knew something she didn't. "Sure we are."

"Zac, there's a thing called doctor—patient confidentiality. My dad gets to talk to Dr. Southern about my sessions, but only because he's my guardian. And I can stop that as soon as I hit eighteen. Nobody else can walk in and ask for them. And I'm just in a regular clinic. Bruno is up in Grove City in a secure hospital that looks like a concrete birthday cake with razor wire for icing."

"How do you know what it looks like?" Zac asked. His expression of surprise hung on the screen for a few seconds, comically detached from his voice as the video card glitched again.

"I checked out some pictures online," Fran said, which she had. After she called up the plans. And before she walked all around the perimeter on Google Earth. She had wanted to be sure he couldn't get out. She knew she wasn't rational when it came to Bruno Picota. He was a black hole sitting dead center in her mind. She kept being pulled toward him, but if she ever fell in all the way she didn't think she'd come back out again.

"So there's no point in asking if we can see Picota's records," she went on, keeping up a careful deadpan. "They'll just say no. They wouldn't be allowed to show them to us even if they wanted to."

"Yeah, I wasn't gonna ride all the way out to Grove City anyway," Zac said.

"What, then?"

"Grant Street."

"Grant Street? What's at Grant Street?"

"The Allegheny County central records office. Which includes court records, because I phoned and asked them."

Fran thought about it. "Oh. But . . ." She thought about it some more. "Really? You think?"

"I don't think, I know. Tapes of Picota talking to his doctors were played out at the trial. And the jury were given full transcripts, which were admitted into evidence. If you were just a member of the public, the records office might redact some of this stuff, because privacy et cetera, but you're not. You're a party to the original case. You could walk down there right now, so long as you've got ID, and they'd have to let you in."

"You're wrong," Fran said. "They wouldn't."

Zac looked downcast. "Why? What did I miss? Did I miss something?"

"We're out of office hours, Sherlock Homeboy." He flipped her the bird, but he was grinning, acknowledging both the joke and the compliment. Fran grinned back, but then straightened her face again because this was, after all, some extremely serious shit they were up to here. "Will you come with me?" she asked him.

"Wouldn't miss it."

"Tomorrow. Right after school."

"I'm there."

"Okay then. Hey, I'd better go. I've still got a Spanish assignment to finish. G'night, Zac."

"Night."

"And thank you."

She cut the connection. She felt a tingle of pleasure as she did it, because having a co-conspirator was nice. A friend, even.

Distracted by these thoughts, she rolled over to put the laptop back on the bedside table and found Jinx's eyes a scant inch from her own. She started back, aware of a flash of vivid white from just underneath that fixed stare.

Jinx's teeth were still bared. Or else they were bared again.

I don't like any of this, Jinx said.

"I can handle it, Lady J. Honest. And if I can't, I'll stop."

You should stop right now.

Fran reached out a hand, pretending to stroke Jinx. Normally Jinx played along with this because they both enjoyed it. This time Jinx deliberately sat up so her insubstantial head went through Fran's hand, making it very clear that she wasn't in the mood for games.

Bruno Picota is our enemy.

"Okay," Fran agreed. "But isn't there a proverb about knowing your enemy? How can that be a bad thing, Jinx?"

Everything about Bruno Picota is bad. He tried to kill you.

"But this—what we're doing—it's just words." Fran gestured

toward the articles open on the laptop's screen. "Words can't hurt you."

Jinx shivered all over, her fur bristling as though there was a cold wind blowing through the room.

No?

"No."

Jinx snarled and leaped. Her gaping jaws snapped shut on Fran's outstretched hand, making her gasp in shock even though Jinx's teeth couldn't hurt her or even touch her.

"Hey," she protested. "Not cool."

Sometimes you don't know what can hurt you until it's too late, Jinx said.

Marc got Liz by the throat and bore her down. Using both hands at first, but then just the one because he was reaching out for one of the sofa cushions with the other. He shoved it over her face, got his forearm onto it and bore down with all his weight. Changing horses in the middle of the murder, suffocating her instead of strangling her. And she had to wonder why. Was it easier to kill her if he didn't have to look her in the face? The question didn't trouble her for very long.

And . . .

She was standing at the sink when Marc moved in from behind and off to her left. She saw the movement out of the corner of her eye, alarmed—momentarily—at how fast he was coming. He punched her on the jaw with spectacular force, her head thrown sideways so it hit the corner of the kitchen cabinet. She was dead when she hit the ground, but whether it was the punch or the ricochet that killed her she never got to know.

And . . .

They were in bed together and an argument about her not putting out for him turned into an argument about love and trust and a dozen other loaded imponderables. The bedside lamp served as punctuation for his final, emphatic statement that she was a cunt! A cunt! A cunt! A cunt! A worthless, cold-hearted cunt!

And . . .

In the car. On the garden plot. In the bathroom. In the kitchen lots of times, when she was cooking or cleaning up after a meal or serving one up, loading the washing machine or scrubbing the countertops. Her death woven into the fabric of their domestic life, the one household chore that Marc took on himself.

Over and over and over again.

The first one of those was mine, Beth told Liz, with no trace of emotion. *The others . . . well, they came afterward. I'm just hitting the highlights here. Believe me, there were a lot more.*

Stop it! Liz protested soundlessly. *Please! I don't want to see this. I don't need to see it. I already know what he's capable of!*

But then she thought: afterward? What does afterward mean?

Instantly, without any pause or transition, she and Beth were face-to-face again in the colorless void that Beth had said was the inside of Liz's own mind. Beth's mouth was set in a tight line and her eyes were hungry as though Liz's reaction to this horrific memory montage was something savory that she was feeding on.

What do you think it means? It's a pretty basic English word. But let me spell this out for you, since you seem to be having a hard time grasping the completely fucking obvious.

He killed me. I died. But I didn't lie down under it, the way you would. No offense. I was fighting him right up to the moment when I ran out of air. Struggling. Trying to get free. Throwing my weight to one side and then the other to push him off balance so I could suck in some oxygen.

And you know what? In some completely messed up way, it worked. I twisted out from under him. I was someplace else.

But someplace else turned out to be not that far.

I was still in my own house. My own bathtub, actually. And I was still dying, just in a different way. Marc's hand was on my face and he was pushing me back down. Holding me under the water.

Drowning is worse than suffocating. Trust me, I'm kind of a connoisseur now when it comes to this stuff. There's nothing quite like that feeling you get when your lungs fill up with water and the last little bits of oxygen bubble up like vomit.

Are you there yet?

Liz didn't answer, but that was irrelevant because Beth didn't pause.

To be fair, I didn't get it myself. Not right away. It took a few more times, a few more deaths, to bring it home. Wham, my head hitting the garage floor. Wham, the kitchen knife being drawn across my throat. Wham, a smack across the back of the head with an electric iron that he bought for me as a goddamned birthday present, which should have been the only hint I needed to ditch him. Rinse. Repeat.

I had a knack I hadn't even suspected. Maybe I never would have known if my husband hadn't decided to kill me. Maybe it took that life-or-death urgency to pull my trigger. Light my fuse. Whatever.

I don't have a word for what I was doing. I don't think there even is one. It wasn't time travel, obviously, because I was jumping sideways. And I started to notice the small details. You know, after the immediate thrill of being a human crash-test dummy started to wear off. The lives I was traveling into were the same as mine, but they were different too.

Every time I had a chance to look around before I checked out, there was something I didn't recognize. Sometimes big things, sometimes small. I died on that sofa a shit ton of times, but sometimes it was patterned, sometimes plain. The upholstery was clean, or else it was dirty. Sometimes it was the New York Times *lying on the coffee table, sometimes it was . . . something else. The* Pittsburgh Post-Gazette. *The* Philadelphia Inquirer. *Or no paper at all, but those were rare because Marc does like to look like he's a thinking man.*

So this was a different kind of impossible. A teleport jump from A to A. I was trying to escape but it was like I was on some kind of a bungee cord. All I could do was bounce back up and I'd be right there. Dying again. The same only different, like it was a TV movie and someone was getting sloppy with the continuity. Can you imagine what that was like?

No, let me answer that one for you. You can't. My great-grandma Scott had twelve children—

My *great-grandma*, Liz thought, before she could stop herself. *She was mine, not yours.*

If Beth heard the interruption, she ignored it. *And I remember one time I did the math for that. She was pregnant for nine years of her life. Nine years of bloating and nausea and heaving that weight around like an overfilled suitcase. I guess if you're looking for a comparison it was a little bit like that. Only I don't know how long I spent dying, again and again and again and again and again. I only know it was a long time. Longer than I'd been alive, maybe.*

And at first it was just confusion, panic, pain, oops. Gone again, back again, before I could even think. But you can get used to anything. Anything at all. Are you listening to me, Liz Kendall? You can get used to it, and you can get through it.

I started to watch Marc's moves. His game.

Because all of those different deaths kept coming back like old favorites, you know? There were recurring themes. And the house—some things changed, but some things didn't. Or usually didn't. I made mental notes.

In the living room, there was almost always a glass ashtray I could break over his head. In the garden, there's a pair of secateurs. In the bathroom, there's usually a packet of razor blades at the back of the medicine cabinet from back when he used to wet-shave.

And in the kitchen, the spilled groceries. You remember those, right?

I got better at it.

I got quicker.

And that night, when you and I met . . . well, that was the breakthrough. I got there a few seconds early. Don't ask me why. Maybe it was because in your world you actually got around to divorcing him. Threw off the cosmic clock by just a little.

Anyway, that was the night when I finally won. I got there in time. I fought him off, I planted that broken bottle in his face, and I didn't die. I won.

Only—and I did not see this coming—I won for you, not for me.

There's no Beth Healey here, there's only you. And right after I got my little moment, you threw me out again. I was in charge for exactly as long as it took to knock that bastard back on his heels, but I couldn't stay in the saddle when things calmed down. I'm crisis management, not business as usual. It's like I was playing musical chairs all this time, with just the one seat, and the seat was taken.

So here we both are, Liz. Lizzie. Liz Kendall. Liz-not-Beth. Me with my mad skills at dying, and not dying.

You with a life.

Liz opened her eyes. It was harder than it should have been, and slower; the message from her brain traveling down through unwilling neurons like the thin, stubborn trickle at the center of a frozen stream.

It was not quite morning. The birds were giving it everything they had out in the yard but the sky was still black at the zenith, whatever might be happening over on the horizon. The inside of Liz's mouth tasted like licorice left too long in the back of a cupboard: an intense and bile-bitter flavor of nothing much at all.

The inside of her head was worse. Her thoughts were bruised and stinging from friction with Beth's thoughts. Remembering was an act that strained imaginary muscles, made her breathing quicken with the shock of unexpected, painful effort.

Only it wasn't just Beth anymore. Her imaginary other selves, her fragments, were now legion. She had told Dr. Southern she didn't have a menagerie inside her. No, she didn't. What she had was more like an anthill, seething with endless variations on a single theme.

Which is worse, Liz thought numbly. Worse, sicker, crazier than she had ever imagined. Normal wasn't anywhere in sight after this.

Normal had sailed off into the sunset long ago. Her madness wasn't just an island she was shipwrecked on, it was a brave new world.

She lay still for a long time without moving, convinced that her body must be as tenderized by trauma as her brain. But flexing her fingers, and then her neck and ankles, brought no damage reports. When she finally sat up, the pain fell away from her as though it was just a trick of perspective. Someone else's pain, cast over her in the way a ventriloquist casts their voice.

She needed to get rid of that taste! She groped for the water glass on her bedside table but couldn't find it. She must have forgotten to bring one in the night before, which maybe was understandable. In reaching for the glass, she discovered that she wasn't alone in the bed. Molly had crawled in next to her at some point in the night and was now pressed up against her left side, snoring very lightly.

Liz grabbed the clock and held it up close until the luminous numbers made sense. It was only 6:00 a.m.: too early to wake the kids for school; too late to try to go back to sleep. Sleep didn't feel like an option now, in any case. She couldn't keep from remembering her own death, refracted and repeated like the endless patterns inside a kaleidoscope.

She disentangled herself gently from her slumbering daughter, climbed out of bed on the wrong side so as not to disturb her and padded soundlessly out of the room. She went through to the kitchen, put some coffee on and sat for a few minutes listening absently to the *plup-plup-plup* sound of the Cona going through its paces. When it wound down, she went over and poured herself a cup. Normally she would have added creamer, but black fitted the mood of the moment.

She drank the coffee down like a sleepwalker, vaguely aware that her tongue and throat were hurting because it was still a little too hot to drink. She was barely tasting it, only just aware of it going down. She could hear occasional footsteps and traffic sounds from the street outside, the faint chug of water in the pipes, the bark of a neighbor's dog. The sounds seemed weirdly flattened and compressed, as though someone had sampled them and taken out half the wavelengths before playing them back.

All those worlds. All those women. Ghosts of possible and impossible lives she hadn't lived. But lives she could have lived, maybe, if things had gone differently. That was the point of this, wasn't it? The whole thrust of the insane delusion she had conjured up and given a name to. That Marc was out to get her and that in every imaginable scenario he was going to succeed.

Liz had watched Carl Sagan's *Cosmos* when the Science Channel re-ran the whole series on its twenty-fifth anniversary. She knew about the cat in the box that was alive and dead at the same time, and she had been broadly sympathetic to the cat's predicament. But that vague, sci-fi-sexy idea of alternate realities must have sunk deeper into her mind than she suspected; must have festered there and turned into this full-blown . . . what?

Psychosis.

Call it like you see it. There was no point in doing anything else.

She had dreamed herself into a crowd, a crew, a multitude—as though she was that guy in the Bible whose name was Legion. But they were a multitude of murder victims. And the enemy, the aggressor, was the man she had loved and married and raised a family with. The man who had defined the shape of her adult life, as though he were a mold and she had poured herself into him until she found her level.

In her mind, in her imaginings, Marc was a mass murderer with a single victim. He was the blind, blank wall at the end of every turn in the maze. He had killed her and killed her and killed her, as though killing her was the real point and purpose of him and everything else was pure accident.

In every world Beth had shown her, he was there. Her life partner, and her executioner.

As Liz turned that over in her mind and thought about what it meant for her mental health, she was filled with frustration and fury that seemed to come bubbling up from nowhere.

No.

Not from nowhere.

From the basement levels of her brain. From Beth.

The horror that followed it was all Liz's own. For a moment she struggled against her own instincts. She wanted to scream out loud: *Get out! Get out! Get out!* At the same time, she wanted to deny that she was feeling anything at all. To pretend Beth wasn't there. Speaking to her, now, while she was awake, filled Liz with a terrible, sickening sense of peril. As though she was crossing a line that shouldn't be crossed.

"Why are you still here?" she demanded at last, her voice high and unsteady.

Is that a trick question?

A shudder went through Liz. She shook her head violently, as if she could dislodge Beth the way a dog gets rid of a flea. She groped for the words to express how wrong this was. "No," she whispered. "No, no, no." She wasn't answering Beth, she was lodging a protest with reality.

Yeah. Good luck with that.

"Leave me alone," Liz begged.

Jesus, don't I wish I could!

"I get why I had to invent you. And I—" She swallowed, with an effort. "Message received. I saw what you had to show me. The warning. What might happen. Now please, just . . . go away. I don't want you here. I only dreamed you up to deal with that one situation. Now I just . . . I want to go back to how I was before."

You can't. We're in this together, babe. You don't trust me, and there's no reason why you should, but I'm here. Like it or not. The only question is what we do next.

"What we . . .?"

About Marc. What we do about Marc.

"That's ridiculous," Liz protested. "I'm not going to do anything based on a . . . a stupid nightmare. And there is no *us*. There's just me. You're only a part of me." She was trying to keep her voice to a whisper, but these words came out loud and hard.

She was suddenly aware of how this must look from the outside. Her sitting alone at the kitchen counter, keeping up one half of an angry confrontation. Falling out with her imaginary friend. She flashed on a memory of reading *Alice in Wonderland* to Zac when he was seven; of Alice right at the end of the book telling her judge and jury that they were only a pack of cards—and then having them rise up and attack her. She tried one last appeal to reason. "Look, I know you helped me. You're the reason why I'm still alive. But I can take it from here. By myself. I want to be me again. I can't cope with being *us*. Please just go back to whichever bit of my . . . my subconscious you came from."

I can't do that. I don't even know how. It's not like there's a button I push. Anyway, you still need my help.

"I do not need your help!"

Seriously, yeah, you do. I'm strong enough to do what needs to be done. You're not.

"No. No." Liz's mouth twisted in revulsion. "You're dangerous and out of control. You almost broke that woman's thumb at Molly's school. You were prepared to put someone's eye out over a parking space!"

For a few moments there was no answer. Down the hall, Zac's alarm clock beeped.

I lost my temper.

Liz gave a hollow, plosive laugh. "Yeah, I think that's fair to say."

I spent a lot of time terrified, and in pain. It does things to you. But I'm fine now.

"There's no point in lying to me. I felt what you were feeling." Liz looked into the hallway to make sure she was still alone—that Zac hadn't come out to grab the bathroom or to wake Molly. She felt a primitive terror of being caught out like this, arguing with an evil twin who demonstrably wasn't there. "You enjoyed that fight. You wanted more." Because that's what I made you for, she thought bleakly. To fight for me. And it's easier to switch you on than to switch you off.

I'm not lying. The words came in a spiky froth of static, Beth's emotions twanging and jangling along Liz's nerves. *What I went through to get here, what I suffered . . . You don't just bounce back from that. How did you feel after he smacked you, or twisted your arm? After he spat in your face? Did you just dust yourself off and get back to whatever it was you were doing? Whistle a happy tune?*

Liz swallowed hard. "No."

No. It piled up inside you like . . . like rocks in your stomach. You thought one more day of it would break you, but you lived with it for years. And those rocks you swallowed are still inside you. Maybe someday you'll be able to spit them out again, but shit, it's not going to be any time soon, is it?

Unwillingly and almost imperceptibly, Liz shook her head.

Is it?

"No."

No. So you don't get to judge me. And I don't feel like I need to apologize to you. Make a penance. Promise to be all kind and friendly next time. I am not kind, and I am nobody's friend. I ditched all that bullshit on the way here, because otherwise I wouldn't have made it and you'd be under the ground with all those other losers I met along the way.

Liz wanted to protest. To say that Beth was just a voice she'd given to an orphaned part of her own personality. That she would have found some way to survive Marc's attack even without dreaming up an ass-kicking variant edition of herself. But she thought of all the evidence stacked against her and she gave it up. All she said was "I want you to leave."

If I leave, Marc will kill you. He's coming for you, and it's going to be soon. The only reason he hasn't come already is that he's figured out he needs you.

"Needs me?"

I know the way his mind works, and so do you. He's not subtle. He was about halfway into his terror campaign, with the car tires and the dead pigeon and all that shit. He was scratching his big itch, which is us, and then the penny dropped that he's about to go to trial. He got derailed. That was him trying to call you last night. I'm sure of it. And I know

182

why, too. But when he's done, he's still going to drag us back onto the killing floor. He can't help himself.

"I'll take my chances," Liz muttered.

Listen to you, all big and brave. You were shitting yourself when you found that dead bird. You know what you're like with him. We both do. You would have given up and died without me. Next time . . .

"We don't know there'll be a next time."

No? Then call that number.

"What?"

The unrecognized number, from last night. Call back, and see who it is.

Liz didn't answer. She was afraid to. She was in danger of believing this paranoid nonsense, and she mustn't. She couldn't let Beth drag her onto her own territory of violence and madness.

Either way, you get your answer. If it's not him, I'll leave. How about that?

"Deal," Liz muttered. She grabbed her phone, went to its history and returned the last call on the list. It rang and rang and nobody answered. Finally she hung up and put the phone down.

"Just a cold caller," Liz said, surer of her ground now. "This is what they do."

Wait for it.

"They want you to ring back because it's a premium line and you end up paying twenty bucks for—"

Her phone rang, cutting her off. She could see from the display that it was the same number she'd just dialed. She snatched it up and stabbed the ANSWER button. "Hello?"

"Hey, Lizzie. How's it going over there?" Marc sounded relaxed and cheerful, as though the last time they'd spoken had just been a few minutes before. As though he'd never attacked her. As though everything was fine between them and always had been. "Sorry, Jamie's still asleep. I had to go out onto the landing."

Liz fought the impulse to throw the phone across the room and back away from it. But everything that had been true at the court-house was true now: making him aware of her fear would be a very bad move. He had too many ways of putting it to use.

"Marc," she said. She heard the tremor in her own voice. She hated that Beth was hearing it too. "You realize you're breaking the law just by talking to me?"

"Yes, sweetheart, I realize that. But I'm not stupid. I'm using a disposable, not my regular phone. If anyone bothers to check, they won't catch me out."

"What do you want?" Liz demanded. Just as she had asked Beth, a few moments before. Something like claustrophobia rose inside her: a sense that she was trapped between their two agendas, with no volition of her own.

"You had company last night," Marc said.

"No." The lie slipped out before Liz could catch it. I'm not afraid of him, she told herself. I'm not. But her heart was tapping her ribs in a quick tattoo.

"I saw the car, Lizzie. It had a flashing light and everything. You called the police."

"Beebee just came by to see how we're doing."

"Beebee? You're on first name terms? That's nice. I've got an assault charge hanging over my head and I'm not allowed to see my kids, and you're having the cop who arrested me over for drinks."

"We didn't drink."

"No? Well, either she came to see you about the case or it was a social occasion. Which is it, Lizzie? Try to keep your story straight."

Part of Liz was amazed at Marc's perfect narcissism. He had threatened her and attacked her, and almost certainly stalked her since, but somehow in his mind her calling the police was a betrayal. Before she could think of what to say to this, he pressed on.

"Lizzie, this is a stupid situation and it's no good for anyone. You've got to cut me a break. If you withdraw your testimony, this is never going to get to court. The state won't prosecute if they can't call you as a witness. I promise I'll keep my temper in future."

He was silent for a moment or two, waiting for her to answer.

When she didn't, he went on as though he'd always meant to. "Lizzie, you don't want me to go to jail. What would that do to the kids? What would it do to us as a family?"

Liz swallowed hard. "We're not a family, Marc," she said, teeth clenched to keep her voice from shaking. "It's been a long time since we've been that. And you trying to throttle me didn't make things any better."

Marc breathed out loud and long, a sigh of exasperation imperfectly suppressed. "I didn't try to throttle you. I just lost it for a moment because you were breaking my balls about bringing the kids back late. Look, if I wanted to hurt you I could have done it any time I wanted, okay? Any time. Last night, even."

I just lost it for a moment. It was almost exactly what Beth had said. Liz suddenly felt surrounded in a way that brought her close to panic.

"Last night?" she echoed. "What do you mean?"

Marc went on talking right over her. "But I don't want that. I'm not some psycho: I'm just a guy who sometimes gets a little bit of a rage on. Name me a man who doesn't."

"You said last night," Liz repeated. "What happened last night?"

"Nothing. You can escalate, I can escalate. I don't want to threaten you, Lizzie. I'm trying to tell you that I care about you, and I want all this to stop. I want us to go back to the way we were. That's what's best for the kids, best for everyone. But it's up to you. There's nothing I can do unless you drop your complaint against me and refuse to testify. That's step one. And then we'll just work it out one step at a time, okay?"

It was hard even now for Liz to find the strength of will to defy Marc to his face, but with Beth hovering around and almost certainly still listening in she forced herself not to flinch. "I'm not doing that," she told him.

"You need to think this through," Marc said, as though she hadn't spoken. He was still speaking in the same tone of sorely tried, long-suffering patience. "Zac and Moll need both of us. Whatever might be going on between you and me, it's not fair to make them suffer for it. And they will suffer, Lizzie. You'll lose my child support, just for starters."

"You barely ever pay the child support. You're four months behind."

"Shit, why would you throw that at me? I always make it up in the end. But you know what, it doesn't even matter. It's not about money, it's about family."

"Marc, I don't—"

"I'm not asking you to lie, Lizzie. Only to drop the complaint. They could still drag you up into the witness box, but they won't. They'll see which way the land lies, and they'll back off. We'll be fine."

Liz groped for words that wouldn't come. She knew that the *we* in "we'll be fine" meant him and him alone. But she struggled in the cast-iron grip of his certainties. Her whole married life had been a series of surrenders, each one prepping and coaching her for the next. She was classically conditioned, like a dog.

May I? Beth asked. *Please?*

It took Liz a second to realize what her other self was asking for. Then her lungs took in a breath without her willing it. Her throat flexed, and her tongue licked her lips.

She could have fought back, as she had during the court hearing, but she let it happen—let the reins slacken, the angle between her mind and her body twist and widen by a tiny fraction. She felt something come in through the gap, like a stiff, cold breeze. But this time she was in control and she only let that breeze blow where she wanted it to.

She felt Beth inflate her lungs. Speak through her lips. Play her, as though she was some weird musical instrument—one with a drone, like a bagpipe. "You heard me, Marc. I'm not dropping the complaint. I'm not letting you off the hook. You tried to kill me and you're going to jail for it."

There was a silence that was somehow live in the way a bared electric cable is live. "That's not fair," Marc said at last, in a tight voice. "I admit—look, I already said this, I said it. I lose my shit sometimes. You know that, and you go all out to set me off. That's always been the way you work. Rile me up and then blame me when I get a little bit out of control. Lizzie, this was both of our faults."

Liz felt the weight of those words—wondered for a short but measurable moment if they might be true. Beth didn't. "Is that how you square it with yourself?" she asked. "Really? You tell yourself your hair trigger is everybody else's responsibility. It isn't, sweetness. It's just yours."

Another silence, longer than the first. As if Marc was walking around that *sweetness* to see what it looked like from different angles.

"It doesn't do any good to cast blame," he said at last.

"Says the asshole who just tried to deal me some." Beth gave a languid chuckle. "But you're wrong, Marc. This is exactly about making sure the blame lands where it belongs. That's what courts are for, right? To determine fault? Well here's a crazy idea. Suppose we just let them do that?"

"Lizzie," Marc said. "Listen to me. Just . . . listen!" His voice was thickening with every syllable, the anger building behind it like water behind a dam. Liz quailed from it despite herself.

Beth basked in it.

"Oh baby, I spent so long listening to you. I was sure you could get a full sentence out sooner or later. But you just kept breaking my heart."

Marc spluttered for a few seconds before he got any kind of traction on his mouth. "What the fuck has gotten into you? I'm trying to salvage something from this situation . . ."

"Yeah. Your own ass."

"Lizzie—"

"Remember when I dug out part of your face with a broken bottle? Come back soon, Marc. I bought in a six-pack."

Over the stream of obscenities that followed, Liz heard Zac's door open behind her and then his footsteps padding softly down the hall. She moved her mind and body back together seamlessly, shutting Beth out. There was no struggle, no aftermath. Beth surrendered at once, dissipated into air, and Liz was in the pilot seat again.

"We'll talk later," she said to Marc, in a gap between curse words.

"I've said all I've got to say," Marc spat out. "If you want to walk again, you better tell that dyke cop you decided second thoughts are best. Otherwise you'll see me soon. I mean it."

The phone went dead, and she set it down.

"Hey, Mom," Zac said, his voice a little hoarse with sleep. "How long have you been up?"

Liz took a few seconds to pull her scattered thoughts, her scattered self, back together. Then she stood, arranged her face into what she hoped was a smile and turned to face him. "Not long," she said. "The coffee's fresh. You want me to pour you a cup?"

Zac shook his head and yawned prodigiously. "I'll stick to juice, thanks."

"Pour some for Moll too. I'll go get her."

She fled back up the hall and into her bedroom, where Molly was still an asymmetrical bump under the sheets, her tousled hair the only part of her that was visible. She closed the door and slumped against it, eyes closed, while her heartbeat went from a tickertape-stutter to something closer to normal.

She had to get on top of this. She had to keep moving, to keep out the fear. The normal and the everyday would be her salvation.

"Wake up, baby girl," she said with hardly any shake in her voice at all. She rounded the bed and reached down to draw back the covers. "Okay, sleepy head, time to—"

A stab of pain from the underside of her foot made her break off with a gasp of surprise. She looked down. She was standing on sodden carpet, scattered with what looked like melting ice cubes. But they weren't ice: they were glass. And the largest piece, a slender curve like a new moon, was embedded in her foot.

She lifted her leg hurriedly, scattering dark red polka dots across the carpet's pale oatmeal.

She must have knocked her water glass over in the night. Or else Molly had when she climbed into the bed. But what had it fallen against to make it shatter? A short fall onto thick-pile carpet shouldn't have been enough to break a sturdy tumbler.

Marc's words came back to her in a rush. *If I wanted to hurt you, I could have done it any time I wanted. Last night, even.*

She had to be crazy. What she was thinking wasn't possible.

Then she saw the photo on the bedside table. The glass that fronted the frame was shattered across where something had hit it, just off-center. In that instant she knew.

Marc had been here. Standing right where she was standing now, looking down on her as she slept. Struggling against his own violent impulses, which she knew from painful experience were strong.

Was it Molly, sleeping right beside her, that had made him hold off? Or had there been some element of reason? Of calculation? For example, the calculation that he needed her alive a little longer to sort out this irritating business of the assault charge before he came back to seal the deal?

Either way, he had grabbed up the tumbler and thrown it down again in order to burn off a little of that violent energy before it overwhelmed him.

Okay.

Get a grip.

Okay.

But Beth had been right about one thing. It wasn't just Marc she was up against: it was her own reaction to him. The thought of him standing by the bed with the tumbler in his hand while she and Molly slept paralyzed her, made her mind sluggish and unwilling.

First things first. Clean up the mess.

She collected up all the pieces of broken glass, using an ornamental bowl as a tray.

Don't let them see you're hurt.

She limped into the bathroom, holding her left leg stiff and unbending not on account of the pain—her brain was so hot and buzzing with adrenaline that the wound barely hurt at all—but to avoid leaving any more blood on the carpet. She dumped the glass in the little waste bin, just for now. She would dispose of it properly later.

She washed the deep cut with warm water from the shower head. Then with her foot up on the side of the bath she applied a little disinfectant before covering the wound with a dressing pad and a strip of Band-Aid.

Business as usual. Clean up the mess. Wake her. Get them both off to school.

Liz hurried back into the bedroom. Then slowed and stopped.

"Son of a bitch!" she whispered. She had thought she was following the promptings of her own inner voice. But it wasn't her voice at all.

Keep moving! You can't wake Molly up until you've cleared the blood off the carpet.

"Beth, would you please just . . . stay out of my head!"

Relax, princess snowflake. I'm not in your head. You pushed me out of there. Right now, the only thing of mine that's in your head is these words.

Which for a moment Liz had mistaken for her own words, her own decisions. A takeover by stealth instead of the violent invasion of the first two times.

Stop being so melodramatic. And clear up the blood!

Why? Liz wondered. Why get rid of the evidence? She couldn't hide this. She shouldn't even be trying.

Yes, we can. We need to. How do you think the kids will feel if they know he can get to them any time he wants to? You're supposed to be able to keep them safe.

But that wasn't the reason. Not the real reason. Something else was stirring a long way down, underneath Beth's words, like a rat in a hole.

Just get the blood wiped up, for God's sake! Moll could wake up any moment now and see it.

That, at least, was the simple truth. Molly was already stirring, smacking her lips as she often did right before waking. So Liz did the cleanup in two stages. First she dropped a towel over the carpet's sudden outbreak of measles, hiding the dark red spots from sight while she roused Molly and hustled her, only just awake and drowsily confused, through into the kitchen.

"Look after your sister for a moment, would you, Zac?" she asked. And she was gone again before he could answer.

There was a can of spray-on stain remover in the hall cupboard— it was almost empty, but hopefully enough for such a small job. Liz scrubbed ferociously with an old washing up brush, turning the dark red to salmon pink. There would still be a stain, but she hoped that nobody looking at it would think of blood.

The kids' voices came very clearly through the open door behind her.

"Which cereal, Moll? Lucky Charms, Corn Flakes or the house special?"

"What's the house special?"

"Corn Flakes with Lucky Charms."

"House special!"

"Coming up."

Liz checked the window of her room, and found it as she had left it. Locked. The front door too, and Molly's window, and Zac's. She knew she had bolted the kitchen door, and even a cat would have trouble fitting through the tiny window in the bathroom.

Business as usual. Right.

Right.

She returned to the kitchen, sat down in between Zac and

Molly and ate breakfast right alongside them. "I'm having the house special!" Molly said proudly.

"Yeah, I heard," Liz said, smiling back at her.

"It's Corn Flakes with Lucky Charms. Zac made it for me."

"Did you say thank you?"

"I did, didn't I, Zac?"

"You sure did, Moll."

The morning routine played out around Liz without touching her. Normally just being with Zac and Molly would have been solace enough to calm her nerves, but right then it was all she could do to keep down the rising panic. She was overwhelmed by a sense of exposure, as though the kitchen was a vast expanse of open ground that offered no cover.

That feeling intensified when they were walking to the car, when they were driving, when she was dropping first Zac and then Molly off at school. Marc's nocturnal visit had turned the world inside out, making familiar places seem like unsprung traps.

When Liz was finally alone in the car, she drove it up to Washington Avenue, parked it in front of the police training academy and took a walk along the southern edge of Highland Park. It was an hour before her shift started, and she really didn't want to go home again right now.

She should have called Beebee.

No. This from Beth, the flat monosyllable landing like a slap. But Beth wasn't the answer to this; she was just another problem Liz had to deal with. She had to think. Marc might have left his fingerprints somewhere. Beebee had advised her to steer clear of reckless allegations, but now . . .

He's not stupid. Think about it. How did he get in?

"Oh, be quiet, Beth!"

It was meant as a whisper, but it came out as a yell. An old woman walking two pug dogs looked across at Liz, startled, then hurried on.

Let's keep this between the two of us, shall we? How do you think he got into the house?

"I don't know," Liz muttered.

Yes, you do. If I know it, then you know it. And hey, you're not going anywhere, so stop pretending you are and sit down. We've got to think this through.

Liz bridled at the brusque commands. She wanted to tell Beth where to shove it, but she couldn't argue with that last point. And in any case, she would only be arguing with herself.

Exactly. First sign of madness.

The *first* sign? That sounded wildly optimistic. Liz was afraid she might have passed the last exit a while back. She sat down heavily on a low wooden frame that had been built around a newly planted sapling, offering it minimal protection against passing dogs and carelessly pushed strollers. Still feeling both out of place and exposed, she massaged her hamstrings as though she was in the middle of a run she wasn't dressed for.

Let's meet topside, Beth told her coldly. *Now.*

"What?"

You know where I mean. The place where we talked before. You remember how to get there, don't you?

"This isn't real," Liz whispered. "None of it. You're not real."

Doesn't matter right now. Tell yourself whatever you need to, but we've got to deal with this and we've got to do it quickly. If we lose the initiative, we're dead.

Liz shook her head. "I don't want to . . . to see you again. We can talk like this."

Yeah, but we're not going to. As we just saw, you have a tendency to run off at the mouth, and this is private. Anyway, we're going to need to start trusting each other sooner or later, and now is as good a time as ever.

"I don't trust you at all," Liz said. "You're exactly the part of me I don't trust."

I'll try my best not to cry. Now move.

It would be the first time Liz had visited the colorless mind-space when she was awake. She had no idea what would happen to her body while her consciousness was busy elsewhere. More than that, though, she hated everything about that eerie void. Not to mention its other inhabitant. And now more than ever it felt like surrendering to her own sickness. How could anything good come from that? Talking to Beth, to the fracture in her mind born out of the very fear she was feeling now. All she was doing was diving that much further down the rabbit hole.

Except what choice did she have, really? If Marc was really out to hurt her, which seemed hard to deny now, Liz was going to need all the help she could get. Beth had such confidence. Such unshakeable self-belief. And such ruthlessness. Face it, she had everything Liz needed right now. Her psychotic breakdown couldn't have come at a better time.

First things first, she told herself. Once she resolved this current crisis, and put it behind her, she would deal with Beth. Until then, she would take the help that was offered and try not to think too much about where it was coming from.

She closed her eyes and tried to find the state of calm self-awareness that she got from the mindfulness meditations. Too much to hope for in her current state, but she moved her thoughts in that direction, a little at a time, like someone inching forward into a darkened room.

She was there before she knew it. The mind-space opened around her, bleak and endless and absolutely empty. There was no sign of Beth.

You've got to let me in, Beth said, *The way you did back home.*

Liz hesitated. Now that she was here, she felt intensely reluctant to do that. Letting Beth borrow her voice had been one thing. Limited, consciously willed and controllable. Liz felt instinctively that allowing her full access to the mind-space would be a very different proposition.

You can stay where you are, she said. Or thought. Or thought she said. In any case she formed the words and meaning passed between the two of them. She had finally figured out how to speak here, although she couldn't have explained even now what it was she was doing. *I like it like this. Me in here, you out there.*

Don't be paranoid. We're on the same side.

So you keep saying. Okay, I know where Marc got the key. He took a copy of Zac's key when the kids were staying over with him.

Exactly. Along with the word came a sense of patronizing approval. Beth was pleased and surprised that Liz had thought it through. *And that should tell you something. Marc is angry now because you got the restraining order and because you're talking to the cops, but he had the key ready and waiting. He was already thinking there might be a time when he wanted to pay you an unsupervised visit.*

Liz said nothing. She tried hard to think of another theory. Nothing came.

So if you think he's going to slip up, you're kidding yourself. He's not just coming at you in a blind rage, he's been working on this. Fingerprints wouldn't help you. He's been in your house legitimately a thousand times. Shit, he bought a burner so he could talk to you without leaving a trail.

Maybe the till receipt . . . Liz offered.

Right. Of course. Because that's what people do when they buy disposable cellphones. They use their credit cards to make sure they leave a nice, wide trail behind them. Probably take out the extended warranty too.

Beebee, Liz thought. Beebee would help if Liz asked her to.

Will you please try to focus? You can only figure out what to do if you know what it is you want.

Liz gave a strangled laugh. Unlike her words, it stayed inside her throat and did not translate. *I want to come out of this alive.*

Good. So let's dig down into that a little. Suppose you call the cops, and they believe you. What's the best outcome?

They arrest Marc.

For what? He hasn't done anything.

He broke into my house! Liz protested. *He violated his restraining order!*

Do we have to go over this again? You can't prove a thing.

Okay, they can give us some protection.

Sure. For a month. Or a week. Or a couple of days. Not forever. So that's not the answer, is it?

I suppose not, Liz said bleakly.

We need to put him away. Make sure he gets jail time, and lots of it.

No suspended sentences, no second chances. County lock-up. If you're lucky, someone shanks him before he gets out. Either way you move so far away he never gets even a smell of you again.

Liz winced to hear it put so baldly into words.

Right? Beth pressed.

Right.

Okay, then. That nest egg you were thinking about last night. The one you were going to use to buy cameras. How much is in it?

About three thousand dollars.

Nice. Very nice. That gives us something to work with. Let me put a proposition to you.

"Well, this isn't a baseball bat," Crusher said almost reverently. "I mean it is, obviously, but it's so much more than that." He hefted the sleek, black baton and swung it to and fro a few times, making an impressive swishing sound in the air. Then he offered it to Liz so she could try it for herself. She took the bat gingerly, feeling Beth's eager interest behind her own queasiness.

"Tilt it in your hands," Crusher invited her.

She did. Left. Right. Left.

"What do you feel?" The store owner's big, bearded face was split horizontally by a tombstone-toothed grin.

"The weight keeps shifting," Liz said. "Is there something inside it that moves?"

"There is!" Crusher applauded her, just with his fingertips. "There surely is! You got it in one, Ms. Kendall."

Liz had picked Paladin Home Defender out of the phonebook on the grounds that their Larimer store was only a few blocks north of the Cineplex. She had started having second thoughts as soon as she looked at the prices, and they metastasized into third and fourth thoughts when she met the store's manager and sole staffer, Ken Crowther. "But you can call me Crusher, ma'am. Seriously. Most folks do."

Crowther certainly looked like a Crusher. He was well over six feet tall and heavyset, with old, blued-out tattoos all the way up both arms in which skulls and daggers featured strongly. But he was soft-spoken, with a New England accent that hinted of old money and prep schools, and when he came in close he smelled of the kind of hard candy that Liz used to buy when she was seven in the form of beads strung on an elastic band to make a necklace. Caught up in the contradictions, her judgment was suspended.

But the most striking thing about Crusher was the pleasure he took in his job. Whenever he picked up any of the weapons in the store to demonstrate them to Liz, he looked like the class nerd handing in his homework. To Liz's pre-emptive "No guns," he had nodded vigorously as though he totally understood—one connoisseur to another—and said, "Our non-lethal section is right over here."

On balance, Liz decided she found him creepy. Beth was contemptuously amused, convinced that at least part of the guy's courtesy and charm was born out of a fervent wish to get inside Liz's pants.

She was pulling against the whole non-lethal thing too. *You've got to be able to put Marc down hard*, she reminded Liz for about the tenth time.

Liz wasn't disputing that. But hard didn't mean permanently.

"So there are two steel sleeves in here," Crusher was saying now, waving his arms over the Baltimore Belter™ in a vivid pantomime, "one inside the other. When you're raising the bat to strike, the inner sleeve goes up and it cantilevers the outer, heavier sleeve downward. So the handle beds into your grip, really strongly. Then you take your swing, the bat comes down, and all that weight goes up to the tip again. It actually accelerates in your hands. When you hit with this, you hit harder than you think you'd be capable of."

Liz tried a few swings, but failed to find a rhythm. It felt like the bat was alive and trying to squirm out of her grip.

Crusher watched her performance with a judicious eye, pursing his lips. "It takes a while to get used to it," he said tactfully. "If you just want the stopping power, though, you need to take a look at this baby." He took down another baton. It was tapered like the Belter, and the color was once again a somber, serious black, but the inspiration here seemed to be a steak tenderizer rather than a baseball bat. The business end of the thing was covered in hard plastic studs like tiny pyramids, blunted at their very tips but still clearly intended to embed themselves in whatever you swiped at. The grip was thicker than the Belter's, and it had a single button situated right by where your thumb would be if you held it one-handed.

"You've got your reaching distance," Crusher said, "which is gonna be close to six feet even for a petite lady like yourself. LED flashlight in the tip. Belt clip here, see, and the balance . . . well, you've only got to feel it."

He put it in Liz's hands so she could feel it. It felt like the baseball bat, more or less, but at least it didn't move of its own accord.

"What's the button for?" she asked.

Crusher gave her another schoolboy smile. "On this model it's a burst function for the flashlight. Point it at your intruder and hit that button, he gets eight thousand lumens—eight treble-zero!— bang smack in his eyes. He won't see a thing for the next ten minutes, guaranteed. Most intruders are going to throw in the towel right there. If he keeps on coming . . . well, you get to play *piñata*."

Liz cringed from that image, but Beth definitely approved.

"On the top-of-the-range T34, though," Crusher said, pointing, "the flashlight is replaced by an eleven-million-volt taser. I personally prefer this model right here, because if I need a taser I'll use a taser, you know? And with the best will in the world, you're not going to aim as well with a weapon that's this heavy. Ergonomically, it's not designed for point-and-shoot. But some people are looking for a Swiss Army knife, I suppose. They want to have all their options bundled in together."

Liz looked at the two price tags. The basic model was $299 plus tax. The T34 added another hundred bucks to that eye-watering figure.

Hey, Beth admonished her. *Think about what it is you're buying.*

A spiky club? Liz thought.

Survival. This is a right-to-life issue. You don't get to live unless you can fight him off when he comes for you.

Liz tried to imagine that, and in spite of everything she failed. She had spent her whole married life deferring to Marc. Whenever there had been any kind of disagreement between them, she had grown used to folding in her will, her ego, to avoid the bruising collisions that resulted from standing up to him, or even seeming to have an opinion of her own. Fighting him was something she could acknowledge as a concept but not summon up as a mental picture.

"Do you want to try them both out against a target dummy?" Crusher asked. He seemed to have interpreted Liz's silence as an inability to choose between blinding her opponent and electrocuting him.

"Thank you," Liz said. "I'm good."

"Or we could look at some pepper sprays. Low-impact, long-distance. And the stronger ones will incapacitate in under a second. Your attacker won't even need to breathe it in. Just the vapor touching his face will seal the deal."

Shit, yes! Beth enthused. *Let's bring some of that stuff to the party, by all means.*

Liz was in the store for almost an hour in the end, and she spent thirteen hundred dollars. That bought her the steak tenderizer in its flashlight configuration, a taser, a plain baseball bat with no cantilevers and a couple of pepper sprays—one of which looked like a BB gun and fired gel pellets that burst into a spray of droplets on impact.

Driving home with the bags beside her on the passenger seat, she felt like a criminal.

See how you feel when you break his face, Beth said.

"Hurting Marc isn't the point of this," Liz muttered.

Never said it was. But it's a sweet little daydream, right?

Liz was alarmed to discover that there was some appeal in the thought. Her grip tightened on the steering wheel. "We just take him down," she said.

Hey, I know the plan. Who came up with it in the first place? You take him down, and you knock him out. Hard. After that, all you need to do is call your cop friend and let her come in and make the arrest. You've got him on a violation of his restraining order, and most likely you've got him on a fresh assault. Whack your face against a cupboard door if you need to, so there's a bruise. He'll go down for five to ten, guaranteed. And you'll be free as a bird.

It sounded so easy.

And so terrifying.

"We don't even know that he'll come."

If he doesn't come, fine. Tomorrow is the trial, and we'll take our chances. But trust me, his head is chock-full of you right now. He's pissed as hell because you won't do what you're told.

"I could just check us all into a hotel somewhere," Liz said. Thinking aloud. Still hoping there might be another way out of this. "If he's found guilty . . ."

He might get a suspended sentence. You know what a smooth, slimy little bastard he is. Or he might get a tag and a home detention. You'd be an idiot to take the risk.

"I can't believe he wants to kill me," Liz muttered, eyes tight shut against the thought, and the images that came with it.

Beth didn't even bother to reply to that one. *Stop at Franklins'*, she said instead. *We need to pick up some paint.*

They took the bus down to the records office right after school. Fran was full of nervous excitement and couldn't stop talking, but Zac wasn't giving her much back.

"We're on the case, Sherlock," she coaxed him. "The game is a cubic yard." He smiled, but with less enthusiasm than she would have expected. "What's the matter?" Fran asked him. Then she guessed. "Your dad's trial."

"Partly," Zac admitted. "Mostly, I guess. It's tomorrow, and I can't be there."

"Well, it is a school day."

"It's not that. Mom wouldn't let me go. She says she doesn't want Dad to see us all ganging up on him, like he's the enemy. It's her case, her complaint, and she wants him to see it that way."

"She's smart, your mom. He's still your dad, even if he's a dick. If he gets an acquittal, you're still gonna have to see him. So making him be the big bad is probably not the greatest idea." Fran hesitated. "So how's she coping?"

"She's doing okay," Zac said. Then he shrugged. "I think she is. She hasn't been around much the last few days. She's been doing a ton of overtime at the Cineplex, then coming home exhausted and falling into bed."

"Probably a good idea," Fran offered. "Take her mind off all the crazy."

"I don't know where her mind is to start with," Zac said sourly, picking at the rubber seal on the bus's window as he stared out at the street. "The last few days, when I try to talk to her, it's fifty-fifty whether she even hears me. She's a million miles away."

Fran let the subject drop. She could see he didn't want to talk about it.

The reception desk at the records office was actually a window in a wall. Iron bars with barley-sugar twists extended from the top to about three-quarters of the way down, leaving a small mailbox-shaped aperture through which to talk and conduct official business.

The lady on the other side of the window looked scary enough that Fran was grateful for the bars. She was whipcord-thin and powerfully permed, and she wore spectacles with tapering points curving up from the outer edge on each side like the horns of an owl. They magnified her bottle-green eyes very alarmingly.

Fran stated her business, said she had called ahead and been given a transaction number, and handed over her birth certificate by way of ID. She also handed over the forms she had printed off from the records office website, and then filled out a couple more that seemed to ask all the same questions over again. Her name, the organization she worked for (*not applicable, I am a private citizen*), her interest in the case, her legal counsel (*still just me*) and much more in the same vein.

The horn-rimmed woman looked the forms over for a very long time, separated out the carbons and counterfoils and stamped what seemed like every square inch of every copy with a library stamp. She did it quickly and with spectacular energy, as though stamping was what she was born for and the rest of her life was just waiting for the next piece of paper to come along and be made all official.

"The main reading room is booked," she said, pushing some of the stamped counterfoils back through the window. You've got to pass security first, then go on down to the basement level. Room 107, first left through the fire doors. A clerk will bring the boxes to you."

"Thank you, ma'am," Fran said, slipping the counterfoils into her jeans pocket.

"Thank you," Zac echoed.

Which was bad timing, because the horn-rimmed lady hadn't noticed him until he spoke. "Is he with you?" she demanded.

Fran confirmed that he was.

"Then he has to sign in too, and fill in a G32. First page. In the box at the right, where it says adjuncts, put the number of *your* G32."

So then there was another bout of form-filling, and more crazy stamping fun, before they were finally allowed to walk through the security checkpoint and into the building proper. Fran waited a moment for Jinx to scamper under the barrier and join them, but Jinx didn't. She was boycotting this whole enterprise.

"Have you seen this place?" Zac marveled.

Fran hadn't, and she had to admit it was something to see. The lobby looked like it belonged in a cathedral rather than a local government building. There were gray stone arches on all sides, one arcade of them built right on top of another, and the ceilings were so high it felt like there should be clouds up there. The lamps, which were lit even though it was daytime, were big glass globes on golden standards taller than a grown man. The city's coat of arms was painted on the wall right across from the security post, the colors as bright as a cartoon. It showed three eagles in big golden bubbles, the gatehouse of a castle, and the words *benigno numine*.

"What does that mean?" Zac asked as they walked past it on the way to the stairs.

"Why would you assume I'd know, Zachary?" Fran asked prissily. He rolled his eyes at her. "Yeah, you're right, I know pretty much everything. *Benigno numine* means 'yay, God's on our team.' We swiped it from a guy named William Pitt, but to be fair we waited until after he was dead. Pitt, as in Pittsburgh, by the way. We swiped his name too."

"I heard about Pitt," Zac said. "Pretty deep guy, by all accounts."

"If that was a joke, it was terrible."

"It'll grow on you. You'll laugh before you know it."

Room 107 was a fifteen-foot cube made almost entirely out of wood. Wooden tiles on the floor, wooden panels on the walls, a very big and solid dark-wood table taking up most of the room. It looked pretty impressive, except that the plaster of the ceiling had an ancient damp stain up in one corner. The smell of beeswax polish was overpowering.

It took about a quarter of an hour before their boxes arrived, wheeled in by a clerk on a little luggage trolley. There were three boxes in total, and they all had the same number on their sides: FP1673812. The United States versus Bruno Martin Picota.

"Doesn't sound like a fair fight," Zac joked.

"Fairer than when it was just him versus me." The words came out sharper than Fran meant them to.

"Sorry," Zac said.

She shook her head. "It's okay. Come on, we're looking for transcripts."

They found them almost immediately because everything in the boxes was indexed, but a second later Zac found something better. In a cardboard container about the size of a shoebox, there was a stack of thirty or forty cassette tapes, each one numbered and cross-referenced to a list. Recordings of every conversation Bruno Picota had had with his court-appointed psychiatrists.

"The bootleg sessions," Zac said. "What do you think?"

"I think we don't have a tape recorder," Fran said, the flippant response covering a twinge of sudden fear.

"But I bet we can get one," Zac said.

And he was right. The horn-rimmed lady came across one for them in exchange for a ten-dollar deposit. "Do you think this thing is even worth ten dollars?" Zac demanded, casting a jaundiced eye over the venerable machine. It was made of plastic colored to look like walnut and it had been manufactured by a company called Crown Electronics some time when dinosaurs still ruled the Earth.

Zac inserted the batteries, slotted in tape number one and hit the PLAY button.

Fran's scalp prickled as a man's voice came out of the machine, half-drowned in a sea of hiss and crackle. "I worked there seven years," the man said, his voice surprisingly high and fragile-sounding. That wasn't how Bruno Picota sounded in Fran's memories of him. "Mr. Ghent was real nice to me."

Zac pressed STOP, and then another button. The voice was replaced by a chunter of busy machinery. "Forgot to rewind," he said.

"Don't," Fran told him quickly.

Zac stopped the tape again.

"I don't want to hear him. It's gonna freak me out. I'm okay with the words, but not in his voice. Sorry."

"No need to be sorry," Zac said. "This is your show."

They put the cassettes aside and went back to the transcripts.

They were bulky. The first session alone ran to eighty-three pages, detailing a conversation that had gone on, with toilet breaks, for more than four hours. Only a few minutes in, Fran started to wonder whether she would be okay after all. Picota's words stirred her emotions in all sorts of ways, some of them less predictable than others.

Maybe the weirdest thing of all was how helpless he was. He kept interrupting the therapists—referred to only by their initials as DH and RTS—to ask where his dad was, when his dad would be coming, if his dad knew where they'd taken him. Fran already knew from that long-ago TV special that Picota had been assessed as having a fairly low mental capacity at the time of the attacks, but they had had an actor voice him, presumably for legal reasons, and the actor had made him sound tough and sinister. The real

Picota came across as scared, bewildered and barely capable of understanding what was happening to him.

```
PICOTA: Is that a tape recorder? Why are you tape
        recordering me?

RTS:    We've got to, Bruno. You remember what we
        told you about what's going to happen now?
        The trial? This is so we can see if you're
        fit to stand trial, and so we can talk at
        the trial about what kind of person you
        are.

PICOTA: I'm a good person.

DH:     But you did some things that don't look
        too good.

PICOTA: I'm a good person. I am. Can I go home
        now?
```

"Jesus!" Fran muttered.

"I know, right?" Zac pointed to a paragraph further down the page. "Look what he says here."

Fran scanned the text. Picota had worked as a janitor at the Perry Friendly Motel, but before that he had worked at a middle school. He preferred the motel, he said, because at the school he had always been scared of the kids.

```
PICOTA: They were mean to me. They didn't like me.
        I tried not to talk to them much and just
        get on with my work but they always would
        ask me questions. Like who's the president
        and what's the longest word I can spell.
        They didn't really want to know the
        answers, they just asked so they could
        laugh at me when I got it wrong.
```

"It's kind of amazing the judge decided he was fit to stand," Zac said. "This isn't how normal people talk."

"Nobody ever said he was normal," Fran said. But she was thinking the same thing: that her bogeyman was turning out differently than she had expected, and maybe—in spite of all he'd done to her—too pathetic to be worthy of her hate.

"This stuff isn't what we're looking for," she said impatiently. "We're looking for what happened between him and me at the motel. Homeopathy, remember?"

"But you said nothing is irrelevant," Zac reminded her.

"I know. But my blind spots are about what he did and what he said. What was going on inside his head doesn't help us all that much. Let's find the parts where he talks about what happened. Here, if we take half each we can go faster."

Fran split the stack of transcripts into two, took one for herself and shoved the other one across the table to Zac. He shot her a glance that had concern and maybe a question in it, but she cast her eyes down and got back to reading.

The first thing that drew her attention was the word Zac had misremembered earlier. The Native American word that didn't quite mean the devil. *Skadegamutc.*

RTS: No, never heard of it. How are you saying
         that again?

PICOTA: With a ch at the end. Ch. Much.

DH: An Indian word.

PICOTA: I think so. Sure. It's, they're real. My
         mom said they're really real.

RTS: And Fran Watts was one of these things?

PICOTA: Yes.

DH: Can you explain, Bruno?

209

PICOTA: It's a ghost witch.

DH: That doesn't really help. Tell us a little
       more, please.

PICOTA: It's, like, the ghost of a witch. A ghost,
       but it, that it's got magic. You know? An
       evil spirit. And you can't ever see how it
       [unclear] where it might have come from.
       You just see that it's there. Maybe she
       had magic when she was alive, you see, but
       you don't know that. And anyway now she's
       dead she's got more. A lot, lot more.

RTS: Now she's dead? I'm sorry, you're saying
       that about Fran Watts? That she's dead?

PICOTA: She is definitely dead.

DH: Did you kill her, Bruno? Is that how you
       remember it?

PICOTA: [unclear]

DH: Is that how you remember it, Bruno?

PICOTA: Sometimes.

Fran's chest had started to tighten up as she read, and it had got
worse and worse until she had to work at breathing through her
clenched muscles. Now that same folding-in-on-yourself feeling
was spreading downward to her stomach. If she just kept on sitting
and reading, she was pretty sure she was going to throw up. Real
soon. She scrambled to her feet, muttered "get some air" and more
or less ran out of the room.

She was afraid Zac was going to follow her, but he didn't.
Again, not so dumb for a boy. She faced the wall, leaning in so
her forehead was against the cold wood. She gave herself permission to cry, but no tears came. The coldness of the wood soothed

her a little, spreading from her forehead down into her flushed face.

She stayed out there for a few minutes, whispering all the worst swearwords she knew under her breath. She was directing them at Bruno Picota, in his cell at the Grove City secure psychiatric facility or wherever he was right then.

"I'm not dead," she told the wall. Remembering the pain of the knife and the *no no no* feeling of shock and denial as it broke her skin. "I'm not fucking, fricking, pissing, shitting, bloody . . . dead!"

Of course you're not, Lady Jinx growled.

Fran turned around with a laugh that was halfway to being a sob. Jinx was standing there in full armor, her hands resting on the hilt of her downturned sword—a heraldic pose taken right out of *The Knights of the Woodland Table*.

Take me to him, Jinx said, *and we'll see who's dead. I'll slice him in pieces, and then I'll cut the pieces into smaller pieces until there's nothing left!*

Fran smiled in spite of herself. "That would be a great plan if you were real."

Don't say that, Fran. You know that hurts my feelings.

"Sorry, Jinx. I'm glad you came."

I came because I knew this would happen. Picota is dangerous. Even finding out about him is dangerous.

"So am I," Fran said with reckless bravado. It was so far from the truth it was actually funny. She was the opposite of dangerous. A skinny little kid who wasn't even right in the head.

She took a few deep breaths, feeling around inside herself for the tightness and nausea. It was still there but it felt like she had it a bit more under control now. She went back inside, leaving the door ajar so Jinx could pad into the room behind her.

Zac looked up from the papers, anxiety written in billboard letters across his face. "Should we stop for today?" he asked. "We can do this any time, you know?"

"Nope, we're doing it now," Fran said. "You come across anything else worthwhile?"

He looked a little shame-faced. "I made a big find. I think. But then I got distracted by the shadow stuff again. Can I show you that first?"

"Okay, go ahead." Fran said. She was determined not to flinch from any of this. The truth was going to set her free, she reminded herself. But only if she didn't run and hide when she saw it.

Zac held up a page of transcript. "This is the first time Picota talks about the shadows. You can see why the news reports went with the big headline and steered clear of the details. It's all ate up with the dumbass."

He put on a goofy voice to go with the goofy street slang, inviting Fran to laugh, but she couldn't quite take up the invitation. He turned his sheaf of papers so she could read it too. It was part of the transcript for session three, and was dated exactly a week after her abduction.

```
PICOTA:  I already told you. Her shadow. Her shadow
         was wrong. That's how you know them.

DH:      How you know who, Bruno? The skadegamutc?

RTS:     Wait a moment, can we stick with the
         shadows? Bruno, you've used that word
         three times now. Wrong. Her shadow was
         wrong. Another time you said it was funny.
         Can you try to explain what you mean?

PICOTA:  I did try.

RTS:     Tell us again.

PICOTA:  I don't want to. God gives it to us so we
         know them when they come. If you can't see
         it, you're not one of the right people.
         Righteous. Right and righteous people.

RTS:     Okay, but Dr. Hemington and me, we're not
```

evil, are we? There's nothing wrong with
our shadows.

PICOTA: No.

RTS: So you can trust us, can't you?

"How long does this go on for?" Fran asked. "Do you want to
just give me the highlights?"

"Here." Zac pointed at the bottom of the page.

PICOTA: It wasn't really her shadow, but that's
        the best way to say it. It's like if you
        were walking in the sun and your shadow
        got up off the ground and turned into you,
        and you turned into your shadow.

DH: So her shadow moved? By itself?

PICOTA: No, it didn't move. It's hard to say it
        right. Like, she carried her shadow along
        with her, all the time. Could be there was
        more than two, though. I didn't count.

RTS: You could see two little girls at the same
        time.

PICOTA: The same girl, but there wasn't just the
        one of her. They were swapping. Switching
        over. The real girl and the shadow girl.

RTS: Okay, but how could you tell when they
        swapped over? I mean, if they were both
        Fran Watts . . .

PICOTA: They got fuzzy. The one who wasn't really
        there got all fuzzy.

Fran let out a sigh. She didn't mean to: it just got out of her.
The tightness came back all at once, clenching her chest like a fist.

Bruno Picota's mind was weirdly in sync with her own. He was describing her hallucinations. Or at least, one specific hallucination. What she saw when she looked at Liz Kendall, Bruno Picota had seen when he looked at her. And it was the reason he had attacked her.

Because she was a demon. A skadegamutc.

"Hey," Zac said. "Are you okay?"

"I'm fine," Fran lied. Wondering if you could catch madness the way you catch a cold. If Bruno Picota had managed to infect her somehow, in those hours they spent together at the Perry Friendly, with . . . something. His sickness. His twisted vision. "You said there was something else," she reminded Zac. "Something big."

She expected him to go forward in the transcript but he took it away. Lying underneath it was the manila file sleeve, with stamps and scribble all over it and the courthouse address and a big CONFIDENTIAL in red letters inside a red rectangle.

"What?" Fran said. "What am I looking at?"

"The consulting psychiatrists," Zac said. "Bottom right."

He put the tip of his finger against the names, and Fran lowered her gaze to read.

DH was Dana Hemington, who she didn't know from Eve.

RTS was Ronald Timothy Southern.

Liz had spent two hours putting a gray undercoat on Zac's bedroom walls. With the bed and desk covered in dustsheets and her son's posters all rolled up and stacked in the hall, the room now looked like a black and white photo of itself.

She was up on an aluminum ladder, working on the ceiling of Molly's room when Zac appeared in the doorway. He looked around with bewilderment and dawning alarm.

"Hey, you," Liz said, heading him off. "How come you're so late?"

"I was with Fran. We were doing research for a project. Mom, what is this? What are you doing?"

Liz tried to keep the tone light. She was acutely aware that she was lying to Zac, even if they were only lies by omission. She had to hope he'd forgive her when it was all over. "You saw I'd bought the paint," she reminded him, forcing a smile. "What did you think it was for?"

"But . . . tonight?" Zac wrinkled his nose as he looked around the room. "Why tonight? You've got to be in court tomorrow. This is stupid!"

"I had a lot of nervous energy inside me," Liz said. That much was true, at least. She came down the ladder, stowed the roller and tray and walked over to him. "I felt like I had to use it on something."

Zac shook his head. He didn't seem impressed with this argument. He checked the door frame for paint before leaning against it, hands thrust sullenly into pockets.

"Sorry about the smell," Liz said.

"I'm not worried about the smell. Where's Moll? Did you paint over her?"

"She's upstairs with the Sethis. They're expecting you too."

"For dinner?"

"Not just for dinner. They've prepped the spare room for the two of you. This way you'll get a decent night's sleep. If you stay down here, you'll be poisoned. And Molly will have an attack."

"What about you?" he asked her.

"I'll join you for dinner. But then I'll sleep down here. With the bedroom door closed and the windows open. I'll be fine. Go get your things and head on up. I'll join you in a half hour or so and eat with you. Then I'll come back down and finish off."

Zac didn't move. His mouth was set in a tight line. Liz ruffled his hair, but he looked away, deliberately refusing to meet her gaze.

"Humor me, Zac," she begged. "Please." She moved sideways so she could see his face, forcing him to look at her—but it was only one quick glance before he dropped his eyes again.

"I think you should have waited and done this after tomorrow." The hurt and frustration in his voice dismayed her.

"I wanted to do it now," she said. "New beginnings. It's kind of an omen."

"You can't make your own omens, Mom. It's only an omen if it happens by itself."

"Says you." Liz smiled again, but Zac's expression stayed serious.

"I want to stay down here," he said. "If you insist on doing this, I'll at least help you finish."

"Not on a school night," Liz said, falling back on that catch-all argument. "You need to do your homework, and you need your rest. I'm burning off steam here and it's doing me good. Really. Go."

Now, finally, he looked at her. "I don't understand," he said. "You're making us go away and be apart from you when we need to be together. You won't let me tell everyone what a shit Dad is, you won't let me be in court and now you're saying I can't even be in the house with you."

"Because . . ." But she had nowhere to go with that sentence. She couldn't tell him the truth, and she had already used up the least implausible lies she could scrape together. "I love you," she said helplessly. "I love you and Molly so much. I want to keep you away from this. Stop it from hurting you."

She put a hand on his shoulder. It slid off again as he retreated.

"This isn't how you stop things from hurting, Mom," he said, really angry now. Liz realized suddenly how much he wanted it to be the other way around, at least some of the time. That he needed to feel that he was being a shield for her, instead of being shielded all the time.

But she had no choice. She couldn't let him be a part of what she was planning.

"Zac, this is what I need right now," she said. "If you want to help, the best way you can help is by looking after Molly and . . ." She tailed off.

"And what?" Zac asked. He looked down at the dustsheets, up at the ladder and the half-painted room, indicating them all with a nod of the head. "Leaving you down here. With this?"

"Yeah," Liz said. "Yes. Exactly. Just for tonight."

"Happy to," he muttered.

He turned and walked away without another word.

"Zac—" Liz called out. The slamming of the door made anything else she might have said irrelevant.

With a heavy heart, she got back to work. She painted for another hour, finishing the undercoat. The job had to be done now she'd started it, even if it was just a smokescreen for something else.

When she finally went upstairs it was to discover that Zac had never arrived at the Sethis. Belatedly she discovered his text, which just said that he would make his own arrangements.

"I'm really sorry," she told Parvesh. "It looks like Zac might not be coming after all. I really upset him. He doesn't understand why I chose such an insane time to do home improvements."

"I don't either, Lizzie," Parvesh said, "but I don't have to. If it's good for you, it's good for us." Pete nodded his agreement, accepting her gift of white Zinfandel as if he didn't know it was the two-buck chuck from Trader Joe's.

Liz excused herself and called Zac. He didn't answer.

Dinner with the Sethis was usually a fairly festive affair. Pete was an amazing cook, and both he and Parvesh told great stories— Parvesh about the branches of his family who still lived in India, Pete about life as a public school teacher in a school so tough it made Julian C. Barry seem like Moominland. They were both on good form tonight, and Liz laughed along at the outrageous anecdotes. Molly laughed too, high and hilarious on the general excitement even though the jokes were flying way over her head.

But the whole time, a part of Liz was lying coiled up and cold like a snake, closed off to these people she loved, insulated from them. She had forgotten how heavy a secret can be. She made her excuses as soon as they were done with the clearing up, thanking the Sethis again for looking after Molly for her.

"It's the least we can do," Parvesh said as she walked out to the stairs. "You know, if Zac is sleeping over with a friend, that frees up the sofa. You shouldn't be on your own with all this crazy shit going down."

"I think I need to be," Liz countered. "Most of the crazy shit is here inside my head, Vesh. I need to make sure it's screwed on straight for tomorrow, you know?"

He gave her a kiss on each cheek. His grave face indicated what he thought of that reasoning, but he didn't try to argue her out of it. "Well, we're here if you change your mind," he said.

Alone in the house with the miasmic smell of silk matt emulsion,

218

she almost did. She called Zac again, and once again got no reply. She wasn't worried for him. Even in his current unhappy state, he was too sensible a boy to do anything reckless or dangerous. Either he would stay over at a friend's house or else he would go back to the Sethis before they locked up for the night. Liz didn't think, given how things had gone between them, that he would come back home.

Still, she was ashamed that she had lied to him and shut him out, however necessary it was. However temporary.

He'll get over it, said Beth with a sneer in her tone. Liz didn't answer. She didn't want to talk to Beth about either of her kids.

She went from room to room, checking windows, closing doors. Her feet crunched on the plastic sheeting, and the sound—all sounds—came back to her with a creepy little susurrus of echoes. The acoustics of the house seemed to have changed far more than could be accounted for by laying down dustsheets and moving a few items of furniture around.

She retreated to the living room. It felt unnaturally bright. The lights were all on in here, as well as in the kitchen and in Zac's bedroom. If Marc was watching, things had to seem normal—and it wasn't normal for the house to go dark in the middle of the evening. She curled up on the sofa and tried to watch TV. It was just sounds and images. She couldn't even tell what kind of show it was. A drama of some kind. Power-dressed men and women in boardrooms and bedrooms, delivering brittle dialogue freighted with subtext Liz was in no condition to guess at.

Getting scared?

"No."

Then relax. Pace yourself. Have a drink.

Just the suggestion caused her stomach to make an acidic rush into her throat. "I'm fine, thanks," she lied.

This is not what fine looks like. If you panic, you'll screw everything up and we'll die.

"I'm not going to panic."

Check where all the weapons are. Make sure you can find them in the dark without groping for them. Seconds are going to count.

"I checked."

You checked with the lights on. Try it in the dark.

Liz ignored the suggestion, but Beth kept on at her, reminding her how high the stakes were as if she didn't already know, as if this wasn't her life she was fighting for. Finally she gave in. With her eyes closed she went from room to room. Touching the gel pistol secreted behind the living room door, the flashlight baton on the kitchen counter, the baseball bat leaning against the bedroom wall. She was wearing the holstered taser on her belt.

"Satisfied?" she muttered sourly.

With the weapons. Not with you.

"Well, I'm what you've got."

Liz decided she might have that drink after all. Returning to the kitchen, she poured a brandy from the bottle she kept for cooking, but just the aroma of it mixed with the paint smell made her queasy all over again. She poured it away. She eyed the kettle instead.

No coffee. If your nerves get jumpy you're bound to screw this up.

"My nerves are . . ." Liz left the sentence hanging. "Fine" was an obvious lie, and "jumpy already" would be a confession. "If you're worried about my nerves, you'll just back off and let me handle this on my own."

There was no answer. The silence stretched.

"Beth?" Liz called softly.

Still nothing. And the intrusive presence, the sense of someone floating behind her shoulder like a bad angel, was suddenly gone.

"Beth?"

Liz hadn't expected to be taken seriously, still less to be obeyed. She called her other self's name a few more times before finally giving up. Of course this wasn't Beth respecting her wishes, she thought grimly. It was Beth rubbing her nose in it, giving her what she had asked for just to prove that it wasn't what she really wanted. Or needed.

"Great," she muttered. "Then I'll do it on my own."

She went back into the lounge and sat down to wait. She didn't

220

try to watch TV anymore: there was no distraction to be found, and no point in kidding herself.

At 10:00 p.m., or a little after, she turned out the lights in both the lounge and the kitchen. She turned on the one in her bedroom for half an hour, then shut that off too.

At 11:00, she made a quick foray to Zac's room and turned out the bedside lamp. She hurried back to her own room as though to a sanctuary, feeling dangerously exposed in the dark.

It wasn't pitch-dark, though. The luminous numbers on her alarm clock were a red blotch on the blackness, and a diffuse and indirect glow from the street lights out front filtered through the partly open curtains. Over the space of ten or fifteen minutes, Liz's eyes adjusted to it. She could see the shape of the bed, the outline of the door, the squat bulk of the chest of drawers. Glancing to the left she located the slanted line of the baseball bat where it leaned against the wall, close enough for her to reach when she needed it.

She sat down on the edge of the bed, facing the open door. Probably wouldn't be long, she told herself. Marc wasn't famous for his impulse control. If he was coming at all, he'd come before midnight.

But an hour passed, and then another. Liz listened to the street sounds, reading sinister narratives into passing footsteps, stray gusts of wind, random creaks of the settling house.

One by one they quieted. She felt herself to be completely alone, even though Molly and the Sethis were sleeping just one floor up and there was a city of a million people right outside her door. She missed Beth, though she was ashamed to admit it to herself. Missed her other self's aggressive confidence and ready rage. She could do with both right now.

She fell into a doze at last. Into a hazy dream that consisted mostly of other people's voices; snatches of conversation that she vaguely felt must have been addressed to her but which she'd failed to catch. She chased them through the dark, down blind corridors made of nothing more tangible than smoke and shadows.

At the end of one of those alleyways, she met herself.

"So you're lost," the other Liz said with cold contempt. "Again."

She wanted to deny it, but it was true. She had no idea, in the dream, where she was or how to retrace her steps. She couldn't even remember why she had come here.

"That's been your problem all along," the other Liz pointed out, shaking her head. "You never had a plan. You let other people take you by the hand and lead you anywhere they wanted. That's why you're in this mess."

It was all true. It had to be, Liz knew, because she wouldn't lie to herself. There wouldn't be any point. She sank to her knees, too tired and too full of self-disgust to go any further. But a spark of defiance made her lift her head to stare herself in the face.

"I'll change," she said.

"Oh yeah?" the other Liz sneered. "How?"

"I'll fight."

Other Liz shivered, broke apart and reformed, like a reflection on the surface of a pond when the wind picks up.

I'll believe it when I see it, Beth said. *But now would be a good time. He's here.*

When the phone rang, Fran somehow knew who it was. Even though it was after ten o'clock, and it was the house phone that was ringing rather than her cell. Jinx knew it too. She perked up from a light doze, growling reflexively at the waking world. *It's that boy*, she snapped. *I can smell him over the wire. Why is he calling you so late?*

Fran raced down the stairs, Jinx loping beside her, but her dad got there first. She heard his "Hello?" as she hit the landing, and when she made the turn of the stairs he was already saying, "May I ask who's calling?"

She was in his line of sight now. She came down the rest of the stairs at a more casual pace, and when she got to the bottom her dad handed her the phone, his face studiously impassive. "It's for you, Frog," he said unnecessarily. "Mr. Zachary Kendall."

Fran smiled weakly. Then waited him out. Gil gave a small grunt of acquiescence, retreating back into the living room so she could take the call in private. He was a stickler for the proprieties, and wouldn't eavesdrop however much he was tempted.

"Hey," she said when she was alone. "How are you doing?"

"I'm fine." Zac's voice was a glum monotone, contradicting the

223

words. Wind whipped and whooped behind him, so he must be out in the open somewhere.

"What was wrong with my cell?"

"It just kept ringing. I couldn't get through."

Fran tutted, at herself rather than him. She remembered that she had turned the sound right down to zero earlier for the dumbest and most embarrassing of reasons: she hadn't wanted a random call to disturb Lady J after she fell asleep.

Excuse me? Why is that dumb? Why is that embarrassing?

"Sorry," Fran said. "I forgot I had it on silent. Is something the matter, Zac? You sound really down."

"My mom kicked us out."

His mom should have done that a long time ago. You don't start growing up until you're hunting for yourself.

Fran blinked. "What? No way!"

"She decided to repaint the entire house. She sent us upstairs to sleep at Vesh and Pete's."

"Well . . . that's not kicking you out, exactly," Fran felt impelled to say.

"Yeah, it is, Fran. She made it so we couldn't sleep in our rooms. That was the only reason she bought the paint."

Then maybe there was some really good reason why she needed to be by herself, Fran thought. Sometimes you couldn't bring the people you loved with you, because of where you were going. The same way she could never have brought her dad to the Perry Friendly. She didn't say any of these things. She just asked Zac where he was. She was afraid she knew.

"That railway platform," he told her. "The one you showed me, between Lenora and Negley Run. I'm going to sleep out."

Fran was appalled. "On concrete? Zac, are you out of your mind?"

"I'll find something I can lie on. Or sit down on, at least. I think we passed a mattress somebody had dumped a little way back from here."

"You'll catch diseases from the mattress and pneumonia from

the wind chill. And you'll probably get mugged for your phone. Do you even have a sleeping bag?"

She heard a stubborn sigh from the other end of the line, and then another blaring, ruffling sound as the wind cut across his words. "I've got my coat."

"You're an idiot."

Yes! He is!

"Thanks."

"Stay on the line, goon. Talk amongst yourself."

Fran muted the phone and went into the living room, where her dad was reading a novel. It was Harold Courlander's *The African*, which he had bought after reading about Courlander's lawsuit against Alex Haley.

He took a lot of persuading.

"Frog, the boy should go home to his mother."

"But his mother made him leave."

"She made him go one floor up. That doesn't make him one of the orphans of the storm."

"He's not gonna go back, Dad. He's gonna sleep rough. And I mean *really* rough. The wind's going crazy out there."

They went back and forth a few more times. Gil made it clear that he didn't like any part of this, but finally he agreed that Zac could come over and sleep on the sofa. One night only, no arguments and no take-backs. "He's not camping out here while he works through his issues, Frog. And he'll have to tell his mom where he is. We're not going behind anyone's back."

Fran gave him a fervent hug. "Thanks, Dad. You're awesome."

"I am," Gil agreed dourly. "It's a heavy burden."

When Zac arrived, he was looking both sheepish and defiant—probably starting to realize that he'd handled a bad situation really badly but not quite ready to admit it yet. It had already come on to rain, and he was pretty well soaked. Jinx sniffed him loudly, stiff with disapproval.

Fran ushered him into the living room, where he said his thanks with downcast eyes. "It's really kind of you, Mr. Watts. I promise it's just a one-off. I had an argument with my mom, but I'm gonna sort it out first thing in the morning."

"That sounds like an excellent plan, son," Gil told him. "Did you get any dinner at all?"

"I'm fine, sir. Thank you. I ate at Little Lou's on Lenora."

"Okay, then. We might as well say our goodnights, since this space is now officially your billet. I'm sorry we don't have a guest room to put you up in, but I've got a desk in there for when I work from home and there's no room for a bed. The sofa's a little bit narrow, but it will have to do."

"The sofa's perfect," Zac said. "I'm grateful. Thank you."

"Once is enough, son. Don't drop too many eggs in the pudding. But you're welcome. If you'll take some friendly advice, though, storming off into the night is a losing game even in fine weather. Do yourself a favor and find another way of relieving your feelings next time."

Zac said he would try, stopped himself in the middle of another thank you and took delivery of some sheets and pillowcases that Fran had brought down for him.

"Sleep well," she said. "Goon."

"Harsh."

"I *am* harsh. You know that about me. I'm the girl who hit you with mashed potato when you tried to be nice to her."

Impulsively, she gave him a hug. It was hella weird with her dad standing right there, watching, but it still felt like the right thing to do. "She'll be okay," she said. "You both will."

"Thanks, Fran. For everything." His voice sounded a little husky. She got out of there fast, knowing her dad would follow right behind. Zac was wound up really tight, and if he broke down in tears in front of her it would be the most intimate thing that had ever happened between them. She wasn't sure she was ready for it, and she knew for sure her dad wasn't.

The hug was just a friend thing. A comfort thing. She felt the imprint of it all along her body, but she wasn't going to pretend it was something it wasn't.

Right. Of course you're not.

"Give me a break, your ladyship," Fran muttered, feeling the blush rise from her collar toward her hairline.

Liz came up from sleep with her heart hammering. Beth's words had been accompanied by a psychic push, hurling her back up into consciousness, but there was something else besides. A sound, tiny but distinct, had just impacted on her attention. Sprawled in the dark, momentarily as lost as she had been in her dream, she tried to replay the sound, to make sense of it. But she couldn't parse it until it came again.

It was the ratcheting whisper of a key entering the lock of the front door.

Liz froze every muscle, straining to hear what would come next. Nothing, at first. At least, nothing up close. But a dog started kicking up a commotion somewhere down the block, and the sound peaked and fell as though a door had opened, letting in the world, and then closed again silently.

She knew beyond any doubt that Marc was inside the house.

Quickly and quietly she came up off the bed and stepped away from it, taking a position where the door as it opened would blindside him. She slipped the taser out of its holster. It took three attempts. Her hands had started to tremble when the key turned in the lock, and now they were shaking badly. She fought to keep them steady, taking aim at the edge of the door. When Marc pushed it fully open and stepped into the room, he would be sideways on to her, an easy target. His eyes wouldn't have had time to adjust, so he wouldn't see her. And he would be moving slowly so she would have plenty of time to aim and shoot.

Something rustled in the hallway. Footsteps? There was no rhythm to the sound: it was just a single scuffle. Then after a few seconds, another.

The dust sheets. She should have rolled them up, at least from out in the hallway. Marc had stopped, trying to figure out what he was walking on. And the longer he hesitated, the more his eyes would adjust to the dark. Liz wanted an ambush, not a fight. He would definitely win in a fight.

Against you. Not against me.

"Beth!" The name escaped her in a hoarse, ragged whisper. "Don't talk to me. Please! I n-need to—"

What, focus? You were out cold until I woke you. You can't do one thing right. Not one!

Now there were footsteps, audible, clear, approaching the door. Liz was still holding the taser out in front of her, her finger on the trigger, her arms wracked with tremors that kept a lockstep with her racing heart.

Shit! Let me in. Let me finish this.

The door opened, and Liz fired. Straight and true.

But too soon. The door was still swinging inward, its movement intersecting her line of fire. The taser's twin tips bounced off the door frame and fell slackly to the floor. Two dull impacts that achieved nothing except to make Marc turn his head in her direction.

He leaned forward, peering into the dark. He had heard the noise, but hadn't seen her. She still had a chance. She leaned sideways, groping for the baseball bat. Her fingertips touched it, but at the wrong angle. It fell with a blunt, accusing thud.

Marc stepped into the room, heading not for the bed now but for Liz. There was something in his hand that might or might not be a knife.

Liz dived for the bat as he raised the thing up and back. Knife or not, he was going to hit her with it. Arm bent at the elbow, thrusting downward.

Her fingers closed on smooth, cold neoprene. She swung the bat in a wild arc, still down on one knee, and caught Marc's conjoined hands a glancing blow. The thing he was holding fell at her feet.

From this close up there was no mistaking it. It was a knife. Not a kitchen knife, but some misbegotten macho thing with a cross-guard and a curved tip. She was staring at the confirmation of everything Beth had said, everything she had fought against believing, from that nightmare montage of her own unhappy endings right down to the present hyper-real, hallucinogenic moment.

Marc had come here to kill her.

With a sob of anguish and protest she rose from the floor—a little quicker than him because he was still trying to figure out what had hit him. His night vision hadn't kicked in properly yet, Liz realized. He didn't know what she'd hit him with, where his knife had gone or where exactly she was in the solid mass of shadow in front of him. She took a second swipe with the bat. It hit him in the side of the head, but not nearly hard enough. She had held back, involuntarily slowing and softening the blow. Afraid of her own violence as much as his.

Nonetheless Marc staggered, backing away and raising his arm to ward off another attack. He didn't need to. Liz just ran, the open door an irresistible temptation. She forgot all her plans in a second: she had to get away, and that was all that mattered.

The knife, you idiot! The knife!

Too late for that. Too late for the baseball bat too. Her elbow hit the door frame as she raced through into the hallway and the agonizing jar made her drop her weapon. She almost tripped on it as it bounced end over end between her feet.

She headed for the kitchen at a dead run. I'm sorry, I'm sorry, I'm sorry, she thought, the words bubbling up in her mind like vomit, impossible to keep down.

"You cunt!" Marc growled, from much too close behind her.

What was in the kitchen? The other baton or the gel pistol? And whichever it was, where had she put it?

The breakfast bar loomed ahead of her, a barely visible dark gray bulk against the lighter gray of the ambient air. She skirted it without slowing. With a whimper of terror she threw herself at the side door and wrestled with the handle. It didn't open. She had locked it herself and put the key . . . somewhere. Not here. Not where she could find it now, with death bearing down on her like a juggernaut, like a train, like the force of gravity.

The flashlight baton.

Let me in!

The flashlight baton was in here somewhere. On the countertop right behind her.

Let me in!

Right behind Marc too. He had been close on her heels when she came into the room and she had lost seconds she didn't have in scrabbling at the locked door. He strode toward her, cutting her off from the countertop, boxing her into a corner that contained nothing. Nothing she could use. Nothing but him, and her.

The knife was in his hand again, but this time he held it low down, the blade angled upward. He would stab her in her stomach, in her chest, in her arms as she tried in vain to fend him off. It would be slow, and bloody, and terrible.

Let me in! Beth screamed and screamed and screamed.

And yeah, Liz thought, despairing. Go ahead. Save me, if you can, because I can't save myself.

Sinking to her knees in surrender. Conditioned by a thousand bruising collisions to fold herself up small and hope the worst knocks landed on parts of her that wouldn't break.

Something rose as she fell. Spread itself like wings through her and above her and around her. A funneled force like a gale hit her full on, snatched her up and hurled her headfirst into a blistering, unbearable cold.

231

She moved away on a curving trajectory, as slowly (it seemed to her) as a flower opening. But the slowness was inside her as well as outside. Her mind sparked feebly and failed to catch.

She was looking at a woman, and the woman was down on her knees. She looked as though she was praying, or maybe just bowing to something inevitable. Her hair hung down over her eyes and her shoulders sagged. A wink of red light from some electronic device (the standby LED on the kitchen microwave, Liz's subconscious supplied) illuminated the curve of her cheek while throwing her eyes into shadow.

But the posture of surrender was an illusion. It was only the strained, strange slo-mo that had sustained it for this long. The woman was rising to her feet. There were muscles moving in those dropped shoulders, and further down still the woman's hands clenched, splayed fingers gathering into fists.

She rose like a rocket, rippling the air, and in rising passed right by Liz's sluggish, floating point of view. Liz got a good look at the nearer of those hands. A bracelet circled its wrist: three small garnets, a larger tourmaline, then three more garnets, all on a band of white gold.

I have a bracelet just like that, Liz thought.

And the truth hit her. Not all at once like an avalanche but in broken pieces, pulses of hectic bright and dark that strobed inside her mind.

This was her own body she was looking at.

She was seeing herself from the outside.

When she had let Beth in, she had imagined that it would be like a telephone call: that Beth would borrow the parts she needed for as long as she needed them.

But it wasn't like that at all. Liz had been expelled, decisively, from her own flesh. She was still drifting away with the force of that sudden, violent push.

And if her body was also still moving (as it clearly was) independently of her (which was impossible to deny), then it was because someone else was now in the cockpit. At the helm. Sitting firm and confident behind those eyes (which to Liz were lakes of darkness in which the glaring red dots of the microwave light now floated like twin buoys).

Beth.

Beth had cast her out.

So—the last domino falling, the last line of the equation—Beth was real. Her existence was not contingent on Liz's, which meant (had to mean) that she was not a part of Liz's sick mind.

That she was, after all, exactly what she said she was.

Another version of Liz, streamlined and perfected by endless pain and unencumbered by pity or mercy, come from a long way off to finish what Marc had started when he killed her.

It felt so good she almost died right there.

It wasn't like the other times. The other times she'd had to work around Liz's conscious mind, leaning in at an awkward angle and straining to make Liz's body do the things that needed to be done. It had been a struggle, and it had tired her out very quickly, which was why she hadn't been able to stay for long. But now . . .

Now Liz's complete abdication, her willed surrender, allowed Beth to step inside her all at once and top to toe. She was putting on Liz's body, sliding herself into every fold and recess, every last particle. The rightness of it was like putting on a glove. She fitted so well, so precisely. She luxuriated in the sensation as though Liz's flesh and blood were warm, fragrant water in which she wallowed.

Then Marc grabbed her by her hair and pulled hard, wrenching her head back. And yes, she was awake again, in charge again, but this was a situation that needed her urgent and earliest attention.

"Bitch!" Marc growled. He raised the knife high over his head. Always an amateur move, Beth thought. He had the killer instinct, no doubt about it, but he indulged his cruelty and his rage in stupid ways. With a knife, you just had to bear in and push hard, making the blade do all the work.

But she had the experience of a thousand deaths to call on, whereas he was always a virgin.

She twisted free of his grip, leaving a clump of hair and probably scalp in his clenched fist. The knife whipped past her face, a blur of silver metal and grim intention. Leaning into the blow, Marc lost his balance and staggered.

There was no time for finesse, or second chances. Beth whiplashed forward, slamming her head into his stomach. With a grunt of pain and shock, Marc folded around the place where she'd connected. He leaned heavily against the wall. Dropping the knife, he pressed both hands to his belly.

Beth scrambled up, groping across the counter until her hand found the vulcanized rubber handle of the flashlight baton.

Marc saw it too—but only when it was swinging at his face.

The first blow broke his jaw.

The second, to the side of his head, dropped him where he stood.

Liz twittered faintly. *What are you doing what are you—*

The third time most likely sealed the deal, because Beth swung with both hands and put all her weight into it. She felt the shock of impact, and when she lifted the baton up again there was a moment's resistance, as though it had embedded itself in something that pulled and held.

No don't do this please don't don't don't

All the many blows that followed were therefore rather celebratory than efficacious. But Beth felt like she had a lot to celebrate and overkill was a concept she could seriously get behind.

When she finally ran out of energy she checked for a pulse, just to be sure. She used the carotid artery, and she pressed hard: it gave her a pleasant thrill to have her hand on Marc's throat. There was no trace of a pulse, which didn't surprise her because there was very little trace of a head. Her fingers came away wet and sticky. That didn't surprise her either, given how many times she had brought the baton down on his face. She stared at the asymmetrical mass that topped his shoulders. The darkness hid the extent of the damage, but she sketched in the details in her imagination.

"You like that, sweetheart?" she whispered. "I sure did. Best it's ever been."

There was a sound of puling and weeping from somewhere nearby. Beth didn't mind. Liz would give up soon enough when she realized how things stood. There was nothing for her here.

An amorphous psychic shriek of panic greeted that thought. Beth winced. "Keep it down," she muttered. "Fuck's sake!"

What have you done?

"What you should have done a long time ago. You're welcome."

She found the light switch and turned it on, steeling herself for another siren-scream when Liz got a good look at the body. But there was nothing. Of course, Liz wasn't in touch with her own flesh right then. Again, this time was different. Instead of the two of them playing a doubles match with the one nervous system, Beth was in sole control.

She feasted her brand-new eyes at leisure. Marc's broken body wasn't much to look at in itself, but the sense of achievement and satisfaction she felt when she looked at it was dizzying. Intoxicating.

You're insane!

"Probably," Beth muttered. "I hear voices."

She searched the body quickly but methodically. The keys were in one of Marc's back pockets. She grinned when she brought them out and felt the satisfying weight of them. The full ring. It was always possible that he had kept his duplicate key to Liz's place separate, since he had no business owning it at all; but no, the cocky bastard had just stuck it in among all the rest of them. Which meant she could proceed with Plan A.

Liz didn't respond in words, but Beth felt her sick horror. Plan A implied a Plan B, which made it clear just how much care and how much time had gone into this.

"Thought I was making it up as I went along?" Beth asked as she fetched one of the dustsheets and laid it out on the kitchen floor. She gave a rich, deep chuckle. "Not a chance. I've been working you, babe. I knew you'd let me in sooner or later if I hung around long enough."

She had to stop talking for a while. It took serious effort to roll Marc's body onto the sheet. His ruined head left soggy clumps of blood and bone and tissue on the floor and on the plastic. She wrapped the sheet around the dead man, sealing it at the ends with duct tape.

You can't do this! You can't!

"Well, technically you did it."

It was you! It was you, not me!

"Really? Fingerprints don't lie."

Oh God, they'll put me in jail! You're leaving me to face a murder charge!

Beth straightened, finally nettled. The whining little shit was so slow on the uptake it was actually kind of funny, but it was also getting on her nerves.

"Who said anything about leaving?" she asked.

Silence, for a moment. The right-after-a-thunderclap kind of silence, where the air sucks itself back into the empty space where the deafening sound just was.

She felt a sensation like a gust of wind and Liz was on her, scrabbling and clawing at the edges of her mind. But she found no purchase there, just slid away like butter off a hot knife.

"Yeah," Beth confirmed. "That's not apt to get you anywhere."

Get out! Get out of there! Let me back in!

"Why? So you can mess your life up some more? To the victor go the spoils, Lizzie girl. That's me—the victor. And this piece of meat I'm wearing is the spoils. You don't figure in the equation at all."

You can't! You can't!

"You're getting a mite repetitive, if you don't mind me saying. Of course I can. What, you think I'm stupid? Anything you can do, I can do better."

Liz didn't waste any more time protesting. She attacked again, trying to squeeze herself through the interstices of Beth's thoughts and back into the driving seat.

Beth held the line but didn't hit back. Hitting back would give Liz something to hold on to. She felt the assault like an attack of pins and needles, prickling her scalp, fizzing along her nerves. It waxed and waned, waxed and waned, but went no further. She was braced for it. She lowered her head and stood with her arms folded while the buffeting wave intensified and peaked and started to fade. Until her other self had spent all her resources in fruitless pushing and thrashing around.

Beth knew from bitter experience how hard it was to keep hold of your sense of yourself when you didn't have a physical body as an ally. Water that's been poured out onto a level surface will spread and spread and spread until it's a thin film just about held together by its own surface tension. Exhaled breath on a cold day starts as a visible cloud, but all that vapor is gone a second later, its shape and substance stolen by the air.

Liz's struggles, never very strong, got weaker. It would have happened in any case, but her pointless, wasteful efforts to get back into her own flesh made it happen faster. She used herself up quickly, until like that exhaled breath she was gone.

I won't let you

I'm going to

You can't do this to

Let me in let me

In let me

And finally silence.
None too fucking soon.

Beth unfolded from the crouched position she had unconsciously adopted, and flexed her fingers. It was a long time before she stirred again after that. Where killing Marc had energized and elated her, she felt as though this second, psychic murder had used up some vital part of herself. She was so depleted that she could barely think. She could only stand there until the feel of cold night air on her skin, cold tiles under her bare feet, brought her back to herself.

She made herself move. She went to the sink and splashed cold water on her face. Then she poured herself a brandy from the bottle Liz had found earlier, and drank it down in a single burning gulp.

There was a lot to do. She'd better get to it.

Cleaning up should probably come first. She looked around the kitchen. Her hard work with the baton had spilled a lot of blood. Fortunately, apart from her own clothes and skin, it had mostly ended up on hard surfaces that would be easy to clean. She filled a bucket with hot water, poured in some disinfectant and got busy, working outward from the body in tight circles. Half an hour was all it took to remove all traces that she could see. The bucket was like the slop-pail at a butcher's shop. She poured it carefully into the disposal, running it at its lowest setting. That would be enough to grind down the detached bits of Marc's brain matter that she had mopped up, but hopefully not enough to wake the kids or the upstairs neighbors. Then she rinsed out and disinfected the bucket itself. And finally the baton, which needed serious work because it had a lot of Marc-stuff congealed onto it and its studded surface held on stubbornly to impacted gobs of hair and tissue.

She set it down at last, pristine and shining. She was going to have to make another pass around the room later, a forensic sweep, but this would do for now. To a casual inspection, the kitchen was clean.

The next hurdle was to get the body into the car. She unlocked the side door and propped it open. Then she went out to the car and opened the trunk. There was a ton of junk in there: old clothes and papers for recycling and an ancient sports bag containing God alone knew what. She transferred it all to the back seat. Measuring the distance from the car to the house, though, she saw it wouldn't do. She couldn't drag a man-sized sack of something thirty yards along the sidewalk and just hope nobody would see. It was too big a risk, even at 3:00 a.m.

So she was going to have to take a smaller one.

She got into the car, leaving the door slightly open so nobody would hear the slam. She reversed up onto the drive as far as she could, almost jamming it up against the side of the house. Now she would only have to move the body about twelve feet. There was relatively little chance of being seen by the Sethis, since only their living room windows faced onto the street and they would be all tucked up in bed by now. The car itself would shield her from people passing by on the sidewalk if anyone was still out walking at such a crazy hour.

All of this had taken way longer than Beth would have liked, but the upside of that was that she had got most of her strength back after the unwelcome and draining task of getting rid of Liz. She pulled Marc's stiffening corpse out of the kitchen and into the side alley by his feet, a few inches at a time, until she had him lying right up against the rear of the car.

The next part would be the hardest. He outweighed her by almost a hundred pounds, and he was taller than her too so the angles would work against her. She approached it like a puzzle. Taking the spare tire out of the car exposed the steel stanchion to which it had been bolted. She looped a length of rope from the garage around the stanchion and tied the free end around Marc's knees. By hauling on the rope, she was able to raise his legs up past the rim of the trunk and fold them so they draped over the edge. She secured them in that position so he couldn't slide down again.

Lifting the upper part of his body was still hard, but it was a lot easier with his lower extremities tied in place. She got him just about high enough, gripping him tightly underneath his shoulders, and leaned in hard, jacking him up by tiny increments until finally he slid over into the trunk. She untied the rope and tossed it in beside him.

The corpse still wasn't lying low enough. She had to peel the duct tape off the plastic sheeting and free Marc's legs so she could fold them back on themselves. After that, she was able to haul him round into a better position and push the trunk's lid closed—which she did as softly as she could.

"Okay," she murmured, to herself alone. "We're good. We're good. We're out of here."

She wondered if she should wash and change before she left. She couldn't see the blood that had congealed on her face but she could smell its bittersweet reek and feel its stickiness on her skin. Even licking her lips brought a battery acid taste. Her clothes hung heavy on her, plastered with Marc's vital fluids. But she was going to get dirtier still, and what she still had to do would take long enough as it was. Better just to wipe off her face and hands and cover the rest with a coat. Preferably one with a hood she could put up to cover her face, in case anyone was watching at the other end of this transaction. She couldn't rely on the lateness of the hour.

She went back into the kitchen. She was headed for the hall closet, but that was as far as she got. Molly was standing right where Marc had fallen, in her pajamas, hair tousled and feet bare. She had her back to Beth, but she turned at the sound of her feet on the tiles.

"Mommy," she said, blinking sleep-dazzled eyes as she stared at the gory apparition in the doorway. "Did you hurt yourself?"

Beth's first instinct was to grab the little girl by the shoulders and shake her violently until she told the truth about how much she'd seen.

Even as she moved, she put the brakes on that panic reaction. This was Molly, for God's sake! Liz might have been the one to squeeze her out in this world, but that didn't change a thing. She was still Beth's kid. *All* Beth's now, and nobody was going to hurt her. Ever. She didn't have to be afraid of a parent's crazy rage, or a stranger's. Not now she had her mommy to protect her.

"Come here, baby," she said, her voice breaking a little. She knelt.

And Molly came trotting docilely, trustingly, into her arms. Beth folded her into a tight embrace—and bit her lip to hold in a gasp of surprise and wonder. The warmth of this little body, the scent of clean cotton, the softness of sleep still on her. It was the first human contact Beth had experienced in what felt like a hundred years that wasn't born out of violent rage. She was overwhelmed, so dizzy with it that she almost overbalanced and dragged them both down onto the tiled floor.

"You smell funny," Molly said, her voice muffled. "And there's all blood. Mommy, why is there blood?"

"It's not blood," Beth lied. "It's cranberry juice. Mommy's all right, Moll."

"Mommy's fine," Molly agreed. "She spilled some juice. All over the floor." Beth laughed in spite of herself. Her daughter's glass-half-full outlook welcomed the lie and made it her own. She wouldn't look any further.

But what the hell was Moll doing here in the first place? And what could Beth do with her now? She had places to be and shit she needed to do. "Baby," she said, "you should be in bed. How did you get down here?"

"I had a bad dream," Molly mumbled, still holding on to her, head on her blood-boltered chest. "I dreamed you were fighting and you got hurt."

Beth's heart jumped and twanged like a broken bedspring. "Fighting?" she repeated stupidly. "Who was I fighting, baby?"

"I couldn't see. But you got hurt and you shouted, and I woke up. I knew it was just a dream because nobody else woke up, but I wanted to make sure you were okay. So I came down."

Beth ruffled her hair. "Well, that was good of you, Moll. And brave. But you're gonna have to go back upstairs now, okay?"

"Okay," Molly said, resigned.

But it wasn't okay. Beth had already started to disentangle herself from the cuddle—reluctant, heartsick, like an addict craving the next fix while she was still coming down from the last one—but she held on to Molly's hands so she couldn't leave.

Because what if she climbed those stairs again and Pete or Parvesh Sethi was waiting for her at the top? What if they asked her where she'd been and she told them how Mommy spilled dark red juice all over herself and all over her clothes? And what if she mentioned the baton, which Beth now realized she'd left out on the kitchen counter, or the plastic sheeting, or even just the fact that Mommy had been outside in the middle of the night? It wasn't wise to let her go now, while the memory of those things was still vivid. And though the alternative felt insane it was probably the lesser of the two evils.

"Would you like to go for a ride with me?" she asked in a low, conspiratorial tone. "In the car?"

Molly looked doubtful. "It's night time," she pointed out. "It's all dark outside."

"I know. But you'll be with Mommy so it will be okay. It will be an adventure. Like Harry and Ron and Hermione in the dragon lands. What do you say, baby girl? Shall we do it?"

243

Molly was sold. She forgot her doubts and nodded vigorously. "Okay! Let's do it!"

"Great stuff," Beth said. "Mommy's just going to wash her face and put a coat on. And we need to dress you up warm too, don't we?"

Which took about ten times as long as any sane person would have guessed. Dressing Molly, like doing anything with Molly, required a running commentary. She told the story of each article of clothing as she selected it and put it on. She also wanted to talk about the paint job. What colors her bedroom was going to be (Beth couldn't even remember, so she said it would be a surprise) and where her pictures and posters would go on the newly painted walls.

Finally Beth got her suited up and into the car. She was still wearing her blood-stiffened sweater, hidden under a Trespass windbreaker. She had scrubbed the blood off her face and hands (the thick strata under her fingernails would have to wait for now) and put on a fresh pair of jeans. She would pass a casual inspection. Anything more than that and she was probably already fucked in any case.

"Where are we going?" Molly asked as she started the car.

"To plant some flowers," Beth told her.

"In the night time?"

"In the night time."

Molly clapped her hands. That sounded good to her.

But the expedition took a long time to get underway, because Beth had forgotten how to drive. She had never driven a Kia, and the dashboard configuration felt strange to her. More seriously, her muscle memories refused to kick in. She knew intellectually what she ought to be doing, but she had to decide on each movement in advance and then send the instructions to her body—whose repertoire she was still relearning—to be executed. The car did a crazy disco dance down the street for the first few hundred yards before she got any kind of a feel for it. After that it got easier, but she took it slowly.

Molly was asleep long before they reached their destination. The vibrations of the car's suspension and the steady rumble of its engine did the job. Beth wished she hadn't said a word about planting flowers. She had been laying the groundwork for further explanations later, when they got to where they were going—as it turned out, unnecessarily.

She pulled up on Mayflower Street, bringing the car right up onto the verge. She wondered whether it was worth worrying about tire tracks. Probably not. It was going to rain again. The verge would be a mud wallow come morning: there wouldn't be any tracks.

There was nobody in sight, which wasn't surprising at this hour but was still both welcome and reassuring. Beth took off the windbreaker and put it over Molly like a blanket. She leaned in to kiss her, but then thought better of it. It would be stupid to disturb her when she was sound asleep.

The urban farm was locked up and silent, but Marc's key—which had remained on his key ring all this time, forgotten by everyone including him—unlocked the side entrance where the garden plots were. Beth propped it open and went back to the car.

Tumbling Marc out of the trunk was easier than getting him in, but not by much. His corpse was stiffer now, and it took more effort to unfold his limbs. Once his torso was mostly upright, though, she leaned on his shoulders and let his weight do the rest of the work, pushing him backward over the trunk's rim until he fell down onto the asphalt.

The car, losing all that ballast at once, rocked and creaked dangerously, but Molly didn't stir and her gentle snore didn't change timbre. Beth locked the car, tugging on the door handle to make sure. It felt wrong to leave the little girl out here on the street, but nobody could get into the car without making a racket that would be heard from a mile off in the still, unpeopled night. If that happened, Beth would come running.

She had given herself the smallest distance she possibly could, but it still took ten minutes or so to haul the body across the grass, in through the gate and down the narrow lane to the garden plots. She thought about borrowing a wheelbarrow, but realized it wouldn't help. She would never be able to keep it steady as it rolled, or get Marc's body up into it in the first place. It would be a wasted effort even to try.

So she kept on hauling. Toting the barge. Lifting the bale. Hating her ex-husband's mortal remains right then almost as much as she'd hated him in life.

She experienced a moment of panic when the gate to Marc's garden plot turned out to be padlocked. But the key was right there on the ring. She opened it up, left the padlock hanging on the hasp and dragged the body inside.

The digging was hard, but it wasn't at all unpleasant. Beth was wired, almost high on adrenaline and nervous energy: it was a relief to be able to burn some of it off. She went out a few times to check on Molly, finding her still fast asleep. This was an insane situation, but it was going okay. For now.

When the hole was deep enough—about four feet—she prepped the body, stripping off first the plastic and then every shred of clothing, cutting it away where she needed to with an X-Acto knife she'd brought along with her precisely for this task. The watch and the wedding ring last of all. She rolled Marc stark naked into the pit and anointed him generously with dolomite lime. Marc had always kept a few bags on hand to sweeten the soil in early spring.

She shoveled the earth in on top of him, and walked all over it for a minute or so to compact it down.

Would his being naked speed up the process? Probably not. Agricultural lime was slower than quicklime, and less caustic. It might not even dissolve Marc's bones. But it was a comfort to Beth to think of the man who had hurt her so much, so often, with such commitment, rotting away inexorably into his component parts. She didn't want any manmade fibers to get in the way of that elegant, organic process. It would spoil her pleasure when she thought about him on future nights, out here, under the ground, sailing away from her without moving.

She went back to the car, filthy, sweat-soaked and stinking, unlocked it and slid in beside her daughter.

"All done, baby," she whispered. "Let's go home."

Molly murmured something, but didn't wake. Her lips were thrust out in a pout of concentration. She was earnestly engaged with some dream or other.

It was safe to dream now. For all of them.

When Beth got back to the house, it was close to 5:00 a.m. There was no point in trying to sleep. She set Molly down in her own bed and lay beside her for a while, listening to the endless symphony of her breathing.

But when the clock showed 5:30 she got up and showered. Blood and mud and other things sloughed off her, leaving behind a heaviness that was both welcome and disturbing. It thrilled her to have such a vivid sense of her brand-new self, the heft and volume of it, but she didn't like to think of herself as having limitations, and a body was a weight you had to carry as well as a citadel you could defend.

She did what needed to be done in terms of putting the house to rights. Her assorted weaponry went into the back of the closet, along with her own bloodied clothes and Marc's in a plastic bag. She would burn them later, but at a time that would look natural, along with a whole lot of innocent garden rubbish. The rest of Marc's things—the wedding ring, the watch, his wallet, two phones (presumably his regular cell and the burner he'd bought to call her) and his key ring—she put in a shoe box on the closet top shelf. She would keep them, for a little while at least. You never knew what might turn out to be useful. Of course they were as incriminating as hell, but Beth wasn't anticipating an investigation—or at least not one that would lead to a search of the house. Marc had absconded the night before his trial. That was a narrative that would play well, she was pretty sure.

She cleaned the kitchen again in case she'd missed any tell-tale stains. Then she picked up all the dustsheets and dumped them in the garage along with the paint, brushes and ladder. The painting would have to be finished at some point, but for now it had served its purpose and she didn't intend to waste any of her time on it.

Her precious time. Her second life. Her triumph.

She went up the stairs and ran into Parvesh Sethi coming down in a flat panic. "Is Molly with you?" he demanded, all out of breath.

"Yeah," Beth said. "Sorry. I was just coming up to tell you. She came down in the night. I only just found her, sound asleep right next to me."

Parvesh sagged in relief. "Oh thank God! Lizzie, I'm so sorry! We should have locked the door. We just didn't think. We threw the bolt, like always, and left it at that. We never dreamed Molly would want to go anywhere in the night."

"It's fine," Beth told him. Better give him his name, she decided as an afterthought. "No harm done, Vesh. I'm sorry you got such a nasty shock. Thanks again for looking after her."

"We're always here, you know that. What about Zac? Is he coming home for breakfast or going straight into school?"

Yeah, that was about enough of that, Beth decided. This guy lived in her building, not in her pocket. "Thanks for everything," she repeated, and went back down the stairs.

"Lizzie," Parvesh called.

She gritted her teeth. *For fuck's sake!* Putting on a fake smile, she turned. "Yeah?"

"You want a lift down to the courthouse?"

"I'm good," Beth said. "Thanks."

"Because we'd be happy to—"

"I've got to get Molly to school. I might as well drive on as come back here."

"Okay, then." Parvesh looked doubtful. Something about her manner had surprised him. "We'll see you down there."

Of course. Of course they would have offered, and of course Liz being Liz would have accepted, pathetically grateful to have a bunch of random assholes holding her up in case she fell down. "It will be really good to have you there," Beth said, still with that plastic smile plastered across her face. "Thanks so much, Vesh."

That seemed to be the right thing to say. He nodded, smiled back at her and let her leave without offering any more help she didn't need.

Getting Molly up and ready for school was an even bigger production than dressing her in the night had been, but this time Beth could let herself relax and enjoy it.

This Molly's rituals were both like and unlike the original Molly's. She still insisted on using the dolphin-shaped sponge to wash her face, pretending that this was a symbiotic deal and she and the dolphin were washing each other. And she still brought Maisie the Mouse into the bathroom with her to sit and watch, as though washing her face and brushing her teeth were an enthralling spectator sport. But she preferred cold cereal to scrambled eggs and waffles. She sat on a high stool at the breakfast bar instead of on one of the ladderbacks at the kitchen table. And she couldn't sing along to Bruce Springsteen's *Born in the USA* because she didn't know the words. It was weird for Beth to watch her and listen to her. It felt as though her own Molly was a light flickering behind this little girl's face. She was there, all right. So precious. So perfect. But mixed with something else.

On the drive into school, Molly kept up a constant stream of chatter from the passenger seat. Stuff from books and comics and TV cartoons and Disney movies all whipped together into a surreal froth. Once again, Beth had that sense of simultaneous recognition and dislocation. Her own Molly had the same weird imagination but tended to deliver it in smaller, more concentrated doses. Talking to her had been like getting teasing glimpses of another world through a door that was barely ajar. With this Molly it was more like you were standing out on main street and the other world was parading past you with drums and trumpets. Beth played along as best she could, suddenly aware on this day of her triumph of everything she had lost and could never get back.

At the school she gave her little girl a kiss on the cheek and a hug. "Bye, Moll," she said. "Have a good day." Was that their farewell ritual? It seemed close enough to do the trick. Molly trotted away up the steps, almost skipping into school.

It was a relief to Beth, as she drove into town, to be able to drop the performance and be herself. There was going to be a lot of bluffing and a lot of winging it in the days to come. It would be a strain, but she had two big advantages. First off, she was already supposed to be under stress because of the trial and all the bullshit that came along with it. If she seemed to be acting strangely, people would most likely put it down to that.

And secondly, the truth of what had happened was so far out there that nobody would believe it on a dare. People might tell each other that Liz had changed in this way or that way, but they wouldn't see it as sinister, and they wouldn't try to work out when or why or how. All she had to do was wait them out.

Sooner rather than later, her own habits and behaviors would become the new normal.

That night Fran had the worst nightmare she'd had in years.

She was back in the Perry Friendly (of course!), in its current rotting state except that it was much, much bigger—an endless maze of lightless rooms that had had their furniture ripped out and their doors nailed shut. She was running through the maze, looking for a way out, and there was something big moving right behind her.

In her last really bad nightmare, Bruno Picota had been a spider. This time he was more like some kind of walrus. He had swollen up to many times his bulk, and he didn't seem to be able to walk. He was dragging himself along with his hands, which were huge even compared to the rest of him, two massive shovel-blades with claws at the end of them.

Picota was gaining on her, even though he was down on his belly. Fran had to find and fumble with each door in the smothering dark, and once she had gotten it open there was no way of closing it again. So each room she ran through narrowed the gap between the two of them. It was only a matter of time before he got close enough to grab hold of her. And Jinx wasn't anywhere to be seen. She was on her own.

The terror of that thought made her turn at last, to face him. And she remembered as she turned that she had a weapon! In her pocket she was carrying the bag of sour worm candies that Zac Kendall had brought up to her room. Ouroborus, the snake that eats its tail.

She pulled out the bag and flung it down on the ground. Sour worms exploded out of it, assembling themselves quickly into tail-eating rings. The rings interlaced to make a chain-link fence, which reared itself up quickly between her and Picota.

Just in time. The walrus-monster flung itself against the barrier, stretching it with his hideous weight. Fran backed away until the wall was right at her back, and Picota came right on after her, the fence stretching and deforming and finally

breaking

breaking into pieces

and every piece was crying out as though it was alive.

Fran realized too late that the fence was somehow Jinx. She had killed Jinx by trying to use her as a barricade against Picota.

She struggled up out of the dream as though it was a tar pit, pitching her sheet and duvet onto the floor in the process. She lay there for a few minutes, coming down slowly, panic-sweat cooling on her skin and panic-thoughts curdling in her brain.

Jinx was beside her on the pillow, her sharp snout nuzzling intangibly into Fran's hair.

I'm fine, she whispered. *I'm fine, Fran. Nothing bad happened to me. It was just a dream.*

"I know that, Lady J," Fran whispered. "But it still felt really bad."

Jinx murmured soothing words to her, trying to make her settle again, but there wasn't much chance of that. Fran got up and slid her feet into her slippers.

You should try to sleep. It's school in the morning.

"I will in a little while, Jinx."

She went downstairs, moving as softly as she could—especially as she passed her dad's room. When she eased the living room door open and stepped into the room, Zac sat up at once. It was as though her dream had woken him too.

That outrageous thought earned a snuffling snort of derision from Jinx. *He doesn't share your dreams. I do!*

"I couldn't sleep," Zac whispered. His bare chest, reflecting the diffuse glow from the upstairs landing, was the lightest thing in the dark room.

"Neither could I. Are you worried about your mom?"

"I'm feeling like an idiot about my mom. I shouldn't have left her on her own. Especially tonight. I just lost it."

"You're allowed to do that from time to time, Zachary. She'll understand."

He shrugged, and she dropped the subject. In Fran's experience, if you were feeling bad about something you'd done, being told it wasn't so terrible just made you impatient. You had to get to that place by yourself, if you got there at all.

She thought about bringing over one of the dining room chairs to sit on, but sat right down on the sofa instead. Inches away from him. "I had a nightmare," she said.

"About Picota?"

"All my nightmares are about Picota."

She wondered whether he would put his arms around her. If he did, she wouldn't pull away. She would lean into it, and it would feel like fate.

Lady Jinx made the pretend-vomiting sound that kids make when they're grossed out. And somehow that did make it gross, because Jinx was like a child in all kinds of ways and if you made out in front of a child then obviously you were a pervert and an asshole. Fran stood up abruptly, and sat on the arm of the sofa, a few feet outside of Zac's reach.

"Anyway," she said, "I had an idea. And I'd like to run it by you, because you're in it. Kind of."

"Go on," Zac said.

But going on was hard. There was no way of taking a run-up at this. Either she would say it or she wouldn't. She glanced over at Jinx, who was sitting back on her haunches with her ears pricked up—still alert in case Fran got too close to Zac again and had to be reminded that he had boy-cooties.

"I want to go and visit him," she said.

Jinx gave a loud yelp.

"Visit Picota? Holy shit!"

You can't! Fran, you can't! He's too dangerous!

"I know it sounds kind of crazy."

Zac sat bolt upright. "Fran, are you sure?"

"I'm sure I don't want to. But it feels like that's the reason why I have to." Jinx was yelping *No! No! No!* but Fran pressed on. "We've been finding out all this stuff, and it hasn't made the fear go away. It's just . . ." She shrugged. "Narrowed it down. Cut away some of the trimmings. I'm not afraid of the Perry Friendly, or knives with that jagged-tooth thing on them, or the dark, or the skadegamutc. I'm just scared of him. So if I want to fix it there's only one place I can go."

Jinx had jumped up onto the back of the sofa to glare into Fran's face. *I can't protect you if you just run headfirst into danger!* she yapped.

We'll talk later, Fran promised Jinx. She was waiting for Zac's answer, but Zac didn't say anything. His hand found hers in the dark, and held it.

It was nice. There were no cooties at all, to speak of. Jinx might have had a different opinion, but the bombshell Fran had just dropped had made her forget all about the terminal disgustingness of boys.

"So anyway," Fran said, "I was wondering if you'd come with me."

"To Grove City?"

"Yeah. I know it's a long—"

"Of course I will. They probably won't let me inside, but I'll go up there with you on the bus and wait outside until you're done. I'll book the tickets, if you want. I've got a student advantage card and I think it will work for both of us."

Fran squeezed his hand. "Cool," she said inadequately. "Thanks. I'm going to see Dr. Southern today to ask him about what we found in the trial transcripts. I'll ask him about this too. What we need to do to set it up."

"There's probably a form you have to fill in."

"Sure. 317-A. Request to visit a psychotic."

"That's 317-B. 317-A is taking a psychotic to Page Dairy and buying him a strawberry float."

Fran laughed out loud. Then clapped both hands to her mouth as she realized that her dad was sleeping right overhead. "I gotta go," she whispered. "Sorry."

Having reclaimed her hand, she didn't feel like she could give it back again. She waved, a little lamely, and whispered goodnight. Zac waved back.

"Sleep tight, goon," she told him.

"On this sofa? I don't have any choice!"

She had to suppress another fit of giggles as she went up the stairs. In spite of everything, she was feeling optimistic and excited.

Then you're an idiot! Jinx growled. *Fran, don't do this. Please don't. We're fine as we are!*

"We've never been fine," Fran said sadly. Jinx opened her mouth to speak, but she caught the emphasis Fran had put on the *we* and closed it again. Fran had been fine before Picota, but before Picota meant before Jinx too. There had never been a time since Jinx arrived when Fran hadn't been medicated or freaking out or both things at once.

Fran opened the door of her room and they both slipped inside. Jinx took up her customary position at the foot of the bed. She was chastened, her shoulders hunched to hide her head, although she peered up at Fran from between her spread front paws. *I understand why you've got to go*, she said. *And I'll come too, so I can guard you. But I'm scared for you.*

Fran knelt so they were on the same level. With one hand she mimed stroking the little fox. "I don't think things can get any worse than they are now, Jinx," she said.

They can always get worse.

"Cynic."

I don't know what that means.

Fran vaguely remembered that etymologically it meant "sort of like a dog" but she thought it would be a bad idea to say so. Instead she said, "We'll go together. I'm not afraid of Bruno Picota if I've got the Lady Jinx to protect me."

The compliment pleased Jinx enough that she didn't argue anymore. But Fran was left wondering where these ventriloquized doubts were coming from. Just once it would be nice if she and her subconscious were on the same page.

Beth was a few minutes late at the courthouse—her imperfect driving skills compounded by an imperfect memory of downtown Pittsburgh. By the time she arrived, everyone was already there, waiting. Everyone except for the star of the show, of course, but he wasn't likely to show any time soon. Jamie Langdon was there, looking at her watch every thirty seconds. She was representing team Marc all by herself: his lawyer, Quaid, was nowhere to be seen. You get what you pay for, Beth thought with grim amusement.

Jeremy Naylor brought Beth up to speed against a backdrop of general nerviness and milling around. "There's no sign of your ex-husband. Apparently his partner hasn't seen him since last night and can't give us any information as to his whereabouts. She's sitting over there, looking like someone pissed in her coffee."

"Well, she's out twenty big ones if he doesn't show," Beth pointed out calmly. Naylor gave her a curious look. Obviously that didn't sound in character. Also, it was stupid. At this point Marc was only ten minutes late. She couldn't afford to be the first person to jump to the conclusion that he had defaulted. Her cue was to play dumb and to be surprised and concerned as the whole thing unfolded, not self-possessed and up ahead of it.

She smiled weakly. "Sorry," she said. "I'm tense as hell. I didn't get a wink of sleep last night."

"Understandable," Naylor said, although he didn't return the smile. "Well, let's see if we can make sure you sleep soundly tonight, Ms. Kendall."

Beebee came over while they were talking. She put her hand on Beth's shoulder and gave her a squeeze. "Last stretch, Liz," she said. "Keep it together."

"I'm good," Beth assured her, playing brave soldier.

"Yeah, well, Ms. Langdon isn't. I just had a little chat with her. It seems she and Marc retired together around half past midnight, and then she woke up at seven and he wasn't there. She wasn't worried at first. He often goes out for walks at night." The cop looked sidelong at Beth and raised her eyebrows. "Be interesting to get the dates of some of those, wouldn't it? Maybe later, after we've got this trial out of the way. Anyway, she called him and the phone went straight to voicemail. Then she waited for him as long as she could and came on over here when he didn't show. She's rattled now. Running out of innocent explanations."

"So what happens?" Beth asked. "If he doesn't come?"

Beebee blew out her cheeks. "Well, that would be some serious shit," she said. "The judge would most likely issue a bench warrant for Marc's arrest. His counsel will argue strongly against that, though, and ask for a stay. Probably say Ms. Langdon has got a better chance of bringing him in if she's given some time to go look for him by herself without the sirens blaring in the background."

"Either way," Naylor summed up, "he's in contempt at the very least and a fugitive felon at the worst. It's bad news for his girlfriend and very good news for us."

"I hope they find him," Beth said demurely, "for Jamie's sake."

"Don't be too noble, Liz," Naylor chided her. "If God gives you an ace, it's a sin not to play it. If you'll excuse me, I have to go and sit on the judge's left shoulder since my learned colleague Mr. Quaid is likely already in position on his right."

Beebee lingered after he'd gone and chatted to Beth some more, mostly about the kids, evidently feeling it was her duty to keep her spirits up. Beth tried hard to keep her frustration and tension from showing in her face. A false step in front of a cop was different from a false step in front of a friend or neighbor. Riskier. Best not to have a cop as a friend in the first place, and she'd see what she could do about that soon, but for now she just had to keep the heroic smile plastered on and make the right noises. Yeah, Zac and Molly were fine. They were holding up well. Zac was cheering her on; Moll was letting it all sail right over her head.

"Like she does most things," Pete Sethi said, strolling up to join them with Parvesh right behind. "Zen Buddhists meditate for years to achieve higher consciousness. Moll was born with it."

"She's not immune, though," Parvesh said more soberly. "I think she's aware on some level that there's some scary stuff going on. Hence the nomadic wanderings in the middle of the night."

"That sounds alarming," Beebee said. And Parvesh recounted the whole story, with a shit ton of unnecessary drama, while Beth stood by with her hands—behind her back—squeezed tightly into fists. Why couldn't any of these people mind their own business? Why did they have to be all up in her life as if they owned a piece of the freehold? Why had even Doormat Liz put up with this shit?

Beth had had friends of her own, of course, before her first life ended. She could barely remember them. Her ordeal had stretched her out too thin and taut for all that stuff. She had traveled lightly from world to world, taken nothing with her except her hate and her determination. That was why she was here. And from here on out, that was how it was going to be. These people could stick around for now, but she would get some distance from all of them as soon as she possibly could. If she didn't, she was going to die from suffocation.

They were finally called into the courtroom just before 11:00 a.m. Judge Giffen, already sitting, apologized to Beth and the other principals for the case not going forward. Obviously this was caused by the non-appearance of the defendant, which there was no getting around. "I've heard submissions from both counsels," the judge said gravely, "and I've decided for the moment not to issue a warrant for Mr. Kendall's arrest. I will give him a grace period of forty-eight hours to present himself to the city police or to his legal counsel. His bail is of course rescinded, and he will be remanded in custody as soon as he's found. However, I will not place a recovery order on the bail monies if he appears within that time. If he doesn't, the sum will be in default. Ms. Langdon, you should consult with your husband's counsel and with the bail agent about what that will mean for you."

The judge rose and exited, leaving them all to replay those few gnomic sentences in their minds. The court had been in session for less than five minutes.

Naylor started putting files and loose documents back in his briefcase. "I guess we're done," he said to Beth. "You know your ex-husband better than I do, Liz. I'm taking the view that he went out on a bender last night and woke up in someone else's bed. Or someone else's gutter. But perhaps he's stupider than he looks."

Beth chose her words with care. "Marc isn't stupid. But he does have poor impulse control sometimes. And he does like his drink. Most likely you're right."

"Then I'm sure we'll be hearing from the Pittsburgh Bureau of Police in due course—and I'll see you back here in a week or two. Just so you know, we were already in a favorable position. Now . . . I'd bet the farm Giffen goes with a custodial sentence."

"Thank you, Mr. Naylor." Beth made a convincing show of being relieved, exhausted, overwhelmed. She took his hand in both of hers, briefly, and got out of the courtroom ahead of both the Sethis and Beebee. She was momentarily torn between giving them the strokes and emotional resolutions they probably wanted and just hitting the highway.

She went with the second of those options. She was planning to terminate Liz's friendships slowly and carefully: no ruptures, just death by gradual neglect. But today was her first day on the job and she deserved a reward after the night's hard labors. She escaped out of a side door before anyone else could grab her and emote at her.

She went home and drew herself a bath, running the water as hot as she could take it. She soaked for more than an hour with a glass of red wine at her right hand, the door wide open, Springsteen's greatest hits drifting in from the hi-fi in the lounge that Liz had hardly ever even switched on. A phone rang somewhere in the middle distance. Most likely it was Liz's, but the sound might be coming from upstairs. She hadn't memorized the ringtone on Liz's phone (*her* phone) yet. Either way she didn't move to answer it. If it was important, whoever it was would ring back. If it wasn't, they could go screw themselves.

The antique hi-fi would have to go. In her own house, Beth had had a fancy digital system with satellite speakers in every room. Admittedly she'd been way behind on the payments for it, but that was what credit cards were for.

Out of the bath, dried and feeling a whole lot more human, she pulled on a bathrobe and went through into the lounge. Slumped decadently in front of the TV, she finished the bottle of red in front of three back-to-back soaps—*Days of Our Lives*, which she'd watched religiously at home, and a couple of others she didn't know from a hole in the ground. Surfing onward with a mild, happy buzz on, she found *The Price Is Right, The Chew* and *Let's Make a Deal*. She drew the line at news shows, though, jumping channel whenever one loomed up in front of her. Too much reality would only harsh the vibe.

Every little thing felt like a pleasure. The scent of pine disinfectant from the kitchen (a legacy of last night's wetwork); the feel of the cushions plumped up under her ass and against her back; even reaching under her dressing gown to scratch an itch. Her body was a musical instrument, strummed by the passing air.

She masturbated, slowly and languidly, then with more urgency and purpose. She would have to find a way to scratch that itch too, and soon. It had been way too long.

She dozed a little, drank and dozed some more. Her phone rang again, and then the house phone. She could have answered but she was reluctant to let the world in. It would come soon enough.

Another bottle? Maybe not. It wouldn't be great to have the kids come home and find her passed out cold. She fixed herself some fresh coffee instead, savoring the dense, layered smell of it as it perked, the plosive song of the coffeemaker, the contrast between warm air on her half-dressed body and cold tiles against her bare feet. Life was full of rich sensations that needed to be appreciated properly.

The flesh of her left heel tugged and tingled as she pulled it free from a sticky patch on the floor. Blood? She squatted down to inspect the tiles. There was no stain that she could see, and she thought she had been thorough, but what else could it be? She touched the floor tentatively with her fingers, probing until she found a small spot that felt tacky to the touch. Then she went and got a bottle of cleaning gel and a cloth and blitzed the whole area, scrubbing vigorously.

While she was still down there, she heard the side door open. She stood up quickly, pulling the bathrobe closed. Zac and Molly were in the doorway, Zac's hand still on the handle. Zac stared at her in amazement. Molly, her sunny self, only smiled.

"I made a map of America!" she announced ringingly. "With all the states."

"Why didn't you answer your phone?" Zac demanded. "I've been trying to call you all day."

"Sorry," Beth said quickly. "Sweetheart, I'm so sorry. The day got by me. After I came back from the courthouse, I just sort of collapsed." She hesitated, pennies dropping one after another. "I should have picked Molly up."

"Yeah." Zac put a heavy emphasis on the word. He looked bewildered. "I got called out of class. It was Moll's principal. He said you hadn't turned up and he called you but got no answer. I was the second emergency number. I told him I'd come right away and get her. I said you were most likely still in court. But you weren't."

Beth felt a twinge of irritation, but she had put herself in the wrong and she had to take the rebuke without kicking. She even managed to put on a smile. "You already got the news?"

"After I couldn't get through to you the second time, I called Beebee."

This business with the cop had to stop! "And she told you that your father was a no-show. It's good news, Zac. It makes our case much stronger if Marc turns out to be the kind of arrogant shit who doesn't even respect the law. A suspended sentence is like the benefit of the doubt, and he just threw that in the trash."

She stopped. Molly was staring at her with big, round eyes. Zac quickly shooed her through into the hallway to take off her coat and put away her school bag. Okay, so using the *s* word in front of Molly had been a bad idea. Even at times like this the decencies had to be defended.

"Mom—" Zac began, as soon as they were alone. He didn't sound angry. It sounded more like he was pleading with her.

"I'm sorry," Beth said again, cutting him off. She put her hand on his arm. She didn't have to lie to him. There would be lies a-plenty, but right now she let her real feelings show. She had missed him—had missed both her children—so much. This moment of reunion had loomed so large in her imagination. She couldn't let it sour because she'd celebrated too hard on her first day back. "Zac, you know what kind of strain I've been under. That nonsense with the house-painting—I was trying to burn all the tension out of me, and at the same time I was trying to keep you away from it." Okay, so she did have to lie, a little, but the emotion was real. "I want us to be a family again. The three of us. We've been stuck for so long in a . . . a situation. Not a life, just a situation. Now it's over and we can live again."

Zac's open, concerned face showed every emotion he was feeling. He believed her, but he was still troubled. "It's not over, Mom," he said. "Just because Dad wasn't there today, it doesn't mean he's gone. Where would he even go to?"

Beth shrugged, as offhandedly as she could. "I don't care, so long as he stays away." But it was true that she couldn't afford to sound so certain, even in front of her kids. "I know, Zac. I know he's bound to come back sooner or later. But today felt like a turning point. I think it was, for all of us. You'll see."

She gave him a hug. After a moment's hesitation he responded, hugging her back. "I hope you're right, Mom," was all he said.

"I'm totally right," Beth assured him. "And I'm going to prove it. What do you say to a movie and a meal deal? Tomorrow I'm back at work and you guys are at school. Tonight we party like crazy animals."

"On a Thursday?" Zac protested.

It was a weak-ass argument and Beth beat it down easily. Thursday was so close to the weekend you could practically smell it. And how long had it been since the three of them went out together? A dog's age, right? "Or the four of us, maybe. Call that girlfriend of yours and bring her along too."

Zac perked up considerably at that suggestion. "You mean Fran? I can ask her."

"Ask her hard. Sweep her off her feet. Girls like that stuff."

"Mom, she's not my . . ."

"I know, I know. Ask her."

That part of the scheme fizzled. Zac called Francine Whatshername, and got no answer. Nobody picked up at the house, either. A few moments later he got a text, which he read but didn't offer to share. "She can't come tonight," he told Beth. "She's got some stuff she needs to do." His casual tone couldn't have been less convincing if he'd added a nonchalant whistle. He was hiding something, and another time Beth might have pressed the point but right then it didn't matter a good goddamn.

It was a great evening in any case. They went to a tiny indie cinema on Sheridan behind the Home Depot and saw *My Neighbor Totoro*, a Japanese cartoon that had been dubbed into English. It was Zac's choice—he had watched a bootleg version on Francine's laptop—but he assured Beth it would be great for Molly. He was right too, although Moll clutched Beth's arm in frantic alarm during the sequence where the younger of the two heroines, Mai, went missing from home. "You know there's no monsters in this movie," Beth whispered to the little girl.

"There's Totoro," Molly muttered, hiding her eyes.

"But he's a good monster. The monster who's one of the family."

Like me, Beth thought, and she had to stop herself from laughing out loud.

At Plum Pan she ordered all their favorites automatically, amazed that she still remembered. Except, of course, that she was remembering two slightly different kids. "Kung po chicken?" Zac asked doubtfully. "I don't think I've ever had that."

"Give it a shot," Beth said. "I think you'll love it."

He wrangled a small piece of chicken with his chopsticks and brought it, dripping with red sauce, to his mouth. His chewing went from experimental to enthusiastic. "That's great!" he said. "It's like spicier sweet and sour."

"Told you," Beth said. "You think I don't know you, Zachary? Moms have eerie powers."

She ordered jasmine tea for the two of them, diet cola for Moll. She had a hankering to order a large glass of red, but she was mellow enough as it was and she had to drive them home. She wasn't going to take stupid risks when she'd only just got her life back. There was always tomorrow.

All the tomorrows.

SITTING IN THE WAITING ROOM AT CARROLL WAY, was what Fran had texted Zac in response to his invitation. IT REALLY, REALLY SUCKS ABOUT YOUR DAD, AND I'D LOVE TO COME OVER AND BE WITH YOU GUYS BUT I'M GONNA BE HERE A WHILE. SORRY.

It might be a long while too, because she had come without an appointment. She couldn't make an appointment without her dad being copied in on the email when the clinic confirmed. It was a legal glitch, something they had to do because she was a minor, and on most days she took it philosophically. Today she wanted a private conversation with Dr. Southern: philosophy could go jump in the lake.

The receptionist was inclined to be snitty when she found out Fran's name wasn't on her list. "I can't guarantee he'll see you," she said.

"If you'd please just ask," Fran said. And then, "Tell him it's about Bruno Picota." Dr. Southern had never refused to see her: she probably didn't need to stack the deck. But she did it anyway.

She sat for half an hour or so while the room emptied out. Soon it was just Fran, an old guy in a motorized wheelchair and a formidable-looking woman with three kids who all sat in a line to the left of her, mousy-quiet and facing front, as if they were soldiers and she was their commanding officer. Fran didn't know the woman but she thought maybe she had seen the kids around; she kept her eyes on the middle distance and did her best to look like someone else entirely.

She was expecting the receptionist to call her name, but Dr. Southern came out himself and beckoned to her to come. She followed him to his office, where he held the door open for her and then closed it behind the two of them. She sat down.

"It's good to see you, Frankie," Dr. Southern said, but his somber face belied the words. "How are you doing with the new dosage?"

"Fine," Fran said. "Thank you."

"Any more bad dreams?"

"Just the one. But that's not what I wanted to see you about."

"Then what can I do for you?"

"I want to talk about Bruno Picota."

Southern nodded. "So I was told. But if you're not dreaming about him . . ."

"I want to talk about the time when he was your patient."

Nothing changed in Southern's face, but his whole body seemed first to be drawn upright with sudden tension and then to sag just a little. This time when he nodded his shoulders were in on it too, almost as though he was bowing his head to something nasty that had become inevitable.

"Ah," he said. And then he didn't say anything else for a while. Finally, he crossed to his chair and sat down in it, making it creak and yaw the way he always did. His hands lay in his lap and he shrugged with them, bringing them up and letting them fall again. "Yes," he said. "Well. That was a long time ago."

Fran waited him out. She could see that he was unhappy and her instinct was to change the subject, to spare him, but she couldn't. She needed to push this stone all the way to the top of the hill, even if it bruised Dr. Southern's toes along the way.

Eventually Southern started to put words together, slowly and haltingly. Fran had the strong sense that he was turning them over in his mind before he spoke, inspecting each one for suspect nuance. "I worked with Picota in the lead-up to the court case. That was a long time before I met you, so I don't believe there was ever any conflict of interest. And he wasn't my patient in the strict sense of the word. I was retained—along with a colleague—to assess his mental competence before the trial and to give testimony about it."

Again, Fran's instinct was to nod and move along. To just let Dr. Southern off the hook, since he was clearly on one. But what he had just given her was sort of the first half of an explanation, and half measures weren't good enough. "Why didn't you tell me?" she asked.

Southern smiled, but the smile came very close to being a wince. "That's a fair question," he admitted. "But I didn't have any sinister motive, I assure you. If you remember, I didn't inherit you from Dr. Kapoor until 2011. Sometime in the summer."

"July fifteenth," Fran supplied. She had started a new notebook, and the first and last dates were on the cover. She could also have told him what time her appointment was, because the fifteenth was a Friday and school would have let out an hour early. On Fridays her appointments were scheduled for 4:30.

"July fifteenth. I'll take your word for it. By then, Bruno Picota was up in Grove City and I hadn't seen him in years. I knew from the insurance forms how your treatment was being financed, and—this was very much in my mind—I was the only psychiatrist working at Carroll Way. I couldn't offer you a reasonable alternative, you see my point? If you didn't want to sign on with me—well, there wasn't anyone else here. It was my way or the highway. And I didn't want to raise a problem for you that I couldn't solve."

Fran started to speak, but Dr. Southern wasn't ready to let her in just yet. "I know, I know. It was wrong. From a professional point of view, it was . . . I'd have to say dubious. I'm not trying to excuse it, Frankie, just to explain what my thinking was. I'm really sorry you had to find out like this, so long after the fact.

And if you feel you need to lodge a complaint with the clinic, or with your insurer, I'll understand."

"I'm not interested in complaining," Fran told him. "I didn't come here for that."

Dr. Southern looked relieved. Actually, he looked like a man who was trying not to look relieved, which was sort of comical if she had been in a mood to laugh about it. "Okay. Well, that's . . . I'm glad to hear it. What can I do for you, then?"

Fran decided it would be better to start with something small, and work her way up to the bombshell by gradual degrees. "I'd like you to tell me what you know about Picota. I'm trying to figure him out." She filled Dr. Southern in on the project—how she had set out to neutralize her fears, first of all through her visit to the Perry Friendly and more recently by learning as much as she could about Picota as a man so she'd be able to stop seeing him as a terrifying monster. She left out all the stuff that had to do with the changes, and the eerie echoes in Picota's transcript relating to her false memories and her hallucinations. She tried to keep it simple, and to make it sound like a project Dr. S could mark in her case file with a big tick and a gold star.

But it didn't seem to be working. The doctor's face, which had been hopeful to start with, got glummer with each sentence. "What?" Fran demanded at last. "What's the matter? This is a good thing to do, right?"

Southern tilted his head, kind of on a diagonal: a movement that was neither a nod nor a shake. "It seems like a really worthwhile project, certainly. But I can't help you with it, Frankie. Not even a little bit. I've got to respect patient confidentiality. I'm not allowed to talk to you about anything we got from Bruno Picota in that room—beyond what went into the court files you already saw. I wouldn't be allowed to practice again anywhere if I did that."

Fran felt a twinge of anger, and she didn't even bother to try to hide it. "So your duty to him trumps your duty to me? We're *both* your patients, Dr. Southern."

Southern grimaced. "No, Frankie," he said quietly. "You're wrong.

You are and he's not. My duty to you is . . . well, it's a thing that actually exists. Here and now, I don't owe Picota anything except the general, minimal respect we owe to anyone we share the planet with. But the rules of my profession still apply, and the law of the land still applies. I can't discuss any insights and impressions I got while I was his therapist. Or nominally his therapist. I'm sorry. I really wish I could, if you think it would help you, but I'm not allowed to do it. Just like I won't discuss you, or your case, with anyone else after you stop being my patient. If it's ten years later, or twenty, or I'm on my death bed confessing my sins to God, I still can't go there."

His earnestness and unhappiness took some of the wind out of Fran's sails, but she was so incredulous she forgot for a moment that this wasn't what she wanted Dr. S to do in any case. All she wanted was for him to broker a meeting. "Wait a second," she said. "You and me, we talk in private. I get that. But you didn't talk to Bruno Picota in private. There were lawyers there, and the lawyers hired you, and you turned over all the transcripts and everything so they could use your opinions in court. The whole point was to get Picota off from being tried for attempted murder. So how can there be confidentiality?"

"Because those were the terms of my engagement, Frankie. That was what I agreed to, and what Picota agreed to. It doesn't mean I can go ahead and talk to third parties without his permission."

"Even his victims."

"Even you, yes."

"Wow," Fran said. "That's . . . I don't have a word for what that is. What did we ever do in this room, Dr. Southern, besides talk about him? But it doesn't matter. I didn't come here for that. What I want you to do is get me in to see him."

Southern blinked. "See him?"

"Yes."

"You want to meet with Bruno Picota?" The doctor's eyebrows had gone all the way up his bald head, joining up in the middle as his forehead went into concertina creases.

271

"Who else are we talking about? I guess you can arrange that, can't you? Ask the doctors at Grove City to let me in?"

Southern seemed stunned by the bare notion of it. "No," he said. "At least . . . I don't think so. I mean, obviously I could ask, but I don't know what kind of argument I could make."

"The argument is I want to see him," Fran said. Her tone was testy, she could hear for herself, but at that she was reining herself in. "He messed up my whole life. It's been ten years and I'm still having nightmares. I'm still seeing things. I may not ever get well, and that's all his fault. So the argument is they should let me in because I've got a right. I've got a right to see him."

"I don't think that's true, Frankie," Southern protested. "Morally, yes, you've got a strong case, but there's no legal requirement. And from a strictly therapeutic standpoint . . ." He ran out of road and stopped talking very suddenly. Fran waited.

"I can see where it might help," he admitted at last. "There are precedents, although in a forensic setting rather than a clinical one. Victims confronting their attackers in court to describe the impact of the crime on their lives." He frowned, thinking so hard it seemed to be causing him actual pain. "I've been saying all along we needed a new approach. This . . . if your symptoms are trauma artifacts . . . it might . . ."

Another silence.

"You're sure?" Southern said. "You're certain you want to do this?"

"I'm sure. I want to get the truth about what happened to me at the Perry Friendly. All of it. I don't think there's anyone else who can tell me."

"And your dad agrees to this?"

"He'll agree when I tell him."

Southern sighed. "Okay then. I'll do my best to persuade Bruno's doctors at Grove City to let you in to see him. I'll suggest that a meeting might be good for him too. Put the main emphasis there."

"Good for *him*?" Fran's voice dripped with disgust.

"That's the only way they'll go for it. If they decide there's a clinical value in it for their patient. Which is Bruno, obviously, not you. You're my patient, and he's theirs."

Fran breathed hard. "Okay," she said. "Thank you, Dr. Southern." She got up, very much on her dignity, but she didn't head for the door. Not straight away. She was thinking about something Southern had said. *What we got from Picota in that room.* He'd mostly been keeping up his consulting voice, which was neutral except when it peaked into calm, rumbly reassurance, but the last two words there—*that room*—had been shoved out of his mouth hard and fast as if he wanted to be rid of them.

"What was he like?" she asked him.

"Frankie, I already explained—"

"Not your diagnosis, Dr. Southern. Just your feeling. What was he like as a person?"

Southern didn't answer for a long time. When he did, it was with another of those hand-shrugs. "What you'd expect. Sick. Troubled. Unhappy. Mostly that—terribly, intensely unhappy. Bruno had his story to tell, and I think he believed it, but he knew how it sounded and by the time I got to meet him it had already started to occur to him that nobody else was going to believe it. That he was out on his own, as it were. He was waving to us from the bottom of a deep, deep pit."

Fran felt a certain degree of satisfaction when she heard this description. If Picota was unhappy, that was fine by her. Of course, this had been the best part of ten years ago. She hoped he was still in that deep pit right now.

"You know he has a learning disability?" Southern said.

"Of course." An expression her dad sometimes used came into Fran's mind. "Slow as a slug in a slump."

Southern didn't smile. "Slow is a good word," he agreed. "That's very much how he seemed to me. Slow to talk, and slow to think his way through what other people were telling him. The conversations I had with him happened over the course of about two months. In that time, I saw a lot of things sink in for him—in

273

slow motion, if you like. What he'd done. What it meant. What the rest of his life would probably be like."

"And it made you sorry for him."

"In some ways. And without trying to mitigate the things he did. Yes."

"Then there's your conflict of interest," Fran said acidly. "If you're still looking for it." It was probably the nastiest thing she had ever said to anyone.

But Dr. Southern only nodded. "I suppose you're right," he said with a bleak smile. "You had a right to expect complete objectivity. I didn't see myself as compromised by knowing Bruno and having treated him, but since I didn't disclose the connection to you that's beside the point. I understand why you're angry."

"I think you've given me the best treatment you could," Fran told him, relenting. "But if you feel bad about not telling me that stuff when you should have, then do this one thing for me."

"I'll try my best, Frankie," Southern said again. "If you're really sure it's what you—"

"We already covered that part, Dr. Southern."

Southern nodded. "So we did."

Beth had had a lot to eat and a lot to drink, all of it on top of a lot of unfamiliar feelings in a body she had almost forgotten how to use. Perhaps that was why her first night back in the flesh was such a broken one.

She dozed shallowly, fretting and turning for two or three hours before finally coming all the way up out of the well of sleep with a ragged yell. She was convinced for a few moments after that waking that someone was in the room with her.

But it had only been a dream. She was alone in the room and the house was silent. Her shout of alarm didn't seem to have roused anyone. No one and nothing was stirring.

She got up and checked anyway. Went and made sure the doors and windows were all locked, the family room and kitchen as she had left them. She had taken up the plastic sheeting: her footsteps made no sound on the thick carpet.

Nothing was moving in the colorless void either. Nobody was sneaking up on her from the other side of reality. She would have felt it.

But would she have felt it in time?

Beth poured a stiff brandy and took it out onto the front porch.

She sipped the booze slowly, relishing its slow-burn sweetness as she rested her folded arms against the rail and looked out into the damp, fragrant night. The world was so full of sensation it was almost too much to take. The feel of the flaking paint under her elbows and forearms. The mingled scents of flowers and petrol and stepped-on city air. The night's cool, touching every inch of her.

None of this had meant very much to her before she died. Now, resurrected, she craved it like an addict. The whole world was her habit. She didn't intend to give it up again, ever.

Which meant she had to be smart. She had to dig herself down into this new life and bed herself in so deep and so strong that nothing could ever uproot her again. Her enemy was gone—both of her enemies, in fact. She had triumphed over Marc and over her other self, although the second of those had hardly been a fight at all.

But suppose some other version of her came roving through the dark, from world to world, and caught her unawares. What she had done to Doormat Liz, some other Beth could do to her.

Beth took another long swig of the brandy and held it in her mouth, letting the hot liquor wend its way down her throat a little at a time.

That would be a stupid way to go, wouldn't it? Pushed out into the cold again because she dropped her guard and let herself be stabbed in the back like an idiot. She was better than that. She had to indulge her appetites carefully so they didn't leave her exposed.

And the other half of that same equation . . . She had been sloppy with the Sethis, with the kids, with the lawyer guy. There was no other word for it. Again and again she had spoken loosely and acted thoughtlessly. If nobody was onto her, it was only because nobody could be expected to guess who she was or what she'd done. But it was foolish and indefensible to arouse needless suspicions. She wanted to take Liz's place without missing a beat or fumbling a catch. Self-respect and self-preservation both pushed her in the same direction.

She would do better. Starting from tomorrow—no, from now—she would be vigilant and she would be smart. Nobody would catch her out again.

With that decided, she drained the brandy and threw the glass against the side wall of the neighboring house, where it shattered spectacularly.

She spent the hours before dawn tidying up the house, which was still showing the after-effects of Operation Marc. She couldn't run the vacuum cleaner so early in the day, but she could dust, sweep and put things back in their places. The kitchen, of course, was already immaculate as a side effect of scrubbing up all the blood. The family room and hall were soon looking great too, and the paint and tools she'd bought for the decorating were stowed away in the garage.

When the kids woke up, they found the kitchen a cave of mundane wonders. Coffee was percolating, juice was squeezed and waffles and syrup were set out for Molly. "You want some omelet?" Beth asked Zac, kissing him on the cheek. "I thought I could chop a little chorizo into it, spice it up. There's frijoles too, but the can was out of date so, you know, fair warning."

"Eggs and ancient beans would be great!" Zac said. He laughed, looking at her in mild suspicion. "What's this about?"

"It's about being nice to each other and getting on with our lives," Beth told him.

"I'm always nice to each other," Molly said, upending a bottle of Mrs. Butterworth's over her already saturated waffles.

"Out of the mouths of babes," Beth said. She tweaked Molly's nose, making her giggle. "Babes who are talking with their mouths full."

"It's only half full!" Molly said gleefully. She opened wide to show them.

"Oh, gross!" Zac protested, but they were all three of them laughing. It was a good start, a good proof of concept. Beth felt the satisfaction you get from solving a puzzle—something coolly intellectual overlaying the warmth of them all being together. It was strange, but not unpleasant.

"You want to throw that invitation out again?" she asked Zac.

"You mean have Fran over to dinner?" he asked. "What, are we going out twice in one week?"

"Nope. I'll cook my carbonara."

Zac laughed incredulously. "You'll cook what now?"

"Spaghetti with cream sauce and bacon," Beth said, dropping the possessive. Liz evidently hadn't had a carbonara. Had she had anything? It was hard to tell. Better to assume she was a cypher and announce every damn thing as a revelation. *I can boil spaghetti now. Can you imagine?* "Go ahead and ask her. I'm assuming she's not Jewish."

Zac laughed again. "I don't think so."

"Well then."

"I'll ask her. Thanks, Mom."

"You're welcome, Zachary. If you're happy, I'm happy."

She got the kids off to school and drove on to the Cineplex. After so long spent eavesdropping on Liz's life, she knew the drill.

Everyone on shift wanted to hear about how her day in court had gone and everyone was shocked when they heard she hadn't had one. Nora DoSanto said it was typical of a man that he couldn't even self-destruct in a straight line but had to ricochet all over and give everyone around him a hard time. By way of showing solidarity, she put Beth up front in one of the ticket windows, which was an easy billet.

Colleagues dropped by in the course of the day to commiserate and to curse Marc out on her behalf. It was cathartic at first, but quickly got to be irritating. Beth liked having people on her side but hated them trying to rub themselves off on her leg. By mid-afternoon, the brave smile she was wearing began to feel like a dead weight, and she longed to throw it down.

But if the day was long, the evening was sweet. Beth's shift ended at 3:00 p.m., which gave her plenty of time to collect Molly from school and then swing by the supermarket on the way home. She turned the shopping trip into a game, making Molly find the right aisles for cream, bacon, pasta and vegetables by spelling out the signs. Molly had pretty good radar for lessons disguised as games but she got into this treasure hunt anyway and was thrilled each time some new ingredient ended up in the shopping cart.

"You got everything," Beth said at last. "You win, genius."

"What do I win?"

"This fine zucchini." She picked one up and offered it to the little girl with both hands, like a trophy.

"I don't want a zookini!" Molly protested, squirming away from it in fits of giggles. "Zac wins the zookini!"

"Okay, then you get to choose dessert."

That was a rash promise but Beth stood by it, adding four tubs of Ben and Jerry's and a caramel cheesecake to the growing pile of groceries in the cart. A couple of Californian merlots went in too. She could handle it so long as she didn't go crazy.

Molly had English homework: a problem sheet that asked her to color in the words of several nursery rhymes. Long vowel sounds had to be colored in red, and short ones in green. Beth spoke the words aloud, drawing out the long vowels ridiculously and reducing Molly to breathless giggles. "Rouuuuuuund and rouuuuuuund the gaaaaaarden, liiiiiiiike a teddyyyyyyyy beaaaaaaaaar . . ."

Zac came home in the middle of this and told them they sounded like complete lunatics. "Compleeeeeeeeeete . . ." Beth echoed, "loooooooooon . . ." Molly laughed herself red in the face and Beth had to stop in case she had an attack.

"So what's the verdict?" she asked Zac. "Am I cooking for four?"

"Three and a half," Zac said. "Add one for Fran, subtract a half because Moll is a pipsqueak."

"I'm rubber, Zac," Molly said prissily, "and you're glue."

"If you're rubber, that's probably why your pips squeak. I told her seven, Mom."

"Then I'd better get started," Beth said. "You want to spell me here?"

She started dinner while Zac and Molly made vowel sounds at each other. Then Zac retired to his room to do teenaged-boy things (homework and masturbation, Beth guessed, but not necessarily in that order) and Molly watched a cartoon.

It was all as normal as normal could be. She had forgotten what normal felt like, its texture in the mind, but here it was: thick and dense, doubled and redoubled on itself until you lost yourself in its folds. To someone who had never known anything else, that weight and solidness might be imperceptible. Beth felt every ounce of it.

The ringing of the front doorbell came dead on seven o'clock, with the pasta draining in the sieve and the sauce at a low simmer, all ready to roll out. Beth turned it off and went to open the door.

The black man who was standing on the porch wasn't anyone she had ever seen before. Her first thought was that he might be a cop, maybe from the Missing Persons department or bureau or precinct or whatever. He had enough height and heft to give that impression. But the polite nod he offered her had the wrong tenor, and his outfit was just the right side of the divide that separates a conservatively minded civilian from a man whose work compels him to dress like one. It looked good on him, either way. This was definitely a man who kept himself in shape. Beth had already guessed who he was before she glanced down and saw Francine Watts hovering just behind him.

"Hi," he said. "Ms. Kendall?"

Beth almost corrected him, but remembered in time. "Yes. I'm Liz Kendall. And you're Fran's father."

"Gilbert. Gilbert Watts. I know I'm not on the guest list, but I was wondering if I could have a quick word."

"Of course," Beth said with false cordiality. "Come on in."

"If you don't mind."

"Of course." She threw the door wide and ushered them inside. "Fran, Zac is in his room. Probably with his headphones on, since he didn't come out when you rang. Would you like to go tell him we're pretty much ready to eat? Mr. Watts, if you want to join us there's plenty of food."

"Gil," he said, as Fran scampered gratefully away down the hall.

"No. Thank you. I just wanted to let you know something before I headed off. It's about the night before last."

Beth suppressed a twinge of disquiet. If he knew she'd spent that night killing her husband, he wouldn't have driven his daughter over here to keep a dinner date. She was careful to keep her smile in place. "What about it?" she asked lightly.

"Well, you may have wondered where your son was that night. Most likely he already told you, but in case he didn't . . ."

Beth hadn't even bothered to ask. That belonged to the era of Liz, which was deader than Ancient Rome in her book.

"I trust my son, Gil," she said by way of a half answer.

"I'm glad to hear it. But still, I think you ought to know that he slept over with us. He called Fran, she asked me, and, yeah, I had my misgivings, but I just wouldn't have been happy with the idea of him sleeping out. So I made up the sofa bed and he slept in my living room."

Beth waited for a few moments, but that seemed to be the end of the recitation. She nodded gravely. "I appreciate you telling me. And I appreciate you putting a roof over his head. We've been through some bad times lately, as a family. I don't know if Zac has told you?"

"I made a point of not asking. It's not my habit to pry."

"Then that's one more thing I've got to thank you for. But I'd like you to know. I had a court appearance the next day. My ex-husband—Zac's father—was arrested for assault a few weeks ago. It was . . . an argument that got physical. And that was the day when the trial was meant to happen. It had been hard on all of us, and that night . . ." Beth hesitated. She found that she wanted Gil Watts to think well of her. That fact surprised her. "We quarreled," she finished. "Zac and I. And he walked out. I would have followed him, but I didn't want to force him to come home if he didn't want to. We were all processing what was happening in our different ways."

It was a long speech. Gil heard her out in silence, not reacting at all, but when she was done he shook his head. "I can't abide a

281

man who resorts to violence when he runs out of words," he said. "Meaning no disrespect, I hope your ex-husband got the book thrown at him and the bookcase as a chaser."

Beth laughed. "He didn't show," she said. "We've got it all to do again. This time I'll try to make sure I keep my kids within doors. I appreciate your frankness, Gil. You're sure you won't stay and eat with us?"

"No, ma'am," Gil said. "Thanks for the invitation, but I've got some work I need to finish for tomorrow, and I had a big lunch. I'll probably just break open a bag of green salad. I need to lose weight in any case."

No, you do not, Beth thought. And on the heels of that she thought about how it would feel to have Gil Watts' weight on top of her, and how long it had been since a man had gone near her with any intent other than to end her.

Put a marker in that one, she decided. And revisit it soon.

"Well, if you're sure."

"I'm sure. But thank you, Ms. . . ."

"Beth." *Damn it!* "Or Liz. Either's good."

"Maybe another time."

"Another time would be good. It was nice to meet you."

"And you."

He gave her one final, respectful nod, then turned and walked away. Beth closed the door, still seeing his face in her mind's eye. His dark eyes, and the doubled arch of his lips. The olive brown of his skin.

Too long.

"Okay," she called out, still savoring that thought. "Dinner is served."

Fran's second visit with the Kendalls was different from the first in a whole lot of ways.

First there was the fact that her dad dropped her off. She had tried to argue him out of it, but he'd said he had to clear the air about Zac having spent the night with them. It was a matter of principle, and he wouldn't budge.

"She won't even mind, Dad. Why would she?"

"I don't know, Frog, and I hope she won't. I'm just not comfortable with the idea of blindsiding her. So I'll say my piece and then I'll get out of your hair."

Fran couldn't argue. She still hadn't told him about her unscheduled appointment with Dr. Southern. She was afraid of how he might react when he found out she'd gone behind his back on something that important. Afraid of Picota too. She had tried to pretend she wasn't, but Jinx kept trying to argue her out of it and that had to be a sign that her subconscious mind was unsettled. From the moment when Dr. S had said he would try to arrange it, she had been wondering if she was making a mistake.

So what with one thing and another, she surrendered meekly, despite her misgivings, and went over to Zac's house in her dad's car. And it turned out it was okay after all. Liz was cooler than cool with the big reveal. Even a few minutes before, that would have left Fran wobbly-kneed with relief. But by then she had other things on her mind.

She saw the change as soon as Liz opened the door, but for a second she wasn't sure what it was she was responding to. Something was different. Something big and obvious and . . .

Then when Liz stepped to one side to let them through into the hall, the penny dropped. And just for a second Fran couldn't keep from gawking like an idiot. Liz had only moved once. Not twice. There was no out-of-sync ghost echo.

It was gone. It was just . . . *gone*. Liz wasn't doubled anymore. There was only the one of her.

Maybe that shouldn't have been such a big surprise: Fran was used to things changing around her, after all. But Liz had been two-in-one every time Fran had seen her. She was almost like Jinx, a symptom that had stuck around long enough to become normal.

Jinx had her own opinion, of course.

One of them killed the other one. That's why there's just the one left now.

Fran didn't answer. Just smiled a sappy smile and scampered off to knock on Zac's door when she was told. She had to knock three times before he answered, and he had the headphones in his hand when he came to the door. He'd been playing some console game, as his mom had guessed.

His face lit up when he saw her. "Hi, Fran," he said. "It's good to see you."

"Likewise, goon," Fran said. "Hey, is your mom . . .?"

She never got to finish the sentence. Molly came barreling out of nowhere and gave Fran's knees an enthusiastic embrace. "Fran!" she yelled. "It's Fran! It's Fran! It's Fran!"

"It's Molly!" Fran yelled back, picking her up and swinging her. "It's Molly! It's Molly!"

"Mommy is making carbonara!"

She put the six-year-old down again. It was hard because Molly was making running-on-the-spot movements and Fran didn't want to make her run into a wall when she touched down. That was normally a problem you only got with cartoon characters. "Cool," she said. "I love carbonara. Do you?"

"I don't know what carbonara is."

"But you like spaghetti, right?"

"Right."

"Then you're probably gonna be fine."

"Let's play Lego!"

"Maybe after dinner."

"Okay, Moll," Zac said. "Scoot, and let the grown-ups talk."

Molly was scornful. "You're not a grown-up, Zac." She trotted back down the hallway and into the living room, her dignity very much intact.

"Wow," Fran said. "Burn."

"I'm used to them. Is my mom what?"

"Sorry?"

"You started to say, 'Is your mom . . .?'"

"Oh. Yeah." But Fran didn't know how to ask the question that was really on her mind. She settled for a more general sounding out of the situation. "Is she okay? I mean, how is she handling all this?"

They both looked along the hallway toward the front door, where Ms. Kendall was still talking to Fran's dad. Zac stepped back inside his room and Fran followed him. Evidently the answer wasn't going to be a simple yes or no.

"She seems okay," Zac said with a noncommittal shrug. "Good, even. She was wound up really tight before the trial, and I thought Dad not showing up would make it worse, because nothing got settled. It was all still up in the air. And yesterday afternoon she was all over the place. She forgot to pick Molly up from school, even. But then she took us all out to dinner, and to see a movie, and she was great. It was like she just decided to put it all behind her."

"That's cool, then," Fran said, remembering how tightly Zac himself had been wound. "Isn't it?"

"I suppose. So long as she doesn't get all bent out of shape again when they find Dad and reschedule the hearing. I mean, she's still got to go through it all sooner or later."

"But it has to be okay now, surely. He skipped bail. He'll do time just for that, I think. It's all good, Zac."

Fran hoped it was true, but the whole while she was talking she was still thinking about Liz. Liz and Bruno Picota. Or at least, Bruno's description of Fran as a skadegamutc. *The same girl, but there wasn't just the one of her. They were swapping. Switching over.*

Liz Kendall had looked like that. Only now she'd managed to fix herself, somehow. So maybe Fran could too.

She killed the other one. You can see it in her face!

No, you can't, Jinx. Don't be ridiculous!

She said the words in her mind, but her lips must have moved too. "What did you say?" Zac asked her.

"Dinner," Fran said quickly. "I forgot, your mom said dinner is ready. We should go sit down."

The spaghetti was really good. Molly dominated the conversation, which meant it was mostly about dragons, but Liz Kendall was in a pretty chatty mood too. She asked Fran about her dad, what he did for a living, what his hobbies were. And about her mom too—like, how long had it been since she died, and how had he been coping since. "Some guys, they just need a woman around, you know? Is that what Gil is like?"

"Nope," Fran said. "He seems to be fine these days with just a football game and the occasional beer or two with the firefighters. There aren't any women around, Ms. Kendall. Unless I count as a woman."

"You don't, honey," Liz assured her. "Not in the sense I mean."

It was said nicely, but it was kind of nasty. Fran didn't realize until then that Ms. Kendall was talking about sex. It was kind of gross that she would do that in front of both her own kids and someone else's. But she said some funny things too, about how things had been between her and her husband before he went away. Like about how one time the family had driven halfway to the Finger Lakes before Mr. Kendall realized he'd forgotten the tent they were going to camp in, but because he couldn't admit that he'd messed up he made out like he'd decided at the last moment to book a hotel instead.

"I don't remember that," Zac said, although he was laughing along at Liz's impersonation of Mr. Kendall as he dithered his way through an increasingly unlikely set of excuses. "We did camp out that time, didn't we?"

"This was another time," his mom said, and she shut him down by offering them all seconds. Which they all said yes to, because the carbonara was awesome.

There was cheesecake and ice cream for dessert, and cinnamon tea that Liz made with fresh cinnamon. Then Zac and Fran did the washing up together while Liz whisked Molly away to bed.

"The camping trip," Fran asked Zac as they worked. "Do you think you were wrong about that?"

Zac looked uncomfortable. "Like Mom said, it must have been another time."

"But you remember camping out at the Finger Lakes?"

"One time, yeah."

Changes, Fran thought. Wrong memories, missing memories and changes. Oh my.

She's just a liar, Lady Jinx growled from under the kitchen table.

But it hadn't sounded like a lie to Fran. Of course people could tell lies with absolute conviction but Zac's mom had clearly been enjoying the story, the memory, as she told it. You could see in her face that she was reliving what happened, adding in new details as they came back to her. In Fran's experience, when liars added in details they did it to make you back off, like card players raising the bid when they had a bad hand. This had been something else.

Liz came back, announcing that Molly wanted both Zac and Fran to come in and kiss her goodnight. Zac went in first because Fran was still drying plates. That left the two women alone in the kitchen for a while.

It reminded Fran of her first visit. She hadn't meant to say anything, but she found she couldn't resist. The happy mood of the meal was still with her. She felt at home in Liz's house, and more even than that she felt that there was a clue to her own big mystery lying right there in front of her, waiting for her to pick it up.

"Ms. Kendall," she began, "I wonder if . . . Can I tell you something about my memories?"

Liz looked at her oddly, maybe even a little warily, but she nodded. "Sure."

"Well, it's not just memories. It's lots of things. I guess I'm talking about my symptoms. You know, I have a condition, kind of? A post-traumatic thing. Because of what happened to me when I was a kid."

Liz didn't pretend not to understand, for which Fran was grateful. She just said, "Okay."

"Well, one of the things that happens sometimes is that things around me will change. Not in crazy ways. Not, like a sofa turning into a giraffe or something. It's more like I might see a red sofa turn into a green sofa, or something like that."

"You mean you're color-blind?"

Fran shook her head. "No, not that. It's not just colors, it can be almost anything. You've got that blouse and those jeans on, but say I turned around for a moment, when I looked back you might be wearing a skirt. Or tracksuit bottoms, or . . . or pretty much anything, really."

Liz was staring at her with blank incomprehension. And something underneath that, maybe a kind of hostility or disapproval, as though she didn't entirely like what she was hearing. "Diving suit?" she suggested. "Ballgown?"

Fran laughed, although the edge in the older woman's voice made her feel a slight pang of unease. Maybe she shouldn't have gotten into this. She was confessing to being a freak, if you wanted to look at it that way. To being mentally ill. Nobody liked being around that. You couldn't catch a mental illness the way you could catch the flu, but Fran had met a lot of people who didn't seem able to make that distinction.

288

"It wouldn't be that extreme," she said. "It would have to be something else you could have worn. Something that's in your closet."

"How do you know what's in my closet?" Liz demanded.

"I . . . I don't," Fran admitted. "But . . ."

"I mean, if you're making stuff up, you can make up anything, right?"

Fran tried again. "Yes, but it always seems to be stuff that doesn't look wrong. Small details, like I said, not big hallucinations."

"But they are hallucinations, sweetheart. All the same. You know that, right?"

Fran had hoped that Liz would say something like "me too!" and that would have given her an opening so she could talk about the other stuff. About being two people in one, or looking like you were. That put-down ought to have warned her off, but having come this far she found she didn't want to just give up, even though the warm and intimate mood was fading fast. "Let me ask you something," she said. "It's going to sound weird, but it's . . . well, it might be important. It might mean something to you. Or . . . or it might not, but I'm going to go ahead and say it anyway, because . . ." She swallowed. "Because I need to."

Liz just stared. She didn't look the least bit enthusiastic, but at least she didn't say no.

"Did something just happen to you?" Fran blurted. "Something that . . . that changed you?"

That got the same deadpan gaze from Liz. And for a second or two she didn't answer. When she did, it was with a single word and it was really no answer at all. "When?"

Fran considered. "Over the last few days. Maybe . . . the night Zac stayed over at my house. Maybe the day you went to court. Around then. Did you . . . did you change, Ms. Kendall? Because you look different to me!"

Fran offered this last insight only because she'd waded in so far without getting a response. It was all or nothing.

And it definitely wasn't nothing. Ms. Kendall's coldly impassive face switched on like a flashlight. Suddenly she was glaring at Fran in furious, cornered rage. Her hands shot up, one of them slamming Fran back against the counter while the other balled into a tight fist.

Fran uttered a yelp of surprise and flinched away from the blow. But the blow didn't come. Liz had control of herself again in an instant. She gave a tinkling laugh, lowering both hands to her sides again as though she'd just been demonstrating a dance move.

"Bless you, dear," she said. "No, nothing happened. And I certainly don't feel any different."

The transformation—the two transformations—were so sudden that Fran wondered if she was hallucinating. But she could still feel the imprint of Liz's hand in the center of her chest. "G-good," she babbled inanely. "That's good. I'm glad."

"What did you think you saw?"

"Nothing. Nothing I can explain. Just . . . nothing, really."

Liz smiled.

Fran stared at her wide-eyed, her heart pounding and her mouth dry. She didn't dare move or take her eyes off Liz, in case Liz changed her mind again and struck.

When Zac came in a moment later to tell Fran that Molly was ready to receive her, she shot out of the kitchen so fast she bumped against him in the doorway. And saying goodnight to Moll gave her a chance to pull herself together a little. But she didn't stick around long after dinner. She was way too shaken up, and she couldn't explain what had happened to Zac because she barely understood it herself. Plus she felt like Liz was watching her now, tracking her whenever she was in the room, making sure that she and Zac were never alone together.

She told Zac she was tired and left for home before it even got dark. Zac was clearly surprised and a little hurt that she was bailing so early. He'd been expecting that they would slip away to his room in the course of the evening so Fran could give him the skinny about how things had gone at the clinic. They sort of had a shared ownership deal with Bruno Picota now. But she wasn't up to talking about that in the light of how bruisingly she had bounced off Zac's mom, and she couldn't think of any way to explain to him that would make it better.

If anything, she made it worse. Her muttered goodbye to Liz, eyes downcast, must have given the impression that she was inexplicably sulking after a spectacular home-cooked meal and a lot of collateral hospitality. She must look like a spoiled brat.

"Well, I'll see you tomorrow," Zac said as he walked her to the door. His face when she glanced sidelong at him was full of unasked questions.

"Tomorrow," she agreed. "Thanks, Zachary."

"I hope you had a good time. Mom's amazing, isn't she? To bounce right back from all the awful shit she's been through lately."

Fran couldn't lie about it. It was pressing hard on every nerve she had. "The meal was great," she said. "I've got to go, Zac. Total collapse. Bye."

She fled off the porch and down the drive without looking behind her. If Zac gave her a final wave, she didn't see it. But most likely, after the show she just put on, there was nothing to see.

I'm just glad you're out of there, Jinx growled. *That woman is dangerous.*

Fran wanted to disagree, but couldn't think of a thing to say. She only wondered what had happened. What was it that had changed Zac's mom?

And what had it changed her into?

So the kid knew something, or had seen something.

But the kid was a freak, Beth reasoned. Nobody was going to listen to her if she spoke up, and she probably knew that well enough herself. There wasn't any danger from that quarter.

There were two options, though, going forward: to wean Zac away from the relationship—tell him to keep his distance from the damaged little girl with the nosy disposition—or else to encourage it and keep a close eye on her. Either was fine, although she had a preference for the second option. If Zac kept up with Fran, Beth could keep up with Fran's father. That raised some very pleasant possibilities.

Absently, she poured herself a glass of wine and took a big swallow. There was nothing to worry about from Fran Watts. Whatever she thought she knew, she couldn't explain it to anyone else in a way that made any sense. She had barely been able to explain it to Beth herself.

Beth emptied the glass and poured another. A fatigue had settled on her in the course of the evening: the body she now wore reminding her of its limitations, which from now on would be hers.

"I'm going to bed, Mom. Goodnight."

She turned and gave Zac a dazzling smile. "Goodnight, dollface," she said tenderly.

He laughed at the unfamiliar endearment which had been part of her interaction with the *first* Zac, many lives and deaths ago. She felt that distance twisting in her gut again as she had when she was driving Molly into school, and she turned away so this other Zac wouldn't see it in her eyes: a grief she couldn't hide, and couldn't explain.

He came over and kissed her. She pressed her fingers against the back of his hand, where it rested on her forearm. "Turn out the light in the hall, would you?" she muttered, still not looking at him.

"Sure. Don't stay up too late."

After his footsteps had receded, she slugged down the second glass of wine, gathered herself and rose. It disturbed her profoundly that, for a few moments there, Zac had gone from being her son to being a stranger. She had to shake off thoughts like that. This was the world she had, and she had fought hard to win it. There was no point in repining for the things she had lost.

She went to her room and prepared for bed. Wearing blue cotton pajamas, she slipped between the sheets, lay down and closed her eyes. But as tired as she was, sleep refused to come. Her awareness prowled around the inside of its new home: her thoughts wouldn't let her rest.

But the body could rest. She slipped free of it and let it lie there, a becalmed ship with nobody on the bridge. Breath and heartbeat regulate themselves, she knew. There was no danger of her physical self hitting a crisis while her mind was elsewhere.

In any case she wouldn't wander far. A part of her was still touching the outer fringes of Liz's nervous system, alert for any warning signals. She floated just above the unconscious flesh, aloof from it but ready to drop back and take over again in an instant.

It was a good compromise. Beth knew very well that lack of sleep was toxic in the long term. The body had to have its down time. Well, the body was getting what it needed. She needed nothing, and could stay awake and on guard.

It was strange that there should be this duality—that her naked will, having once fought its way free of her own dying body, remained a thing apart from this new body she had won. She could put it on and take it off, and still be herself.

The ghost in the machine.

The monster that was part of the family.

The best of both worlds, she told herself. The very best.

The next day, Beth got on with the wider project of becoming Liz. Family life had a shape that she barely remembered, and it was fractal. There were things that happened every morning or every day or every week or only came around once in a while, and she was going to have to get her head around all of them— partly helped and partly hindered by her own memories of a subtly different set of routines with her original family.

The day-to-day stuff was the most urgent and the most obvious. Liz's day—like her own before she died—was built around things that wouldn't move. Breakfast and drop-off for the kids, a stint at the Cineplex—just half a shift today, 10:00 a.m. till 2:00 p.m.—and another trip to Giant Eagle so she could fix dinner.

She needed to get better at this, obviously. You didn't drop by the supermarket every day: you planned your meals in advance and bought for the week. And when you were on a fixed income, you didn't resort to takeout or restaurant outings very often. These limitations chafed her. She wanted to celebrate her return with hedonistic excess, not sensible housekeeping.

She was interested, though, in how this Giant Eagle was different from the one she remembered in her own neighborhood. The produce aisle was in the right place but everything else was shifted around, and there was a pharmacy in the back where her own store had had a deli counter. She couldn't help feeling that the original store had been better. More choice, cleaner light and the prices . . .

She had to derail that thought and laugh at herself. It was like impostor syndrome in reverse: she was seeing the entire world as an inferior replica of her own world, when it was just different. If it didn't seem to measure up, that was because the present moment never did: memory's rose-tinted airbrush was too powerful.

Beth shrugged off the whole stupid issue and filled her basket with fine foods. Tonight she would cook a cassoulet with medallions of lamb and Italian sausage. The kids wouldn't know what had hit them. There was a ton of ice cream left, but she added a key lime pie—something she hadn't tasted since her resurrection and suddenly felt a hankering for.

As she transferred the groceries to the trunk of the car, she got another attack of impostor syndrome. Her former ride had been a Nissan Rogue. Liz's Rio was like Liz herself: underpowered and self-effacing, a car that begged you not to take any notice of it. Every time Beth climbed inside it, she felt like she was putting on a piece of Liz's damp, crushed personality.

Okay, that was a project for another day.

Maybe tomorrow.

Preoccupied with these thoughts, she ignored for a few seconds the sense of déjà vu that had just crept over her. Out of the corner of her eye she had seen something—or someone—she recognized. She looked around and realized at once what it was.

A blonde woman had just stepped out of a big black SUV, parked a few spots along. It was the woman Beth had rumbled with at the school: not Eileen Garaldi, but the other, blonder one whose name she had never learned.

Beth watched the woman walk into the store, oblivious, her fat ass wobbling as she went. My goodness me, she thought. No need to check my watch, because it's obviously payback time.

She briefly considered some options involving matches and firelighters. Giant Eagle would sell both, but there were CCTV cameras all over the parking lot and arson was a crime for which the camera footage would be pulled and scrutinized, no doubt.

Keying wasn't.

Beth circled the SUV a couple of times, incising shallow, concentric ruts in its bodywork. It was restful and cathartic, and it gave her time to come up with other ideas. On the third pass, she had a lightbulb moment.

There was a toolbox in the Rio's trunk, one of the cheap black plastic ones the Triple-A used to give out with memberships. She went back to the car and took a couple of items out of the box— an adjustable wrench and a tiny Maglite. She went back to the SUV, the tools held close to her side so nobody passing by would get a glimpse of them. Not that anyone was looking.

Back when she was seventeen and stupid, Beth had had a brief fling with a guy named Byron Bruce, whose father owned a garage. Byron had been around cars since he could walk, and intended to follow in his dad's footsteps. Beth had had to feign an interest in cars in order to hang with him, and she had picked up some stuff almost by accident.

With a final look around to make sure nobody was in her line of sight, she dropped down and squirmed her way under the SUV. Groping with both hands, holding the Maglite in her teeth, she eventually found the oil filter screw and twisted it loose. Not all the way: just enough for a slow ooze of oil to appear along the lower edge of the filter. She ducked her head away quickly as the first couple of drops spattered down.

The car would still drive. It would get Blondie home again tonight, and maybe it would last through the school run in the morning. Sometime tomorrow, though, or the next day at the latest, the engine would start to run hot. Once it got going it would overheat very quickly, because it would be running without lube. Finding the leak would be easy enough, and you could stop it just by tightening the screw up again, but you had a really short window in which to register what was happening, stop the car and deal with the problem. Otherwise the parts of the engine that were meant to slide frictionlessly across one another would fuse together and stop moving for good and all.

Beth snaked and shimmied her way out from under the car, collected her tools and hit the road. Her hands were filthy, and there was a broad, glistening streak of oil across the front of her blouse. She could feel some on her face too: she hadn't been quick enough to get out of the way when the valve loosened. Lucky for her the oil had cooled down enough so she didn't get burned. All the same, and knowing that she looked like a homeless person, she felt a sense of well-being. Some of the universe's infinite mountain of shit had been shifted back to where it belonged.

The warm, fuzzy feelings stayed with her all the way home. She was practically smirking as she grabbed the groceries out of the trunk and headed on up the drive toward the house. It was nearly two hours yet before she had to go pick Molly up from school. Plenty of time to change, and put some coffee on.

"Ms. Kendall?"

She hadn't even registered that there was someone waiting on the porch until the figure—dressed in a bright yellow raincoat with red trim, like a walking hazard sign—popped up right in front of her. She took a step back and dropped the groceries so her hands would be free to fight.

But as the onions and cans of flageolet beans rolled back down toward the road, she relaxed again. A little, anyway, but not too much. There might still be a fight looming. For now, though, the woman held up both hands in the universal gesture of declared harmlessness.

"I just want to talk," said Jamie Langdon. "If that's okay?"

During study hall, Fran found Zac waiting for her at their usual table in the library, in the reference bay where nobody liked to sit because it was in full view of the librarians' station.

"Pull up a chair," he said. "First round is on the house."

More sour worms. Her dream loomed up in her mind and her stomach lurched. "I'm good, thanks," she said hastily.

"So, are you ready to go to work?" Zac asked. "I think we should start with the Smoot—Hawley Tariff Act, then move on to Mrs. Keith's grammar exercise if the excitement gets too much for us."

"Sure," Fran agreed. "Sounds like a plan. *When Smoot Met Hawley* is my favorite movie."

"It's everyone's favorite."

They went on as they usually did, taking alternate sections of their dry-as-dust textbook and reducing each to keynote-style prompts. The excitement never even threatened to reach dangerous levels, but the boredom was amicable enough. It was only spoiled by the fact that Fran knew in advance they wouldn't just stick to homework. She owed Zac a progress report. And something else besides that he didn't expect and wouldn't welcome.

She kept hesitating, putting off the moment, until he got tired of waiting. "Fill me in on what happened with Dr. Southern," he said at last, propping the history book up on its broken spine.

"He said he'll write to Picota's doctors at Grove City. Try to set something up."

Zac's enthusiasm was instant, and overwhelming. He let out an incredulous gasp that turned into a laugh. "Sweet! We're off to the races?"

Fran tried to moderate his expectations. "He just said he'd try. It's ten to one nothing will happen. The shrinks at Grove City would have to believe it would be good for Bruno to talk to me, and I can't see how they'd get to that conclusion. I'm the kid he almost killed. Even just seeing me would most likely have him crawling on the ceiling."

Zac waved these pragmatic objections away. "But there's got to be a chance. And if it goes ahead . . . Fran, it's perfect! Being in a room with Bruno would be a million times better than just going back to the motel."

Or a million times worse, Fran thought glumly. It might not just be Bruno who was crawling on the ceiling. Aloud she repeated, "It's most likely not going to happen."

Zac didn't even seem to be listening. "What we should do," he said, getting out his tablet, "first thing, is we should get our research on. We need to read up on the skadegamutc, so we can talk to Picota on his own terms. Match the radius of his fruit loops. I looked it up on Wikipedia. The tribe that had that story was the Abenaki. So it's a fair bet that was the tribe Picota's mom belonged to. Want to see what else we can find out about them?"

Fran didn't. Quickly she put out a hand and covered the tablet's power button so Zac couldn't turn it on.

"Actually," she said, "I wanted to tell you about something else."

What had happened with Liz had been bobbing up in her thoughts again and again since the night before. She wasn't sure how Zac was going to take this new helping of weird shit on top of so much else, but she was certain about one thing: he had a right to know.

300

"Tell me what?" Zac looked surprised, then concerned. Probably he could read her tension in her face.

She took a deep breath, and just went for it.

"You remember the first time I saw you and your mom at Carroll Way?"

"Sure."

"Do you remember me staring?"

"Yeah. I was staring too. I didn't expect to meet anyone from school there."

"Okay, but it was more than that. On my side, I mean. I was staring because I was seeing something maximally strange."

This didn't feel like a time for half-measures. What she was about to say wouldn't make any sense at all unless he knew everything. This would be the hardest thing she had ever done, except maybe for going back to the Perry Friendly, but she owed it to Zac not to hold back.

So she told him everything. She reminded him about the changes, first of all: her own weird problem that probably went all the way back to her abduction. Then she told him what she had seen the day they had all met up at the clinic, going right the way through to his mom's brief but major league freak-out the night before. She tried to describe it the way she would write down an incident in her notebook, with no emotion or commentary, as if it had happened to someone else. She thought it might sound more believable that way.

But she was watching Zac's face while she talked, and she could see it wasn't working. He just looked puzzled at first. Then his frown deepened and turned into something else.

Fran remembered now all the times they'd talked about Zac's mom. How protective he was of her, and how much he wanted to stand between her and the world. Which—when the world meant his father—Liz had never allowed him to do. Maybe she should have thought about these things before she opened her mouth. It was too late now.

After she'd finished, she waited for Zac to speak. He didn't seem

301

to be in any hurry. "I know it all sounds kind of bad sci-fi," Fran said to fill up the strained silence. "But it's true. Swear to God."

"Sorry," Zac told her with no inflection to his voice. "I don't even know what that story was about."

"It's about your mom maybe being the same as me."

"The same as you, Fran? How, exactly?" The idea seemed to offend him, which in turn gave Fran a vicious twinge of hurt she didn't want to examine right then.

"I'd love to find out," Fran said. "But she didn't seem to want to talk about it."

Zac closed up his books. It looked like study hall was over, at least for the two of them. "Well hey, do you think it might be because she didn't understand the question?"

"Zac—"

"I mean, it must have sounded pretty funny, coming out of the blue like that. 'You used to have a trademark visual effect, but now you don't.' I'm not sure I'd know how to react to that, if I'm honest."

He'd raised his voice. It made Mrs. Schuler cast a hard look in their direction—the prelude to an intervention. Under the table, Lady Jinx growled: a sudden, indelicate eruption of sound. Fran felt much the same.

"Look," she said, "I'm not saying I understand it. I just wanted you to know what happened."

"What you think happened," Zac corrected her. "That's not always the same thing, is it?"

Fran did the slow-blink-and-then-refocus that you did when somebody was being a humongous dick. "Wow," she said.

"Don't look at me like that, Fran. You get hallucinations. You told me all about them."

"I do, yes. But I know how they work."

"How they usually work." Zac's tone was flat, unequivocal.

"Exactly. This was different."

"That doesn't mean you weren't having some kind of episode." Maybe it was the hard emphasis he put on the word, so it sounded like a curse-word. Or maybe it was the grim set of his face.

"I'm not saying your mom is crazy," Fran muttered. Mrs. Schuler was giving them the stink eye again, so she kept her voice as low and level as she could—as though they were still just talking trade protectionism. "I'm not even saying there's anything wrong with her. I'm thinking it might be the opposite. She seems a lot happier now than she was before. A lot . . . stronger, somehow. More confident. But one way or another, she changed. When I first met her, she looked . . . well, exactly the way I looked to Bruno Picota. There were two of her. Now there's just the one, and I was hoping I could ask her why. But she shut me down hard when I mentioned it. I wanted you to know in case you could find out more. But if you don't want to, that is totally your choice."

"Yeah," Zac agreed, his tone almost snide. "It is, isn't it?"

Fran had an irrational urge to tip the bag of gummy worms over his head. She knew he was angry, but she had thought him incapable of that kind of petty sniping. "Well, I gave you the facts," she said. "You can do what you like with them. Including nothing, obviously."

She gathered her things, blinking away a tear she fervently wished wasn't there. She was a lot more angry than she was unhappy.

"The facts?" Zac said. Only now he wasn't saying it to her. He was saying it to the room, in a big, ringing voice. "I don't know how to thank you, Fran. You know everything, obviously. You see such a shit-ton of stuff that nobody else can see. It must be a big responsibility, having that kind of a gift."

"Zachary Kendall," Mrs. Schuler said sharply. "If you raise your voice one more time I'm going to ask you to leave."

Fran looked at him in wonder. It was as though she had never even seen him at all until then. The revelation that he was capable of that much cruelty somehow took away any of the pain she would have expected to feel from the betrayal.

"Asshole," she said without any heat at all. "Have a nice life."

She stuffed the last of her books and notes back in her bag.

"Fran—" Zac said in a voice much more like his own. Now that he had determinedly pushed things to a crisis, he seemed surprised at where they had landed up.

"Don't bother," Fran suggested. "Work hard and play hard, goon."

Which was a pretty good exit line, at least. Unfortunately it wasn't actually her exit. She still had to do the walk of shame, past all the other tables, watched by dozens of her curious classmates who had seen her arguing with Zac and were making no secret of their amusement. Freaky Frankie was always good for some improvised entertainment.

There were a few whistles and catcalls, which Mrs. Schuler ineffectually tried to shush.

Fran kept her head down and kept right on going. Lady Jinx guarded her back with a magic sword that—newsflash—didn't really exist.

"He'd been really tense," Jamie said, "as the appeal got closer. He was pretty hard to live with, to be honest."

Beth could think of a million answers to that one but she just laughed, amused in spite of herself. "Yeah, tell me about it."

The two of them were sitting in the living room—the worst option by far unless you counted all the others. Going into the kitchen and sitting up at the counter was what you'd do if a friend called, an invitation to intimacy, so to hell with that. Staying out on the porch ran the risk of someone overhearing what Jamie had to say. Parvesh Sethi, to name but one, worked from home and kept his windows open.

So the living room it was. But Beth hadn't bothered to fix coffee. The best way forward here was to hear her out and shine her on, but that didn't require Beth to be hospitable. The last thing she wanted was for Jamie to get comfortable.

To be fair, Jamie looked anything but. She kept smoothing down the hem of her raincoat, which she hadn't taken off, and her dark eyes darted around like they couldn't find anything they liked enough to settle on. She had a thin face and a tall, angular body. She was a goddamn clothes horse, more or less, with the arms folded out at asymmetrical angles. Christ only knew what Marc had seen in her.

"I know," Jamie said. "You had it a lot worse than me. He never hit me. I didn't believe what you were saying to start with, but as the trial went on I kind of had to accept . . . you know, that there was another side to him. We talked. About you, and what he'd done to you. He swore to me he'd changed, and he could never be like that again."

Beth raised an eyebrow, allowing her skepticism to show. "Lovely," she said. "He told me that too. Couple of times a month on average. Is this what you wanted to talk to me about, because really, that's between you and him."

A nice touch, she thought, that present tense.

"No," Jamie said with a faint, unhappy smile. "No, I don't think it would be right to ask you to talk to me about any of that. I'm just scared for him, that's all. I know everyone's assuming he ran away to avoid going to jail, but that doesn't make any sense to me."

"No?" Beth asked, openly sarcastic.

"No. He didn't pack. Not a thing. I mean, like, not even his toothbrush or his shaver. It's not as though he's rich, Ms. Kendall. Far from it. Most of the time he's not bringing in a red cent, and we just live on what I can make from my mail order business. We've got a few hundred bucks in a savings account, but I looked and he didn't touch it. If he ran, he ran with maybe twenty dollars and some change in his pocket."

"Maybe he wanted to make a fresh start. Or maybe he had some funds you didn't know about."

Jamie picked at her hem some more. She shook her head slowly. "Maybe," she admitted. "I think there were a lot of things I didn't know. He used to go out at night sometimes, and if I was awake when he got back in he said he'd just been out walking because he couldn't get to sleep. But I could see how tense he was when he said it, like he was ready to lose his temper if I took it any further. So I knew there was more to it than that."

She looked straight at Beth for the first time since she'd sat down. "But he loves those kids," she said. "I can't imagine him leaving them."

Can you imagine him killing them? Beth thought. I can.

This was easy. It would only have been hard if she had any respect for this woman, and she wasn't in any danger of that. "So you were still tiptoeing around his temper," she said, "even after he promised he was a changed man. What does that tell you?"

Jamie was still staring at her—a troubled gaze, not an accusing one. "I told you: he never hit me. That was the truth. I would have left him if he had. And he was never cruel to the kids. I wouldn't have stood for that either."

"Good for you. Best way of keeping the kids safe, though? Don't let him near them in the first place." Beth didn't try to hide her contempt. She still didn't feel like she needed to.

Jamie sighed and looked away at last—down at her hands. "Okay," she said softly. "I guess that answers that."

"What?" Beth felt a small twinge of alarm. What had she given away? She had felt in control until now.

Jamie looked up again. In spite of Beth's snarking tone, her expression was still calm and sad. "I didn't know how to ask, but . . . I thought he might have been with you. When he was sneaking out. That he might be coming round here. That the two of you might be . . . you know."

It was such a grotesque suggestion that Beth gasped out loud. "Jesus!"

"I know. It sounds ridiculous when you were dragging him up on assault charges. But he really believed he could persuade you to change your mind. And I . . ." She hesitated.

"You thought his methods of persuasion might include sex?" Beth stood up involuntarily. The alarm was gone, replaced by pure, white-hot indignation. Underneath that, her stomach lurched with nausea at the bare thought of it. "You thought I'd let him touch me? Let him do me?"

"I'm sorry." Jamie held up her hands again, the way she had out on the driveway. "I never intended to give offense. I'm just trying to make sense of all this."

"Get out," Beth said. "Get the hell out, right now, before I slap your stupid face off."

Jamie seemed astonished at her sudden vehemence. Clearly she didn't appreciate the enormity of what she'd just suggested. "Okay," she said.

She picked up her things hastily, but Beth was already wrestling with herself, trying to damp down that flaring filament of rage. There was too much at stake here. Spiking Blondie's car was one thing, but Jamie could cause genuine trouble for her. She had to be careful.

"I'm sorry," she said with an immense effort. "That was rude. Seriously, though, I would never let Marc within a mile of me. There's a court order, so I'm sure he would have had more sense than to come, but we're through in any case. We were through a long time ago. Please don't make any mistake about that."

Jamie stood irresolute, relieved at the change in Beth's tone but still thrown off balance—as much by how quickly she had calmed as by how suddenly she had flared up.

"I believe you," she said. "And I . . . I'm sorry to have taken up so much of your time. Like I said, I'm just worried for him."

She wasn't making any move toward the door. "Was there something else?" Beth asked, trying not to make it sound like just another way of saying "get the hell out."

Jamie gestured toward her purse. "I brought some gifts for Molly and Zac," she said. "I haven't seen them in ages, and . . . well, it's not likely I'll be seeing them any time soon, is it? But I wanted them to know I'm thinking about them. And if they want to call me, they can. Any time. I hope they know that."

"Gifts?"

"They're nothing much, to be honest. Just little things."

"Leave them on the counter," Beth told her.

Jamie took two small parcels out of her purse. Paper bags from a store somewhere, folded over and taped shut. She set them down side by side.

"Thank you," she said.

"You're welcome."

"And if Marc should get in touch with you—"

"The police will be the first to know. You'll be the second."

"You've got my number, then?" Jamie seemed surprised.

"I can get it from Zac."

"Oh. Right."

Jamie took the hint at last and left, asking Beth to pass on her love to Zac and Molly. "Of course," Beth assured her.

Alone at last, Beth ripped off the wrappings and looked at the two gifts. A braided bracelet for Molly; a puzzle ring for Zac. They both had a homespun look to them: probably Jamie had made them herself.

Beth threw them in the trash and started dinner.

But Jamie Langdon had left a mood of unease in her wake, and it persisted. Did I miss anything? Beth asked herself as she chopped onions, bringing the knife down with more force than was strictly needed. She thought not, but probably every murderer since Cain had made the same calculation and got the same result.

Maybe she should go over to the garden plot and check on how Marc was decomposing. But there were lots of reasons not to. She'd buried him as deep as she could, and layered in a lot of strong-smelling fertilizer to mask the scent of his decomposition. Winter was coming, so nobody would be out on their plots for the next few months. When they came back in the spring, it was likely that Marc would have rendered down nicely.

Plus there was a chance she might be seen, and she had no right at all to be there. The garden plot key had been Marc's. She shouldn't even have held on to it after she was done burying him. But there it was in back of her closet along with his two cell-phones (sans batteries), his wallet and all of her assorted weaponry. That stuff would take some explaining if the apartment was ever searched. She really needed to get rid of it. But a part of her refused to contemplate throwing away things that might still turn out to be useful—and that applied to Marc's effects as well as to the weapons.

You never knew.

Fran got home before her dad, which happened a lot. Tonight she was grateful: it gave her a chance to recover from the day.

She kind of hated that she needed to recover. She had had to be self-sufficient for most of her life after learning way back in second grade how irrevocably her cards were marked. If you were known to be a weirdo, if that was the basis of your social identity as it was for her, nobody would cut you any slack. They might pity you, but they wouldn't want to hang out with you and they mostly wouldn't go out on a limb by defending or befriending you. The chess club had become the closest thing she had to a tribe, and she enjoyed a fairly high status there because she had better game than any of them, but that guarded respect was as far as it went.

So it shouldn't have hurt so much to be blown off by Zac Kendall. Their friendship had still had its training wheels on. It shouldn't have built up enough velocity to do any real damage when it hit the wall. Fran didn't feel undamaged, though. She felt bruised and resentful and full of useless self-pity.

Also, for the first time in ages, she felt a little bit helpless. She had already been having doubts about her ability to face Bruno Picota. Now she was sure she couldn't do it. Not alone.

311

But it was about one chance in a million that Dr. Southern could get her in there anyway, so there was probably no point in worrying about it.

It had been a memorable summer, and an eventful fall. But winter would be the same as it always was. In Pittsburgh you just turned up your collar and went to sleep a little, inside, until the good weather came back again.

Time moved on, but in a lot of ways it seemed not to.

Beth continued to savor the pleasures that came with being alive and in the world. The taste and smell of food, the feel of fabrics on her skin, the music and TV shows she'd missed, the turning of the seasons, the warmth of the house after a brisk walk on a cold day, booze and weed and dark chocolate.

Sometimes, though, she caught herself sinking into a kind of trance. She had forgotten how much of life was about boredom. About slogging on through things that didn't have any intrinsic interest while you waited patiently for the things that did. That wasn't what she wanted. She had spent too much effort and pain in getting here to sit around and waste her time now she'd arrived.

So she fought back against the insidious threat of routine. And she enlisted Zac and Molly in the fight by instituting a relentless regime of treats. She took them out to movies and to bowling, state parks and Six Flags, museums once or twice when there was nothing better she could think of. They enjoyed themselves a lot. They rediscovered what being together as a family really meant.

(They weren't her family, but she tried not to think about that.) Then there were treats that were just her own. Red wine, and sometimes white, and sometimes spirits. A blunt at the end of the day, scored from her co-worker Tandy whose brother was a dealer. She got herself laid at least once a week, under cover of going out with the girls from work, leaving Zac to babysit his sister. Always one-night stands: no names, no pack drill, no questions asked or quarter given. Just wham, bam, thank you Sam. That was the only way if you wanted to avoid getting saddled with a loser or a psycho. Her plan to make a move on Gil Watts had come apart when Zac and Francine's friendship broke up without warning, but that was probably for the best. Might have been hard to keep that one clean and simple, and clean and simple were her watchwords now.

Sleep still eluded her. The body slept, but Beth's consciousness never went offline. She just let the body fall away from her for a few hours and spent the night in watching and thinking. Once or twice, when she was in this untethered state, she drifted through the walls of the condo to spy on the neighbors. But their lives were suffocatingly dull, and she always felt exposed when she was away from her flesh-and-blood nest for very long. Anything might happen to it while she was away.

She had read somewhere that you couldn't survive indefinitely without rest. Probably that was true for most people. For her, though, flesh and spirit seemed to have reached an accommodation that worked for both. Body and soul could spend the night apart, then come together again and be none the worse. She felt a little ragged and raw in the early morning sometimes, but she burned that off soon enough if she kept moving.

And she *did* keep moving. Constant activity was an antidote for a lot of things, including thought. There were many topics it didn't do to think about too much when it came down to it: this wasn't her world, and the fit was never going to be perfect. Whenever the kids reminded her of some treasured moment she had no memory of, the parallax chafed her. When some trick of Molly's speech or a fleeting expression on Zac's face reminded her of her own kids (guaranteed original and genuine), and how their sweet lexicon of words and actions had died with them, it hurt her heart.

She was still wedged into this life at a slightly awkward angle.

But she was alive. That was the salient point. She intended to stay that way.

She managed to hide her vacillations from the children. If anything, her awareness of the secret gulf between them made her more attentive to their needs. She tried to tie herself to their lives by a thousand slender threads, since the big cables of consanguinity were gone for good.

Some of those threads were material things, gifts she'd bought them. Maybe that idea had grown out of Jamie Langdon's visit, but Beth suspected it was another symptom of her dislocation, her sense of being out of place. Money felt no more real than anything else did, so she spent a whole lot more of it than she had. She bought Zac a new electric guitar and amplifier ("You want to follow in the family tradition, right?"), and Molly a bike. Not forgetting her gifts to herself, of course. She had a new black leather jacket, a Patrizia Pepe with two rows of silver studs bracketing the diagonal slash of the zipper. The black Nissan Rogue sitting in the driveway set it off really nicely, and consoled her every time she climbed behind the wheel.

The other thing that gave her a great deal of satisfaction was how smoothly she had managed to extricate herself from Liz's pre-existing friendships and obligations. The informal network of play dates depended on reciprocity, so all she had to do there was stop having other people's kids round to play and the invites had quickly stopped coming. The Sethis had been harder to dislodge, but it was all a question of finding the right lever. She had had to refuse about a dozen invitations for lunch, dinner and impromptu parties, but the couple had finally got the message when Beth started telling them jokes with homophobic punchlines. Visibly hurt and puzzled, they had retreated into their own space.

Beebee would be next, but as long as the search for Marc continued it was safer to stay on the cop's good side. At least this way Beth got progress reports—the progress, thankfully, being entirely in the wrong direction. Illusory sightings in St. Clair, Philly and distant Ithaca kept the local cops scampering like mice while Marc rendered down quietly and inexorably a few blocks north.

Jamie was the only irritant who refused to go away. She called Beth at least once a week to ask if there had been any news, always in the same meek and stolid tone, ready to be disappointed and accepting the curt thumbs-down without argument every time. She hinted once or twice that she would love to see Zac and Molly if they wanted to come over. "Maybe spell you for a night or two, if you want to go away. It would be no trouble . . ."

Right, Beth thought. Borrow my kids, debrief them at your leisure. Where does Mommy go? Who does she see? What happened on the night of . . .? No trouble at all.

"I'll ask them," Beth said every time. And didn't. She had nothing to gain from that transaction.

She was doing great, all things considered. But she didn't let her guard down, and she took nothing for granted. So when the shit and the fan did finally stage a short reunion tour, around mid-November, she wasn't caught out. It was almost as though she'd been expecting it all along.

It was about one in the morning. The kids had crashed out hours ago, but Beth was still awake. Or rather she was awake again. Having tried and failed to get to sleep, she was propped up on her pillows, working her way through season ninety-three of some bullshit crime drama.

Out of nowhere, the screen of the tiny flatscreen flickered for a second and then righted itself. That was all the warning she got, but she was instantly alert. The flicker was inside her eye, not inside the TV. Something had tried to slip past her guard into her mind, but it hadn't gotten very far at all.

She didn't sleep again that night. She turned out the light in the end for the sake of appearances, but she couldn't even bring herself to close her eyes. She sat unblinking in the dark and waited for an attack that didn't come.

The next day she had a full shift. She tried to shrug off her exhaustion as a body thing, but it dogged her through the day.

Everything seemed to take twice as long as it should, and to be about three times as irritating.

The flicker at the corner of her eyes didn't recur at the Cineplex, or on the drive home, but it was there again as soon as Beth opened the front door. As though it had been waiting for her.

Well now.

She cooked and served a meal, her mind elsewhere. The potatoes were half-raw and the meat cooked dry. When Molly bitched about it, Beth didn't even respond.

"I think it's too tough for her to chew, Mom," Zac said.

"Make her something else, then," Beth muttered. She took herself away to her own room and locked the door. Could she be wrong? She wasn't wrong. She felt it again, a tentative touch. Saw it way off at the very edge of her visual field, a virtual ripple trying to pretend it wasn't there at all.

"Well, hey there, girl," Beth murmured. "It's been a while." She kept her voice cold and casual, almost inflectionless.

The ripple went through a few shivery permutations without resolving into a definite shape.

"You're looking good, Lizzie," Beth said. "Have you lost weight or something?"

She waited for a response. When it didn't come, she started to doubt herself all over again. The stain on the air was so faint it could be no more than an after-image. Still, the things that had gotten her this far included a healthy—maybe more than healthy—dose of paranoia. Better to assume the worst and go from there.

"You think you're ready for round two?" Beth said aloud. "I can promise you, you're not."

That was just stating a fact. If this tiny optical illusion *was* Liz, there was no way she could push Beth out and take her place now that Beth was alert and armed against her. Hell, she couldn't have done it even with a surprise attack. Beth was way stronger than her to start with and she had the advantage of position.

But under that certainty there was a doubt. If this *was* Liz, then

Liz was more tenacious than she seemed. She should have faded away like a bad fart a long time ago.

Beth sat up, keeping the same iron-hard expression on her face, the same indifferent tone in her voice. "Ring the bell and come out punching," she said. "By all means. Whenever you feel the urge. I'll chew you up and spit you out, you sad little fuck."

She waited for a long time, but nothing at all happened. After maybe half an hour, she went back out to the kids. Zac had made Molly an omelet. Molly had eaten it, and now wanted to talk about it: unedited highlights, play-by-play and color commentary both. Beth watched TV and pretended to listen.

"Is everything okay?" Zac asked.

"Just a headache," Beth said. "Thanks for picking up the slack there."

"You want some Tylenol?"

"I just want to sit."

She endured another sleepless night. The next day she was feeling wrung out by mid-morning. She grabbed a half-hour nap in the car after she finished her shift, not caring if anybody saw. It was the house where she had to be on her guard. That was the only place where the crappy little special effect manifested itself.

Enough was enough. She needed to shut this shit down before it went any further. The question was how.

Assume the worst and go from there. If this was Liz, then Beth needed something that would make her back off or come on strong: something that would decide the issue once and for all.

She had an idea what that something might look like. Liz was just Beth without balls. Her reactions might be different but her buttons were more or less in the same places.

That evening she bided her time. Did some laundry. Watched some soaps. Went through the motions with the kids. But keeping one eye open the whole time for the tiny spots of turbulence in the air that announced her invisible house guest. She was there, off at the edge of things but never entirely out of sight. Clearly she was settling in to become a permanent fixture.

Over my dead body, Beth thought.

She put Molly to bed. Kissed Zac goodnight, telling him not to stay up too late—then stayed up herself until the light under his door went out. The house made stretching and creaking noises as it cooled around her.

She sat in the kitchen, dragging the short, thin blade of a paring knife through the sharpener again and again.

When the air moved in the corner of the room, the smallest possible shimmer like a heat haze that couldn't get its act together, Beth nodded a welcome.

"Just the two of us now," she said. "Girls together. Much more cozy."

She held up the knife. Its edge had a blue shine to it. "You think that's sharp enough?" she asked.

No answer from the special effect.

"I know," Beth said. "Sharp enough for what, right? Can't use it on you, obviously. You're way too thin to cut."

She paused, licking lips that felt a little dry. "That is you, isn't it, Lizzie? You came back, even though it was obvious nobody was missing you. The kids are safer with me. Happier too. You should see all the stuff I've bought them. The fun we have. They don't need you. Nobody ever did."

She got to her feet slowly. "But you're never going to believe that, are you? Never going to take the hint. So let me show you something. One mother to another."

Her heart was beating faster than she would have liked. She refused to admit the possibility that she was afraid of Liz. Liz was, after all, a doormat, a woman who could be relied on to surrender when the going got even a little bit arduous. But Beth wanted her gone all the same. Not conditionally or temporarily, not pushed down into some sinkhole from which she could crawl up again at her leisure. Gone forever.

She walked to the door, through it, down the hallway. Past Zac's door to Molly's. The stain in the air followed her, although it moved so slowly that it almost seemed to be standing still. *Got you good, didn't I?* Beth thought. *You can barely even crawl. I bet it took you a month or so just to scrape yourself off the pavement. Why the hell would you think you stand a chance against me now?*

She opened the door and stepped inside, leaving it just ajar behind her. A ragged rumble of breathing, not quite a snore, came from the bed where Molly was a small bump in a large expanse of duvet. Some nights, because of her bronchiectasis, Molly snored like a chain saw. Tonight she was relatively quiet.

Beth sat on the edge of the bed and pulled the duvet down a little, exposing Molly's head and neck and her left arm, thrown across the pillow with the hand curled into a tight, emphatic fist. Molly even had excess energy when she slept.

"Look at her," Beth said, keeping her voice low. "Did you ever see anything so beautiful in the whole world? Answer is you didn't, because there's nothing out there that comes close."

She drew the knife lightly across the tiny nubs of Molly's vertebrae, barely touching them. The little girl shivered in her sleep and shifted a little.

"Sorry, sweetheart," Beth muttered. She reversed the knife in her hand, gripping it hard now, the blade pointing down between the first and second of those tiny bumps, beneath which ran the precious conduits of her little girl's blood and breath; the slender cord that made movement possible.

Don't!

It was a wail of utter despair.

Finally! But Beth didn't yield at once. She waited while that milky smudge at her shoulder bobbed and rippled, groping for a semblance of shape and not finding it.

Don't hurt her! Please!

"Why would I want to hurt her?" Beth demanded in the same soft, level tone. "I love her as much as you do. She's my baby girl, and there's nothing in the world that's more precious to me. But listen to me, Liz Kendall. Listen to me, and believe me. I will rip her wide open and watch her bleed out on the ground before I

320

give her up to you. She's mine. Your whole life is mine. I won it fair and square and I'm not giving it back.

"So I'm telling you to get the fuck out of here, and not come back. If you push me, if you make me think for a moment that you're going to take what's mine, what happens next is on you. All of it."

The stain in the air said nothing. It made a sound, but you couldn't mistake the sound for a word, or even an idea. It was a shapeless articulation of pain, and of surrender.

Slowly, almost imperceptibly, it faded. Beth waited until there was nothing left. Only then did she remove the knife from Molly's neck. It fell from her hand onto the bedroom floor. She was trembling all over where a second ago her hand had been steady as a rock. All her self-control collapsed at once. A sudden rush of nausea took her by surprise, her throat filling up with sour bile that she forced down again with a huge effort. In its wake came quick, strangled sobs.

"I didn't mean it," she gasped. "Oh baby, I didn't mean a word of it. Not one fucking word. I would never— I couldn't ever—"

She gathered the little girl up in her arms and squeezed her tight. Molly squirmed and cried out as she woke, with no idea of what was happening or who was holding her.

"It's all right now," Beth told her again and again. As if it had been someone else's hand holding the knife, as if she were the protector rather than the threat. "It's all right now, baby girl."

Liz made it as far as the bottom of the street.

Well, almost. A hundred yards shy of East Liberty, she drifted to a halt and more or less ceased to exist. She was so close to nothing the difference didn't seem to matter: a weightless, dimensionless pinprick of despair. Cars passed through her infrequently. The noise of their engines passed through her too, no more substantial and no less.

The world penetrated and dismantled her like an endless parade of camels padding serenely through the eye of the same damn needle, which couldn't move or evade or close itself or do anything very much except endure.

It had taken her so long to get this far! After the sucker punch that threw her out of her own body, she had fallen for an endless time, and lost herself along the way. Her thoughts had scattered like raindrops in a squall, had settled wherever the wind took them, so each little thought had had to crawl for miles to find its neighbors.

She had collected herself the way you collect roadside garbage. Made a junk sculpture of her own mind, which she was now using to think. With no brain to keep her thoughts in, it was the best she could do.

She had found herself in darkness at first, and wondered if she was in hell. But the glaring yellow lights that bore down on her, two by two, and turned sullen red as they passed, made it clear at last that this was not the afterlife but the Fort Pitt Tunnel. She had crossed the Monongahela River, not the Styx. That was miles from Larimer. How had she come so far? Maybe distances worked differently when you were a ghost. And dead or not, that was what Liz now was. The ghost of herself, exorcised and dispossessed. Maybe not even a full ghost at that. Just the bits she could find and bring together.

She couldn't even move at first. She didn't know how to interact with the space around her, since she didn't fill any space to start with. She was like a camera feed without a camera, a space into which the world emptied its images of itself.

And then, slowly and imperfectly, its sounds. Dopplered engine roar; fluting wind; the thud-space-thud of tires hitting a pothole.

But if Liz could see without eyes and hear without ears, why shouldn't she walk without legs? The invisible pinprick had invisible resources of its own. Over the space of days, measured by the coming and the waning of the light, she worked and worked at shifting her point of view, furiously pushing at the margins of reality until they gave just a little.

She moved. Ponderously, painfully, as if she was the most massive thing in the world rather than the least. But still, a win was a win.

She found her way home. Slower than molasses, a tiny ship that left no wake, she forged on mile after mile until she was back among familiar streets.

The door gave her some problems, but that was because she still wasn't thinking straight—or thinking much at all (the urgency that filled her and dragged her through the night came from somewhere deep and unexamined). It seemed to her that a door must still be a barrier when really it was an irrelevance. After staring at it from almost zero distance for a day and most of a night, she pushed herself straight through it. There was a brief interval of darkness and she was on the other side with no loss of momentum.

She drifted up the hall, steering by the faint, warm glow from under her bedroom door. She was through the maze at last. The only thing left to do was to confront the minotaur.

And, after all that effort, Beth had vanquished her in the space of a minute. She had forgotten, somehow, in her endless, painfully protracted battle charge that she had no weapons to fight with, no advantage to push, no plan.

She wasn't fighting a monster; she was trying to lay single-handed siege to a fortress. So naturally she had failed. What was worse, and completely unexpected, was *how* she had failed. By threatening Molly, Beth had won this battle and all possible future battles. Liz wouldn't dare to go near her after this, or even to enter the house.

Which meant she was leaving her kids in the care of a woman who was prepared to use them as hostages to save herself.

I can't even cry, Liz thought in blank despair. *I can't even scream.* What did that leave?

In the days and weeks after her second decisive victory over Liz, Beth was riding higher than ever. She rewarded herself in all the ways she could think of, luxuriating in the feeling that she was now, finally, safely embedded in her new life.

The paranoid part of her played up from time to time even then: it reminded her that a feeling of invulnerability was dangerous. In the absence of an enemy, you could defeat yourself just by becoming too cocksure, too arrogant. But arrogance was in her nature, as was hedonism. She gave them both free rein in spite of that nagging inner voice. There was so much to enjoy in this brave new Pittsburgh, and lots of lost time to make up for.

Increasingly, though, her pleasures were solitary. She had to admit to herself that her relationship with Zac and Molly had soured a little.

It had already started before that night with the knife and the ultimatum. The steady diet of treats was bound to pall in the long run, leaving all of them a little spent and exhausted. But when it did, Beth was caught unawares. She hadn't realized how much she had come to rely on the frantic partying as a shield, holding the kids at one remove with moments of regimented enjoyment.

When they were all together in the house, she kept being reminded—at moments when she least expected it—of how strange these two children were to her. As familiar to her as her own right and left hand, but still . . . alien. A word here. A gesture there. A laugh. A frown. A headshake. A tone of voice. All of them just a little off, but a miss was as good as a mile.

Molly still slept with her night light on. Beth had been through this with the real Molly before she turned five, not wanting to indulge her in things that would only make her weak. Of course, weak was fine in Liz Kendall's family. Weak was the house style.

Zac was just as bad. She had watched, with contemptuous amusement, while he picked the hot jalapeño slices out of his chili before he ate it. The real Zac would have slathered hot sauce over the top and asked for more.

But when you came right down to it, it really wasn't about these small details. It was about the sense, the unshakeable instinct, that lay underneath them—and it expressed itself through those telling words. *The real Molly. The real Zac.* They weren't around anymore to plead their case. To be the yardstick against which every other Zac and Molly had to be measured. They were dead. The only place where they persisted was in Beth's mind.

That thought inserted itself like the edge of a crowbar between her and her comforts. Between her and this life. The distance was almost too small to see, but it was like the gap that sat at your heel if you didn't lace your shoe up tight enough: chafing and scraping until it drove you insane, not so much with the pain as the inevitability. Every step you took brought it back, again and again and again.

But the whole business with the knife somehow brought things to a head. When she held the knife to Molly's neck, she was telling herself the whole time that she didn't mean it. That was the only way she could do it at all. But even as a bluff, it left an aftertaste. Whenever she touched Molly, or talked to her, it rose between them like a wall. Beth couldn't have done that to her own child. She would have had to be insane. But she wasn't insane, and she had done it. The paradox dragged her against her will toward an unpalatable truth.

When Molly was playing her endless, pointless games. When Zac was playing guitar. When the three of them were eating together, or driving to school, or watching TV. These things were no more than smoke and mirrors. Beth ate, and drove, and watched, woke, slept and walked alone.

For Fran, time went forward in a way that brought no change and didn't even make any promises.

The week after she and Zac stopped counting each other as friends, he sent her a long email that was chock-full of apologies. She knew him well enough to believe all or most of them. He hadn't meant to hit out at her. He just reacted badly to anything that threatened his mother, and the timing had been especially disastrous because he was still bouncing back from that big row he'd had with his mom on the night before the trial-that-never-was. He hated himself that he'd brought up Fran's mental health problems against her. He hated that he'd abused things she'd said to him in confidence. He would never forgive himself for hurting her.

It wasn't easy to write back to him, but she made herself do it.

Hey, Zac. Don't worry about it. I know you're a good person, and it makes sense that you'd beat yourself up for doing shitty things. But the shitty things are still there, and they're not going to go away. I can't forget them anymore than you can, and frankly I can't see myself ever talking to you about stuff that matters anymore. We can still talk about everyday stuff, obviously. Say hi to me any time you like, and I'll say hi right back. I'm not going to blank you or anything. And if you need a spare pen or a quarter for the drinks machine, I've got you covered. That's as far as it goes, though, okay? We blew the rest of it, which is too bad because I liked hanging out with you. Give Molly a hug from me, goon, and take one for yourself. No hard feelings.

Fran

She almost wrote *Francine*, but that would just have been histrionics. She pressed SEND and shut the lid of the laptop right away. The alternative would have been to sit there hitting the refresh key every twenty seconds in case he sent a reply. If he did, there wouldn't even be any point in reading it. It wasn't like she could change her mind after setting it all out so reasonably and clearly.

She had ambushed herself with her own eloquence.

In every other respect, life went back to what counted as normal. She had a few episodes, but they didn't escalate. If anything, they became less intense with time. She went back to her old dosage but carried the spare pack of risperidone around with her all the time in case she needed to step it up.

And Jinx was just Jinx—her old self, unfailingly sweet and supportive. Since the threatened visit to Grove City hadn't come off, there were no bones of contention between her and Fran anymore. So Fran still had one BFF. Or none, depending how you counted.

It was easiest not to think about it. Any of it. Along with the narrowing of the days that winter brings, Fran felt her mind narrow, and she didn't particularly resist. School and homework and chess club were her horizons now.

In spite of everything, though, she had the sense that something was in the air, still impending. Her dad would have said that the other shoe still hadn't dropped. Fran had no idea what that really meant, but it conjured up a picture in her mind of a heavy boot sailing down through the sky, heading straight for her. That was a pretty good description of how she felt.

Maybe for that reason, she kept her head down even more than she usually did and tried not to do or say anything that would attract the lightning. She stayed home a lot. She handed in all her assignments bang on time as though God was going to be signing off on her report card. When she saw Zac Kendall coming, she turned and walked the other way. Lady Jinx covered her retreat with Oatkipper at the ready.

Sometime in early November, Dr. Southern called her on her cell. This was unusual. He almost always used email to contact her, with a cc automatically going to Gil. So she knew before he even said a word what this was about.

"Grove City said yes," he told her, sounding both pleased and apprehensive. "They asked me to fix a time with you."

Caught on the hop with no cover in sight, Fran temporized. "I've got a lot of work to do before the end of the semester. We'll have to wait a while."

Dr. Southern was nonplussed. "I got the impression you felt really strongly about this, Frankie," he said. "I sold it to the Grove City guys very hard. We went back and forth for weeks while they bounced it up the ladder to their senior clinician—a guy named Trestle who is seriously hard to get hold of. And he had it out with Bruno Picota, and—to my absolute amazement—came back with a yes. They think it's a done deal. They're expecting me to confirm a time."

Fran felt bad for Dr. Southern, and ashamed of her own cowardice, but she held her ground. "I can't do it right now," she said, which was the simple truth even though the stuff about being too busy with school assignments was just nonsense. She was way out in front of her work and could make it to the Christmas vacation at a stroll. What she couldn't do—or didn't think she could do—was face Bruno Picota all on her lonesome own.

She thanked Dr. S for his help and hung up as soon as she could.

Was that the other shoe dropping? She thought not.

Then Zac made a second attempt at an apology, and he did it in a way that was heavy-handed and kind of stupid. He sent her flowers, and since they arrived while she was at school Gil opened the door to the delivery guy and signed for them. He was bemused and inclined to disapprove.

"I didn't know you and Mr. Kendall were divorced," he said to Fran when he handed the flowers over. It was a big bouquet and must have cost a lot, which only made it worse.

"He disrespected me," Fran said.

Gil nodded slowly, solemn-faced. "Did he now? Anything I should know about?"

"No. It's all good. But we're done." She had used that highly formal word to stop her dad from making any more jokes on the subject, and it worked. He took her at her word and left it right there.

He also went to the door when Zac called at the house a few days later. Fran didn't hear the words that passed between them, but she heard her father's tone and she was pretty sure Zac wouldn't come round again.

Good riddance! Lady Jinx growled from under Fran's bed.

"Yeah," Fran said bleakly. "Absolutely."

For better or worse, things pushed themselves into new configurations.

Beth found that there was a limit to how much bullshit she was prepared to take. The next time Molly dragged her heels getting dressed in the morning, floating around the kitchen like she had all the time in the world, Beth grabbed her shoulder, led her back to her bedroom and shoved her inside, telling her sharply to get her ass in gear and then closing the door on her.

Then a few days after that, Beth was watching some show or other and the kid came trotting up to bend her ear with some story about what had happened when la-di-da pulled yak yak yak's hair and then blah blah blah and et cetera got involved, and . . .

"Mommy's busy," Beth said. "Just go away and play with your toys, okay?"

Molly looked bemused for a second, like that couldn't be right, but then momentum carried her onward. "And Miss Summerson said—"

Beth never got to hear what Miss Summerson said. She planted her hand dead center on Molly's chest and pushed her backward.

She hadn't meant to knock the kid down. She just misjudged the mass by a little, forgetting how slight Molly was and how little force was required to destabilize her. The little girl went over hard.

That shut her up okay, but her face clouded up with hurt and bewilderment and her lower lip was quivering. It was clear that once she got over the shock and disbelief she was going to get loud about it.

Beth was appalled at what she'd done, and doubly appalled at the thought of Zac finding out. She jumped up out of her chair, knelt down next to the six-year-old and scooped her up, kissing her cheeks and forehead.

"I'm sorry, sweetheart," she said quickly. "That was an accident. It's okay, it's okay. Don't cry now. Tell me about . . . that stuff. What happened at school? I'm listening."

Zac came running in at that point, alerted by the loud thud and wanting to know what had happened. "Nothing," Beth told him. "Moll took a fall, is all. She was running and she fell. Isn't that right, baby girl?"

"I took a fall," Molly quavered. And Beth laughed and gave her a huge hug, making it absolutely clear to Zac and Molly and most of all herself how much she loved her little girl.

"You okay, Moll?" Zac asked.

"Yes," Molly confirmed.

It passed off okay. Molly threw out a few half-assed sniffles but she didn't howl. And Zac went back to his room none the wiser. Crisis averted.

Except that it wasn't. Not really. Beth felt the way Liz must have felt the first time Beth welled up from inside her like fresh lava and spilled out into the world. *Was that me? Was all that rage inside me? Where did it come from?*

And what does it want?

Liz was starting to dissolve, a little at a time. It wasn't entirely unpleasant, or frightening. Dissolution was just there all the time, spread underneath her like a safety net, tempting her with the promise that all her pain and confusion could end at once.

It was becoming increasingly difficult for her to think. Ironically, thought was the closest to physical effort she could come. It was as though she was carrying bundles of ideas from synapse to synapse, loading them up and pushing them on their way, then trudging a little further along her train of thought to do the same thing all over again.

Mostly she thought about the immediate past. Marc's murder, her eviction from her own body, Beth's terrifying strength of will and her own helplessness. It was a short meditation, endlessly repeated. In some ways it was like the mindfulness meditations from Dr. Southern's book, except that in this case the end product was despair. *Know That You're Here, and This Is Now.*

Zac and Molly saved her. Molly came skipping toward her one day, holding Zac's hand, the two of them wrapped up warm in scarves and gloves against the first inroads of winter.

"It's a jerboa!" Molly was saying.

"A gerbil?"

"No, a jerboa. It's a gerbil that lives in the desert. He can jump like a kangaroo."

"Wow, that sounds amazing, Moll."

Liz was rapt, drinking in the sight of them, the sound of their voices—an oasis in the desert of those arid, empty thoughts. When they walked by her, without even suspecting that she was there, she turned and followed them down the street, straining her imaginary nerves to keep them in sight for as long as possible.

They outdistanced her very quickly, turned a corner and were gone. But they left her with a hunger that energized her.

After that day, she moved up the block, stationing herself as close to the house as she dared. When Beth appeared, she kept absolutely still and prayed not to be noticed. When Zac came out alone, or when Zac and Molly came out together, she followed them.

Only a little way at first. She was as slow as a drifting balloon and couldn't keep up. But she got a little bit faster every time, and time was a thing she had in abundance.

It was, of course, the only thing she had. She knew that Beth's psychic ambush had left her badly damaged, and she was healing very slowly if she was healing at all. But Beth had honed her skills over hundreds, maybe thousands of worlds. Liz felt that if she kept at it, there was a chance she would get better at this.

When she had a little more control over her speed and direction, she finessed the situation a little. She spent the night hours drifting across the city, block after endless block, until she got to Worth Harbor Elementary or Julian C. Barry. That let her be with the kids for hours at a time. Alternating between Zac and Molly, she spent the whole of the school day with each in turn.

The journey home, when school let out, took her the rest of the daylight hours. Liz couldn't take the bus, or hop a lift in one of the many cars. She had tried, but there must be some trick to it that she hadn't worked out yet. Getting in through the bus's open door was just about possible, even at her slowly drifting pace.

When the bus moved off, though, it passed right through her and left her standing where she was.

But again, she felt that she was getting faster each time. At full stretch she could match a normal man or woman's walking speed for minutes at a time.

In the evenings, Molly mostly stayed home. Home was off-limits to Liz while Beth was there. She took up a vantage point a few houses down the street and waited out the hours of darkness there. Unless Zac left the house. If he left the house, she went with him. She watched his back, though she couldn't protect him from anything at all.

A hackneyed expression came into her mind from time to time: what doesn't kill us, makes us strong. Now making herself strong, in these strictly limited ways, was helping her not to die.

Amazingly, the flowers and the house call were not the end of the matter. Fran got a Snapchat picture a few nights later, and she opened it before she saw who it was from. It was a shot of the notice board at the half-built station behind Lenora. Next to JAZ SUCKS BALLS was a new notice bearing just three words in Zac's scrawly handwriting.

Fran read the words several times over. Then she looked out of the window. It was already getting dark, and the wires from the telegraph pole across the street were dancing in a stiff wind. The forecast was for an overnight low of four below zero. Only an idiot would wait out there in the gathering dusk and freeze their ass off in the hope of a conversation.

Don't! He's tricking you!

"I don't think he is. Look what he said."

It doesn't matter what he said! It's a trick!

Fran went downstairs and suited up for the cold. Gil had been working in his tiny study: he left his keyboard and came to the door to watch her. "Little late for a walk, Frog," he observed.

"I was feeling a bit cooped up, is all," Fran said. "I just want to walk around the block a couple of times."

Liar!

Fran didn't need Jinx's accusation to feel ashamed. She hated hiding anything from her dad, but this would be way too hard to explain.

"Put a hat on," he told her. "And a scarf."

"Way ahead of you, Dad-of-mine." She gave him a hug and fled, keeping her face turned away so he wouldn't see it and guess that there was more to this than she was saying.

There was already a serious bite to the air, so she walked quickly. At first she thought Jinx hadn't come along at all, but then she realized the fox was keeping a long way behind, muttering low in her throat. Fran didn't try to catch the words: she already knew Jinx's opinion of what she was doing.

The streets were mostly empty as she headed up toward Lenora. One of the homeless guys who pitched their one-man tents along the stretch of wire fence behind Saint Peter and Paul yelled something at her, but it didn't sound threatening. He waved a blanket or a coat, like maybe he was offering her something to keep herself warm. She kept on walking and didn't answer in case he was offering something else.

Once she threaded her way through the bushes behind the playground and stepped down onto the tracks, the night closed in on her for real. The nearest streetlights were just a vague glow on the horizon now, and the dark seemed to bring the cold to bear in some weird way. The air was just chillier here.

In spite of the dark, it was easy to follow the railway line. It was a lighter strip, as neat and regular as an airplane runway, between the walls of solid black that were the bushes. This would still be a great place to get mugged, though.

There's nobody here, Jinx told her coldly. *Just him. Nobody else.*

From a long way away, as she approached the platform, she could see a moving pinprick of light, small but very bright. It was the screen of Zac's phone, she realized. He had it on flashlight mode and he was waving it around in his hand as he walked rapidly up and down the platform to keep warm.

She was suddenly aware that Jinx had stopped moving. Glancing down, she saw that the fox was sitting back on her haunches, staring ahead of her. Not straight ahead, though: not at Zac's light, but off to one side of it.

"What?" Fran asked.

Jinx shivered and shook herself. *I don't know*, she said. *I thought . . . it doesn't matter.* She trotted on again, her body low to the ground as if she were stalking prey.

By the phone's light, as she stepped up onto the end of the platform, Fran could see the sign Zac had made: the three words that had dragged her out into the dark and brought her here.

YOU WERE RIGHT.

He had seen her coming too, and turned to face her. The phone lit up his face from underneath, so his smile of welcome looked sinister and horrible.

"Hey, Fran," he said. "It's really good to see you."

"That's nice to hear, Zac. But my ass is freezing off and it's a school night. You've got five minutes. Go."

Zac nodded, accepting her terms without argument. "You said my mom had changed. She has."

Fran indicated the sign with a brusque gesture. "I already got that much," she said testily. "Specifics."

"It's really hard to explain. She's kind of . . . not there, a lot of the time, even when she's with us. She's thinking about other stuff, not listening when we talk. If I call her on it, she loses her temper and says she's got a lot on her mind."

"And?"

"She doesn't bother to cook dinner anymore. Most nights she just orders takeout, or if she's going out she tells us to fix something for ourselves. If she's staying home she goes into her room, right after dinner, and watches TV with the door closed. A lot of times, though, she goes out and leaves us to it. Comes back after midnight. A few times she's even stayed out all night and I've had to get Molly ready for school in the morning and walk in with her."

It was clear from Zac's face that there was more. In the biting cold Fran wasn't inclined to be patient. She made a winding-up gesture, even though she hated when people did that to her and it made her feel like kind of a douche.

"She doesn't do any grocery shopping, either. I have to do it. And I had to re-up Molly's inhalers when they ran out. She didn't even mark it on the calendar, which she always does, like, three months out."

"So she's making you take a bit more responsibility. That's not such a—"

"I think she's hitting Molly."

Fran left her half-finished sentence hanging in the air, all her impatience and irritation draining away at once in the shock of what she'd heard. The expression on Zac's face was almost worse than the words. He looked like he'd just said *God is dead* or something—like there was a hole in the world and he'd given it a name.

"You think?" Fran asked.

"Yeah."

"You don't know?"

"I didn't see it with my own eyes, no."

"Then what makes you think it's happening?"

"I sort of heard it. At least, I heard something. I was in my room, doing homework with some music playing. And there was a sound like a bang, and then Molly saying 'ow,' and it fell right in a quiet bit of the song so I heard it really clearly. I jumped right up and came out of my room. They were both in the family room. Mom was holding on to Molly, rocking her a little. She said Molly fell over while she was playing or something."

"What did Molly say."

"She said she fell down. But that was *all* she said. You know how she is. Every tiny thing is a story with her. But this . . . she didn't have a single thing to say about it. She was just standing there, with Mom's arms around her, stiff as a board and not saying

340

a word. She didn't even look at me when I asked her if she was okay. She looked down at the floor.

"Her eyes were red like she'd been crying, or maybe like she wanted to cry. I asked her if she was okay and she said yes. Just that one word. Yes. Then she turned her face away so I couldn't see it."

Zac looked off into the darkness as though he was re-enacting the scene as he remembered it. His face was still lit up all pale and ghastly by the light from the phone.

"It just wasn't like her," he muttered. "She should have been the one telling me all about it at the top of her voice, and Mom should have been the one shushing her and telling her not to make such a big deal. It felt like the whole thing was the wrong way round.

"I asked Moll about it again the next morning when I walked her into school. She didn't say anything. I mean, she wouldn't answer me at all. She zipped right up. That's when I started thinking maybe it wasn't just that one time. You don't get scared like that after just one time.

"Most days Mom picks her up from school, you know? Unless she's on full shift. And then it's just the two of them until I get there. I'm scared of . . . I don't know. What could be happening when I'm not there."

"That's awful, Zac," Fran said. In spite of herself she reached out and put a hand on his arm. Jinx gave a low growl from the very edge of the platform where she had planted herself like a watchdog. Fran thought it was because of the physical contact, but then Jinx dived right off the edge and disappeared into the dark.

"Yeah, it's awful," Zac agreed, pulling her attention back to him. "But also it doesn't make any sense. It's not . . . she can't *do* this stuff. You know about my dad, right? How he used to lose his temper sometimes and hit out? Not at us—at Mom. But Mom was always afraid he might hurt us too. She used to put herself in between in case . . ." His hands completed the sentence, pantomiming something the dark hid from her—and dislodging her

341

hand in the process. "So it makes no sense that she would ever, ever hurt Moll. Or me. She couldn't do that. I mean, I thought she couldn't. And I still can't figure any of it out. So here I am. And I guess I'm coming to you because you seemed to spot it before it even happened."

Fran glanced off into the darkness. Jinx had vanished from sight out there. Maybe she'd seen or heard something and was investigating it. More likely she was just washing her hands of all this.

She looked at Zac again. His hangdog face, his slumped shoulders, begging for help he couldn't ask for in actual words because he knew he didn't have any right to.

And if it had just been him, then maybe Fran could have walked away. But she knew she couldn't walk away from Molly.

Zac was still watching her, waiting for an answer. She already knew, pretty much, what she was going to say to him, but she had to set him straight on a couple of things first.

"I didn't spot it before it happened," she told him. "It just happened earlier than you think. I think it was the night you slept at my house. The night before the trial. But I don't have any idea what it was that changed or what it meant. I'm pretty sure your mom knows, because of how angry she got when I asked her about it, but there was no way she was going to spill the beans to me. If you want the truth, maybe you should just ask her."

"I can't do that," Zac protested, appalled. "I'm scared for her, Fran. Really scared. I feel like I'd just be adding to the pressure."

"The pressure?"

"Well, because . . ." The light from the phone went all over the place as he shrugged or waved his hands or something. "She wouldn't act this way if she was herself. If she was right with herself. Something has to be weighing on her. Bending her all out of shape."

The all-purpose *something* again. It was hard to imagine what that something could be. It cast such a long, sick shadow.

"All the more reason to ask her," Fran said. But she didn't really think Zac would get anything out of Liz. She didn't really think he would ask the question. It was down to Fran. It was always going to be, because it was her question too.

"I'm going to see what I can find out," she said.

"How?" Zac asked. "Find out from who?" And then, after a very long silence, he said, "You're going to talk to Picota?"

"Yes."

"You still think all of this is connected?"

"Yes. And you still don't see how it can be."

"No. Of course not."

"Then why come to me, Zac?"

He shook his head slowly, as though the logic of it escaped him. "I just felt like I had to tell you," he said, his voice only just above a mumble. "Because you tried to warn me, and I hurt you. I felt like I owed you the truth."

Lady Jinx trotted out of the darkness again and jumped up onto the platform. She looked from Fran to Zac, then back again without a word.

"You don't owe me anything," Fran said.

"Not even an apology?"

"No. You gave me that, and I accepted it. Remember?"

"But I . . . I'd like us to be—"

"We're good," Fran said. "Don't sweat it."

She turned on her heel and walked away. It must have seemed pretty abrupt, even rude, but she didn't want Zac to see that she'd started crying. He looked so sad, and so bewildered, and however this came out it wasn't going to make him any happier. The best she could hope to find in Grove City was an explanation—or a clue that would lead her to an explanation. It wouldn't be some kind of magic medicine that would change Liz Kendall back to the way she was before.

But Fran had to hope that the magic medicine existed. Because she and Liz were linked by something that nobody but she and Bruno Picota could see. Liz was her future.

And if that was how she was going to end up, maybe Bruno had been right after all.

Maybe she *was* a skadegamutc.

Liz was a silent witness to this meeting, standing in the densest of the sumac thickets as though she was something shameful and unnatural that had to hide from the light. She was completely invisible, but that was still a queasy novelty to her.

Tonight, when Zac left the house, she had followed him to the desolate, unfinished railway siding behind Lenora Street, and she had waited with him on the bare concrete platform until Fran Watts arrived. She had no idea until she came who it was he was waiting for, but she was pleased to see the girl. It perplexed her that Fran seemed to have slipped out of Zac's life. They had seemed to be such fast friends, and so good for each other.

But Fran didn't come alone. There was a small dog loping along at her side. A dog, or else . . .

It was a fox. A very strange fox with a long, slender body and an impossibly luxuriant brush. In her amazement, Liz shifted all her attention from the girl to the animal. Which was when something even weirder happened.

The fox checked and sat up on its haunches. It looked straight toward Liz, its ears pricking up. The girl noticed this too, and stopped in her tracks to talk to the fox, bending a little to bring herself down to its level.

That first direct glance seemed to have been a fluke. The fox looked around in all directions, almost comically quizzical. If it was aware of Liz's presence, the awareness seemed to be based on something other than actually seeing her.

Fran and the fox continued on together. Zac greeted the girl and ignored the animal, whose existence he didn't seem to suspect. Liz tried to ignore it too, since it seemed to have become aware of her existence when she first looked at it and thought about it.

But as she drifted closer so she could listen in on the conversation, the fox tugged at her attention more and more. From this close up, it was a very strange creature indeed, its features simplified and exaggerated in the manner of a children's cartoon. The texture of its fur was odd too, seeming mostly to be a single block of color across which narrow chevrons moved to simulate the effect of fur rippling in the wind. Except that the wind in this narrow, manmade gulley blew resolutely from west to east: the chevrons just did their own thing at random intervals.

Once Zac and Fran started to talk, though, Liz forgot the anomalous animal altogether. They were talking about Beth. Zac had noticed she was acting strangely, and he had news that was more recent than anything Liz had seen herself.

Then she heard the thing that twisted her thoughts into tangles of terror and despair. "I think she's hitting Molly."

It was too much to bear. It was like a weight placed on her soul, so heavy that it bent in two. It reduced Liz's floating consciousness, for long moments, to a rolling boil of anguish and confusion.

Caught up in that crisis, she lowered her guard. She didn't register the fox's movement until after it jumped. In an instant, it had passed right through her.

Fleeting though it was, the contact jarred Liz to the core. If she had a mouth and a voice, she would have gasped or screamed. She hadn't felt pain or any other physical sensation since the night she had been locked out of her body. And what she felt now wasn't pain exactly: it was a discharge of energy, like the static charge that shot into your fingers sometimes when you touched your car's door handle on a warm day.

The fox seemed taken aback too. It landed awkwardly, its outlines blurring for a moment. Before it could collect itself, Liz recoiled, pure instinct carrying her backward more quickly than she would have thought possible. From the platform into the bushes, then through them and through the fence behind into the back yard of a house, past a swing set and some rose bushes from which the flowers had fallen long before, in among thorns and weeds and broken, discarded plant pots.

To her horror, the fox was now coming after her. Its eyes glowed amber in the dark like cat's eyes on the interstate. Its jaw was gaping, its long pink tongue hanging down to taste the air.

Liz sank down into the damp and cluttered undergrowth and stayed very still. She didn't think the fox could bite her, but it had hurt her just by touching her. It might look like a cartoon but she was sure it represented an actual threat.

Fortunately, it seemed to have lost track of her again. It padded back and forth along the flower beds a few times, then sat still at the edge of the lawn, its narrow face ranging from left to right and back again.

Finally, it gave up and loped off in the direction from which it had come, back through the fence toward the railway line. Liz stayed where she was for a long time after that, only coming out at last when Zac—alone now—emerged from the bushes into the alley on the north side of Lenora.

She hovered in the air, irresolute. Her first instinct was to stay with Zac as long as she could. To walk beside him as far as the front door of the house, then turn away and wait for morning.

But what about Fran Watts and her animal familiar?

Fran could see the fox, and the fox had been able to see Liz. There was a chain that led from Liz all the way back into the real world. But the fox had attacked her on sight. Could she possibly tame it? Make it accept her? How did you pacify a ghost animal, or win its trust?

And what was Fran, if ghost animals consorted with her?

Wrestling with wild speculations, she slowed to a halt. She would lose Zac in any case once he got home and stepped inside. Perhaps she could do more if she stayed with the girl and her phantom guardian.

She turned and went in the opposite direction, back through the fence onto the railway line. The two retreating figures were still just about in sight. Accelerating to her pathetic top speed of about three miles an hour, Liz followed them.

Lady Jinx knew very well that she and Fran were being followed.

When she had seen the weird little thing, the turbulence in the air, the almost nothing, she had been only a little curious. But when it looked back at her, she was on the alert at once.

And she had pounced on it, because an almost-nothing hiding in the dark was sure to be up to no good. It probably wanted to hurt Fran. Anything that tried to hurt Fran would end up in Jinx's jaws or on the end of Jinx's sword. That was what Jinx was for.

But when she jumped, the almost-nothing ran away and hid. The scent of it was still strong, but it was hard for Jinx to tell which direction it had taken. There had been a moment when her teeth had all but closed in on the thing, when she could have dragged it down and bitten it until it stopped moving. Then, almost immediately, it was gone.

Frustrated and out of temper, she returned to the railway plat-form where Fran and the boy were still talking. She licked her front paw and pretended nothing had happened while she thought the whole incident through.

Fran would want to know about it for sure, but Jinx was afraid of what Fran would do if she found out. She seemed addicted to risk these days: telling her secrets to a stupid boy, going back to that terrible place and now talking about meeting . . . *him*. She was already putting herself in terrible danger. And now she was being tracked by an almost-nothing that came out at night and hid in the dark.

Jinx had sworn her oath and she knew her duties. Sometimes you protected people with your sharp, sharp teeth, but sometimes you did it by not opening your mouth in the first place. She decided to say nothing. If Fran asked her why she had run off into the dark, she would say she had been chasing birds, or bats, or fireflies.

But Fran was still engrossed in silly nonsense talk with Zac Kendall, and she didn't even seem to have noticed that Jinx had been away. Jinx felt a pang of unhappiness and resentment at that. Who *was* Zac Kendall anyway? Had he sat by Fran's bed every night, guarding her against her own past? Had he tracked down the scary memories nesting in her mind and eaten them whole before they could hurt her? Had he pledged his sword and his heart to her the way Jinx had?

No. He hadn't. He probably didn't even *have* a sword.

The conversation seemed to go on forever, but eventually it wound down.

"You don't owe me anything."

"Not even an apology?"

"No. You gave me that, and I accepted it. Remember?"

"But I . . . I'd like us to be—"

"We're good. Don't sweat it."

Fran turned and left. At last! Jinx went with her, giving Zac Kendall an insulting wiggle of her hind quarters as she stalked away. Ha ha ha! He didn't even know she'd mooned him.

There wasn't much to laugh about, though. Fran wasn't happy about the stuff Zac had told her, and Jinx wasn't happy because all of this was dangerous and stupid and the exact opposite of what Fran should do. They walked along in silence. Fran had her hands jammed into her pockets and her head down against the cold: in solidarity, Jinx leaned hard into the wind she didn't feel.

Then she realized with a thrill of indignation and excitement that the scent from the railway platform was in her mind again. Just a fugitive whiff of it, coming and going at the limit of her perception. The almost-nothing was creeping along behind them, keeping its distance and hoping not to be noticed. She didn't know Lady Jinx!

But Jinx had to be clever. The thing was so close to being nothing that it could hide very easily. If Jinx turned and attacked, she would probably fare no better than last time. She had to trap her enemy, and she knew the way to do it.

She slackened her pace, falling behind Fran little by little. Fran was so wrapped up in her thoughts that she didn't notice. The almost-nothing probably did, but it had no choice. It had to slow down too, or else it would soon come within reach of Jinx's strong jaws.

Now came the trick. Jinx hunched up her shoulders and lowered her head, her huge brush waving behind her like a hypnotist's pocket watch.

First you step, then you slide, back to front and side to side. Her practiced paws came down exactly where they needed to, advancing by gradual degrees into the un-places she had explored as a cub, so many years before.

The almost-nothing followed, not knowing that it was being led astray. The world was falling away one small detail at a time, and if you didn't know what was happening it was easy to miss it. Everything that was lost was replaced by a gray haze that was neither light nor dark.

Ha ha ha!

Jinx sped up again, breaking into a rapid trot. And now the almost-nothing followed because it had to. Because there wasn't anything else here but the two of them, and if she lost sight of Jinx she would be left alone in the gray.

Which was closing in on all sides.

Jinx broke into a dash. The almost-nothing sped along in her wake. It must be desperate now, realizing how Jinx had tricked it but knowing that Jinx was now its only hope. If it got lost here, it might stay lost forever. Perhaps it thought that Jinx was deliberately trying to shake it off. Nothing could be further from the truth. Up ahead of them in this no-place, there was a place that Jinx had hollowed out with her paws and her furious will.

She dived into it now, and the almost-nothing arrived close behind her. When it came, Jinx was waiting. Her front paw came down on it and pinned it in place. They were in her den now, and her rules were the only ones that mattered. In the real world, she had jumped right through the almost-nothing as if it wasn't there at all. Here, if she wanted it to be solid, it would be solid.

She couldn't make it show its face, though. It was still only a squidgy mass, almost invisible to the eye, but pungent and obvious to Jinx's other senses.

Oh good, she growled. *Just when I was starting to feel hungry.*

Don't! the almost-nothing cried. *Please don't! I'm not your enemy!*

No, you're not. You're my dinner.

Oh God! Listen to me, I . . . I'm Liz Kendall! I'm Zac's mom!

Don't lie. I've seen her. You're too small to be her.

This is . . . part of me. What was left after she—

Don't tell me. I don't care. Zac's mom is a monster.

The other one is a monster. I'm the real Liz Kendall. Her name is Beth. She stole my body and she won't let me back in!

Jinx squeezed harder, and the almost-nothing spasmed in pain. *You're not fooling me,* Jinx told it coldly. *Nobody fools me. I won't let you get close to her.*

To . . .?

Fran. You won't hurt her. Not while I'm here.

I don't want to hurt her. I just want to get my life back!

Jinx snuffled contemptuously. *Why should I care about that even if I believed you? You and the other one are both the same to me.*

The almost-nothing didn't like that. It squirmed under Jinx's paw, but couldn't get free.

All right, it said at last. *Just let me go please. And I won't go near Fran again. I promise.*

You promise? Jinx gave a cold laugh. *Why would I believe anything you say? You won't go near Fran again because you'll be here, forever and ever. Or until I eat you.*

She took her paw off the thing, but at the same time she swatted it across the den with her other paw, so it sank into the soft walls and was stuck there.

By the time it struggled free, Jinx was gone. She heard its scream as she trotted quickly away.

You mad little bitch! Let me go let me go let me

That takes care of you, Jinx muttered smugly. *Monster.*

"I'm really sorry to bother you," the cheerful man said.

He was standing at Beth's table, leaning right in, showing her a state of Pennsylvania private investigator's license in the name of Arthur Vance. Showing, too, no inclination at all to move.

Vance didn't look the way a private detective was meant to look. He had the uncanny cleanliness of a Mormon door-knocker, white shirt and gaudy tie included. He wasn't wearing the backpack, but he was sure as hell wearing the smile. And carrying a venti cup of coffee, as though he was daring Beth not to invite him to sit down.

Her co-workers were looking on with undisguised fascination. The food court in the middle of the morning was less than half-full, and most of the people on the tables closest to Beth were people she knew. People she had to work with. Maybe Arthur Vance was relying on that fact to keep her tractable and quiet while he asked his questions. If so, he was on the lower slopes of a steep learning curve.

"What's this about?" she demanded. "I'm on my break here."

Which was stating the obvious, but then again it was a sore point. Beth had almost decided not to bother going in that day. She was on a half-shift, which meant hauling her ass across to

Bakery Square for the pleasure of spending four hours vacuuming carpets and unblocking toilets. There was still some slack in the credit cards, and the dark clouds had a lock on the sky that made staying indoors and firing up a blunt seem like a great idea.

But she had done the responsible thing, and this was her reward. This smirking apparition jumping right up in her face, all sandy hair and freckles and perfect teeth.

"You'll be doing me a huge favor, Ms. Kendall," he said, "but if this isn't convenient . . ."

The people all around were still half-swiveled in their seats to face in Beth's direction, their curiosity pinning their good manners to the mat. Whatever she said was going to have an enthusiastic audience. But she needed to know what this bullshit was all about, and sooner was better than later.

"Sure," she said. "Whatever. Sit down, why don't you? But I've only got ten minutes."

Vance thanked her kindly and sat down with alacrity. Leaving his coffee untouched, like a prop that had served its purpose, he set out his stall.

"I've been engaged by Ms. Jamie Langdon to find her former partner and your ex-husband, Marc Kendall. She believes he may have met with some kind of foul play. That he could have been murdered or abducted. She wants me to get to the truth in any case, and to tell her whether he's alive or dead."

Vance's tone was irritatingly patronizing, as though he was explaining all this to a child. Beth felt like she had to push back a little, just for the sake of her self-respect.

"Most people think he just ran out on his bail bond," she said. "You know, rather than go to jail."

"Ms. Langdon is well aware of that possibility. And she understands why the police consider it to be the most likely scenario."

"But she doesn't buy it."

"No, she does not. And she's of the opinion that the official investigation—since it started from that assumption—has failed to thoroughly explore other avenues."

Such as that Marc is now fertilizer in his own garden plot, Beth thought.

"I don't think I can help you, Mr. Vance," she told him. "I don't believe my ex-husband got croaked or kidnapped. I just think he's in hiding."

"May I ask if he's been in touch with you?"

"No. I would have told the police if he had."

"And he hasn't contacted Ms. Langdon either. Or anyone else in his family who she's spoken to."

Beth felt a sudden, cold shiver of anger. Jamie was way too free and easy about strolling into other people's lives. "She got in touch with Marc's mother?"

"And his step-sister. And some gentlemen he used to drink with over in East Liberty. Fellow entrepreneurs."

Beth gave a short laugh. She just couldn't keep it in. "Entrepreneurs? That's a polite word for what Marc was." She caught herself on that last word, the suggestive use of the past continuous, but decided to let it lie rather than draw attention to it by correcting herself.

"Honestly, I don't have an opinion on that," Vance said, holding up his hand like he was bearing witness to God. "You and Mr. Kendall had your disagreements, obviously. But he belongs to a community, of sorts, and Ms. Langdon thinks it's significant—telling, even—that he hasn't made contact with anyone in that community. Or anyone at all, for that matter. When you skip bail it's sensible to lie low, but it's unusual for an absconder to cut himself off from every aspect of his former life. I mean, you'd expect him to reach out to his mother just to reassure her that he was still okay. Ms. Langdon too, arguably, especially as his failure to deliver himself to the court put her in severe financial difficulties."

"She still had enough money put by to hire you," Beth observed sourly.

Vance gave her a Mormon smile. "Actually, they're all throwing in together. Ms. Langdon, Mrs. Kendall senior, Marc's sister Vera. They've agreed to split my fee into equal thirds. That is unless you'd like to come in too, in which case you'd have full access to anything I—"

"No."

"Anything I find out, I was going to say."

"Absolutely not. I can't afford even a quarter of you."

Another smile. "No problem. I get paid either way, obviously, so it's not an issue for me. I just thought there might be some advantage in the arrangement for you, since you'd get the services of a professional investigator at a fraction of the cost you'd normally expect to pay."

"The cost I'm expecting to pay is nothing," Beth said. "Can you give me a discount on that?"

Vance laughed heartily. "No, that's too hard a bargain for me. You win." He got serious suddenly, the way con artists do when they want to throw you a curveball. "I wonder if you have any ideas, though, where your ex-husband might have gone to ground? I mean, if the police are right and he's just keeping his head down rather than face trial. Are there any places you went to together that he might have an attachment to? Or any friends I might not know about who he could be staying with?"

"Sorry," Beth said. "I don't think there's anything I can add to what you already know."

"No? Well, that's a pity." Vance finally took a sip of his coffee, drawing it out to cover the pause—which was made all the more obvious by the lack of any other conversations in their immediate vicinity. It was another con man trick, leaving a hole in the conversation in the hope that she'd feel a need to fill it. Beth just worked on her meatball sandwich until he was finally forced to start up again.

"How did your ex-husband seem to you the last time you saw him?" he asked. "Happy? Unhappy?"

Dead. Covered in his own blood for once, instead of mine. It looked good on him, I've got to say.

"The last time I saw him was at the courthouse when I got an injunction requiring him to stay the hell away from me."

"Sorry, I meant to say the last time you spoke to him."

Had Liz and Marc talked at the courthouse? Beth didn't think so, but she couldn't be sure. Liz had fended her off pretty effectively that day, and she hadn't been able to stick around for the whole show. She took a punt. "That would have been the night he attacked me," she said. "The night he was arrested."

Vance's brow furrowed just a little. "Are you sure?" he asked.

"Of course I'm sure."

"Only, the reason I ask is you made a complaint to the police a few days prior to Marc's disappearance. About a stalker. A guy who was pranking your car and turning up at your house when you weren't there."

Beth gave the man a blank stare. "Yes. So?"

"So didn't you think that might have been your ex-husband?"

Beth hesitated. The phone calls between Marc and Liz . . . those had all been on the disposable burner Marc had bought, surely? And the burner was still in the back of her closet along with Marc's regular cell, next to their batteries which she'd taken out and dumped in a Ziploc bag. Vance was just fishing without any bait on his hook.

"It crossed my mind," she said.

"What do you think now? You reckon it was him?"

"I have no idea."

"Because, you know, the night he disappeared he didn't take his car. And it was a cold night. He was going someplace that was close."

"Or maybe he took a cab."

"Maybe. But I don't think so. No cabbie remembers taking him, and the phone records I got from his network provider don't have him calling a cab. He would have had to hail one on the street, which, you know, in Larimer after midnight . . ."

He left another pause, but Beth was done with speculating. "He didn't come anywhere near my house," she said.

"That's weird. Because he definitely set off in that direction."

It wasn't hard to keep her face straight. If Vance had anything solid he would have led with it. You only threw out a teaser if you were looking to get a reaction. She didn't give him one. "Really?" was all she said.

"Really. We've got him on CCTV footage, heading east on Lincoln. That would have taken him round your neck of the woods, wouldn't it?"

"It would have taken him a lot of places," Beth said. "Including the Allegheny River. It's a pretty long road." She took another bite out of her sandwich, dumped the rest and wiped her fingers.

"That it is," Vance said with a chuckle. "But we have him walking, like I said. So it's not likely he went all that far. I'm thinking your house holds up pretty well as a possible destination."

"I never saw him," Beth repeated. "Not that night. If I had, I would have told the police at the time. If he was heading my way, maybe he was trying to get a glimpse of the kids. If he was about to skip town, it would have been the last time he saw them in a while."

Vance mulled this one over, tilting his head one way and then the other. "I can see that," he said. "It was pretty late, though. After midnight. Doesn't seem likely the kids would still have been up. Were they?"

Beth blinked. The memory of Molly standing in the bloody kitchen had just come back to her very vividly. "No. Of course not."

"Sorry." The detective rotated his coffee cup idly, using just the tips of his fingers. "I wasn't trying to imply anything about your parenting, just asking for clarity's sake. Returning to the substantive point, if Marc had been leaving town I'd expect to see some signs of planning. Preparation. He left his toothbrush and his electric shaver behind. His phone charger. He didn't even pack a change of underwear."

"I'm not an expert on the state of his underwear. You'd have to ask Jamie Langdon about that." Beth stood. She felt she'd heard as much as she needed to. "I need to get back to work," she said.

"Of course." Vance pushed the coffee cup away and got to his feet. "I'm really grateful to you for taking the time to talk to me. Can I drop by again if I turn up anything interesting?"

Beth just wanted rid of him now. "If it's interesting, I assume you'll tell the police. I'll find out through them."

"Are those my marching orders, Ms. Kendall?"

Enough was enough, she suddenly decided. "Healey," she snapped.

"I'm sorry?"

"I'm taking back my maiden name. Ms. Elizabeth Healey. Fuck knows, it took me long enough to get there."

"Touched a nerve," Vance said, breaking out a smile that was even wider than the ones he'd displayed before. "I am genuinely sorry. Just so you know, I'm not on anyone's side in this. Certainly not your ex-husband's. I work to a brief, that's all."

"I'm sure," Beth said.

"Good day to you, Ms. Healey. I can get down to the street if I just keep going straight, right? Thanks again for all your help. It's very much appreciated."

And he was gone, leaving Beth with the unpleasant sense of shock you get when someone jostles you on the sidewalk and keeps on going without any apology or acknowledgment, as if you weren't even there. The women on the surrounding tables were watching her openly now, some of them talking in low murmurs— probably discussing the highlights of what had just happened. Beth was about to say something about the matinee being over, but one of the women, Alice Folger, gave her a thumbs-up and a nod of respect. Some of them—maybe all of them—were on her side in this. The goodwill of a bunch of minimum-wagers maybe didn't mean a whole lot, but it was better to have it than not. Especially if the Mormons came back in force.

For the rest of her shift, she was serving chili dogs and cheese fries at one of the snack food stations. A welcome step up from cleaning, but Jesus! What did that say about her life? She'd had ambitions once. Now here she was about half a notch above the street, living day-to-day and hand-to-mouth and never looking even an inch over the horizon.

What was wrong with this picture?

Partly, she knew, the frustration was just a reaction to Vance showing up and rubbing her nose in her own mistakes. She was still brooding about it when she clocked off at the end of her shift and drove home.

Except she didn't go there straight away. She was suddenly filled with a sense of claustrophobia at the thought of spending another evening trapped in the same narrow space with two people who, although she had been with them every moment of their lives and knew every inch of their skin, were still total strangers to her.

She had read online, in a not-so-idle moment, a sensationalistic article about a mental illness called Capgras delusion. Sufferers became convinced that their loved ones were impostors, that some hideous substitution had been carried out while they slept so they woke up surrounded by strangers disguised as spouses, lovers, parents, children.

Beth had enough objectivity to self-diagnose. What she was feeling now was like Capgras except that it wasn't a delusion—because Zac and Molly both were and weren't her kids. She had been able to make herself believe the disconnect wouldn't matter, that she could love them just as much as the children she had lost. But that plan had unraveled, leaving her at first indifferent to the Liz-variant Zac and the Liz-variant Molly and then, increasingly, revolted and unnerved by them.

But she had managed to hide her ambivalence, at least most of the time. Yeah, there was that one time when she'd pushed Molly and sent her sprawling, but she'd been careful not to let that happen again. She wasn't a violent sadist like Marc. She didn't revel in other people's pain and humiliation, especially if they were helpless. She just freaked out a little, sometimes, if the fake kids came too suddenly and unexpectedly into her space. And after her encounter with Vance the private dick, she really didn't need that shit right now.

Yielding to a sudden impulse, she took a right onto Stanton and drove up to the Full Pint Wild Side. She and Marc had drunk there a few times in their first few months at the city. Before things went bad. Beth wasn't going for the nostalgia, though: it was just far enough from her usual haunts that she wouldn't be recognized there. She went inside and ordered a screwdriver: a double, with Greenhook gin and freshly squeezed juice.

She sat in a booth in a quiet corner of the room and stared at the drink for a long time while recent events replayed on a loop behind her eyes. Tense as hell, her nerves jangling like tiny bells, she set her parted lips to the glass. Tilted it up, so the alcohol washed against the tip of her tongue.

She drank the whole thing in a couple of swallows. When the bartender brought her a bowl of peanuts, she ordered another double and drank it more slowly, pondering. Was Vance nothing, or were the chickens coming home? What was the worst that could happen here?

If Jamie kept poking away at Marc's disappearance, she could easily end up convincing the police there was something worth investigating. They wouldn't find the garden plot. Nobody knew about that. All the same, Beth thought, it would be nice if she could think of a way to nip this whole thing in the bud.

She glared at her drink, waiting for a workable idea to arrive. But to count as workable, the idea had to do two things. It had to give some weight to the theory that Marc was still alive, and it had to make Jamie lose her appetite for the chase so she called off her Mormon.

Pretty tall order. She sat there a long time and nothing came— except for a man in a Led Zeppelin T-shirt, shaven-headed and extensively tattooed, who tried to hit on her. Another time she would have gone for it. The guy was perfectly okay for a little afternoon delight, if nothing else. When it came to really casual sex, you had to relax your standards a little: the best was the enemy of the good.

But right then she had other things on her mind.

"Surely a lovely lady like you isn't drinking alone?" was Mr. Zeppelin's opening line.

"You see anyone else?"

"Nope."

"Then your eyes are working just fine. And mine are too, so you're out of fucking luck."

The man flushed red, with embarrassment or anger. "There's no need to be like that," he said in a tight voice. He retreated back to the bar, where he'd been sitting by himself.

Men and their damn appetites. They just didn't know how to turn it off.

A thought came to her suddenly, out of nowhere—or at least the leading edge of a thought. It had the merit of simplicity, and it ought to leave Jamie with much less enthusiasm for picking up Marc's trail. Since she insisted on leading with her chin, it would feel pretty good to smack her in the face, and it would hurt her all the more because it would seem to come out of kindness rather than cruelty.

She had it coming.

When Beth got home, she went to the closet and got out Marc's phone. Not the burner, his regular phone. She attached a charger and poured herself a glass of pinot while it warmed itself up after its weeks of hibernation.

As soon as the screen lit up, she tried Marc's old security swipe—a capital M, starting at lower left and ending at bottom right. If he had changed it, this idea would be a non-starter and she would have to think of something else. But it worked just fine.

She typed slowly and carefully, fortifying herself with occasional sips of the rich red wine.

Hey, Jags. This is me. Apologizing for once in my life. I should have gotten in touch sooner, but the truth is I was kind of ashamed to. I let you down, I know, and I left you in a bad situation with the bail bond and everything. I wish I could have figured out some other way, but I couldn't. I've been seeing this girl for a few months now. I met her one night when you were at your evening class. We got talking, and we were just on the same wavelength. I'm not going to tell you her name, because I don't want you to come looking for me. You'd be wasting your time in any case. I'm a long way away from anywhere you'd be likely to look. Anyway, it seemed to me like if I didn't leave when I did I might never leave at all. This way you don't have to wait for me to get out of jail only to find that I'm with someone else. It's better for both of us, I hope you see that. Goodbye and good luck, babe, and thanks for everything. I won't forget you. Marc

When she was finished she read it through three times from beginning to end. It read pretty well, she thought, but it wasn't perfect. Or maybe it was, and that was the problem. She took another pass, adding in a few typos of the sort that people were liable to make when their fingers were moving quickly across a tiny virtual keyboard.

Then she hit SEND, because there was no point in overthinking it. Jamie wasn't a mastermind: she was a scrawny little rabbit who'd poked the wrong bear.

There was only one way to get the Grove City visit back on the agenda. Fran had to come clean to her dad.

She picked her moment: a Friday night after homemade chili and an episode of *Stranger Things*. She told him everything, or at least the portion of everything that she could actually explain. The part about trying to come to terms with her fear, first by visiting the abandoned hulk of the motel, then by reading the transcripts from Bruno Picota's trial and now by going to see him in person. "If that's okay, Dad. If you let me go."

Gil's face went through many degrees of unhappiness while she was talking. His first questions were logistical ones. How long ago did all this start? How many times had she been back to the Perry Friendly? When had she spoken to Dr. Southern?

She could see that what hurt him more than anything was that she hadn't told him. That she had carried this for so long without asking him to help. Fran tried to explain that he *had* helped, always, just by being there and by loving her. If she hadn't told him, that was mainly because she hadn't felt right about demanding more from him when he had already done so much. She wouldn't have been able to do this sprint by herself if the two of them hadn't run a marathon together.

Gil made the right noises to all of this, but it was only about a half of the truth and he knew what the other half was. She hadn't trusted him to give his consent to things that would put her in danger, and she had chosen the easiest way around that problem when she decided not to tell him.

He didn't say any of that, though. He didn't reproach her by so much as a word. "If you think this will help, Frog, then I'm all for it. But I'm not sending you up to Grove City by yourself."

"Dr. Southern will come," Fran told him. She assumed he would, anyway. She couldn't see him missing out on something like this. His current patient and his former one, face-to-face: the match of the century! The insurance wouldn't cover it but somehow she didn't doubt that he would find a way to be there.

"Fine. But I'm coming too," Gil said.

"Okay."

"But you're sure, Fran? This is something you want to do? Not something Southern dreamed up to justify his fee?"

"I'm sure, Dad. It wasn't his idea—it was mine."

"Good for you," Gil said with a sad smile. The smile said he'd raised her well and maybe wished he hadn't. "I'm coming along," he repeated. "No arguments."

Fran didn't offer any. She emailed Dr. Southern before she went to bed to tell him that the trip was on after all. *I mean, if I haven't already missed it. If they didn't take back the offer.* She added that her dad was coming with her, and that he would need at least three days' notice so he could get the time off work. She said she was sorry if she'd dicked him around, and she thanked him in advance for making all the arrangements.

Remember to bring plenty of donuts, Jinx said scathingly.

"Don't be mean," Fran scolded her.

The reply came almost at once. Dr. Southern must be monitoring his clinic emails from home. *Okay*, he wrote. *I'll see what I can do. Back at you soon.*

Fran met up with Zac in the library the next day and brought him up to speed. Right away he offered to come up to Grove City with her. That made her sad because it had been her plan way back when she'd first asked Dr. Southern to set this up. But things between them had changed too much. Even though he needed the answers almost as much as she did, she didn't want him to be there when she asked the questions. They had started the quest together, but she would finish it by herself.

"My dad's going to be there," she told him by way of shorthand. "He doesn't really approve of me seeing you anymore."

"I wish you approved," Zac said. "And I wish you believed me when I said I was sorry."

"How many times did your dad tell your mom he was sorry, Zac?"

His face filled with hurt. "That's not fair."

And it really wasn't. Fran knew that. But she couldn't make herself feel differently than she did. "I'll see you when I get back," she said. "I promise I'll tell you everything I find out."

When she got home from school there was a second email from Dr. S. *They can do Saturday. 1:00 p.m. Seems like that might be okay. You don't have to miss school, and it's probably more convenient for your dad too. Let me know.*

"Works for me," Gil said.

So they were on. Too late to go back now, even if she wanted to.

That thought brought another one: she wanted to so badly.

After only an hour or so in the fox's den, Liz lost all track of time.

Desperation made every minute seem endless. She was agonizingly aware that every moment she spent here left her children at the mercy of a monster. And she knew better than anyone what the monster was capable of.

Looked at another way, the time seemed weirdly suspended. There was no sun here, no day or night to measure by. There was nothing that changed or could change. She could have been there for years, or just a few heartbeats. There was no way of knowing.

This was a terrible place. Oppressive and claustrophobic, even though it had no walls. When she tried to leave, the inexplicable gray stuff that the den was made of pushed back against her, gradually becoming denser and harder until she was forced to give up. There must be a doorway somewhere through which she and the fox had entered, but tracing the walls revealed no obvious breaks.

Liz wondered if this gray endlessness had anything in common with the colorless void where she had met Beth. But that place had been inside her own mind, while this was . . . somewhere else. In the fox's mind, perhaps. That might be why she and Beth had had a presence in that other place, visible face and form, while here she was nothing at all until the fox wanted to lay its paws on her, when she suddenly had just enough substance to make her vulnerable.

Dealer's choice. It seemed that whoever lived in these scary hinterlands got to decide how they worked. It was all a matter of will power. But will power had always been Liz's problem. Even when she had still been in her own body, she had drifted along for years as if the world could push at her but it wasn't her place to push back. If she ever got out of here, she would do everything in her power to change that.

In the meantime, she filed the thought away and made another circuit of the walls, hoping to find the exit that had eluded her the first time around. It was easy to believe that she had been led astray. The topography of the place was so strange that anything was possible. How could you stick to a straight line when everything was the same monotone gray and wasn't even there until you touched it?

She didn't find the door, but she did find . . . pictures. There was no other word Liz could use, although *pictures* didn't seem to cover it. Woven into the fabric of the den there were hundreds of still-life tableaux: everyday scenes for the most part, including some of places Liz actually knew. A children's playground in Highland Park; a street corner on Larimer Avenue; the Costco on Meadow Street.

The things were fascinating, and very hard to look away from. The colors seemed shockingly brilliant in this monochrome place, and it warmed Liz just to see familiar, normal things again. It was hard to tell what exactly these images were, or how they had been formed. In places they seemed to have the detail and accuracy of a photograph, but it was mainly the figures in the foreground who showed up in this way. The backgrounds blurred quickly into abstract collages of shape and color.

As Liz looked at them, the figures started to move.

Mesmerized, she drifted in closer. Wasn't that the schoolyard at Julian C. Barry? It certainly seemed to be. Kids were milling around the way they did at recess, forming knots and clusters and then drifting apart again. A froth of voices rose around her. A shout. A snatch of song, slightly off-key, the tune one she had never heard and instantly forgot again.

Abruptly and without warning, Liz was transported. She lay on her stomach on hard asphalt. The heels of her hands throbbed as though they were on fire. Mocking laughter sounded from all around her in different timbres.

It hurt her, that laughter—more than the ache in her hands, or in her hip which was throbbing too. She hated it and she was afraid of it, because it meant that they (Which *they*? Who were *they*?) were only getting started. Fear rose up in the front of her mind, dense and cloying. She knew the drill, and she had no expectations that anyone would help her out of this.

"How'd you like that, bitch?" a girl's voice shouted.

"She's not a bitch," someone else said with gleeful spite. "You've got to have something going on to be a bitch. She's just a freak!"

Liz tried to roll over so she could get back up onto her feet. Nothing happened. She had a body again, somehow, but she was forced to accept that it wasn't hers. It wouldn't do the things she asked it to. Even the basic things.

And as she pulled on the puppet strings of its nerves, and as they refused to respond, she was shaken free. Back to the dank, pervasive grayness of the fox's den.

She fled.

That had been real, a real moment that someone else had lived, and however it had come to be here there was something obscene and wrong about her going into it and reliving it (leaving aside the question of how that was even possible!). There was no way she was going to do it again.

She stuck to that resolve for a very long time (it felt long; again, there was no way of knowing). Finally, though, when the sheer emptiness and the knowledge of how helpless she was threatened to overwhelm her, she sneaked back to the pictures and looked again. She was ashamed, but she had to escape from this place, even if it was only for a few seconds.

371

Choosing at random, she found herself peering into a room. There was a window that looked out onto a tiny yard. Four flower boxes evenly spaced along the edge of a cement-floored patio. The side of another house and the uprights of a kids' swing set. It was a sunny day. The sunlight shining through the open curtains was what drew her, and then—as her other senses started to engage— the sound of birdsong.

It happened again, just like before. Without any transition, she was inside the picture. Inside the room. The heavy, sour reek took her by surprise: a smell of sweat and vomit cut with the astringency of disinfectant.

The eyes she was looking through now had no interest in the sunlight outside the window. They were looking at a single bed, and at a woman lying in the bed. The woman had brown skin like burnt parchment. It was a face she knew well and loved more than any other. She felt those things, strongly and undeniably. At the same time, the woman was a complete stranger. Liz had never met her and had no feelings about her at all. The feelings belonged to someone else.

The woman was struggling to talk. It was clear that she was very weak, that the effort was exhausting her. And it was wasted in any case, because her voice was so thick and silted up with sickness that the words were unintelligible. The woman's claw-like hand was much more eloquent, squeezing Liz's hand tightly, holding on to that contact as the world folded itself down to this moment and this room.

And then it was over. The woman's eyes didn't close and her grip was still tight, but she was very obviously dead. It was as though a door had slammed shut. One moment she was there, and the next . . . nothing Where there had been something, where there had been so much, nothing. And Liz sank to her knees, reduced to nothing herself, crying out wordlessly.

But the sound meant *Stay with me! Stay with me! Don't be gone!*

Numbed, Liz fell out of the vision and into herself. Grief pulled her down, paralyzed her for long moments. She felt its rounded outline within herself like a new planet with its own gravity.

Why did I love you? Why am I lost without you? What am I now?

Those were all, every one of them, the wrong questions. It hadn't been her in that room; it had been somebody else. A child, she thought. The woman's hand had enclosed hers easily, and she had felt what it was like to be enclosed, to be small and safe and wrapped up in that warm, endless presence.

She had no lips or tongue, no mouth, but a word shaped itself within her. *Mommy.*

She should have stopped right there. There was no excuse for going on except that she was an exile from her own body, tethered to nothing and terrified of dissipating altogether like an exhaled breath. These grim, indelible tableaux, as she relived them, gave her the precious illusion of weight and substance.

But they *were* grim. There wasn't a single happy moment in the entire gallery. Everything here was of a piece, a torture chamber of humiliations, fears, accidents, defeats and disappointments, betrayals, injuries, disasters natural and otherwise.

Either the fox had found these stolen, human memories here and built this part of its den around them or else it had purposefully brought them from somewhere else.

In which case the relevant question had to be: what did it use them for?

On Saturday they set off early. Gil was driving, and he had told
Dr. Southern to be at the house for 9:30 a.m. By 9:35 they were
on the road. Fran rode shotgun, while Dr. Southern sat alone in
the back.

There was no small talk in the car. Dr. Southern essayed some
observations on the Steelers' front lineup, but Gil wasn't in the
mood and his responses were monosyllabic. After the first few miles,
Fran asked if she could turn the radio on. She found a soft rock
channel, and it stayed on for the rest of the journey.

Fran had been afraid that Lady Jinx wouldn't come, given how
strongly she disapproved of this expedition. She certainly wasn't
with them when they started out. But a few miles along the road,
Fran saw her out of the corner of her eye, sitting in the back seat
next to Dr. S. She was wearing a sullen scowl and making a big
show of being wedged into a corner by Southern's bulk.

It's like sitting next to a big enormous pig, she growled. *And he just
farted, so he even smells like one.*

Grove City turned out to be a town rather than a city, and a pretty
nice one at that. Fran had been expecting razor wire and checkpoints:
instead they drove past the spacious gardens of the Christian college,

a movie theater with an old-fashioned marquee display above its front door and a big monument to Richard "Dick" Stevenson, former congressman and local benefactor. There was a statue of "Dick" with his arms half spread out like he was explaining something. The sun gleamed off the statue's bronze forehead, making it look just a little bit like the dead congressman had got himself into a sweat.

Even the psychiatric hospital, when they finally got to it, seemed very bland and ordinary from the outside. It had a very high wall, but painted on the wall was an awesome mural. The mural depicted dinosaurs in a Jurassic paradise, sunning themselves on the banks of a mighty river. Fran knew that there had been some important archaeological finds along the Ohio and its many tributaries, but the closest the Ohio came to Grove City was about fifty miles. "Yeah," Dr. Southern said when she pointed this out. "I think maybe whoever commissioned that picture had an ax to grind against the Christian college."

Gil laughed out loud at that. Fran didn't get it, but was glad that some of the tension in the car had finally been released.

They parked up in a lot where there were flower beds rather than concrete dividers separating the rows of cars, and went on into the reception area. That was where the facility stopped trying to pretend it was something it wasn't. They found themselves in a tiny, wedge-shaped space, with a window in the wall on one side and a sliding grille of thick bars on the other. The bars had been painted vivid sky-blue, and there was a sign above them that read SALLY PORT EGRESS MUST BE CLEAR AT ALL TIMES. The word CLEAR was in bright red.

Dr. Southern told the man at the window that they were expected, and handed over the letter he'd gotten from Dr. Trestle, Bruno Picota's senior clinician. The man looked more like a prison guard than a receptionist. He was six feet tall or so, well muscled, and he stood at his desk even though there was a chair right behind him, as though he was standing to attention. His hair was cut very short and although he was clean-shaven, the lower half of his face was dark with virtual stubble.

The man said he would notify Dr. Trestle that they'd arrived. In the meantime, he asked for their ID. Fran's dad and Dr. Southern handed over their passports, but all Fran had was her birth certificate. The man took them away and made photocopies of them, then handed them back along with three little keys. He pointed to a bank of wide, shallow lockers like safe deposit boxes on the wall next to where they'd come in. He told them to put all the things they had with them in the lockers, especially their phones and anything else they had that was electronic. Then he took the keys back because they weren't even allowed to have the keys with them when they went through to the other side of the blue bars.

After they had done all that, they still had to wait because Dr. Trestle hadn't shown up. Since there were no chairs, they just stood in a line. Gil asked Fran if she was okay for about the twentieth time, and she told him again that she was. It was a lie. She was actually really scared, though she was comforted a little when she saw that Lady Jinx had put her armor on and was standing on guard next to the blue gate.

Which was now sliding open at last, making no noise at all except for the sound of a motor rumbling inside the wall—and then a single heavy clang as the gate hit the unpadded end of its track.

A man stepped through and walked straight over to them, looking calm and unhurried, no matter that he'd made them wait so long. Fran's first thought was that he had to be a nurse or an assistant of some kind, both because he was young and because he was physically very small and slight. But when she got a good look at his face she revised that estimate. There was an intensity about his expression that seemed like it had to go along with some kind of authority: you couldn't walk around a psychiatric hospital looking like that unless you were either a doctor or an inmate—and since he was wearing a white coat (admittedly over jeans and a T-shirt) the first was more likely than the second. His dark eyes darted left, right, center, ending on Fran.

"Neither of these gentlemen looks like a Francine," he said, "so I'm thinking that has to be you. Welcome to Grove City, Ms. Watts. I'm Kenneth Trestle."

He put out a hand and Fran took it automatically. The shake was brief but vigorous. Mostly in Fran's experience men only shook hands with other men. But Dr. Trestle didn't offer to shake with Dr. Southern or her dad. He took a while even to acknowledge that they were there. When he did, he just looked at them both expectantly, waiting for them to introduce themselves.

Dr. Southern did that for both of them, and then he started to thank Dr. Trestle for allowing them to visit his patient. Dr. Trestle shook his head quickly, cutting him off. "Let's not take anything for granted just yet," he said, "shall we?"

Fran's dad looked from Trestle to Southern and back again. He frowned. "Okay, I must be missing something," he said. "We just drove sixty miles to get here because you said this was on."

Trestle wagged his finger like a teacher warning a little kid not to misbehave. "What I said was that I would allow Ms. Watts to have a meeting with Bruno Picota. That I would give my approval for that to happen."

Gil's scowl deepened. He didn't seem to like having Dr. Trestle's finger up in his face. "Yes," he agreed. "Exactly."

"What I didn't say, therefore, was that you could just push her in there and slam the door. She and I, we need to have a little talk first."

"About what?" Gil demanded.

"Ships and shoes and sealing wax. But mostly Bruno Picota."

Trestle ran a hand through his thick black hair. The hair stood up after the hand's passage and didn't lie down again. "I think many good things could come out of this meeting," he said. "I'm hopeful, as far as outcomes are concerned. But Bruno is fragile. I'm prepared to say that on the record. He's fragile, and his recovery is a work in progress. And Ms. Watts—" He gave her a nod, not offhand but respectful, as if he didn't want to talk about her in the third person without acknowledging that she was still in the room.

377

"—well, she's still very much a part of his delusional system. It's hard to predict what might happen when he sees her, but I want her to be aware of some of the possibilities."

"So you'd like to brief us," Dr. Southern summarized, "before the meeting."

Dr. Trestle wagged his finger again. "Her, my esteemed colleague. I would like to brief her, not you. As far as you and Mr. Watts are concerned, I intend to observe full patient confidentiality. You've had all you're going to get from me. But I'll talk to Ms. Watts about Bruno, if she wants to hear it, and I'll grant her fully supervised access if she wants to take it. Up to half an hour, depending on how things go.

"That's the deal, and it's not negotiable. So give me a yes or a no and we'll take it from there."

For a few seconds, nobody said anything at all in reply to this speech. Fran had come here with mixed feelings in the first place, and Dr. Trestle's words played on her worst fears. Picota was still as nutty as a fruit bat, was what she was hearing, and he was still fixated on her. But she hadn't come all this way to turn around and go back again, and she needed to know what Picota could tell her. So she wanted to blurt out a *yes!* straight away. But she knew she needed at least one of the grown-ups to say yes too, and grown-ups—even her dad—were apt to think they knew better than you did what was good for you. She could ruin everything by jumping in too fast.

So she waited for someone else to speak first, and the someone else turned out to be Gil. He was still mad about the finger thing, evidently, because the look he gave Dr. Trestle would have stripped paint off a wall. "You're pretty fond of your own opinions, aren't you, Dr. Trestle?" he demanded in a voice that was one up from a growl.

"Generally," Trestle said. "Until I hear better ones."

"So if I agree to this, what? My daughter goes in to meet that man on her own?"

"No. I'll be there. But you won't be, and neither will Dr. Southern.

I'll find you a room with a water cooler in it and you can watch the water cool until we're done."

"With respect," Dr. Southern said stiffly, "your duty to your patient doesn't obviate my duty toward mine. I need to be present at this meeting for the same reason you do—to evaluate how Francine is coping and to pull the plug if I think it's necessary."

Trestle puffed out his cheek. "I understand your feelings," he said. "Still not negotiable. Sorry."

"That seems somewhat arbitrary," Dr. S said stiffly, "if you don't mind my saying so."

"Not at all. My client is a notorious criminal. I fend off book offers on a regular basis. Your first-hand account of a meeting with him would be worth a lot of money. I need to protect him from that."

"Then make me sign an NDA."

"There's no way to make that binding on third parties. You talk, somebody listens, it hits the news and I have no control over that whatsoever."

Dr. Southern was as angry as Fran's dad now, or maybe more so. "I won't," he snapped, "talk. To any third parties. I'm a professional, just like you are."

Trestle looked at him hard. "So your decision to take Ms. Watts on as a patient," he said. "That wasn't motivated by any possible desire to write up your thoughts and feelings about the Picota case and make a little nest egg for your retirement?"

"No. It wasn't."

"And you were entirely honest with the family about your prior connections to the case?"

Dr. Southern's mouth moved but no sound came out of it.

"Thought so," said Trestle, deadpan.

"What?" Gil said, looking more pissed off than ever. "What prior connections? What are you talking about?"

"It doesn't matter," Fran said quickly. This wasn't a good time to pull on that loose thread. "None of it matters." She looked at Dr. Trestle until he looked at her. It didn't take long. She sensed

379

that she was the only person here he was even a little bit interested in. "I'm going in to talk to Bruno Picota on my own," she said to him and to everyone else. "If I go in at all."

Dr. Trestle gave her a pained smile. "Well, that's an interesting theory. But the last time I checked, I was still the senior clinician here."

"Bruno Picota wants to see me," Fran said. "He told you that, didn't he?"

There was a moment of extremely brittle silence. Since nobody else seemed to want to break it, and since Dr. Trestle looked like he'd just bitten down on something sour, Fran went on. "You only said yes because he said yes. If he didn't, you couldn't make him do it. And I don't think you're allowed to stop him. I mean, not just by saying so. Not if we both want it to happen."

Trestle didn't give her the schoolmarmish finger-wag, but he did stare at her very hard. If Fran had been in his class, there would probably have been a detention coming her way. "He didn't say anything about seeing you alone, though," he pointed out.

"No," Fran agreed. "It's me that's saying that."

Dr. Trestle went back to just looking again, as if a googly-eyed stare would make her back down after she'd gotten this far.

"I believe she's right," Dr. Southern said. He seemed to have gotten his temper back under control while this exchange was going on, so his voice was much more calm and reasonable. "Assuming you already added her name to the approved visitor list. You can't take it off again without due cause. This young lady just put both of us in our places, Dr. Trestle. I'd advise that you take it with good grace."

Fran looked to her dad—the one adult here who'd been left out of that equation. His eyes were wet, but he gave her a discreet thumbs-up, his hand staying down at his side. She knew him well enough to get both messages: that he was on her side all the way and that he wanted none of this to be happening.

Dr. Trestle still wasn't done. "There's a security issue," he said primly. "Especially if I'm not present. Bruno's behavior is erratic and his health is poor. If he's totally unattended, there's a two-fold danger."

"This being the kind of institution it is," Dr. Southern said mildly, "I assume you've got humane restraints and male nurses. Mitigate the risk however you want."

Dr. Trestle finally gave it up. "Fine," he said. "If you'd like to follow me."

They went inside, through the blue gate, which closed behind them, and then through a red one that opened in front of them. Dr. Trestle led the way and Lady Jinx brought up the rear. She held Oatkipper in a two-handed grip. They were going into enemy territory.

Dr. Trestle led Fran down corridor after corridor, through a building that looked increasingly like what it was: a prison disguised as a hospital. The walls were painted in institutional green and the floors were shiny linoleum with a pebble-dash pattern. It sucked at the soles of her shoes a little, so they made a clicking sound as she raised them again, a Morse-code punctuation to their walking.

They had left Dr. Southern and Gil sitting on two straight-backed chairs in a bare hallway, between a fire extinguisher and a dispenser for liquid disinfectant. There were no luxury car magazines to keep them entertained.

"He wants to say he's sorry," Dr. Trestle said to Fran as he unlocked a sally port and ushered her through. He sounded inexplicably angry.

Fran glanced up at his intent face. He hadn't looked at her once since they all went through the security gate. "Excuse me?"

"Bruno," Dr. Trestle said testily. "That's why he wants to see you. So he can tell you he's sorry. And that's the only reason I agreed. I've worked really hard to break down his delusional systems, and the fact that he's prepared to apologize to you is a huge accomplishment. The culmination of a lot of effort. But I can't capitalize on it fully if I'm not there."

Well then, Fran thought, it sucks to be you. But her conversation with Bruno Picota was likely to be pushing in a very different direction, and after all that Picota had taken from her she felt entitled to grab this little bit back. So she said nothing and just walked beside Dr. Trestle to where they were going.

Whenever she had imagined being face-to-face with Bruno Picota, the setting was always the same. She would meet him in a room whose walls had been upholstered like overstuffed sofa cushions, the padding held in by recessed studs so there were dimples every foot or so and ballooning swags of thick fabric between the dimples. The overall effect, in Fran's imaginings, was kind of like a bounce house, mostly because she had been on plenty of those but had never set foot in a restraint cell. And Bruno was invariably slumped in the corner of the bounce house, in a straitjacket that had about a hundred or so leather straps all over everywhere, tying his arms crosswise to his chest. Sometimes he had a Hannibal-style muzzle too.

The room that Dr. Trestle took her to was nothing like her imaginings. It was just a room, really. It had regular walls, with posters on them: nature scenes, mostly, along with one official notice listing rules for visits. Rule 11 stood out to Fran because it was at her head height.

11. An inmate authorized a contact visit may be permitted a brief embrace and kiss at the beginning and end of a visit, but excessive intimacy shall be strictly prohibited.

Shouldn't be a problem, she thought slightly hysterically.

Bruno was restrained, but not in a straitjacket. He was wearing a pair of handcuffs with a long chain between them instead of a hinge. The chain was threaded through a steel bar set into the table at which Bruno sat. There was a chair on the other side of the table so Fran could sit facing him, a long way outside the furthest reach of his arms.

This place wasn't a bounce house, clearly, and it wasn't a padded cell either: it was more like a police interview room. But of course it would be, Fran thought. The Grove City Hospital was full of convicted criminals, after all, so this layout made sense.

Picota didn't.

She knew her mental image of him was way out—crazily distorted and hyped up by memory and by fear. She had used the photos of him that she'd found on the internet to adjust the image back down to something a little closer to human, but real-world Picota had still been terrifying. As big as a bear, with dark hollows under his eyes and a stare that made you think he was looking at something horrible in his head that he wanted to do to someone.

This Picota was like someone had let the air out of the old Picota, waited until he was two-thirds deflated and then put the stopper back in. He was a small man living in the ruins of a big man's body. The skin of his face hung slack, and his mouth was lost in a sort of slow-motion treacly pour of collapsing chins. His skin was gray, except for a big red sore on his cheek that had its own hinterland of angry skin all around it. The shoulders of his green hospital-issued jumpsuit came quite a long way down his forearms.

He licked his lips, where there was a fringe of dry skin. His tongue looked gray too.

Two men wearing white hospital gowns over white shirts and trousers stood behind him, one on either side. They looked straight ahead of them, not meeting Fran's gaze, and they kept their hands clasped behind their backs. One of the two was white and the other one was black, but they had the same stolid faces and the same build: they were as big and solidly built as linebackers.

"Bruno," Dr. Trestle said in a voice carefully devoid of emotion, "this is Francine Watts. Francine, Bruno Picota."

Picota nodded, but didn't say anything.

Dr. Trestle turned to the nearer of the two linebackers. "Lionel, if Bruno becomes upset or agitated, take him back to his room at once. Don't hesitate, okay? I trust you to make that call."

The big black man nodded. "You got it, Dr. Trestle," he said. He had a high voice that sounded strange coming from that deep chest.

"Thank you. The same goes for you, Bruno. If you feel distressed or afraid, tell Lionel or Niklaus and they'll make sure you're okay." Only on his way out of the room did he finally look around at Fran. "I'll leave you to your visit," he said. "Enjoy."

Fran would have loved to return those insincere good wishes with a sweet thank you, but she was way too keyed up. She crossed to the chair—on legs that felt slightly shaky—and sat down. Lady Jinx hesitated in the doorway for a second or two, then scuttled in behind her, keeping Fran in between herself and Picota until she could tuck herself out of sight under the chair. Once she was there, though, Fran heard the *SHINNNNNNG* sound of Oatkipper being drawn. Jinx wasn't scared: she was just making intelligent use of the terrain.

Fran did the same thing. She didn't want to look directly at Picota. Not from this close up. He was still scary, even if he was all shriveled and fallen in on himself. Instead she turned to glance at the black man. Lionel.

"May I please have a glass of water?" she asked.

Lionel blinked twice, as if the unexpected question had just bounced off his nose. "I'm sorry, miss," he said. "You most certainly can. Nickie, can you put your head out?"

While Fran sat with her head down and her hands folded in her lap, the other man did exactly that. He went to the door, opened it partway and thrust his head and shoulders through the gap. "Pitcher of water in VS3," he shouted at the top of his voice. "Please."

After which he returned to his place.

It was a small thing, trivial even, but somehow it worked. Fran had imposed herself on the room. She had made something happen. Emboldened, she raised her head and looked straight at Picota for the first time.

She was prepared for him to stare her out, but what happened was the opposite of that. He seemed to shrink a little under her gaze. "Bruno," he mumbled. "I'm . . . you know who I am. They told you. I'm Bruno. And you're Francine. I'm very pleased to meet you." His voice was thick and gravelly, as though he had a chesty cough that had left his throat raw.

In spite of everything—the setting, her residual fear and the urgency of what had brought her here—Fran almost laughed. *I'm very pleased to meet you.* It was just such a stupid thing for him to say.

And she almost answered. *It's good to meet you too.* Good manners were a trap you fell into, especially if you'd lived most of your life hiding what you were really feeling so people wouldn't think you were a freak.

The arrival of the water saved her from that pratfall. A third male nurse brought it, in a plastic pitcher with a hinged lid and two paper cups stacked on top of it. He set it down in front of Fran and she murmured a thank you. The man nodded, but he didn't say anything. He just headed for the door and closed it behind him.

Fran poured herself a drink from the pitcher, framing words inside her head as she did so. But Picota spoke again before she could figure out an opening line.

"I wanted to say I'm sorry," he said in the same uneven raspy tone that rose and fell as though his throat was a bumpy road, "that I hurt you. It was a long time ago, I know it was, but . . ." He licked his lips again. "I'm still sorry. I'll always be sorry. It was a bad thing to have done. Especially to a . . . a . . . you know, a kid. I'm glad you got better."

For a second, Picota glanced at the black nurse, Lionel, as though he'd forgotten his lines and needed a prompt. When he looked back at Fran, his mouth and eyes had drooped a little more. She couldn't tell if it was unhappiness that dragged them down or if he was just tired. "It was a long time ago and I was a different person. I had a lot of bad thoughts in my head, and sometimes I didn't always know what was real. I imagined . . . all kinds of things."

"But you know now," Fran said. It took a huge effort to speak. Her chest was full of something bulky and tremulous. She was afraid she might burst into tears, and she was afraid that her voice would come out as a Mickey Mouse squeak. But the conversation wouldn't go anywhere unless she picked up her half of it. "You know what's real, and what isn't."

Picota raised his eyebrows. "Oh yes."

"So that means you know why you're here . . ." She had no idea what to call him, settled for ". . . Mr. Picota?"

"I do."

That was enough of a run-up. Fran got to the point. "When you kidnapped me, you did it because you thought I was some kind of monster."

Picota winced and glanced away, ducking his head below his shoulder. "I was sick," he murmured thickly. "I was a different person and it was a long time ago. I'm not good at telling how long but it must have been a lot of years because look at how grown-up you are now." He gestured vaguely, not turning to face her. The chain clanked as his hands came up, reaching the limit of its travel, which was very tight. "You were just a little girl before. So it must be a really long time."

He drew a long, snuffling breath. "I used to try to count but then I stopped counting because it was a big number and it made me scared. I haven't seen my dad, you know? I used to see him every day, but since I came here I didn't see him at all. They told me he passed, but even when he was alive he didn't want to come up and see me. Not after what I did."

All of this came out at an even, inexorable pace—kind of like a slow rush. It seemed to be forced out of Bruno under pressure but it was sluggish because his mind was slow. Fran felt a momentary nausea at the thought of what might be going on in there. What it might be like to be a crazy man growing old in a hospital that was really a prison, all alone and forgotten and shunned by the people who used to love him. The person, rather. Maybe there had only ever been the one.

Lady Jinx growled from under the chair. Picota unfolded and turned, looking around in bewilderment as though he'd heard that animal sound. Most likely he just lost his train of thought. Fran suspected it was a very short train with no driver.

"You mean because of what you did to me?" she asked him. Out of the corner of her eye she saw Lionel's hand clench slowly into a fist, although the expression on his face stayed the same, solemn and calm. She knew that men who hurt children had a bad time in prison. She wondered if that was also true in places like this.

Bruno closed his eyes and kept them closed for a few seconds. "Yes."

"Because you kidnapped me and almost killed me?"

"Yes. That's right." He delivered that statement with strong emphasis, but stumbled over the next words and almost couldn't get them out at all. "I d-d-d-did that, yes. I did that. I'm gl-glad it was only almost. Glad you . . . that you're not dead. That you got better, after all. I was sick, in my opinion, and I was mistaking you. I thought you were . . . something. Something that's not even real."

"Skadegamutc," Fran said, and Jinx growled again. Picota moaned in his throat, a sound of undisguised distress.

"I was mistaking you," he said again. His face was more animated now, his forehead wrinkling and clearing as though thoughts were zigzagging around behind there and making a mark each time they hit. Fran thought maybe she could just wait him out because that sense of pressure was so palpable: she was almost certain now that Bruno Picota had some things he really wanted to say. But he just kept looking at the ceiling and then down at the tabletop, like he'd gotten stuck in some kind of loop and couldn't get out of it.

"Why did you attack me?" Fran asked him. "What did I look like to you?"

Picota passed a hand across his face. He had to duck down a little to do it because of the tightness of the cuffs. "I'm doing all right," he muttered under his breath. It seemed like this was for his own benefit rather than hers, and it seemed like it didn't do the job because he said it again. "I'm doing okay. Okay. Okay."

"What did I look like to you, Mr. Picota?" Fran asked again.

Picota dropped his hands back onto the table. He drew a deep breath, his narrow chest inflating visibly. The tips of his fingers curled. "Monster," he said. All that breath left him again as he said it, as though it was something heavy that he had to lift up out of himself and dump down on the table between them. "You said it. You said the word, and you were right. I thought you were a monster."

"Why?" Fran demanded.

"Because there were so many of you."

"You can see there's only one of me."

Picota seemed close to tears. He shook his head slowly. Fran didn't think he was disagreeing. It seemed more like he was dismayed at the difficulty of the task she'd set for him. How did you describe your own madness, your own visions that you'd now disavowed? "That's what everyone thinks, and most people are right. I thought about it since then." His voice went lower and speeded up at the same time. "I should have thought if it goes one way or two ways. Like, what do I look like in the mirror, or if I'm standing in front of the mirror but with my eyes closed. Does the other me close its eyes too? You can't ever know for sure. So what I see in you—does that go for you when you look at me? Am I the Bruno in the mirror, or all those Brunos in all those mirrors, or am I just me? It's obvious, really, but I never thought. If things are changing one way then maybe they're changing the other way too. Am I?"

The question came out of nowhere. Fran took a moment to realize it was addressed at her. "Are you what?" she asked him.

"Changing." He stared at her with a sudden, surprising urgency. "Am I changing?"

"No. You're not."

Picota breathed out heavily again. He looked relieved. Then he did something that freaked Fran out a little. He leaned down sideways and looked under the table. There was nothing there but Jinx. For a long moment they were almost nose-to-nose.

Finally Picota straightened up again. "Where do you live?" he asked Fran.

The white nurse, Niklaus, jumped in quickly. "You don't need to know that, Bruno. You shouldn't ask that."

"It's okay," Fran said. "I still live in Larimer, Mr. Picota. Just off Lincoln Avenue."

"Lincoln," Picota repeated, nodding his head. "So you were very close to it. That makes sense."

Fran felt a shiver go through her. "What do you mean?" she demanded. "Close to what?"

The lids of Picota's eyes came halfway down as if he was looking at something that was too bright. "The place," he said.

"What place?"

"The place where things get squishy. It's got a name but I don't like to say it. I wish I'd never gone there, because when you come out again . . ."

His voice trailed off. He was staring right at Fran from under those lowered lids, but she didn't think he saw her. He was staring inward, not out.

"When you come out again?"

"You know," Picota murmured. "You were there too, but I was there for longer. Much, much longer. Years. Doing okay, Bruno. I thought it was magic and it had to be really bad. Deviltries, like my mom said. Like she said the ghost witches do. Like you were the ghost of . . . of a . . . " His hands tried to shape something in the air, the chain clanking as it sawed back and forth in its bracket. "But it's not. It's only that place, and what it does to you. If you stay too long you get squishy too. It touches you, I guess. It sticks to you if you're a certain kind of person. Like you. Like me. If you look like there are two of you, it doesn't mean you're bad."

"What does it mean, then?" Fran gave the two male nurses a panicked glance, aware of how crazy all this must sound. "What do you *think* it means?" she amended.

"I *think*," Picota said, copying her emphasis exactly, "it means you could have happened different. Or you did already."

Fran didn't understand at first. Then she did, and her brain felt as though it was momentarily too big for her head, pressing against the inside of her skull with dangerous pressure. "Different," she said. The word came out strained and high. Different, as in *changes*. As in the things she saw when she had an episode.

"Little bit," Picota said. "Or a lot. Maybe I had oatmeal instead of corn flakes. Maybe I wore yesterday's socks one more day because they didn't smell so bad. Maybe I lost a quarter out of my allowance and couldn't buy a soda on free choice day."

He looked her square in the eyes.

"Maybe I killed you. Sometimes I remember it that way."

A shiver went through Fran, starting at the top of her head and traveling down through her body, making her shake so hard she couldn't hide it. When it got to her stomach it melted. She thought she might be about to pee herself and hoped—please, please, please!—that she could hold it in.

"You didn't kill me, Mr. Picota," she said as calmly as she could manage. "That's obvious. I'm not a ghost. But I . . . I know it's hard, sometimes, to remember things right." She swallowed, licked her dry lips, gave the two nurses another frightened glance and finally just went for it. "Suppose someone looked different, the way you said. If there were two of them. But then you saw them again a little while later, and they . . . they just went back to looking normal, like . . . like regular people. What would you think about that? What might have happened to them?"

She kept her eyes fixed just on Picota now: she didn't want to look at the nurses in case they stepped in to shut her down. She knew she must sound as crazy, as damaged, as Picota did, and they'd been told to pull the plug on this if their patient got distressed. Was she distressing him? It didn't matter either way because she couldn't stop. Either she was going to get to the truth now or she never would.

Picota closed his eyes completely and kept them closed for a long time. When he opened them again he did it very slowly, as if he was coming out from cover. As if he was hoping she might not still be there. "Doing okay," he whispered.

"What would you think, Mr. Picota?"

Picota shook his head.

"Tell me," Fran demanded. And she forced herself to add "Please."

Another head-shake. Picota didn't want to say it.

Niklaus finally took that as his cue to intervene.

"Miss," he said flatly, "I think we may need to wrap this up now. Bruno, lay your hands on the table, either side of the ring."

"Tell me," Fran said. Yelled, almost, because they were going to take him away and she needed an answer.

"I saw it," Picota said. "Okay. Okay. You don't have to tell me. I saw it soon as you came in."

Niklaus looked at Lionel and gave him a *WTF?* shrug. Lionel nodded in reply. The two nurses stepped forward and took Picota's arms.

"What?" Fran demanded, bewildered. "What did you see? What do you mean?"

Lionel brought Picota's wrists right up together and Niklaus snapped a regular, hinged pair of handcuffs onto him right behind the pair he was already wearing. Then he unlocked the original, chained pair. In a matter of seconds Picota was no longer shackled to the table, but his freedom of movement was actually less than it was before. His hands were pressed together as though he was praying.

Picota was still talking through all of this manhandling. "One moves in, the other moves out. Isn't that what happened to you?"

"Nothing happened to me!" Fran said. "I wasn't asking about me!" Something he'd said earlier—said twice—suddenly registered. "Wait, what did you mean when you said I got better? Got better from what?"

The nurses lifted Picota gently out of his seat and set him on his feet. He went limp in their hands, absolutely passive and unresisting—but he was still looking at Fran. "From there being two of you," he said. "There's just you now. But I think the other one is under the chair there, pretending to be a dog."

Lady Jinx gave a blood-curdling yell. She shot out sideways from under the chair and rose onto her hind paws—in full armor and with Oatkipper raised to strike.

"Let's go," Lionel said. He stepped in and put a reassuring arm on Picota's shoulder. "Say goodbye, Bruno."

Picota was staring at Jinx, his eyes as wide as they could go. He laughed in incredulous delight. "She's got a knife!" he said. "She's lovely!"

Jinx lunged at him, the sword passing through Lionel's back and Picota's chest. The little fox swung Oatkipper around again and again. The blade went through and through Picota from every angle.

Die, villain! she yipped. *Die, false knight!*

"What do you call her?" Picota asked. "Does she have a name?"

Die die die die die die die die die!

"Just wait here a moment, miss," Lionel said to Fran. "I'll be right back to let you out."

The two big men hustled Picota out of the room. He was watching Jinx the whole time, not just unafraid of her attempts to slaughter him but thrilled. "Good doggie," he said. "Come on. Come on, little doggie." As he passed out of sight, he was trying to whistle, the sound issuing in truncated, discontinuous notes from between his dry lips, like it broke into pieces inside his mouth.

Jinx chased him all the way to the door of the room, swiping at him the whole time, but she paused on the threshold, tottering there as though she was in danger of losing her balance.

She turned to stare at Fran, her dark eyes as wide as pools and her muzzle gaping wide. Fran stared back, terrified. The violence hadn't been any less disturbing for being futile. Jinx had meant to kill Picota. And Jinx was . . .

Jinx was . . .

Picota's words had canceled gravity, not in the real world but inside Fran's mind. All the thoughts in there had risen up at once and now they were floating around, bumping into each other. And the shock of those collisions went through her whole body.

Don't say anything! Lady Jinx commanded her.

The snake Ouroboros, that eats its own tail.

He was lying. He's a dirty liar!

The cartoon she loved. The character she loved. The name of the sword, even, not as Lady Jinx in the show said it but as Fran herself had said it when she was a lisping six-year-old girl.

Stop it! Jinx advanced on Fran. She was still holding Oatkipper in a two-handed grip, but then she threw it down and spread her claws—which somehow was a lot worse. The magic sword disappeared as it hit the floor. Jinx's bared teeth snapped and snarled.

Don't talk anymore!

Fran wasn't talking in the first place, but she couldn't stop the thoughts as they crashed back down, one by one, in their new configuration. I wouldn't have let him cut you, Jinx had said. And Fran had answered: I didn't know you then. You came afterward.

Immediately afterward.

Jinx threw back her head and howled. There was no real sound, of course, but inside Fran's head it reverberated from wall to wall and met itself coming back.

Bruno Picota had said: maybe I killed you. Sometimes I remember it that way. And sometimes Fran did too.

Another howl from Lady Jinx, even louder.

"Jinx!" Fran gasped. "Jinx, listen to me, please. Do you remember when you took your oath?"

Jinx glared up at her. Her hackles were standing up and her lips were drawn back on a rictus grin of terror and misery.

What has that got to do with anything?

"A knight gets her name when she takes her oath. That's true for everyone who sits at the Woodland Table. Isn't it? Sir Querin was Andrew the page. Lady Essen was Lorissa the innkeeper's daughter. Right? And Sir Stronghand was Boris the woodcutter."

So? Jinx snarled.

"So that must have been true for you too. You knelt before the queen and you took your oath, and she gave you your name and your sword. Remember?"

Yes!

"And that was a great day. The best day for any knight."

Yes!

"What was your oath, Lady J?"

To keep you safe! To stay with you forever and not let anything hurt you!

"Okay. And before that, before you became the Lady Jinx, who were you? What was your name?"

Jinx jumped as if someone had shot current through her. She backed away from Fran, growling between her teeth.

"Don't be scared, Jinx! Please!" Fran put out a hand, gentling her. Jinx slashed at the hand with her unsheathed claws. She did no damage at all, but tears welled up in Fran's eyes all the same.

Jinx was on all fours, trying to run, but her paws didn't seem to find any traction. She and Fran were glued together. They always had been, from the moment when Jinx first arrived.

"Was your name . . .? Was it the same as mine?"

Stop it! Jinx was writhing horribly, her little body twisting as she tried repeatedly to bolt but made no headway. Pieces of armor fell from her like rain. She was just an animal again. An animal caught in an invisible trap, unable to get free or even to understand what was hurting her.

She whined, long and drawn out, on a shrill and rising pitch.

Fran sank to her knees, trying to get as close as she could to whisper reassuring words. To stop the pain and bring her back. But Jinx was fading quickly. She had found a way to get free after all, but not in any of the usual three dimensions.

"Jinx, stay with me!" Fran cried out. "I won't hurt you! I promise! Jinx!"

But Jinx had been hurt past saving a long time before, in the same moment that Fran had.

In this world . . . Bruno Picota's knife touched her side, but then he stopped. For some reason, he stopped right there.

But somewhere else, the knife had kept right on going.

And another six-year-old, feeling that terrible pain, her feet windmilling in the air as the life-blood left her, had run in the only direction she could. Which was sideways.

Surrendered her shape, and her name, just to stay close to the life she'd known.

The life she'd lost.

"Jinx—" Fran sobbed. "I'm sorry! Don't go!"

She was talking to herself. With a final effortful heave, kicking at the air like a hanged man, Jinx was out of there.

Her vanishing allowed Fran to see Dr. Trestle standing in the doorway. He was looking at her with a face that had no expression in it at all.

"I hope you got something out of that, Ms. Watts," he said. "From Bruno's point of view, it seems to have been an utter disaster. Let me see you out."

Beth thought she had handled Mr. Vance the Mormon detective pretty well all things considered. She judged her success by the sudden, resounding silence coming from Jamie Langdon. Yeah, she thought smugly. Lost your appetite for finding your lost sheep now you know what color his wool is.

The thought removed some of her tension. It did nothing to improve her relationship with Zac and Molly, though, but that felt like a lost cause. Once Beth's mind had settled on the proofs of their alienness, the effect was exponential and out of her control. She couldn't make herself see them as her own anymore. They were Liz's. Her own kids were dead and worlds away: she would never even be able to leave flowers on their graves. These liars who wore their faces were just insults to their memory, and the less she saw of them the better.

But she was making headway with that. Withdrawing more and more each day from domestic chores and responsibilities, she had coaxed Zac without ever asking him outright to take up the slack. He was giving Molly her breakfast and taking her into school every day now, and picking her up at the end of the day. All Beth had had to do was to sign the form for an hour of homework club, which gave him time to get over from his own school to Molly's. He was cooking dinner, washing up, doing the laundry and generally finding his inner mom, which was all good as far as Beth was concerned. It left her free to pursue her pleasures.

She did this with a kind of urgency that hadn't been there before. Hedonism held thought at bay, so she spent and drank and screwed and played hooky from the Cineplex, and generally left tomorrow to take care of itself.

Until it finally arrived, one day early, in the form of a phone call from officer Bernadette Brophy. The call came through in the middle of the afternoon on a day when Beth should have been on-shift but wasn't. She had called in sick instead and driven the car across the Monongahela to the South Side Flats, intending to get a tarot reading at the Gypsy Café and maybe fall into the way of a casual hook-up. But the Gypsy was all closed up and had been for years, which made her feel both old and seriously pissed off. A sheet of corrugated iron was nailed up over the frontage and there was a cutesy note bidding farewell to former patrons that had been there long enough to bleach. Was the Gypsy still serving back in her own world? She was never going to know.

So in the middle of the afternoon, Beth was sitting in a bar called Fat Head's, nursing a strawberry daiquiri. The tarot reading was moot, but she hadn't given up on the other half of that game plan: there were several men in the place who looked like possibles.

Then the phone rang, and her day hit the rocks. "This is Beebee," Brophy said, sounding as always bright and brisk and full of pop'n'fresh cheeriness. "How are you doing?"

"I'm good," Beth said. "I'm sorry I haven't been in touch, but I've pulled a lot of extra shifts. With no maintenance coming in from Marc . . ."

"Sure," Beebee said. "I'm happy to help, you know. You just have to ask."

"I will," Beth lied. "Thanks, Beebee."

"You're welcome. Actually, though, Marc is why I called. We've kind of got a lead on him."

Beth couldn't keep from grinning, though she made sure her voice sounded innocently surprised. "Really? Where is he?"

"Well, we don't know that yet. But someone was using his phone last week, pretending to be him."

Beth had her next line all ready. It was going to be "Poor Jamie? Seriously? That bastard!" Now all that fake emotion was stuck in her throat like a chicken bone.

"Pretending?" she said instead as soon as she could actually speak. "I don't understand."

"Jamie Langdon came into the precinct to show us a message she'd received from Marc's phone. Whoever sent it was trying very hard to convince her they were Marc. In fact they succeeded. She was sure it was from him, until she noticed something weird about the message itself. Whoever sent it must know your ex-husband very well because they got the tone exactly right. Except that he said he was sorry. Jamie said the more she thought about it, the less that sounded like him."

Jesus, Beth thought, am I not allowed even a little bit of artistic license? She had imagined a Marc who had walked away from his entire life and then found there was a single splinter of functional conscience sticking in his skin. "He said sorry to me a lot," she said in a carefully neutral tone. "Pretty much every time he beat me."

"Yeah, I honestly wouldn't have put a lot of store by what Ms. Langdon had to say on that score. But the fact is, we already had a subpoena on the phone number so the text was forwarded to us right after it went to her. Only we got all the GPS records along with it, and that was a lot more interesting than the message was, frankly."

"In what way?" Beth asked.

"It was sent from right here in Pittsburgh. Whoever sent the text talked about being a long way away, but when they said it they were somewhere in Larimer. Probably within walking distance of your house. The phone mast the message pinged off is at the corner of Carver Street and Ashley."

Beth had taken herself and her phone out into the street by this time. The bar room soundscape could easily have been the Cineplex food court, but she felt a little hunted just the same and decided to put a stop to it. She leaned against the wall outside, her head back against the cold stone, the October chill undoing all the good the booze had done. "It makes sense for Marc to lie about where he is," she ventured. "He's got to know there's a search out for him."

"It makes total sense," Beebee agreed. "But our data monkeys had a little talk with the phone company and the signal history is really interesting too. As in, there isn't any. Marc turned his phone on in this one place in Larimer, sent the message and turned it off again."

"So . . .?"

"So that's a really strange mix of smart and dumb. If it's genuinely him then he's been using a different phone over the past few weeks since he disappeared. Most likely a disposable. And obviously sending Jamie a message from that new phone would run the risk of revealing the number to us. But firing up the old phone tells us where he's at in any case. So he's being paranoid, but not nearly paranoid enough."

Beth squeezed her eyes tight shut. *Shit, shit, shit!* "Yeah, but," she said, "it's only dumb if you think he really is living in Larimer. If he drove in from someplace else . . ." She let the thought tail off. She couldn't afford to argue for a busted hypothesis. It just made her look like a suspect. "I guess you thought of that," she said.

"Yeah, we did. Makes you wonder, though, if he wanted to give the impression he was still in town, why he'd go out of his way to say in the text that he wasn't. But in any case, we're not taking it for granted that the message was genuinely coming from Marc. And if it wasn't, then it was someone leaning over backward to convince Jamie—or us, maybe—that Marc is still alive and well and living in Pennsylvania."

"You think . . .?" Beth swallowed bile. "You think he's not?"

"We don't know what to think at this stage. But we're morally certain he hasn't been hanging out in Larimer. And we're leaning toward the view that there might be a third party—maybe more than one—involved in his going off the radar."

"Meaning . . .?"

"Meaning we're looking at abduction and murder as possible scenarios as well as bail-jumping."

"Right," Beth said. "Okay." And then, for the look of the thing, "Oh Jesus." One domino after another, she thought in sour wonder. But that was the wrong metaphor. You try to fix a drip and you knock the pipes with your shoulder, making a worse leak than before. Now the basement's flooding with water and you've got to do something, but you know that as soon as you move . . .

"I'm sorry if this has upset you, Liz. I know there was no love lost between the two of you, but it's still a horrible thing to have to think about."

"It is."

"If you want a shoulder to cry on, or someone to get drunk with . . .?"

"I'll be fine, Beebee. Thank you."

"No problem. But I'm going to be paying you a visit anyway, so we'll get to see each other. I'll need to take statements from you and the kids."

"The kids?" Beth repeated. "How come? Beebee, I'd like to keep them out of this."

"I understand that, Liz, honest to God. But there's ground that has to be covered. I need to ask them about the last time they saw Marc, how he seemed to them, if he said anything that might be pertinent to his disappearance. I'll be careful not to say anything that will scare them. Well, Molly, I mean. Zac's a big boy, right? He can handle this?"

"Let me . . ." Beth tried to pull her thoughts into some kind of shape. "Give me a little time to prepare them. Could you do that? They're still adjusting to not having their dad in their lives anymore. I don't want to pile any more on them, or not all at once."

"I'll be tactful, Liz. You know that, right?"

Liz didn't answer, which Beebee seemed to take as an answer in itself. "I can wait a day or two," she said, sounding a little hurt. "If you think it will help."

"Thanks," Beth said. "Thank you. I'd better go. It's the end of my break."

She hung up without any farewells, and almost threw the phone down in the gutter. Her muscles were twitching with the need to do something, anything, but there was nothing to do. And that was how she had messed up in the first place: by doing the wrong thing when all that was needed was to sit on her hands and wait.

Now the police were sniffing around again. They had followed the fake bait she had thrown out but in the wrong direction, all the way back to her door.

So what now? Beebee could talk to Zac until the cows creamed their pants, but it would be a bad idea to let her interview Molly. Molly loved her stories, and there were any number of ways in which the crazy story of that midnight jaunt to the garden plots might surface.

She had let herself get seduced into temporary fixes, when what she needed was an endgame.

Saturday night was the coldest night of the year so far, although obviously there was a lot worse to come. In the morning Fran opened her window to find that the bowl of milk she had left out on the ledge had formed a crust of ice overnight.

And it had not lured Jinx back.

She showered, brushed her teeth and dressed in a sort of trance, a fug of misery. It was hard even to move, and impossible to think. Inside her head she was wailing all the time. *Come back! Come back and I won't ask you any more questions, not as long as I live.*

It did no good. Jinx didn't answer, and wasn't anywhere.

Fran had got more than she bargained for out of Bruno Picota: all the answers she could use, and then some. But the price had been too high and there was no way now to call off the deal or unlearn what she knew.

She had ridden all the way back from Grove City in silence. Dr. Trestle had handed her back into her dad's care without a word, and after one look at her tear-stained face her dad had asked no questions about how the meeting had gone. Only hugged her and said, "Let's go home, sweetheart."

She had texted Zac from the car. GOT SOMETHING FOR

YOU. TALK SOON. She left it at that for now. The rest would be hard and she wasn't nearly up to it yet.

Home didn't feel like home when they finally arrived. Jinx took up no space at all when she was there, but her absence was vast and palpable.

Through Sunday Fran kept to her room, pretending to read. Her phone buzzed a few times during the day, but it was Zac every time and she still hadn't thought of how to break the news to him. *Your mom is not your mom, she's an interloper from a parallel universe* was going to be a big pill for him to swallow, and most likely would just make him lose his shit with her again. Especially since the only proof she could offer was the absence of an imaginary fox. Not exactly a smoking gun, however you looked at it.

Your mom is not your mom, and Jinx is me. A different me, from another world. But I don't know how that happened, and I chased her away by asking her. Now I'm more alone than I've ever been in my life, and I don't know if I can bear it.

Around three o'clock, with the afternoon and then the evening stretching ahead of her like a desert without any waterholes in it, she succumbed at last to the temptation she'd been feeling all day. She went onto YouTube, found *The Knights of the Woodland Table* and binged her way through it. For most of the time she was crying, but it still gave her some comfort to see Jinx on the screen. It made her seem a little bit closer. And it made it easier to think about what she had learned.

Why had she ever thought Jinx was imaginary?

Because it was easier than accepting that she was real. That Fran really was having conversations with a cartoon fox—or someone who had disguised herself as one. It was the difference between pretending you were eccentric and admitting you were crazy.

Next question: if Jinx was what Picota said she was, then how could Fran ever hope to make that right? Knowing what she now knew, what could she do?

How could they go back to being Freaky Fran and Lady J when really they were Schrödinger's cat in its two most popular flavors?

She was still chasing her thoughts one by one down the same drain when her dad knocked on the door and poked his head in. "Hey, Frog," he said.

"No frogs here," she said. "I changed back into a tadpole." It had been her old riposte from way back when her mom was still alive, and it made him smile as she had known it would. She wanted to deflect his concern for her, his transparent unhappiness. It was too much to deal with on top of her own.

But Gil didn't leave. He came on into the room instead and sat on the edge of the bed. Fran was cross-legged on the mat, watching the cartoon on the screen of her laptop.

"I thought we could go out and watch a movie tonight," Gil said. "If you were up for it. That superhero thing just opened."

The outside world was the last place Fran wanted to be right now, but she could see what was behind the invitation and she didn't want to crush his hopes by turning it down. "I'd like that," she lied.

"Coolio." He said that word with an attempt at brightness, but then his voice dropped a little—a warning sign that he was about to get serious. "Fran . . ."

"I'm okay, Dad."

"I know that's not true. But I think it will be soon. I wanted to say something to you about yesterday. Maybe you don't want to hear it, but I'm going to say it anyway."

Gil's broad face creased with a kind of soft urgency. He rubbed a hand across his chin, then dropped it back into his lap. "It took a ton of courage to do what you did yesterday. More courage than you knew you had, I bet. And maybe it didn't turn out the way you were hoping, but still it was an amazing thing to have done. And I think you'll find that that old fear lifts off you now, not all at once but a little bit at a time. You put a crack in that wall, a big one, and it can't stand up the way it did. You'll see I'm right."

"Okay," Fran said. She didn't want to say any more in case she started crying again. He must be able to see how red her eyes were, but he was pretending not to notice.

"Okay then. A movie followed by pizza. With maybe a beer for me and a chocolate shake for you."

"And cookie dough for dessert," Fran suggested.

"You drive a hard bargain, Frog, but that could be arranged." He ruffled her hair and left. She unpaused the cartoon and—of course!—started crying again.

"Oh, pull yourself together!" she muttered aloud. She didn't watch to the end of the season. She already knew how it ended, with the serpent knight Lady Subtle betraying her oath and tricking everyone so they thought Queen Yuleia was evil. With the Woodland Table falling apart and all the good knights ready to fight each other instead of the bad guy.

Just like real life. And who the hell needed any more of that?

She got out her math homework, which was due in on Monday. She stared at the equations with unfocused eyes for the better part of an hour before giving it up and taking a walk around the block. Maybe Jinx was nearby. She never wandered far, except when she sneaked away to her secret den.

Pittsburgh was beautiful in the fall, but the best of fall was over now. The trees were no longer in their party dresses, but naked. And when they were naked they were thin and angular and spiky and altogether sad to look at. Just like me, Fran thought glumly. The wind poked at her like a bony finger.

But there was the movie to look forward to. Or rather, not the movie so much as her dad's attention and kindness and concern for her, which was comforting. It might make her forget, for a couple of hours, the scariness of not knowing where Jinx was or what to do about Liz Kendall.

Without meaning to, she had been walking west all this time. Toward Homewood. She stopped when she came to the bridge. Beyond lay the Perry Friendly. Just the thought of that place made her shudder as though someone had walked over her grave.

Someone did, she thought. And it was me.

Cursing herself for an idiot, she turned around and went home. When she got there, Gil was in his coat and looking for his car keys. "Thought you were going to stand me up, Frog," he chided her.

"I lost track of time," Fran said. "Sorry."

"No need to be sorry. Just jump in the car. We need to go give our thirty dollars to Marvel Comics and another twenty or so to Big Popcorn."

He was working hard to make her smile, and he kept on doing it all the way to the Cineplex. Calling out to every in-joke they'd ever shared and keeping up both halves of the conversation because Fran wasn't able to hit the ball back to him more than a couple of times.

They bought a ridiculously huge bucket of popcorn and two rain barrels full of Coke and went inside. "You'll have to tell me who everybody is," Gil insisted. "I don't know the Mighty Thor from the Pillsbury Doughboy." He was inviting Fran to indulge in one of her favorite vices, which was to give lectures on how the Marvel Cinematic Universe was different from the comics. She let herself go, and forgot to be unhappy for a while.

But the Coke took its toll, and she had to sneak out of the theater during a second act lull so she could hit the bathroom. Then on her way back she got lost and turned around somehow and ended up in the wrong auditorium—one that was being cleaned up between performances. A woman in Cineplex livery was threading her way between the rows, collecting popcorn cartons, cups and discarded ticket stubs and dumping them in a bulging white trash bag.

"Excuse me," Fran said, moving to intercept the woman at the end of a row. "Do you know which screen—?"

The woman turned to face her and the rest of the sentence slipped all the way back down her throat as she saw who it was.

"Oh hey, Francine," Liz Kendall said in a voice that was way sweeter than popcorn. "We've missed you, sweetheart. What's doing?"

Fran clenched her fist and drew back her arm. She did it without even thinking about it. Her *body* did these things, and her mind gave its approval a few milliseconds later. *Goodbye, clenched fist. We all wish you well on your ultra-short journey to—*

The impact jarred her arm all the way to the shoulder. It even jolted her neck, like being in a car that braked too quickly and threw you forward, then back again.

"Well now," Liz Kendall said, smiling through the blood that was welling up from her split lip. "We know where we stand."

Fran backed away in a hurry, as much from her own unexpected violence as from the woman she had just assaulted.

"I know what you are!" she blurted. "And I know what you did! All of it!"

"No, you don't." Liz made no move to retaliate. She just set down her trash bag as if she was acknowledging that they might be here for a while. She sounded almost bored. "You don't know a damn thing. If you did, you wouldn't have hit me in an empty room where it's just the two of us and I can kick the crap out of you without anyone being the wiser."

Fran realized too late that she had retreated toward the rear of the theater rather than toward the exits. Liz was between her and the door. But there was a whole maze of seats she could flee through if she had to, and she would probably be more agile in those narrow spaces than a grown woman. "You wouldn't dare," she said, trying to sound like she believed that. "You touch me and I'll scream, Ms. Kendall. Really loud."

She was standing on the balls of her feet, ready to bolt the moment Liz made a move toward her. But Liz didn't. She sat down instead. And she laughed, a long, throaty chuckle, as though all of this was a rich joke at someone else's expense.

"It's Beth, honey," she said. "And I'm not going to hurt you. But we should definitely talk, don't you think?"

Fran measured the distance to the door. She was almost certain she could run past Ms. Kendall before she got to her feet again. But she didn't try yet, just in case. If she waited long enough, maybe someone else would come in and she'd be safe.

Wait a second. *Beth?*

Was she admitting . . .?

"Relax," the woman said. "You attacked me, remember. Not the other way around. I admit I lost my temper there for a moment, but I've got nothing against you." She raised her hand to her mouth and wiped it, then held them up to show the dark red smear on her palm. "Nothing except this, and I probably had that coming. I put a real scare into you that night in the kitchen, didn't I? And I called you a crazy person, or as good as. Let's say we're even."

Fran still didn't move. "We're not even," she said, her voice tight.

"No? Well, I'm sorry, honey, but only the first one is free. If you want any more, we go knock for knock, and I'll knock you so far you'll have to get a ride home on the space shuttle. You want to sit down?"

She indicated a seat right next to her.

Fran shook her head. "No way."

"Please yourself. Look, you've obviously got some idea in your head about me. I don't know what it is . . ."

"Then I'll tell you," said Fran. "You're not Ms. Kendall. Not the real one. You come from somewhere else and you took her over somehow. Got control of her." Fran faltered. She suddenly remembered what Jinx had said, about how this Liz—Beth, rather had eaten the other one. Jinx had been warning her. Trying to protect her, if only she'd listened.

Beth shifted in her seat, making herself more comfortable. She crossed her legs, sticking them out into the aisle. "Well now, that does sound like a crazy person talking, if you don't mind me saying so."

"I don't care," Fran said. "It's true. And I don't know what else you've done since but I know you're hurting Molly and I'm going to stop you."

"That'll be a neat trick without any proof, won't it?"

"I've got proof! Zac is onto you too. Everybody is onto you. You're not as clever as you think you are!" It occurred to her after she'd already said it that bringing Zac into this was probably a stupid thing to do, and a wrong thing in any case because she didn't have his permission. She'd just blurted out something that had been told to her in confidence. She shifted tack quickly. "I'll call child protection. They'll send an inspector."

Beth was unmoved. "They'll find a well-fed, healthy kid who loves her mom. No cuts, no bruises, no history of trips and falls, absences from school or any of that shit. I gave her a push and she fell over, that's all. I'm not Charles Manson. And if you think Zac will give evidence against me, you don't know Zac. He loves his mother, that boy."

"You're not her!" Fran said. It came out as a shout.

"No," Beth said. "I'm not. But he doesn't know that, does he?"

The flat admission took the wind out of Fran's sails. She wasn't sure where else to go with this. She clenched her fists again. The one she'd used to hit Beth was throbbing painfully and didn't close all the way. "You've got to bring Liz back," she said.

"You think so? Why?"

Fran groped for words. All the reasons were so obvious there was no easy way of saying them. "Because you don't belong here, and she does."

"You ever hear that thing about possession being nine-tenths of the law?"

Fran's mind was racing. Her phone had a voice recording app. Could she activate it without looking at the screen? Probably not, but maybe she could pretend her phone was on vibrate, and take it out of her pocket, then—

411

"I'd like it a lot better if you sat down," Beth said. "I'm not going to hurt you." She considered. "Well, probably not. Unless you do something to piss me off, in which case it's on you."

Fran shook her head. Her dad must already be wondering what had happened to her. She had to make her break for the door soon, and it would be a lot easier to do that if she was standing up.

Beth was looking at her strangely. For a long time she said nothing at all, but her expression was one of intense thought.

"You don't know me," she said at last, much more softly than before. "Shit, you barely knew her. But if you did know me you wouldn't be giving me arguments about what's right or what belongs. Believe me, I know better than you do where I belong, and I can't ever get back there. But this is where I wound up, and I'm not about to leave because it makes you unhappy." She paused, her cold stare fixed hard on Fran. "You really should back off, kid. That's a friendly warning. You've got your life to live, and I've got mine. They don't have to overlap."

"It's not your life. You've stolen someone else's life," Fran reminded her grimly.

Beth tossed her head, consigning that objection to oblivion—or to her bag of trash. "The stuff I've got, including this body, I got it by fighting for it. All she had to do was be born."

"That's stupid," Fran scoffed. "What, so if someone else fought you and beat you and took it away from you, then it would suddenly be theirs?"

"If they beat me, believe me they would have had to earn it. I'm a tough act to follow. Say, just for instance I was interested in doing a number on you. The first thing I'd do is scream real loud, then when someone comes I'd point to this split lip and say you gave it to me. You could say you didn't, but you've got my blood on your knuckles and a long, rich history of mental instability. Doesn't look good, does it?"

Fran didn't like the look of calculation in Beth's eyes. She was still tensed and ready to run, but she felt as though the threat had just shifted a little—from something she could see to something that was invisible and therefore much more dangerous.

"I'd tell the truth," Fran said. "At least people would be watching you then. You'd have to stop beating your own kid, for one thing."

Beth scowled and got to her feet again. She settled the trash bag a little more carefully, as if she was making sure it didn't accidentally get tipped over. Fran stepped back a few more feet. "I'm a little sick of hearing about that," Beth said. "I told you, I pushed her once. I didn't beat her. I would never intentionally hurt a child. Even you."

She advanced on Fran, her arms thrown wide with the palms open. Fran wasn't fooled for a second. She backed away even further, then picked her moment and sprinted for the door.

Beth was too quick for her. She barreled in on an intercept course and thrust out her foot, tripping Fran so she went sprawling on the carpet. Then she knelt astride her, her knee in the small of Fran's back, one of her hands gripping Fran by her braided hair while the other hooked under her chin and squeezed hard.

Fran struggled to get free, but Beth's weight would have been too much for her even if she hadn't been in a headlock. She opened her mouth to scream, but Beth's grip on her throat tightened. Only a tiny clicking noise came out of her mouth, made by her jawbone being pushed sideways by the heel of Beth's hand. She couldn't utter a sound.

Beth leaned down and set her mouth against Fran's ear. Fran could feel the heat and wetness of her breath. "I was lying about that, obviously," she said. "I am totally up for hurting you." She didn't hiss or growl or snarl. She didn't even sound angry. If anything, her tone was gentle.

Panic came out of nowhere, eclipsing Fran's mind. She tried to break free again, shifting her weight furiously from left to right to left, trying to dislodge Beth from her back. Beth just bore down harder and pulled Fran's head up and back. Fran was going to choke if she didn't stop fighting. She went limp, and Beth loosened her grip a fraction.

"Better," Beth said. "Now I am thoroughly pissed off with you, little girl, and killing you would be the easiest thing in the world. But I've got other battles to fight, and some of them actually matter. My ex-husband is missing, and the slut he was living with is twisting my tits like you wouldn't believe. I don't want to have to keep one eye on you while I'm dealing with that.

"So I'm cutting you a break, just this once. Unrepeatable special offer. You pick your little tush up off the ground and you take it out of here, and you never, ever, come within a mile of me or mine as long as you live. If you do, I swear to God I will kill you, dismantle you and stow you where nobody will ever fucking find you. And if your dad comes looking, I'll do the same to him. Do you believe me?"

She loosened her grip more so Fran could answer. Fran was too terrified to speak at first, but when Beth shook her she managed a hoarse croak. "Yes!"

"Good. I knew there was a little grain of sense in there somewhere."

Suddenly the pressure was gone. There was no sound as Beth moved, but her fingers were no longer around Fran's throat and her knee wasn't in Fran's back. Fran crawled a few feet forward before climbing to her feet.

Beth was already standing, arms folded across her chest as if to say she was done with this. Done with Fran. "Now get the fuck out of here," she said.

Fran fled, out of the empty theater, along a corridor that curved like the inside of a shell, down some stairs. She had no idea where she was running to: she just had to get as much distance from Beth as she could manage. When she reached a fire door she sank down, crouched into a ball and burst into tears.

She had never felt so helpless. She had all the answers she needed, but she couldn't do anything with them. She had lost Jinx, and now she had lost this battle.

She realized with a sickening feeling, like vertigo, that she had never been remotely equipped to fight it.

Beth finished out her shift in a thoughtful mood. And she wore her feelings on her face, so none of her co-workers came near. She liked it better that way in any case.

When she got home and found the house empty, she fired up her son's laptop and read every article she could find on Fran Watts' kidnapping. It didn't trouble her that Zac and Molly were nowhere to be found. Presumably Zac had taken his kid sister out for a walk or a treat. She checked her phone and found no messages there, so it wasn't an emergency of any kind. That being the case, she didn't much care when they came back. The later the better, really.

The media had had a field day with the Picota case. Picota made a great bogeyman, and the six-year-old Fran the perfect victim. Beauty and the Beast. Unsurprisingly, most of the articles were about Picota's psychology rather than Fran's, but there were plenty of insights to be gleaned from the prurient reconstructions of the crime. Well, that and the fact that when Fran had met Liz for the first time it had been at the Carroll Way Medical Center, where they had both been waiting in line for a session with the same shrink. Ten years after her abduction, Fran Watts was still in therapy.

What was it she had said to Liz? That it was good to be able to find things when you needed them. Important, even. A pretty banal comment, Beth had thought at the time. But in Fran's case it was probably more like a cry for help. That early trauma reverberated down through her life, stirring echoes that never quite faded.

Useful to know.

Beth heard the key turn in the lock of the front door and shut down the browser window. She put the laptop back where she had found it on Zac's bedside table, and went out to meet her kids as they walked in, Molly all bundled up in woolly hat and gloves and outdoor coat so she was twice her usual size. Holding Zac's hand and trotting along in his wake, a tiny perpetual motion machine.

"We went to the park!" she exclaimed. "And fed the ducks. And went in a rowboat."

Zac gave Beth a guarded smile.

"Wow," Beth said. "That sounds exciting. I wish you'd waited for me. I love rowboats. I'm the rowboat queen of Pennsylvania."

Zac's face flushed. "I didn't know when you'd be back," he said. "And it was already starting to get dark."

"It's fine," Beth said. "You're a good big brother." She gave him a hug, then picked Molly up and hugged her too. It wasn't faked. Maybe it started off that way, but something real and raw welled up inside her and it was all she could do not to cry.

"I love you both," she said with a catch in her voice. "You know that, right?"

"We know!" Molly sing-songed, pressing her cheek—still cold from the outside air—against Beth's warm indoor cheek.

"We love you too, Mom," Zac said. It didn't sound as heartfelt as she would have liked. She had taken his devotion for granted and leaned on it pretty hard. But he was a genuinely good kid and he didn't know jack shit about anything under the sun. No matter what Fran Watts had said, no matter what she thought, he was never going to lose faith in his mother, or stop trusting her.

416

Which, again, was a good and extremely useful thing. "Oh hey," she said to him, as though it was an afterthought, "I ran into your friend today."

"Which friend?"

"Francine Watts. She was at the Cineplex. Got herself all lost and confused and I pointed her in the right direction."

Zac just stared at her for a moment or two, nonplussed.

"Did she . . . say anything?" he asked.

"Just sent her love to you both. She looked upset, though. Really unhappy. Like something was weighing on her mind. Is everything okay with her, Zachary?"

"As far as I know."

"Poor kid. She's been through so much. It's amazing it didn't drive her right out of her mind."

Zac made his escape, muttering about having an assignment to finish. Beth let him go for now. They would return to that theme soon.

She started to fix dinner. In fact she went to town. Cutting some aged rib-eye into strips, she rubbed it with a little salt and then prepared a marinade of soy sauce, chili, black pepper, garlic and lime. She immersed the steaks and left them to steep.

Then she went and read to Molly in the living room—much to the six-year old's puzzlement. "It's not my bedtime yet!" she exclaimed.

"I know," Beth said. "But stories aren't just for bedtime, baby girl. They're for whenever you want to tell them."

With Molly nestled in her lap, she read all her old favorites one after another. *Fox in Socks*, *Bear Hunt*, *If You Give a Mouse a Cookie*. Zac was in his room, but the door was open: even if he wasn't listening in on purpose he'd still get most of the highlights.

"Why is your voice funny?" Molly asked. "Are you okay, Mommy?"

"I'm fine, sweetheart," Beth answered with a break on the last word. She held Molly for a minute or so without saying anything, then finished the story, kissed her on the top of her head and set her down gently. "Mommy's got to go make dinner," she said. She closed the door behind her as she left the room: Zac was up next.

In the kitchen, she opened a bottle of red and poured herself a very full glass. She held it in her hand for a second or two before opening her fingers and letting it fall. It shattered on the tiles, the sound easily loud enough to carry.

When Zac ran in, he found Beth on her knees, picking the larger pieces of glass out of the mess on the floor, her fingers dripping red.

"Mom!" he cried. "Are you all right?"

"I'm fine," she said. But she shook her head, turning slowly to meet his gaze. She put on a bewildered expression—one that would have looked right at home on Liz's face. "Zac, I don't know. I've done some really bad things and I don't have any idea how to make it right again between us."

He crossed the room and knelt down beside her, throwing his arms around her. "You've been stressed out," he said, "for ages now."

"That doesn't make it okay," Beth said. She turned on the waterworks and Zac held her until she turned them off again. With an eye on the time, she moved on to her confession, telling him in anguished tones how in a moment of blind misery, panic and a whole lot of other feelings she couldn't even explain she'd actually hurt Molly. "I pushed her and she fell. I can't believe I did that, Zac! What kind of a monster am I?"

And so on, and so forth. By running herself down she forced him into running her up again, and she extorted forgiveness out of him by refusing to forgive herself. Once she had him in that emotional corner, the rest was easy. They moved to the breakfast bar, leaving the spilled wine and broken glass where they lay.

She had let him down, Beth said. She had let them all down. And not just her own family but that poor girl, Francine Watts, who was family in all but name. "What is it with her, Zac? What's making her so unhappy?"

It wasn't plain sailing even then. Zac was reluctant to give away things the kid had told him in confidence. Beth had to work him hard to get him to talk, and he talked about the facts of what had happened to Fran rather than the more intimate terrain of her feelings.

But one of the facts was very pertinent indeed. The kid had just made a personal pilgrimage up to Grove City to meet her nemesis, Bruno Picota, face-to-face. That evil old shit was still alive up there, it seemed, and Fran had hoped that by talking to him she might be able to work through what was left of her childhood trauma.

Beth suspected there was more to this whole thing with Picota than Zac was telling her, but that was fine. He'd given her plenty to work with. With her arms around him, she promised that she would do better. Be the person she used to be, only more so, and never neglect or hit out at the ones she loved ever again. She was intending to do a little more crying by way of a finale, but Zac beat her to it. They held each other and sobbed and were reconciled, and old hurts stopped hurting.

Or whatever.

Beth sent Zac in to check on his sister while she cleared up the mess she'd made and finished dinner. She congratulated herself on a part well played, but she was also genuinely exhausted. To get that authentic feel, she had plumbed memories that she hadn't gone near in a long time. The life she'd lost hung over her like a cloud, making the life she'd won darker and bleaker. Draining it of some of its savor and its meaning.

But Beth was a survivor, and the key word here was life. That was what she was fighting for. In the end, it legitimized everything she had already done.

And the terrible thing she was about to do next.

Jinx just kept running. She had no idea where. The important thing was to get away. But in the end, she ran to the place where she always ran to, the place that was hers and had been hers ever since the night she was born.

Which had been a time of blood and breaking and inexplicable terror. But birth was probably like that for everyone.

She limped into her den on her last legs, exhausted, starting and snapping at nothing. She fell into the rank softness of the place, wrapped it around her and closed her eyes. She thought she would sleep. Sleep forever, maybe, so she never had to think or feel or talk to anyone ever again.

Hey!

The shock of a voice here, in this secret place, was electrifying. Jinx jumped up and turned around to face the threat, whatever it was, her hackles up and her fangs bared. She had forgotten her armor and her sword for the moment: she was all instinct.

But it was just the almost-nothing. She sagged almost down to the ground and shook herself all over as though the movement could flick away the fear and the fury and the fight-readiness like drops of water.

Go away, stupid thing, she snarled. *Or I'll eat you! You shouldn't even be here.*

You brought me here! the almost-nothing said. *And then you went and left me. I didn't know if you were ever coming back.*

Jinx turned her back on the thing and lay down again. She folded her brush over herself like a blanket, which she thought was a pretty clear indication that she didn't want to be bothered.

The almost-nothing refused to take the hint. It kept on talking, talking, talking. Jinx stopped listening. The noise was an irritant but she could shut out the meaning, so it just became a sound like the whining of a mosquito. Not even that, really: just an imagining of what a sound would be like if she allowed it to be one.

She had had to run away. Fran had begged her to stay, and she was still in the same building as Picota (*Picota! Picota! Picota!*) but Jinx had had no choice. The questions right then were the bigger danger. Sometimes you protected people with your teeth, or your sword. Sometimes you protected them by running away.

From the things you couldn't think of. The things you couldn't say.

Does she know you're lobotomizing her? The almost-nothing asked.

Jinx shuddered again, from her nose all the way down to her tail. *You'd really better be quiet now,* she rumbled. Her eyes were closed and her head was down tight against her chest.

Those are her memories, right? Francine's? You took them right out of her head and brought them here. Why? Are they your food or something? Do you eat other people's—?

Jinx reared up and turned and jumped, so quickly that the almost-nothing had no chance to back away. She bore it down, putting her full weight on it. And she gave it a bite, just to prove she could. It cried out in shock and pain.

I should kill you just for saying that, Jinx snarled. *As if I'd ever . . . As if I could . . . I took away the things that hurt her! I made her be happy again when she was sad or scared. I love her more than anyone and that's why I'm always on guard. Always ready in case bad things happen. You, though: I'll eat you in one bite if you don't shut up!*

421

She was suddenly aware of how easy that would be. The almost-nothing had no way of fighting back or defending itself. It might be a monster, but it was a pathetic monster that had no real way of hurting anyone even if it wanted to.

Jinx found a little space, even in the vastness of her self-pity and her concern for Fran, to be ashamed. She pushed the almost-nothing away, but she did so gently, trying not to harm it any more than she had.

Just leave me alone, she said again.

She curled around herself and lay down. The almost-nothing was quiet, but it wasn't dead. The throb of its thoughts persisted. It even spoke from time to time, but very softly, most likely just to itself. After a while, it even became soothing. Jinx would have to kill the thing in the end anyway, because it knew where her den was. But she would do it as quickly and painlessly as she could.

She sank into a sort of doze, thinking about happier times when she lay at the foot of Fran's bed and listened to the rise and fall of her sweet breath, hour after hour after hour.

She was so attuned to threat that she was slow to realize what was happening as the tentative cadences touched her ears and then the edges of her awareness, until finally she let herself acknowledge them for what they were.

The almost-nothing was singing to her.

Fran made it through the rest of the movie, but she had no idea what she was watching or listening to. Her dad's plans to cheer her up and bring her out of herself had been shipwrecked on the hidden rocks of Zac's evil mom.

That agenda was ongoing, though. After the movie Gil took her to one of the many pizzerias around Bakery Square—she didn't even register which one it was—and plied her with medicinal chit-chat.

"So the one with the shield is Star-Lord? Why do they call him that?"

"They don't, Dad. They call him Captain America."

"Then which one is Star-Lord?"

Fran tried her best to play along, and succeeded well enough to keep the game going all through dinner. The only respite was when the Steelers game came up on the restaurant's massive wide-screen TV and her dad's attention wandered.

That was when Zac's first text came through. The first of many, as it turned out.

SHE SAID SHE SAW YOU. WHAT HAPPENED???

Fran almost didn't reply. She really didn't feel up to going there just yet. But she had promised Zac answers and then spent the whole weekend hiding from him.

NOTHING HAPPENED, she messaged him back. WE JUST TALKED.

She waited, knowing he wouldn't leave it at that. She didn't have to wait long. The next text dropped almost immediately.

SHE'S IN A WEIRD MOOD. SHE CRIED.

Wow, Fran thought. That was about the last thing she could imagine Beth doing. What would possibly make her cry? She just texted a question mark.

"Oh, good job!" Gil exclaimed, still watching the TV. The chime of another message sounded at the same time.

SHE SAID SHE'S SORRY. SHE'LL BE DIFFERENT FROM NOW ON.

Fran thought long and hard about that one. There were so many possible answers. In the end she settled for three words. They seemed like the best she could do.

DON'T TRUST HER.

"I hope that's not some boy," Gil said. "You've got to be careful when you're on the rebound, Frog."

He had no way of knowing how many raw nerves he was touching with that one stupid joke. Fran smiled weakly, but she didn't attempt a laugh: in the mood she was in right then it might have come out sounding like hysteria. She put the phone away and didn't look at it throughout the rest of the meal.

In the car on the way home, though, she stole another glance. Just the one. Zac had messaged her three times, the texts about ten minutes apart. First, the bald WHAT DO YOU MEAN? Then FRAN WHAT DO U MEAN? And finally WHY SHOULDN'T I TRUST HER? COME ON EXPLAIN.

But she couldn't. Not right then. And maybe never. Beth's threat came back into her mind along with a sudden, physical chill of fear, as though someone had dropped her heart and her lungs into an ice bucket. *I will kill you, dismantle you and stow you.*

"What's with this traffic?" Gil muttered. "I'll try Washington."

And if your dad comes looking . . .

"On a Sunday, for Pete's sake. Where's everybody going?"

If your dad . . .

"Okay, that guy is blocking a hydrant. I hope he gets a ticket."

I'll do the same to him.

Panic welled up inside her. She turned off the phone, on the third attempt because her hands were shaking. She couldn't tell how much of the fear she was feeling was for herself, and how much was for her dad. She imagined Beth walking up to him, smiling at him, and then . . . no. Nothing, nothing, nothing! She wrenched her mind away from terrible, formless thoughts.

The evening went by in a daze. She played cards with her dad, first gin rummy and then cribbage. Her mind was all over the place and she lost the best part of a million dollars even though she was pretty sure her dad was trying to let her win. In the end he gave up the unequal struggle.

"Do you want to call it a night?" he asked.

"I think I do," Fran said. "Sorry, Dad. I'm all wiped out."

"But today was good, right?"

"It was great." She gave him a weak smile. "You're the best, Daddo." She kissed him on the cheek. "The very best. Always." She wished she could be happy for his sake, after he had worked so hard.

And—now it was too late—she wished she could be honest. But to tell him the truth now would mean exposing him to Beth. He wouldn't stand a chance against her. He was too good, and too gentle.

Fran went up to her room. She hadn't lied about being tired. She felt as though she had been walking around all day with a boulder on her back. She lay down and closed her eyes.

But the panic was right there where she had left it. It surged up again from the bottom of her mind, stronger than ever, and she sat up in a hurry. Something terrible was happening or was going to happen. She felt it, like a pointy splinter of certainty in the general squishy mess of her thoughts.

There wasn't anywhere she could go, or anything she could do, to get away from that feeling. In the end, with bleak resignation, she turned her phone back on.

She found what she expected to find. Lots more texts from Zac, each a little shoutier and crazier than the one before. He had gone right on messaging her through the evening, hoping that the thirtieth text might succeed where the twenty-ninth had failed.

The last message didn't have any words. It was just a jpeg. Full of misgivings, Fran opened it.

The photo showed a small, bare room. Seven words had been scrawled in black marker pen on a white wall pocked with blooms of mildew. IM GONNA WAIT HERE TIL YOU COME. The open door of the room was just visible on the left-hand side of the picture. The room was dark. When Zac took the photo, he had had to use his phone's flashlight, which was barely up to the job. The flash had also picked up the number on the door, reflecting off the dull metal so the two digits shone with white witch-light. 22.

Of course.

"Thank you, Zachary," she muttered. "Thank you so much." Obviously he lost a few marks for repeating the same dumb stunt he'd pulled on her last time. But on the other hand, he got extra credit for choosing the Perry Friendly rather than the railway platform. He knew she wasn't going to leave him to spend the night all alone in that place. Classy, very. It was like holding a gun to your own head and saying, "Hand over your money or the kid gets it."

With a heavy heart Fran got up and put on her outdoor clothes. Her watch said it was still pretty early, only just after nine o'clock. Even so, she was sure her dad wouldn't be happy with her going out alone, especially since she couldn't tell him where she was going. She was left with the choice of whether to lie to him (again) or just sneak out without him seeing.

"Jinx," she said, keeping her voice low. "Jinx, are you there?"

There was no answer. Fran hadn't really been expecting one.

She went down the stairs slowly and carefully, holding her boots in her hand. As she stole past the door of the den the sound of the TV came through the half-open door: not a football game but a news broadcast or maybe a documentary. "Of all nature's wonders," a cultured male voice was saying, "few are more majestic than—"

Fran went out through the back door, pulling it closed behind her about a millimeter at a time until the lock clicked. Then she sat on the step to put her boots on. It was butt-numbingly cold, but she needed to be careful not to make a sound. The window of the den was only three feet to her left.

She had to pass under that window to get to the side passage. She did it in a low crouch, her legs bent almost double and her head tucked in under her shoulders. The blinds were down, but their neighbor's security light shone right into the yard and she might accidentally cast a shadow as she moved.

That thought brought Bruno Picota into her mind very much against her will. She tried to push the thought away, but it stayed with her as she rounded the back and side of the house, crossed the front lawn—again very carefully and quietly—and finally stepped out onto the street. It was completely empty, which she found reassuring and unnerving in about equal measure.

She walked quickly, coat zipped up all the way and head down. Picota's gray, sagging face hung in front of her eyes. He had talked about a place where things got squishy. *It sticks to you if you're a certain kind of person,* he said. Had he meant the Perry Friendly? Yeah, of course he had. Where else could it have been? *You were there too, but I was there for longer.*

And now she was going back there. At night. Even though Beth had warned her what would happen if she didn't stay out of her business. Fran was amazed at her own stupidity. It didn't feel like courage. At best, it was a reluctance to leave Zac hanging after promising to share what she found out. He had set her on this road in the first place: he deserved to know where it had led even if he didn't believe her. Even if he hated her for what she was about to tell him.

There was still some traffic on Washington as she crossed the bridge. Fran stayed in the center of the walkway, feeling too visible and too vulnerable in the light of the streetlamps, so she didn't even see the cars on the highway below her; she just heard them pass, the boom-hiss of their tires on the asphalt sounding like the tide going out on a distant beach.

She stepped off the bridge at the Homewood end and walked on into darkness. Most of the streetlights here were broken. The tidal roar was hushed. She felt as though she was going underwater.

Everything was different at night, but she remembered the way. She was walking quickly now, partly because she thought she was less likely to be accosted if she looked as though she was going somewhere, but mostly as a way of fighting the strong urge she felt to turn around and run away.

The motel's driveway loomed ahead of her. The wrought iron, hectic with rust like an embarrassing infection; the lightbox with its empty promises. Fran walked right in. She crossed the parking lot, picking her way with care in case she tripped on the concrete dividers in the dark. The arch that led through to the courtyard was right in front of her now: a deeper darkness beyond, and a silence that seemed to swallow every sound.

"Jinx?" she whispered again. Just in case because you never knew. Because there had never been a time before this when she called on Jinx and Jinx forsook her. And because she really, really didn't want to step through that arch on her own.

But Jinx didn't answer and didn't appear. Fran could have shouted out to Zac, but she found she didn't want to. Suppose someone else was out there too, closer than him? Suppose the Perry Friendly at night had residents who didn't show themselves in the daylight?

This was no good at all. She couldn't come all this way and then let her own imagination defeat her. She made herself step forward, through the arch and into the rear courtyard.

There was a paved path that led off to her left in a long curve all the way to the other end of the courtyard where room 22 was. But taking the path would mean walking in front of each room in turn, past each blind window and bolted door. Fran couldn't make herself do that even though the going would be easier and safer. She waded out into the weeds instead, once more feeling her way a step at a time. She tried not to make any noise, but the weeds swished and rustled as she moved and occasionally a thicker stem broke with a wet click under her foot. Nobody could accuse her of stealth.

The door of room 22 was open but there was no light inside. Fran felt a twinge of doubt. Had Zac led her here as some kind of cruel joke, bailing as soon as he'd sent the message so she would arrive and find the whole place deserted? No, she didn't believe that. He'd only ever been cruel to her once, and that was in the heat of a bad moment. He wouldn't trick her in such a nasty, sadistic way. He wasn't like that.

So she screwed up her courage and headed right for that open door. But she stopped a few feet short of it. The darkness and the silence felt like a barrier she was pushing against, and she couldn't make herself go any further.

"Zac?" she whispered.

A light went on inside the room, and then off again at once. It was a vivid, blue-white rectangle: the light from a phone's screen as someone checked for messages or maybe just looked to see what time it was.

Weak and almost sick with relief, Fran stepped forward. "Next time I'm gonna choose the venue, goon," she said. "I had about three heart attacks getting here."

"Next time?" said a voice out of the dark. "Oh, sweetheart, I hate to be first with the bad news."

It wasn't Zac's voice. It was Beth's.

Fran jumped like a startled fawn. But when she came down she didn't waste any time trying to figure out how this could be happening. She knew in that instant that this was a trap and she'd walked right into it. She turned and ran. All she needed to do was get out into the middle of the weeds and duck down. Beth couldn't see in the dark any better than she could.

The taser hit her right between the shoulder blades. The world lit up like a million fireworks, the colors all blending into a pure white light that was made of nothing but pain.

It wasn't much of a leap, really.

A child's memories. A fox that looked more like a child's drawing than a real animal. A fox that had childlike features and a sweet soprano voice with a child's lisp to it.

Liz sang "Morningtown" first. She had used it as a lullaby on Zac and Molly both, and the fox seemed overwhelmingly tired. Then she just went for whatever felt right. "You Are the Everything," "Danny Boy," "The First Time Ever I Saw Your Face." Songs about love, and about longing.

She wished she had a hand to touch the little animal's head and neck. It was lying on its side, all curled up, its belly half-exposed. A real animal lying like that would be inviting a human touch, a human scratch or stroke or caress. Liz tried to make the words do it instead.

The fox didn't react in any visible way. Six or seven songs in, Liz stopped, thinking the experiment had been a failure. She was an outsider here, a prisoner, and she couldn't change her status or negotiate her freedom with REM and Roberta Flack.

Suzanne, the fox growled.

What? Liz wanted to make sure she'd heard right.

Sing "Suzanne" next.

Liz did. Then she went on to "If I Didn't Have Your Love to Make it Real" and "Hey, That's No Way to Say Goodbye." She would never have gone to Leonard Cohen by herself: there was always so much sadness underneath even his sweetest songs. But the fox seemed happy with those choices. Its breathing deepened and slowed, and it lay quiet until she was done. Its eyes were closed, and Liz thought it might actually be asleep until it spoke.

All right, it said. *I won't eat you.*

That's very kind. Thank you.

If I let you go, you have to promise never to come back. If you come back, I'll bite you or kill you with my sword. Or if you tell anyone else how to get here.

I promise.

After a little while, when the fox hadn't moved from beside her or said anything else, Liz ventured, *Is it okay if I ask what your name is?*

Lady Jinx.

A vague memory stirred and came halfway into focus. *Wasn't she a . . .? I mean, were you a knight? In a forest somewhere? With a . . . a queen and a bunch of other knights?*

Yes. I was. Then I came here.

Okay. I'm pleased to meet you, Lady Jinx. I'm Liz.

Liz Kendall.

Yes.

Zac's mom.

That's right. Do you know Zac?

You know I do. You were there on the railway platform.

Yes, I saw you there. But you didn't talk to him so I wasn't sure.

I only talk to Fran.

And to me.

You don't count.

Liz wasn't about to argue that one. Actually she was careful not to disagree with anything Lady Jinx said. She was convinced now that she was dealing with a child; a child of around Molly's age but in some ways less mature, less in control of herself. So she used the same strategies she would have used with Molly, coaxing and gentling. Making her feel safe and helping her to find the way back to her better self whenever she was inclined to sulk or throw a tantrum.

She told Jinx about Zac and Molly. How much she loved them. How much she missed them. Moments she treasured from back when she was still with them.

And she let Jinx talk, when she was ready, about the trip to Grove City. Walking into the lair of her worst enemy, Bruno Picota. Wanting to protect Fran from the man who had already hurt her so much. Failing in her greatest test. Being exposed, and running away.

I can't go back, Jinx lamented. *If I go back, she'll ask me again. I don't want to tell her! I can't! But even if I don't say it, she'll know it when she looks at me.*

Liz didn't understand this part. She knew the little animal had a secret, and whatever it was Fran had figured it out because of something Bruno Picota had said. She reassured Jinx as best she could, reminding her how much Fran loved her and how long they had been together. Their relationship wouldn't change on account of something that had happened in the distant past.

Think of all the things you've done for her. Watching by her bed at night. Being there for her after her mom died. Taking away the bad memories.

It's true, Jinx said, a little consoled. *I did do all those things.*

Exactly. And that counts for more than anything, doesn't it? Liz hated herself for what she was doing, but she couldn't let the opportunity slip. There might never be another one. *I'm amazed, really,* she said softly, *that you were able to do it at all. You must be very brave. And very clever.*

Jinx gave her a wary look. Clearly that had been laying it on a bit too thick. She plunged on anyway. *I don't think it's something I could have done. Taking away all those bad memories. Was it hard?*

Yes, Jinx said. *It was very hard.*

433

If Fran had known what you were doing, it might have scared her. I suppose you had to be very quiet, and very careful.

Yes.

Going all the way into her mind, and all the way out again, without ever making a sound. So she didn't have the slightest idea. So she never even knew you'd been there.

Jinx was just looking at her now. Waiting. She'd gotten to the conclusion already and was waiting for Liz to come out from hiding and join her there. Being a child didn't make her stupid or naive.

Will you teach me? Liz asked anyway. *Please?*

Jinx scowled and bared her teeth. *No,* she said. *I won't. That's like saying can I borrow your sword I won't do any harm I just want to feel how sharp it is.*

But I won't, Liz protested. *I won't do any harm. Not to Fran, I swear. I just want to—*

The fox rose and shook itself. *I know what you want,* it said. *Do you know what I want?*

A multicolored haze enveloped her for a second. When it faded Jinx was standing on her hind legs—and dressed from neck to toe in silver armor. A broadsword hung at her waist. There must be a hole in the back of the armor for her brush, which rose higher than her head and flickered as though it was on fire.

Liz was awed in spite of herself. Everything in this place was like a dream, but she had never in her life had a dream as vivid as this. Jinx as a knight was imposing and beautiful. There was still something simplified and cartoonish about her, but she looked the part, all the same. A warrior, standing on her dignity.

To keep Fran safe, Liz guessed. Because duh.

To keep Fran safe. And telling you how to get into her mind and take pieces out of it won't do that, will it? I'm not going to tell that to anyone.

Liz had allowed herself to hope. The flat refusal almost plunged her back into despair, except that despair was a luxury she couldn't allow herself. Not while her children were in Beth's hands. She would have to find some other way of fighting her.

All right, she said. *I understand. If you'll just show me the way home, then . . .* She faltered and stopped. Jinx was shaking her head slowly. *You said you'd let me go!*

That was before you started asking me those questions. About Fran, and how to get into her thoughts.

No! Not Fran's thoughts. Beth's thoughts!

It's all the same. You just want power. Like Lady Subtle when she betrayed Queen Yuleia. I'm sorry, Liz. I won't hurt you, but I'm not going to let you go. You're clever and you tried to trick me. It's better if you stay here.

Liz felt a wave of fury and frustration. She fought her way through it. Jinx was just a little girl. A little girl who happened to have the power of life and death over her. She had messed up badly by underestimating both the fox's intelligence and her paranoia. Which meant she had blown the only chance she had of getting out of here.

She groped desperately, wildly, for another argument to throw into the scales. Jinx was turning away, preparing to leave. What could she do or say to change the decision she'd already made?

Will you at least give Fran a message from me? Ask her to pass it along to Zac?

No. If Beth is a monster, Fran should stay away from her. I won't tell her anything about you.

Liz almost screamed. The logic was impregnable. She needed to make Jinx an ally, but Jinx's priorities were simple, rigid and remorseless. There was only room in her head and heart for one thing.

But that one thing did come in a candy-coated, cartoon wrapper. It occurred to Liz, in a moment of chilling calm, that there was an obvious way of finessing Jinx. It was the same way Jinx finessed herself. You didn't get around a knight by being devious. Knights had a code. They came pre-programmed.

All right, she said quickly. *I understand. I won't ask you to trust me.*

Good, Jinx muttered. She was already walking away. The conversation was over.

But you belong to the forest table, Liz called out. *And they're sworn to protect the innocent. Or did I miss a memo? Do you just do what the hell you feel like now?*

The fox slowed. Stopped. She turned to face Liz with something like a warning written on her face. *It's the Woodland Table. We're the shield of the righteous and the sword of the defenseless.*

Well, that's exactly what my children are, Jinx. They're righteous and they're defenseless. They're trapped in a monster's dungeon with nobody to save them or care whether they live or die. Please say you'll keep them safe. Swear to me on your honor that you'll go to them and keep them safe.

Jinx hesitated. Liz saw the doubt in her hyper-expressive, cartoon face and pressed her advantage. *I'm asking you to do your duty as a knight. You can't say no. If you say no, you'll be shamed in front of—of the whole table. All the other knights. Your queen. Can you imagine what your queen will think of you?*

A shiver ran through the little fox. Liz could see she was pressing the right buttons; also that what she was asking Jinx to do was hard. Very hard. It pulled her away from the one task that defined her and made sense of her, which was protecting Fran.

But it played into the narrative suggested by the armor and the sword, however insane and inexplicable those things were.

You have to, she finished. *You're their only hope, Lady Jinx. I don't have anyone else to turn to.*

Something happened to Jinx's stance over the space of half a dozen heartbeats. She stood up straighter. Her right hand slid down, almost imperceptibly, until it rested on her sword hilt. Her chest expanded as though she was drawing in a deep, slow breath.

I swear on my honor, she said. Her eyes were wide and her teeth were bared. She seemed surprised, and not in a good way, by the words she was saying. *I swear on my sword, Oathkeeper, whose touch no evil thing can withstand, that I will keep your children safe. The monster Beth will not have them.*

Thank you, Liz said. Feeling the insanity of the moment almost like a flavor, a salt-sea tang in the gray air. *Thank you, Lady Jinx.*

When the fox turned and walked away from her, fading quickly into nothingness, she tried to follow. But the walls closed in around her again and she was alone.

Some of the details had only come clear to Beth when she was already embarked on the plan, but the broad shape of it was there from the start. The start being the moment when that little streak of muddy pump water looked her in the eye and said, "I know what you are!"

Oh, she played it cool. Of course she did. The Bakery Square Cineplex was not the right place to have this out. The best Beth could do was to put a scare into said little streak, and at the same time to leave her with the sense that that was *all* she was going to do. A very minimal, very precisely judged act of violence, and a few carefully chosen words: *I'm cutting you a break.* Send the kid away feeling like she'd gotten off with a mild spanking this time.

But now . . . well, now Beth had to deal with it. Really deal with it so the problem (or problems, plural, because Beebee Brophy and the Pittsburgh City Police were looming in the middle distance too) would go away forever.

Alone at home, before Zac and Molly got back from their boating adventure, she thought it out coldly and dispassionately. She could see the shape of a solution, but she approached it with extreme caution, examining it from every angle. She was afraid she

438

might be doing a number on herself, dragging unrelated things together to propel herself down a certain road so she could say afterward that she had no choice.

There was a story that would play well, up to a point. The story was a tragedy in one act. Francine Watts, a fruitcake of long standing, goes up to Grove City to confront her nemesis, Bruno Picota. It does not go well. She comes home to Pittsburgh in a highly agitated state, and over the next twenty-four hours or so she sinks deeper and deeper into depression. Finally she kills herself, putting a sad but unsurprising end to a tortured and fucked-up life. She does this in the very place where her life was derailed ten years before: the Perry Friendly, a conveniently secluded and deserted site that could be stage-dressed in any way Beth thought appropriate.

But after Fran had been found, some worms might start to spill out of cans. Zac knew all about the kid's trip up to Grove City and what she was trying to do there. He might not be convinced by a suicide scenario, and he might have suspicions. If he shared those suspicions with the police, the whole thing could easily unravel.

And then there was Molly, who was soon to be questioned by the police about the night of Marc's disappearance. If she remembered even half of what had happened that night—or even a single salient detail like the blood all over Mommy's face—then Beth was cooked.

She followed these troubling ideas as they grew from thin trickles of possibility into a broad, inexorable torrent. But there was a part of her that was flailing and fighting the current. She couldn't name what she was thinking, even to herself. She could only play it out in her mind in wordless images. Three kids at the Perry Friendly, not one. A suicide pact. The older kids drugging the little one, then bashing her head in with a rock before cutting their own wrists and bleeding out, side by side, on rotted linoleum.

Her stomach twisted. She ran into the bathroom, bowed down in front of the toilet like a supplicant while waves of nausea cramped and sweated her. But when the crisis passed, the picture was still etched on her eyes. The three sprawled shapes. The silence. No risk of exposure, now or ever.

No. No no no. Not her kids.

Exactly. They were not her kids.

But at the same time they absolutely were. That she couldn't love them, that she had come almost to hate them and fear their touch wasn't their fault. It was hers. She had run from her own death, again and again and again, until finally she ended up here. Back where she started, except that the road she ran turned out to be a Moebius strip and now she was upside down to everything that mattered.

They weren't her kids.

They were, but they were not.

And this was life or death. Life after death, that she had grabbed and held on to in the face of a whole frothing, flaring universe of random agony. She had walked into the promised land across a thousand stepping stones, each and every one of them a death. She wasn't ready—wasn't able—to give up what she had now and go back down into the dark.

Beth had given up doubt a long time ago. She had only survived so long by paring herself down to a fine edge of utter certainty and self-belief. That paring wasn't something she could undo or step away from. The edge was inside her now.

She would do this awful thing. And she would hate herself for a long time, perhaps forever. But she would survive that too.

Once she had decided, she went about it methodically. She researched Fran Watts. She lulled Zac's suspicions and interrogated him. She prepared dinner, which was no small part of the plan. And in her head, she worked out the logistics. The best way was the simplest, which meant dividing first and conquering afterward.

She claimed to have lost her phone, and borrowed Zac's. She intended to put it to use immediately, opening up a dialogue with Fran. Texts were the perfect medium because they were terse as hell and only came in one flavor. Lying was a lot easier if you didn't have to worry about nuance. But before she plunged in, she

440

scrolled back through previous messages to get a feel for the rhythms of Zac's messaged prose. She was glad she did. There were rich pickings there that sparked new ideas.

But all she needed to do for now was to give things a little push to get them moving. SHE SAID SHE SAW YOU, she typed. WHAT HAPPENED???

Fran replied at once, which made it even easier. Now she had something to play off. They batted the unspoken ball back and forth a little. DON'T TRUST HER was interesting. It validated everything Beth was doing. The threat hadn't taken. If she hadn't decided to act, the kid would now be rallying her own family against her.

When Fran stopped responding, Beth flung a few more text messages into the void and then returned to the other half of her plan. There was still plenty of time. She fried up the steak, baked up the rice and called the kids to table.

"Wow," Zac marveled as he tucked into the meltingly tender meat. "This is amazing, Mom! What's it called?"

"Weeping tiger," Beth told him. "It's from Thailand."

"Is it made of tiger?" Molly asked, thrilled.

"No, baby girl, just regular cow. But they have to find a cow that's got tiger stripes."

This lame joke made Molly giggle fit to bust. Beth ruffled her hair and let the hand rest there for a moment or two, tears and emotions welling up despite herself.

"Can I have my phone back?" Zac asked.

"No phones at the table, mister. You know that."

Except for her. She slipped away a couple of times under the pretext of preparing something mysterious for dessert. Actually she was just texting Fran again and again, laying the groundwork for the big finale.

"I'm sleepy," Molly complained, chasing a piece of steak lethargically around the plate with her fork. Beth took the fork from her, speared the meat and held it to the little girl's lips. "No dessert unless you clear your plate," she chided. Molly opened her mouth

441

and accepted the morsel without complaint. She chewed on it for a long time, decelerando.

"Mom," Zac mumbled. "I feel kind of weird."

"You'll be fine, dollface," Beth told him. "Don't be scared."

Molly's eyes were glazing over. The half-chewed meat slid out of her mouth and fell down onto her plate. A moment later, she fell sideways off her chair. Beth caught her before she hit the floor and lowered her gently down. When she looked up again, Zac was slumped at an angle, his eyes half-closed, his posture unnaturally still.

Beth checked his pulse with a finger at his throat and was reassured. It was important to her that the children didn't suffer any more than was necessary: to that end she had ground up eight temazepam tablets, using the handle of a knife as a pestle, and added them to the marinade. The intense spices hid the bitterness very well.

Loading the kids into the car was a great deal easier than it had been when she did the same thing with Marc. They were lighter, for one thing: even Zac wasn't too heavy for her to lift and carry over a short distance, and Molly was a piece of cake. The Rogue helped a lot too. It was a bigger and frankly a better car than the Kia had been, with a capacious trunk into which—once she folded the back seats down—two inert bodies fitted without any fuss or strain.

Nissan should build that into their advertising, Beth thought.

Before she set out, she sent a couple more texts in Fran's direction. The coup de grâce would come later, but it was no bad thing to keep the channel open. Beth hoped it was open. If Fran had just turned her phone off for the night, this could all fall apart on her.

Either way, she couldn't afford to dawdle from here on out. She locked up the house, got into the car and drove, not toward Lenora but toward Washington—and then across it into Homewood.

She hadn't been to the Perry Friendly Motel since before she was married, and she wasn't entirely sure of the way. She could have used the car's built-in GPS system, but that seemed like a bad idea for any number of reasons. She just drove slowly, following her instincts and turning in whenever she saw anything that looked familiar. She missed it on the first pass, but the lightbox sign and the wrought-iron gateposts registered a second after she drove past it. She turned around and found the lightless access road almost at once. She kept an eye out for headlights, but there were no other vehicles in sight as she turned in off the street and bumped and rocked her way up the crumbling flags of the driveway to the Perry Friendly.

The abandoned motel was a sinister place after dark. Shit, it was probably sinister in broad daylight. No wonder Bruno Picota had chosen to bring his kidnap victim there. The ambience was perfect. Of course, Beth was seeing it as a ruin. Maybe it had been a happening place back in the day.

It would have been possible, just about, to drive the car across the weed-choked lot and park it in the rear courtyard, but the crushed-down and ripped-up weeds would have left a spectacularly visible trail. Instead, she parked at the end of the driveway, where the undergrowth began in earnest. She would have to carry the kids one by one through the arch and across the courtyard to room 22.

The cold air hit her as she got out of the car. It seemed much chillier here than it had been back at the house. Her breath steamed against the backdrop of the headlight beams like writhing ghosts, and the crunch of her feet on the gravel chased up echoes that seemed to come from unlikely directions. Beth changed her mind: open or closed, this place had always been a creepy fucking dive. Even its name, the Perry Friendly, was trying suspiciously hard. You didn't give your establishment a name like that if people got a positive vibe as they walked in.

Zac and Molly still hadn't stirred. Beth took Zac first, carrying him slung over her shoulder in a fireman's carry. Over this longer distance the weight quickly started to tell. Putting one foot in front of the other required a real effort, especially since she had to place her feet carefully to avoid trip hazards buried in the weeds.

By the time she laid Zac down on the floor of room 22, she was sweating like a Sumo wrestler and breathing like Molly on a bad night. She needed to take a short rest. She used the time to write her message for Fran on the wall in black marker, using multiple strokes to thicken each letter so they would show up better in the photo.

Then she went and fetched Molly, which was a stroll in the park after carrying Zac. She laid the little girl down next to her brother, careful not to jolt or bruise her even though she was so deeply asleep she wouldn't have felt a thing.

In fact, she wouldn't feel anything again, ever. That thought brought a wrenching sob into Beth's throat, so powerful it was almost like vomiting. She didn't want to have to do this. She wished there was any other way, any route to her own safety that didn't involve the children's deaths. But there wasn't. She had to see it through or else surrender everything she'd won. Go to jail for Marc's murder, or flee into the void and leave Doormat Liz to face the music for her.

No. She had fought too hard and suffered too much. She had bought this life with her own blood, a whole ocean of it. And now that interest was due, she would pay in someone else's.

She took a photo of the message on the wall, following the template she had already found in the message history on Zac's phone. It would either work or it wouldn't. If Fran Watts took the bait, this ended tonight and the rest of Beth's life began. Until then, there was nothing she could do but wait.

She sat down just inside the door. From this vantage point she could look out into the courtyard while keeping one eye on her unconscious kids. Time went by very slowly. The crickets sang and occasionally some animal, most likely a rat, scratched against the wall behind her or scampered across the floor. She used Zac's phone at first to keep track of time, since the face of her watch couldn't be seen in the near-perfect dark. But she forced herself to stop when three successive glances, seemingly long minutes apart, all showed the time to be 10:43 p.m.

Beth had read about what happened to people in sensory deprivation tanks. Their brains responded to the complete absence of information from the outside world by filling in the blanks with vivid hallucinations. Something like that started to happen to her now. She heard sounds out in the courtyard. A bleat of tinny music, a woman's laugh. Those noises could have been carried on the wind from some house nearby, Beth told herself. But there were no houses: that was what made this place so well suited to her needs. Then from the room next door she heard a creak of bedsprings, followed by an unmistakably sexual moan.

She scrambled to her feet and stepped outside. The door to the adjacent room was nailed shut and there was no light or sound from inside. Just nerves, then. She had never suffered from them before now, but this body had been Liz's for a long time before it was hers. Maybe nerves had a memory the same way muscles did.

She returned to room 22 and her vigil, trying to ignore the sense that the space around her was somehow aware of her. That the Perry Friendly, so long abandoned, wasn't dead at all but just now waking from a light, unquiet sleep.

Finally she heard the sound of someone approaching, rustling and stumbling their way across the courtyard. She dropped her hand to the taser, which she was wearing on her belt, and waited patiently.

The sounds stopped. Whoever was out there—and this time Beth was sure somebody actually was—had slowed to a halt, almost certainly looking toward room 22 for signs of life. Should she provide some? Better to hold still and wait.

"Zac?" The whisper came from close by, but it was hard to say in the dark exactly where the whisperer was standing. Beth needed Fran to be right up close when she fired. Inspiration came when she shifted her weight and felt Zac's phone move in her hip pocket.

She took it out and turned it on, then off again at once.

It worked. The footsteps walked right up to the door of the room.

"Next time I'm gonna choose the venue, goon," Fran Watts said, sounding relieved. "I had about three heart attacks getting here."

She was standing square in the doorway, outlined very conveniently against the lesser gloom of the outside air. Beth raised the taser, slowly and silently, and took careful aim.

Normally when Jinx left her den and headed back to the real world, Fran was her beacon. Jinx's sense of her was strong and highly directional, and Fran was always the destination she was heading for. Now, for the first time ever, she turned away from that intense, steady signal and followed a different trail entirely.

She went to Liz's house, steering by memory: her recollections, powerful and recent, of the house where Zac Kendall lived, together with the tiny cub called Molly and the monster who looked like their mother. She breached from the void into their family room.

The house was empty, but it smelled of recent occupation. The children had been here, and so had the monster. But not Fran. The monster hadn't lured her to this place. Full of relief, Jinx padded from room to room to interrogate the smells some more.

They weren't really smells, she knew that: she was sensitive to the way people thought and felt, and the residue of thought and feeling was what she was looking for now. What she found was confusing. The monster had thought sad thoughts, and cunning thoughts. She had thought of her children, and she had thought of blood. In the midst of all this, she had thought—very strongly and clearly—about Fran.

Considerably more alarmed now, Jinx ran through the house from room to room. The scents were strongest in the kitchen, but there was no way of telling what had happened there. The scent of Liz's two children was very weak. They weren't feeling anything much at all. But the monster's spoor was strong, and rich with turbulent emotions.

She should go to Fran, she knew. She needed to check that Fran was safe. But she had promised Liz, on her honor as a knight, that she would protect the children. She had to keep that promise, now more than ever. It was very clear that the monster meant them harm.

Jinx loped straight through the wall, down the driveway of the house and out onto the road. They had lingered for quite some time in the driveway, but Jinx didn't. She followed the trail, running hard with her head down through people and cars, houses and streets and gardens. She didn't look where she was going because she didn't have to: nothing could stand in her way.

The monster had taken Zac and Molly, preying on the weak and helpless the way monsters did. But now the monster would reckon with Lady Jinx, and it would beg for mercy before it died. She allowed herself a brief imagining of that moment—when Oathkeeper's blade cut off the monster's head. It felt so good that she imagined it again and again, with different words from her and different wails and shrieks from the monster.

She wasn't looking or thinking. She was careless. The evil rose up ahead of her, a curtain of filthy smog that the eye couldn't see. She was running too fast to stop in time, even if she had realized, and by the time she realized it was all around her. Her headlong gallop lost its rhythm as her feet scrambled on caked blackness. She staggered blindly back, eyes tight shut, to the perimeter, where she lay helpless, a trembling mass, until her thoughts gradually came back to her.

The Perry Friendly. The trail led right to it.

Or rather the trails. There were two now. The monster had passed right through this gate only a little while before. And so, even more recently, had Fran. Fran had followed Beth here, to the one place in the whole world where Jinx couldn't go.

Jinx couldn't help herself. She threw back her head and howled, first like a fox and then, as the dams within her broke one by one, like a little girl.

Fran woke, sick and groggy, to find that she couldn't move or speak. She was lying on a solid floor—presumably the floor of room 22. Her hands were down by her sides, somehow pinned or held in place, and something had been taped or tied across her mouth.

Beth was kneeling nearby, facing away from Fran. She was rummaging in a big canvas holdall, whose contents clunked and rattled and occasionally creaked. The smell in the room was a lot worse than before. Along with the mildew and damp there was an eye-watering reek of rot. Some animal must have died in here since the time when she and Zac had made their visit.

Fran tried to tilt her head so she could see what was pinning her hands, but although there was now some light in the room it wasn't falling on her. All she could see was Beth—and then, as Beth moved, Zac and Molly. They were lying side by side on the floor a little way away. They weren't moving. Fran couldn't tell if they were even breathing, but a milky drool was coming from the corner of Zac's mouth.

Beth unzipped her leather jacket and set it aside. Was she feeling too hot despite the biting chill in the air? No, Fran realized, it wasn't that at all. She didn't want the jacket, which looked very expensive, to get dirty. That meant she was about to do something she knew would make a mess.

Fran's mind flashed brilliant white with sudden abject terror. She didn't want to die here! Not here of all places!

Where was the light coming from? It must be on the floor somewhere, because Beth's shadow, huge and shapeless, crawled across the ceiling as she moved. Staring up at it, Fran wondered suddenly if all her dreams had not been dreams at all, but memories of this moment that somehow got played out of sequence.

Beth stepped in front of Fran and squatted down so suddenly it was as if the shadow had congealed into flesh and blood. In her right hand there was an X-Acto knife. Fran gave a muffled grunt of alarm and tried to squirm away, but with her arms and legs immobilized all she could do was writhe uselessly on the spot.

"Easy, girl," Beth murmured. "I'm not going to cut you. Take it easy. If you do what you're told, none of this has to hurt."

She frowned, as though she disapproved of Fran's fear. As though Fran was just being a baby and needed to grow up and be sensible. She leaned in with the knife, at the same time gripping Fran's shoulder and rolling her over.

Fran screamed behind her gag, making almost no sound at all. Beth made three passes with the knife. On the first two times it caught and she had to put some effort into it. With the third pass, something gave.

It was Fran's right arm. She realized that she could move her hand now. Just her right hand, and her right arm as far as the elbow. A trailing end of duct tape dangled from her sleeve. There must be a whole lot more wrapped around her, stopping her from standing up or moving her left arm at all. Maybe that was what was gagging her too.

Beth leaned in close to her. "Now are you going to give me any trouble, sweetheart?" she asked matter-of-factly. "There are other ways of doing this, and they'll hurt more. We're going to play a little game, is all. Are you up for that?"

Fran made a sound into the gag. It didn't mean yes. It didn't mean anything.

Beth took it for a yes anyway. She was kneeling behind Fran now, and her knees were in the small of Fran's back, propping her up on her side. She reached out with one hand and picked up something Fran couldn't see. The black blot of her shadow spread across the ceiling and down the walls as she moved the thing closer: a storm lantern, the kind that's electric but has been made to look like something old-fashioned that has a candle inside it.

By its light, Beth laid three items down in front of Fran. The X-Acto knife. A white cardboard packet a little longer and wider than a pack of cigarettes. And a red plastic dragon that Fran recognized from one of Molly's Lego sets.

Fran's gaze went from the three objects to Beth's hands as she arranged them in a line. Beth's hands were yellow in the storm lantern's glow. Yellow and shiny. She was wearing washing-up gloves.

"Here's how this works," Beth said. "I'm thinking of one of these three things. You've just got to guess which one. Pick it up and show me. If you guess right, you get a gold star and a pat on the head. If you get it wrong, I'm going to cut you.

"Ready when you are, sweetheart."

This time, when the fox returned it wasn't gradual or mysterious. She shot straight out of nowhere, as if the air had spat her out, and tumbled end-over-end as she tried to right herself. Even before she was on her feet again she was babbling at Liz in a voice that seemed subtly changed.

Come you've got to come you've got to save her. Please save her. I can't go there, but you can. You've got to come right now!

Actually it wasn't even subtle. That was Fran's voice. It was younger and higher, but the similarity was unmistakable In her moment of crisis, Jinx's disguise was breaking down.

Whoa, there! Liz said *Slow down. Tell me what—*

The monster's got her! The monster's got all of them! But there's a place I can't go! She took them to the place I can't go! If you don't come she's going to eat them!

Beth? You mean Beth? Liz moved as quickly as she could toward the little animal. She hovered right over her, a roil of troubled air like a tiny thunderhead. *What has she done? Tell me!*

But Jinx could hardly talk at all now. She was convulsing with panic, ripples chasing themselves down her body as if she was a bad picture on an old TV screen. She spilled the story out in pieces, fragments of sentences like broken teeth. The empty house. The chase through the night to the Perry Friendly. Fran's trail, cutting across the monster's, going in after her.

Why? Why would she go there again? Beth is going to kill them! I smelled her thinking it! Come quickly, Liz! Come right now!

Liz didn't need any urging. The fox's panic had infected her. *Show me the way*, she told Jinx. *But you'll have to go slow enough for me to follow you.*

If I go slowly, it will be too late!

Jinx, we don't have a choice. I can't run.

Then curl yourself up small. As small as you can.

Liz didn't hesitate. Jinx had been a ghost for a whole lot longer than her and had a better grasp of the rules.

It wasn't hard. Even in this place, where Liz had enough substance to feel the solidity of the walls when she tried to break through them, there was almost nothing to her. She folded in on herself, again and again, closed and held herself like a fist.

Okay, now what do I—?

Jinx opened her mouth wide and swallowed her.

Not all the way down, just into the middle of her throat. Liz felt herself both engulfed and held in place. Stifling a scream, she kept her rigid, folded posture and braced herself.

There was a sense of rushing, headlong motion. It went on for a long time, but any time at all would have felt long given where they were going. Who they would face there. What would happen if they arrived too late.

Then she felt a different kind of movement, jerky and spasmodic. Jinx regurgitated her like a cat coughing up a hairball, with effortful heaves and hacks. Liz was spat out onto cracked asphalt, intact apart from her dignity.

It was night and they were at the edge of the world. A low, sprawling building rose up in front of them, a cut-out paper silhouette. Between them was nothing but the broad, slightly curving line of a driveway and the dead ground of an overgrown parking lot. Something about the quality of the air—not its smell or its

454

taste since Liz couldn't access those things—suggested bruised ripeness turning into rot. The whole world souring, the way milk soured.

She would have known what this place was even if Jinx hadn't told her. There was no other place it could possibly be. And if Beth had brought her children here, it was for one reason only.

I can't go in, Jinx said again. Pleading. *When I get close to that place I just freeze up and I can't even move. Please, please help her! Save her!*

Then tell me how you do it, Liz demanded urgently. *Quickly! How do I get inside her head?*

You've got to use words.

You mean it's like a magic spell? That's ridiculous. I can't—

Her words. Wait until she's talking, and slide in. Ride the breath, and the thought of it, all the way back to the place inside.

She'll see me coming.

Not if you're really slow, and really quiet.

It was unfathomable and stupid at the same time. But then, Liz was talking to a cartoon fox about the best way to break into her own body. It made about as much sense as anything else would have done at this stage.

Jinx was trembling all over. Even her outline was blurring. Liz gave it up. There was no time. She had to do something and she had to do it now, before it was too late.

Focusing all her attention on the Perry Friendly, she began to move in that direction. Her kids were in there. She drifted across the parking lot, gathering speed, a weightless bubble of wrath and vengeance.

A knife. A plastic dragon. A piece of cardboard.

Fran tried to pick up a coherent idea as fear stampeded her thoughts, sent them running through her brain and away, out through her ears and her wide eyes and her flared nostrils.

Which one was right? Which one would stop Beth from hurting her?

The knife was a weapon. If she picked that, Beth might take it from her and use it. The dragon was a toy, so maybe that meant *let's play a game*. The packet . . .

The packet had a prescription label on it in the name of Elizabeth Kendall. Above that, in a neat Courier font, the word *temazepam*.

Fran understood then, and she knew there were no wrong answers. Beth just needed Fran's fingerprints on all these things. Preferably prints that had been made by her consciously picking the things up, and gripping them, rather than having them pressed into her hand after she was dead. When they autopsied you, they could probably tell that kind of thing. This was all going to be used as evidence of . . . something. Something really bad that included drugs and wounding and (*oh God!*) Molly. Fran clenched her fist and lowered her hand.

"I'm not going to ask you again," Beth said. "Choose one and pick it up. Otherwise I'm going to have to hurt you."

Fran was staring at the X-Acto knife. It seemed to get bigger and bigger as she looked at it. Her breath was trapped inside her so she felt she was getting bigger too, blowing up like a balloon that was ready to burst. She was going to die here. In the Perry Friendly, where she had always been meant to die. Where some of her had died already. There was nothing she could do to stop it.

But she could resist it with everything she had.

She picked up the X-Acto knife. Drawing back her arm, she threw it away across the room. She couldn't throw it far because her right arm was only halfway free and didn't have much travel, but outside the little circle of the storm light the darkness was absolute. Good luck finding that, she thought.

"Okay," Beth said. "That's one. Let's go for two. Which one am I thinking about now?" She seemed completely unfazed. But of course she had all the time in the world to find the knife again. Or she could just leave it where it lay. A police forensics team would find it later, like something out of *CSI*, and someone would say, "Let's check this baby for prints."

Fran made a clenched fist again and tucked her hand in against her chest. For good measure she rolled over onto her stomach, trapping the hand underneath it. She would make this as hard for Beth as she possibly could.

Beth got a good grip on Fran's shoulder and her waist and tried to turn her back. Fran twisted and writhed, trying to squirm out of her grasp. They wrestled in silence for a few seconds, but it was obvious that Fran couldn't win. Beth was much stronger than her. The fact that she was drawing this out, unfolding and turning her an inch at a time, didn't mean Fran had a chance. All it meant was that Beth was trying not to hurt her.

No. Not that. Trying not to *damage* her.

Fran's mind started to race. Beth had decided to kill Zac and Molly. There was no mistaking that. And she wanted Fran's fingerprints on everything so it would look like Fran had done this.

Done what, though? Coaxed Molly here with the toy. Got both her and Zac to eat sleeping pills. Used the knife to murder them. And finally killed herself. Nobody would believe that, would they?

Maybe. Maybe they would. Freaky Fran had a mental illness. Her weirdness and isolation were a legend. And it was always the lonely, messed-up kids who had the starring role in every high school massacre. When lonely, messed-up kids turn up dead, you've got your explanation ready to hand.

Her dad. Her dad would believe, and it would break his heart.

She couldn't get free. Couldn't fight. The only thing she could think of to do was to throw in a few details that didn't fit. Put some cracks in the story and hope someone saw through them.

Twisting free from Beth's grip, she threw herself down on the floor again as hard as she could. Her pinky finger was held out straight in front of her and she let it take all of her weight.

Agony shot through her and she screamed behind the gag.

Beth saw what Fran was doing, but too late to intervene.

With a muttered "Shit!" she threw the kid over on her back and knelt astride her, pinning her free hand to the floor with one knee. The broken finger stuck out almost at right angles to the rest. Fran's chest heaved with huge panic breaths as the pain hit.

"You stupid little bitch!" Beth snarled. She raised her hand to smack Fran across the face, but had enough will power to fight the impulse and lower it again. There was no point in making a bad situation worse.

And it hadn't been stupid at all. Actually Beth couldn't help but admire the quality of the kid's lateral thinking. A broken finger was an anomaly. It spoke of coercion rather than suicide.

So now, instead of planting evidence, Beth would be forced to erase it. Fortunately she'd planned for that contingency too.

She stood up, planting one foot on Fran's chest so she still couldn't move, and reached into the bag. There it was. A half-gallon can of Sunoco 260, unopened. She unscrewed the can's cap and flicked it over her shoulder. She was aware that the girl on the floor could see the can, and probably smell the gasoline inside it.

459

She didn't mind that much at all. If you went fishing for trouble, you got to bring home your whole catch.

"Yeah, you see what you did?" she asked. "Didn't have to be this bad if you just did as you were told." She poured about half the gasoline out on the floor around the girl and on the girl herself. The rest she kept so she could Molotov it and set the fire going when she was done.

She recapped the can and set it down.

Fran just stared at her, her dark eyes impossibly wide. Her chest was still working hard. Was she suffocating rather than just gagging on the stench of the gas? Some people had trouble breathing through their noses. Molly would be dead inside of a minute if anyone gagged her.

That thought derailed Beth for a moment. Her mind flooded with memories of the real Molly, and hot tears blurred out the world for a moment or two. "I'll kill you first," she muttered, turning away. She meant it as a reassurance. *I'll make it quick and clean, as close to painless as I can manage, and only burn you afterward.*

She stopped talking. There had been a strange reverb on her words just then, as though someone else was repeating them a little out of synch. She was all done with words in any case. Done with finessing the evidence too. Let it fall where it would. If the whole place burned to the ground, nobody would be able to prove a damn thing after.

But first things first.

In the absence of a knife, she had to use her hands. She fastened them around Fran's neck, thumbs together just under her chin, and squeezed.

Wait until she's talking and slide in, Jinx had said. But when Liz arrived, Beth wasn't talking at all. Nobody was.

She had lost too much time. There had been the driveway, and then the courtyard, and all the screaming urgency in her mind didn't speed up her leisurely drifting by the smallest fraction.

And then there were the rooms. She had forgotten to ask where exactly in the sprawling ruin Beth was to be found, and going back would waste more time than she had. So she made a complete circuit, traveling at the same remorseless amble through one room after another until she found herself in the furthest corner.

In room 22.

She slid through the wall without slowing and realized as soon as she saw the glow from the storm lantern that she was in the right place. By its light she saw her children, sprawled motionless on the ground. And Beth beside them, kneeling over a third prone figure.

It was Fran Watts. And Beth was strangling her.

Her mind was screaming at her to check on Zac and Molly, but if she stopped to do that Fran would certainly die. Liz came up behind Beth, unnoticed. The woman didn't even turn. Her mind was on the task, her head hunched down between her shoulders, panting with effort as her locked hands pressed down hard on Fran's throat. Fran's eyes were bulging out. Her face was red, deepening to purple.

And there were no words. There was no entry point Liz could use.

Or maybe there was. Jinx had said to ride the breath and the thought. She had one out of two.

She placed herself beside Beth's lips. She folded herself smaller and smaller as she had when Jinx carried her in her mouth. She waited for an in-breath. It had to be on the in-breath so Beth didn't feel herself invaded: so she felt only the natural flow of air.

And not what it carried.

Liz was plucked out of light into darkness.

In darkness she unfolded, all at once, and launched herself upward with all the force she could dredge together; all her fears and outrage; the fury that had been building in her as she went from empty room to empty room.

She used her memory of following Jinx from the real world into the nowhere of the den. And muscle memory too, although muscles weren't her destination now. This was her home, her flesh. Nobody knew it like she did, not even the monster who had stolen it.

She broke free into a pallid radiance of no earthly color. She carried Beth with her, sending her spinning a long way away across the dimensionless void. The effort left her hanging helpless, drained of all strength by that convulsive push, but she was rewarded by the look of utter consternation and disbelief on Beth's face as she sailed away end over end.

(She had a face! They both had faces! Here, in the cathedral of her body's nerves, they were mirrors of each other as they had been before.)

Surprise, Liz managed to say.

One moment Fran was dying. Her throat slammed shut, all the oxygen piling up outside and nothing inside but a throbbing black stain that spilled out from the corners of her eyes to swallow up her brain.

Then Beth slumped forward as though someone had bashed her on the back of the head. All the strength went out of her hands and Fran was able to breathe again.

She pushed herself backward, sucking in air through her nose in an endless rush even though she was probably poisoning herself with gasoline fumes. Beth was having some kind of seizure. She was down on her hands and knees, her body wracked by tremors. Whatever was happening, it meant Fran had a chance.

But only if she got herself free. She pulled at the duct tape that bound her left hand to her side. There were too many thicknesses, and her hands were drenched in Sunoco so everything was slippery. She couldn't find the end of the tape, and even if she did it would take ages to unwind it. The tape around her ankles was even thicker.

She looked around frantically for the X-Acto knife. It had seemed like such a great idea to throw it away. Now she wished fervently she had played Beth's game by Beth's rules and put it back where she'd found it, in the light.

But she knew roughly where she had thrown it. She snaked her way across the floor, away from Beth, into the darkness. Pushing with her bound feet, scooping and shoveling with her hand, she slithered along what she thought was the right line. Every foot or so, she stopped to sweep her hand around in a circle, hoping it would connect with the knife.

When it finally did, her hand was moving too fast and she swatted it further away into the shadows. She heard it hit something with a hollow clunk and come to rest. Fran yelled in frustration, the sound completely smothered by the gag.

She risked a look over her shoulder. Beth was still on her knees but the trembling had stopped. She was eerily still now, her hair hanging over her face like a curtain so Fran couldn't see or guess what was going on there.

But then, very slowly, she raised her head. The face that gazed across the room at Fran had eyes that were just hollows full of darkness, but the mouth curved upward in a line, widening gradually into a crescent-moon grin.

Surprise, Liz said.

Beth's body twisted and turned, orienting itself to the same plane as Liz's, the same imaginary vertical.

What, that you're hanging around like a bad smell? Beth intoned, her lips not moving. *I'd be surprised if you did anything else. You look like shit, girl. Give me a second, though, and you'll look like nothing at all.*

She advanced on Liz, gliding without effort, a galleon whose sails were filled with her own invincible will.

But Liz had a plan and she had been working on it from the moment she entered this weird arena. She had learned a lot when she was trapped in Jinx's den. In the real world, she had drifted through doors and walls as though they weren't there, but Jinx had made her solid enough to touch just by wanting it. Deciding it. It was Jinx's space, and Jinx made the rules.

And this is my space, Liz thought furiously. *It was mine before it was hers. I'm solid. Like steel, like concrete, like a wrecking ball. I weigh as much as the fucking moon, and when I hit her it will be like the moon falling out of the sky.*

Beth bore down on her, arms spread wide and teeth bared.

Liz swung.

And connected.

It wasn't like the moon falling out of the sky. It was more like a bag of warm oatmeal hitting a kitchen counter. The impact was muted and softened, way too soft to hurt.

But it took Beth in the stomach and it stopped her charge. And the follow-up, to the point of her chin, made her reel back in shock.

Liz pressed her advantage, throwing wild punches as she advanced—much faster here than she had been back in the real world. A fierce charge was the only strategy she could think of. Maybe if she built up enough momentum she could force Beth right out of her body and take over again.

And at first it seemed to be working. Beth was driven back, slowly but perceptibly, each punch making her yield an inch or two. She wasn't retreating from Liz: it was just the force of each blow pushing her backward, like hammer blows driving in a nail.

But then she stopped. She took Liz's punches on her face, her shoulders, her chest and her stomach, turning her head a little to the side but otherwise just enduring. Assimilating. Thinking it through.

Her fist clenched and her arm drew back. Liz had no thought to spare for defending herself: she was still pinning her hopes on the barrage.

Beth's punch sank into her midriff more deeply than Liz would have thought was possible. She opened her mouth to gasp, but in a place where there was no air to breathe that wasn't an option. She folded in around the pain, throwing up her hands to ward off any further attacks.

Beth lowered her head and butted her. This time, the interpenetration was deeper, and indisputably real. For a second, or part of a second, their foreheads occupied the same space.

Liz's entire body exploded with agony so intense that her nerves shut down for a second or two. When sensation came back, she was drifting backward in the line of the attack, her head and neck dipping backward as her legs curled up toward a fetal crouch. She forced them down again, tried to right herself.

Beth must have felt some of that pain too, but she recovered more quickly. Just as Liz struggled back to the vertical she advanced again, this time not even bothering to make a fist as she glided in to the attack. She just threw out her open hand, punching it through the center of Liz's chest.

It was like being set on fire from the inside out. The pain made any kind of thought or strategy impossible. Liz tried to withdraw, but her movements were slow and clumsy. Beth followed hard, alternating right hand and left, going first for Liz's head and then her torso so Liz's clumsy defense was always out of the line of the attack.

But this must be hurting her too, surely. Liz flailed blindly with both arms, in a windmilling motion. She connected with . . . something. Something tenuous and barely there, gone as soon as she touched it. But she sensed that she had done some damage.

A second later, the impossible pain blossomed inside her again, filling her to the brim in an instant, freezing her on the spot again. Beth had stepped right through her.

You didn't think this through, did you? Beth asked her. *No weapons here. Nothing but what we are. And I'm better than you. I always was.*

She reached out with both hands and brought them together inside Liz's head. This time, at least, the pain had an end point. Unfortunately, so did Liz.

Jinx couldn't see or hear anything of what was going on in the rear courtyard of the Perry Friendly, but she could smell it. The same sense that let her track people by their thoughts was wide awake now to the boil of fierce emotions coming from inside the darkened building.

Most clearly of all, she smelled Fran's fear and misery. She hid her face behind her paws, trying to shut the feelings out. Liz would save Fran. Liz was strong enough and clever enough to do everything that needed to be done.

Except that Liz was afraid too. And in pain. And then, very suddenly, not there at all.

Jinx whined, long and low. There was no help for it. Fran needed her, and Fran was her only friend. Her only home. The keeper of her face and name and all that was left of her.

She made herself walk. Then she made herself run.

The knife, Fran thought. I've got to get to the knife. But she was out of time. Beth shook herself like a dog, and walked toward her.

It was a very small room, Fran realized suddenly. In her imagination it had always been immense, a place so vast that if you stood in the middle of it you could barely see the walls. But now Beth crossed it in three strides.

Fran looked along Beth's trajectory and saw the knife. She lunged for it at the same time Beth did, but Beth was faster and got there first, bending down to scoop it up just as Fran's groping fingers closed on the handle.

Beth straightened again, the X-Acto knife in her hand. She slid the blade out to its full length of about two inches.

"Close your eyes, sweetheart," she muttered. "I can tell you, based on a fuck-ton of experience, it's better if you don't see this coming."

The knife dipped, and Fran rolled aside. The blade sank into her shoulder instead of her throat. There was a moment when it didn't hurt at all. She used that moment to pull her knees right back into her chest.

When Beth leaned in again to finish what she'd started, Fran kicked out as hard as she could. Her feet slammed into Beth's knee. There was no sound, but the contact felt solid and jarring. Beth toppled forward with a hiss of pain and surprise.

But she kept hold of the knife. And since she fell almost on top of Fran, there was nowhere Fran could go to escape the next thrust. Or the one after that. The knife went into her side, and then into her stomach.

Even now it didn't hurt all that much. What took the fight out of Fran was the sheer, queasy astonishment of the knife blade puncturing her skin, sliding around below the surface of her where it had no right to be. The strength drained out of her as though it was pouring through the shallow wounds along with her blood.

Beth paused, either to shift her balance or just to gauge the effect of that last blow. For a second, they were just staring into each other's eyes, close enough so that Beth's panting breath ruffled Fran's hair. She lined up the knife again, under Fran's chin. Fran brought up her hand, but with no force or momentum. It touched Beth's forearm like a caress.

Then Fran looked past Beth, her eyes widening. Beth didn't turn. Wasn't about to fall for such an obvious trick.

So when Jinx leaped and hit her right in the center of her back, she had no warning at all.

Jinx went right through her, the same way she'd gone through Bruno Picota. And like Bruno Picota, Beth could see her. A fox in full career, her red-orange brush like a wildfire, turning as she landed and howling her battle howl.

She attacked again, diving right through Beth's abdomen. This time, seeing her coming, Beth threw out her arms to fend off the weird little animal. She scrambled backward. Her left arm bumped against the storm lantern and knocked it over.

And she dropped the knife.

Fran was in no condition to leap. She could scarcely move at all. She crawled toward the knife in agonizing slow motion, sliding through the spreading pool of her own blood.

Jinx couldn't fight the monster. She couldn't even touch her. She felt the familiar jolt of static shock in the moment that they occupied the same space, but that was all. Her hope of invading and conquering, of taking the fight to Beth in the fortress of her own body, came instantly to nothing.

She realized the truth too late. That there was only one mind she was welcome in, one dream where she could find purchase. She and Fran were two halves of the same person, so of course Fran's body and soul were a home for her when she needed them. It was the same thing, more or less, that let the monster sneak inside Liz. Because the monster *was* Liz in the same way that Jinx was Fran. But Jinx and the monster had no such kinship.

Jinx knew in that moment that she had failed. Fran was alone and defenseless.

The monster stared at her, and shook its head. Her face and the gesture said the same thing: whatever Jinx was, she wasn't going to worry about it now. She was going to finish the job she came here to do.

Behind Beth, Fran was crawling across the floor, slowly and awkwardly, supporting herself on one hand with the other bound at her side. Perhaps, if the monster were to be distracted for a few more seconds, she might escape into the dark outside and not be found.

Jinx had one trick left and she used it now. Rearing up on her hind legs she transformed from plain Jinx to Lady Jinx, armed and armored. She drew Oathkeeper and held it high.

The monster's jaw dropped. A half-laugh of pure amazement was forced from her lips.

You see me now, creature, Jinx cried ringingly. At least in her own mind it was ringing. She hoped the monster could hear her as well as see her. *I am the Lady Jinx, of the Woodland Table, and this blade in my hand is Oathkeeper, forged before time began to strike thee down.*

Beth shook her head. "You have got to be shitting me!" she muttered.

Jinx advanced in a series of shuffling steps, quartering with the long, broad blade as she came. As with Picota, it just went through Beth without hurting her. But it held her unbelieving gaze for a few precious seconds.

Suddenly the monster threw back her head and screamed. Terrified, Jinx crouched back and hunkered down. She thought Beth must have a battle howl too, and this was it.

But when the monster looked down, Jinx followed her gaze – to the calf of her leg and the little knife that was sticking out of her. Fran's hand was gripping the other end of the knife, twisting it in the wound she'd made. When she pulled it out, the spray of blood that followed it seemed more black than red in the dim light.

Fran reared up on her tied-together legs and thrust again, this time at waist height. But the monster caught her wrist, grabbed hold of her and they went down together. Fran was trying to stab with the knife and at the same time to keep it out of Beth's reach. Beth was trying to take it away from her without being wounded again. And they were doing this in near-total darkness because of the fallen lantern.

Jinx's legs shook. Her every nerve was shouting at her to jump into the fight. To help Fran. But she knew there wasn't anything she could do.

A hand touched her shoulder. She gave a startled yelp, and turned.

Liz hadn't died under Beth's merciless assault. She had lost consciousness, lost focus, and fallen—right out of her own body and into the external world, where she lay too weak and spent to move. She could only watch as Beth turned her attention back to Fran, as she stabbed her with the knife, and then as Jinx attacked.

She was too weak and too damaged even now from her first dispossession to beat Beth at her own game. There was just too little of her.

But there was *something*. When she moved, she discovered with shock and excitement that she didn't just float now: she moved in the ways that a human body moved, with limbs and a head and torso that seemed to be extended through space in the normal shape and configuration. She was still a phantom, but in falling out of the gray space she had managed to keep some semblance or memory of human shape.

She forced herself to her feet. She lumbered forward, one step, and then two. For something so slight and so vestigial, she found it a tremendous effort to move. It was as if she were lifting up the world.

Lady Jinx lay crouched between her and Beth. She leaned down, and touched Jinx's shoulder.

Jinx yelped, and spun to face her. When she saw who it was she shrank away from Liz, afraid. She had only ever seen Liz before as a spiritual puffball. This half-human apparition was something new and frightening.

Liz held out her hand, palm open. Jinx stared at it for long moments before she finally understood.

She handed over her sword without a word.

Beth finally succeeded in getting a double-handed grip on Fran's wrist. She slammed it against the floor, once, twice, three times. The knife fell free at last, and Beth picked it up. Fran was going for it too, but a solid punch to the side of her head put a stop to that nonsense. It laid the little girl out cold, which Beth wished she'd done long ago.

She reversed the knife, feeling for the line of Fran's jaw and for the little pulsing artery.

Hey, a voice said. It was her own voice, which was not something she was expecting to hear again until she used it herself. A strange emotion flooded her, a mixture of resignation and boiling, thrilling rage. On the one hand, when was this bitch going to realize she was beaten and just lie the fuck down? On the other, Liz was to Beth the perfect enemy, being everything about herself that she had ever hated. When they fought, when she hurt Liz and beat her down, it was the purest pleasure she had felt since she killed Marc. It filled the void in her the way nothing else could hope to fill it.

She stood, gathering herself, and turned.

The thing that was standing behind her was a ghost only a little more convincing than the ones kids make at Halloween by cutting eyeholes in sheets. The face it wore—Liz's face—was a blurred smear. But it was carrying a medieval broadsword: carrying it effortfully and awkwardly in both hands, the way an old woman might carry a shopping bag that was much too heavy for her.

It was the sword the fucked-up little fox-thing had used on Beth to no effect at all.

Liz jabbed with the sword, slowly and clumsily. Beth raised her hand to meet it as it came, the way you might pass your finger through a candle flame, mocking its inability to hurt her.

The blade passed through her forearm: a spike of terrible, bone-shattering cold. Her scream of agony shattered what was left of the glass in the room's already broken window.

The sword was so heavy it felt to Liz as though she should be sinking into the earth with each step she took. How did Jinx hold it one-handed, twist and swing and slice the air with it as though it weighed nothing at all?

The answer was obvious. Because it was a piece of her soul, given shape. It was no different from the armor she wore, the fur on her back, her arms and legs and face. It was made of her.

But in Jinx's hands, the sword had been useless against Beth. It had passed through her harmlessly, and Beth had barely noticed. Liz had gambled everything on a hunch—that it might be different if the hand holding the sword was hers. That she might be able to close the circuit in a way that Jinx couldn't. It was a kind of sympathetic magic, or at least she hoped it was: you could only touch the things that were of the same nature as you, whether to help or to hurt, protect or destroy. She and Beth, they were two pieces of one thing, resonating on a single frequency.

And she had been right. When Liz touched the sword, the power flowed. When the sword touched Beth, Beth felt it. The shriek of pain and the shattered glass were proof of that.

Now if only Liz could move a little faster! She had landed one blow, but only because Beth hadn't been afraid of her. Hadn't even tried to move aside. She wasn't going to be caught the same way twice, not by a shambling, weightless thing that walked like a puppet with half its strings cut. They turned a slow circuit, the limits of their battleground marked out by the three bodies stretched on the ground.

Liz swung again—or poked, rather, unable to bring the sword any higher than her waist no matter how hard she pulled against its dreadful weight. Beth ducked aside with arrogant ease and stepped past her, heading for Fran.

Liz turned, but too slowly. Trying to bring the sword around and strike again was like trying to turn an ocean liner. It wallowed in the air.

But then a hand slid through Liz's—literally through it—to grip the sword's hilt. The hand had only three fingers. A thin white streak ran through the red-brown fur that covered it.

Together, Jinx said. She had stepped right up alongside Liz, partially overlapping her. Liz's right side pricked and tingled where they touched.

Together. They turned. Jinx took the weight and Liz took care of the aim. The sword still felt to her like a mountain on the move, but it moved where she wanted it to and that was all that mattered.

As Beth bent down over Fran's unmoving body, the X-Acto knife once more in her hand, Liz took her with a scything, upward thrust that entered her chest and ripped its way out through her head.

There was no wound. The blade was as insubstantial as air. But Beth felt herself torn, sliced open along a seam she hadn't known she possessed. There was no pain, but there was something worse than pain. The truth of her, the essence of her, spilled out like water from a shattered dam.

She crashed to her knees. Diminishing. Memories were boiling and subliming out of her as if that gossamer blade was white-hot and had set the core of her on fire. Her children's faces flared and faded. When they were gone, they would be gone forever. She reached for them and felt only the edges of the hole that was left behind. Their names, even, were gone. Neither the sound nor the sense of them remained. Just an aching nothingness, a bereavement that was evaporating in its turn. Nothing. Nothing would be left.

And then, when Beth had sublimed away into the air like a sigh on a cold day, Liz would step in again and take up where she had left off. As though, in spite of all she had done, all she had suffered, Beth had never even been there at all.

No way, she thought grimly. No fucking way. Why should anyone else have the happiness she'd lost? Why, much more importantly, should Liz?

She forced herself to move. She still had the knife, so that part wrote itself. She cut her left wrist with a deep lateral slash. Her hands were starting to shake, and the world was running like water. Focus. Focus. She could do this. Transferring the knife to her left hand she excavated three deep gouges in her right wrist.

The tremors were building, not just in her hands but in her whole body. The knife slipped from her fingers, but she didn't need it anymore.

Liz was screaming in her ear, scrabbling once again to get a hold on her, to climb inside her and into the driving seat, but Liz's best chance of taking her had been when she was looking the other way. Even now, even dying and dissolving, Beth could hold her off for a few seconds longer. For as long as it took. The fox was yelling at Liz to pick up the sword again. Its voice was as shrill as a child's.

Reaching into her jeans pocket, Beth fished out—with a great deal of effort—the box of Diamond safety matches she had tucked in there before she left home.

Liz shrieked and cursed and laid siege to her. The fox howled. None of it mattered.

Getting the box open took forever. An eternity of groping and swiping, her shaking hands slick with fresh blood, pulsing with exquisite pain. Drawing a match out was beyond her, so she just upended the whole box and pawed at the little pile of splinters until one of them stayed attached to her fingers somehow.

Please! Liz screamed. *Don't!*

Beth didn't have any breath to spare on a reply. She was fading fast. She let the match speak for her. Dragged it along the safety strip until the stinging heat against the heel of her hand told her it had sparked.

She dropped it to the floor, the last, hot seed of her hatred, hoping with all her heart that it would find some fertile ground.

That done, she gave herself over to nonexistence. She did it with a sort of resigned contempt, like someone flinging down their last hand of cards as they left the table and not bothering even to check whether or not they came out ahead.

Dying was something she knew how to do.

When Fran recovered consciousness, she thought for a second that it was summer. The hot air on her face and the dazzling brightness made her imagine she was sitting in a park somewhere on a day in mid-August, and that it was way past time to find some shade.

Then she inhaled the complex, choking bouquet of combustion and realized the truth. She opened her eyes, blinking to get the sweat and tears out of them, and looked around the room.

It was on fire, and so was she.

The pain in her shoulder and side was terrible, and so was the weakness. She had to force her aching body to move, and it moved like a bad stop-motion effect. She rolled over onto her belly and then onto her back, trying to put out the spreading splotches of flame on her clothes. It actually worked, to her dull amazement.

But that wasn't going to matter in a minute or so. The fire was taking some time to spread in the center of the room because the carpets were steeped in damp and stewed in mildew, but the bare boards where the carpet had been rolled back had caught nicely and had passed the blaze along to the wooden frames of the doors and windows. The skeletal curtains were going up like fireworks.

Beth was slumped beside her, on her face. When Fran nudged

her with her foot, and then kicked her, she didn't wake. Zac and Molly hadn't moved an inch from their earlier positions.

Fran couldn't even see the knife from where she was. It had to be close, but even if she found it and freed her hands and feet in time, she couldn't carry the other three out of here. She felt the muscle-deep ache of her fresh wounds and the stickiness of her own blood pooled under her. She didn't have the strength. Even on her best day it would have been a big ask. Bound and bleeding out, she knew better than to try.

She turned her head—wincing as the wound in her shoulder reported in with a sharp stab of agony—to look at the room's only other occupant. Jinx's sharp, almost triangular face was creased with anguish. She was squatting beside Fran, keening very softly. That was probably what had woken her.

She went inside! Jinx wept. *She went inside and she hasn't come out.*

Fran had no idea what that meant. The room was thick with smoke now. The air she was breathing was as warm as soup and stank like barbecued garbage. She looked around again to try to find the knife, but now she couldn't even see Beth lying right beside her.

Because Beth wasn't on the floor anymore. She was standing up.

Fran scrambled back as Beth leaned down, both hands groping blindly. She readied herself to claw at Beth's eyes if she only came within range. She would have to do it one-handed. Her left arm didn't seem to be working anymore.

Don't, Jinx yipped. *Don't, Fran! It's the good one! It's Liz!*

Liz was looking around her with a dazed, myopic stare. It wasn't just the smoke: she seemed to have forgotten where she was and how her body worked. Blood dripped freely from her lacerated wrists. Her upper body slumped at an angle as if someone was lifting her up from behind with a hand around her waist.

Fran ripped the duct tape from her mouth, sticky shreds of it still holding her lips together at the corners.

"There," she gasped. She pointed with her one free hand to Zac and Molly. She was trying not to breathe in because breathing was like sipping coffee that turned out to be fresh out of the machine, bitter and boiling hot and once it was in your mouth impossible either to swallow or to spit out. She jabbed her finger urgently at the two prone bodies. "Over there. Go. Go!"

Liz turned and saw. Eventually. Everything seemed to be happening too slowly now, while the world consumed itself like kindling around them. She staggered away at last, shifting her weight carefully with each step as if she was walking a tightrope. But at least she was heading in the right direction.

Fran tried to pull herself on her good arm toward the open doorway, but she didn't get far. The pain from her side and stomach when she moved was awful, and it made her think she might faint. She didn't want that. Conscious, there were still things she could do.

And here was one of them. The X-Acto knife had fallen half in and half out of the flames. She tried to pick it up, but dropped it again with a yelp of shock and pain. It was already too hot to touch.

Liz staggered and stumbled out through the door, cradling a tiny, shapeless burden. Molly. After a long moment she came back inside, ducking her head away from the door's flaming lintel.

Fran found Beth's discarded jacket. There was a splash of bright red on the sleeve that looked a little like blood, and for a moment she was confused. She had wounded Beth in the leg, and anyway it had been after she took off the jacket. Then she saw the puddle of red plastic on the carpet. Molly's dragon had melted, and the molten goop had splashed Beth's sleeve.

Liz went out again for a second time. More slowly this time. She was pulling Zac by his shoulders, a few inches at a time, with agonizingly long rests in between. The blood from her slashed wrists still flowed freely over everything she touched, forced out by her exertions and by the heat of the blaze. She was all but used up now, forcing herself to move.

Fran slipped her hand partway into the sleeve of Beth's jacket. She used it like an oven glove to pick up the knife which was now glowing red-hot in places. It still hurt, even through the leather, but she made herself hold on to it. She wouldn't need it for long.

She didn't have to cut through the duct tape on her legs and left arm. It vanished at the touch of the hot blade like a magic trick. She managed to get back up on her knees, maneuvering her unwilling body with terrible care and patience. The wounds were like an internal maze she was threading as she moved.

When Liz came back for her, Fran had the X-Acto knife in her hand, the jacket wound around her wrists about a hundred times to keep out the worst of the heat.

"Your wrists," she croaked.

Liz didn't seem to realize what she meant until Fran touched the flat of the blade to the deep wound on the heel of her left hand.

There was a sizzling sound, like bacon on a griddle. Liz gave an anguished grunt, the rush of her out-breath punching a brief hole in the roiling smoke. But when Fran stopped she held up the other hand. Fran cauterized that wound too, holding the knife hard against it until the flesh blistered.

They staggered out of the Perry Friendly together, holding each other up like soldiers in the First World War who had survived a charge across no-man's-land. The ceiling fell in right behind them, sending gusts of sparks twisting and eddying around their ankles.

There was darkness for a little while. It was very welcome. Liz wrapped it around her like a blanket and prepared to sleep.

But she was shaken awake again, repeatedly. Someone was calling her name again and again, louder and more urgently each time.

"Liz," she confirmed. "Yes. Here." One word at a time was all she could manage. There were jagged splinters in her throat, a taste in her mouth like soot and rancid oil.

She lifted up her bleared and sticky eyelids, blinked until she could see halfway clear. Actually a little less than halfway. Smoke hung in the air in horizontal layers like badly folded blankets. It was the acrid taste of it that was in her mouth

She was lying in the courtyard of the Perry Friendly on a bed of wet weeds. Fran was sitting beside her, one hand pressed to her own stomach. It was Fran who was shaking her and shouting at her. She looked like she was coming home from a hard day at the abattoir, the whole front of her sweatshirt dark with blood.

And the Perry Friendly was burning, thousands of sparks rising up out of the roof to pour like an inverted waterfall into the midnight sky. Their collective radiance was what made details like the blood visible, even though it was the middle of the night.

It hurt to move, but Fran was insisting that she had to. "Now, Liz. Before they come."

Liz looked down at her wrists. The pain was worst there, and she could see why. The burns that ran from the heels of her hands to halfway up her forearms were still fresh enough that the blisters were forming and bursting as she watched.

Fran Watts had cauterized the wounds on her wrists with the blade of a knife. That one fact brought an avalanche of memories down on her all at once.

"Molly!" she panted. "Zac!" The smoke had got to her throat. She couldn't shape the words properly. But Fran understood, and pointed. The kids were lying a little way away. Their eyes were closed.

"They're breathing," Fran said, her voice a wheezing whisper. "I checked. I think they're going to be okay. Ms. Kendall. Liz. You've got to go. Someone will have seen the flames by now. You can't be here when they come."

She told Liz what she meant to do. Told her more than once, because it was hard for Liz to make her mind work. But she got it, finally. And Fran was right: there really was no other way. Or at least, the other way was a lot worse for all of them. Especially Liz herself.

She carried the kids to the car. She did it alone; Fran couldn't stand. It was harder this time because she was that much weaker now and because there was nothing to shield her blistered hands and arms. Every contact sent a paralyzing shock of agony through her and lit up her head with synesthetic lightning bolts.

Would she even be able to drive the car? Her hands felt like dead weights. Her fingers, when she made them move, bent halfway and then stopped. Her thumbs didn't move at all.

She returned to Fran, who was still lying exactly where she had left her. Her hands were pressed to the wounds in her shoulder and side. The drying blood on them made it look as though she was wearing black gloves. Liz knelt beside her, or rather fell down onto her knees.

"Are you sure you'll be okay?" she asked. Her voice was ugly, a dry rasp with barely enough breath to carry it. "What if they don't come?"

"They're coming now," Fran said. She raised a gory finger. A single siren was already whooping, still distant but getting closer. "That one's a fire truck, but the police will be right behind it. Go!"

Liz went.

Getting the car started was an ordeal that went on forever. She had to use both hands to turn the key, again and again until the engine caught. She could barely see, partly because of the smoke and partly because her eyes kept trying to close. When she finally started moving, she put too much of her clumsy weight down on the accelerator and launched the car straight at the Perry Friendly's gatepost. She swerved at the last moment and only raked the side of the car along the post. It made a sound like a scream, unless that sound was inside Liz's head. Either way, she kept right on going.

As she turned onto Washington Avenue, Molly rolled over in her sleep and coughed.

The story Fran told had the virtue of simplicity. It had very few moving parts.

She had been feeling restless and unhappy after her encounter with Bruno Picota, she said. Unable to put him out of her mind, she decided to go for a late-night walk. She wasn't thinking about where she was going. She crossed the bridge into Homewood and found herself, completely to her surprise, in front of the Perry Friendly Motel.

Curious, she went inside to see what the place looked like at night. She hadn't thought to tell anyone what she was doing. She hadn't suspected any danger.

But a man came out of nowhere and attacked her. He must have been living in one of the rooms of the boarded-up motel, and Fran had surprised him. He was either high or crazy or maybe both. Thinking that Fran was threatening him, he stabbed her three times with a stubby little knife of some kind. Maybe a box-cutter or something like that.

Fran passed out, and when she woke up the motel was on fire. She got outside into the courtyard just as the first fire engines were rolling up.

That was all of it. To any questions outside of that threadbare scenario she answered, "I don't remember." She said the same thing when the police officers who came to the hospital to interview her asked for a description of her nonexistent attacker, and when they asked her about the fresh tire tracks on the motel's driveway. No, Fran said, she hadn't seen any cars. If a car had been there, it had nothing to do with what had happened to her.

She was in hospital for nine days. None of her wounds had punctured an organ or a major artery, but even so she had lost more blood than she could easily spare and suffered a lot of general bruising and battering. Plus, although nobody exactly came out and said this, they were concerned about her mental state, which was known to be fragile. She was a kidnap survivor, after all, the victim of a prior trauma whose relationship to this present trauma was complicated and concerning.

Perhaps for that reason, the solemn-faced officers stopped pressing her after a while when she told them her mind was blank. Blank was far from the worst thing it could be.

Her dad was similarly tentative, and gentle to a fault. He tried his best not to let Fran see how much this fresh catastrophe was tearing him up. Though his eyes were bloodshot most of the time, she never saw him cry. It was hard to lie to him. Almost unbearable. But Fran didn't think she could ever make him believe, or understand. If she told him the truth, he would call the cops and tell them to arrest Liz Kendall.

When she got better, she told herself, he would stop grieving. And she *would* get better now. The Perry Friendly was ash on the wind. She had faced Bruno Picota and seen how small and sad he was, then she had faced down a bigger, badder monster by far. The world's relentless changes held no fears for her now.

Zac Kendall was the only one who got the whole truth. Fran had made him a promise, after all. He came to visit her every day, bringing something different each time: red grapes, gummy worms, F. Scott Fitzgerald's collected short stories. But it wasn't until her third day in the hospital that Fran felt up to telling him exactly what had happened. He'd already heard a lot of it from his mom by this time, but Fran was able to fill in some of the missing details. Most importantly, she was able to explain to him how her own story and Liz's came to intersect. How so many of the things that seemed like coincidences were nothing of the kind.

"It was the place. The Perry Friendly. It got hold of all of us, just in different ways. Bruno Picota worked there for years, so I think he got it worse than anyone. Your mom and me, we only got the edge of it, but it changed us just the same."

Zac was still having a hard time with this stuff. He looked as though he was biting down on something sour. "Changed you, meaning . . .?"

"We're just a looser fit than most people. We're still in the world, but we're loose. Sometimes we see the worlds on either side. Sometimes we can even go there. That's what Beth did. She kept on looking until she found a world where she was still alive, and then she moved in. Jinx did the same, but she was sweet and gentle and she didn't try to hurt me. She stayed with me because . . . well, because I was the life she knew. I was her, the way she used to be."

Zac nodded slowly, almost reluctantly. "I think I understand that part. Well, kind of. Most of it. But there's something that doesn't make any sense to me at all, even if I believe everything you and Mom have told me."

"Share your thoughts, Mr. Holmes."

Fran was trying to make a joke out of it, as far as she could, but Zac didn't smile. "Okay," he said. "It's this. The first time Bruno Picota ever met you, he already saw something weird about you. Extra shadows, whatever. You were already different. But that was before the other you—Jinx?—came along. It was before you'd even seen the Perry Friendly. In fact, you only went there because he took you there. How does that make any sense?"

Fran fished two gummy worms out of the packet, a red one and a green one, and twined them together. Actually, you could make an Ouroboros out of just one, but it was cooler if two snakes chased each other round the circle, each eating its own tail. "It's like this," she said. "I guess."

She couldn't explain it any better. She and Liz and Bruno Picota were a loose fit in time, as well as space. When you looked into the next world along, you saw things at a weird angle. And when it looked back into you . . .

Fran remembered Picota's knife entering her heart. Picota remembered killing her—some of the time, at least. Liz had told Fran she used to stay at the motel back when it was still open, and one time she heard what sounded like an argument going on in the next room. She was pretty sure now that what she had heard that time was their showdown with Beth. A fight that wasn't going to happen for another twenty years.

In the light of all that, it didn't strike Fran as weird that Picota had seen Jinx inside her before Jinx ever came to live with her. What was weird, maybe, was how the dream and the reality slotted together like two halves of the same thing. How the things Picota did to her, in this world and the other, had made what he saw come true.

Ouroboros.

But there was one other thing that had come back to her, as she lay in the hospital bed with nothing else to do besides think. "You remember that public speaking competition?" she asked Zac. "In sixth grade?"

"The one where we got to the semi-finals? What about it?"

"The hall was in Homewood. On the same street as the Perry Friendly. Right next door, in fact."

Zac looked sick. "What, so we've got another evil building to worry about?"

Fran shook her head slowly. "I don't think it's the building, exactly. It's . . . the place. The place was always there, Zac. When the Abenaki Indians told their stories about the skadegamutc, there wasn't any Perry Friendly. No Larimer, no Homewood, no Pittsburgh. There was just a place, and some bad things that happened there. And I guess they never stopped happening."

493

Zac was still looking troubled. "It's best not to think about it too much," Fran told him. What she didn't say was: *because you've been there too, and so has Molly. Maybe it's in you. Maybe you'll meet some other Zac down the road somewhere, and either be best friends or try to kill each other. I'd recommend the first of those options, but you might not get to choose.*

Jinx only came in the middle of the night when all the other visitors were gone. She was still a little skittish around Fran, and Fran knew why.

"The holes in my memories were you, weren't they?" she asked on the night of the fifth day. "Tell me, Jinx. A knight of the woodland table is honest, brave and true. You can't lie."

I'm sorry, Jinx said, hanging her head. *I thought I was protecting you from things that would hurt you.*

"Sometimes things that are gonna hurt you are still things you need. Like, I needed to remember the time when my mom was dying."

I know. Please don't be mad with me.

"And the time when Picota took me, and right after. When you came. If I'd remembered that stuff I might have known who you were."

I thought if you knew, you might be scared of me. I was a ghost, after all.

"Yeah, you were *my* ghost. And there I was, living your life, having everything you'd lost. You should have hated me. But instead you became my best friend. The best friend anyone has ever had."

I couldn't ever hate you.

"I'd understand if you did. I'm living the life you were meant to live."

I want this life. I want to be with you.

"I want that too, Jinx. But let's get a few things straight. No more sleeping at the foot of the bed. You live in here now." Fran pointed to her own forehead. "We'll work out the details later. Like, there might be times when one of us wants a little peace and quiet and the other one has to take a walk around the block. Or go hang out in the den for a while, if you don't mind showing me where that is. But apart from that it's share and share alike, always. Deal?"

Deal, Jinx whispered.

Her heart was singing as Fran welcomed her in.

It took Liz a long time to find her life again. Most of it was where she had left it, but the pieces didn't always fit together in quite the way they should.

The Sethis were cool to her, bordering on frigid, presumably on account of something that Beth had said or done. It was clear that they no longer saw her as a friend. She had to win them back a little bit at a time, with small courtesies and kindnesses. More than a year passed before they all sat down at the same table again.

Beebee Brophy seemed wary of her too at first. When she came to take the kids' statements about the night of Marc's disappearance, she kept a formal distance. Liz was as warm as she could be, and the ice had started to melt a little by the time Beebee left. There was more work to be done, but this was a newer friendship with fewer rules and expectations. A fresh start wasn't such a big ask.

Well, depending how the investigation came out. It was still ongoing, despite the fact that Molly remembered absolutely nothing from the night of Marc's death. Not the blood, not the midnight ride, not any of it. Sometimes, Liz knew, the things that happen when you're nodding off or when you've only just awakened take on the texture of your dreams and fade just as quickly. She was glad of it in this case, for Molly's sake as much as her own, but she didn't kid herself that she was in the clear. Beebee was still doggedly looking for a body.

In the spring, Liz wrote to Jamie Langdon to invite her to dinner. *I know it might feel weird*, she wrote, *but I thought maybe we could give it a try. The kids miss you, and they'd love to see you again. Or if you prefer, you could take them out somewhere for the day. Let me know.*

Jamie went for option B that first time and every subsequent time. Liz understood, and didn't begrudge. There were too many things standing in the way of their being friends. Too many truths that couldn't be told and debts that couldn't be paid back.

Debts were a common theme in her life right around then. Her other self had maxed out every credit card she had, then got some new ones and maxed them out too. Selling the Rogue helped some, but not enough. Liz had to sell some pieces of jewelry her mom had left her, shunt the remaining debt into a new credit plan and switch to a fifty-hour week for the foreseeable future. She just barely held on to the duplex.

And then there was the nightmare. For three months it visited her every night. Sometimes it came just once; other times it was a hideous punctuation that woke her sweating and sobbing every couple of hours. The details never varied. She was outside her body, without weight or mass, drifting helplessly while terrible things happened (she knew) elsewhere.

She beat her fears in the end by surrendering to them. Before trying to sleep, she would slip quietly into the children's rooms and sit by their beds for a little while, watching their chests rise and fall as they breathed. If Molly's bronchiectasis made her snore, as it often did, Liz savored the sound like sweet music.

They were alive, and they were together again. Nothing could possibly matter more than that.

Sometimes late in the evening, after Molly had been put to bed, she and Zac would sit together in the family room and talk about the other Liz, who Zac called "that thing" rather than Beth. In a weird way it was consoling to share those memories, terrible though they were. Unspoken, they felt too much like hallucinations. Signs of madness. By retelling the story, they reassured each other that they were sane.

Zac was angry with himself that he hadn't seen Beth for what she was. He seemed to feel that he had failed his real mom by not spotting the fake. He told Liz too, shame-faced and halting, about his other failure, when Fran had tried to warn him and he had jeered at her in the school library, humiliating her in front of their classmates. He said he would never stop blaming himself for that betrayal.

"You thought you were taking my side," Liz said, stroking his arm. "And she forgave you, didn't she?"

"I don't know that she did," Zac said glumly. "She just did the right thing because she's amazing."

"Tell her that," Liz suggested. "Tell her so she knows you mean it. You can't stop being friends after all you've been through together."

That was a lie, of course. Liz knew better than anyone how easy it was to lose something precious, either because you didn't fight hard enough to keep it or because you didn't realize it was precious until after it was gone.

But given the storm that had just passed over them, she kind of felt like they were on a roll.

Acknowledgements

The only reason I know Pittsburgh at all, and had the effrontery to set a novel there, is because of the boundless generosity of Johanna Drickman and her family over the past forty years. They've been the kindest of hosts on many occasions, and I feel very privileged to have them as my friends. I'd also like to thank them for being sounding boards for the story as it developed. Thanks, too, to my patient, meticulous and insightful editors, who among other things helped me to shape Beth's arc and to eliminate rogue Britishisms when they occurred. Thanks to Meg, my ever-supportive and supernaturally brilliant agent, for always being there to nudge me back onto the rails when I'm wobbling (I wobble more than somewhat). And thanks to Lin, Lou, Davey, Ben and Cam, who had to listen to me ranting on about the work in progress, and sometimes listen to it or read it, and offer helpful opinions instead of braining me with a tea-tray. Greater love hath nobody, in my opinion.

extras

www.orbitbooks.net

about the author

M. R. Carey has been making up stories for most of his life. His novel *The Girl With All the Gifts* has sold over a million copies and became a major motion picture, based on his own BAFTA Award-nominated screenplay. Under the name Mike Carey he has written for both DC and Marvel, including critically acclaimed runs on *Lucifer*, *Hellblazer* and *X-Men*. His creator-owned books regularly appear in the *New York Times* bestseller list. He also has several previous novels including the Felix Castor series (written as Mike Carey), two radio plays and a number of TV and movie screenplays to his credit.

Find out more about M. R. Carey and other Orbit authors by registering for the free monthly newsletter at www.orbitbooks.net.

if you enjoyed
SOMEONE LIKE ME

look out for

A BOY AND HIS DOG AT THE END OF THE WORLD

by

C. A. Fletcher

My name's Griz. I've never been to school, I've never had friends and in my whole life I've not met enough people to play a game of football. My parents told me how crowded the world used to be, before all the people went away, but we were never lonely on our remote island. We had each other, and our dogs.

Then the thief came.

He told stories of the deserted towns and cities beyond our horizons. I liked him – until I woke to find he had stolen my dog. So I chased him out into the ruins of the world.

I just want to get my dog back, but I found more than I ever imagined was possible. More about how the world ended. More about what my family's real story is. More about what really matters.

Chapter 1

The end

Dogs were with us from the very beginning.

When we were hunters and gatherers and walked out of Africa and began to spread across the world, they came with us. They guarded our fires as we slept and they helped us bring down prey in the long dawn when we chased our meals instead of growing them. And later, when we did become farmers, they guarded our fields and watched over our herds. They looked after us, and we looked after them. Later still, they shared our homes and our families when we built towns and cities and suburbs. Of all the animals that travelled the long road through the ages with us, dogs always walked closest.

And those that remain are still with us now, here at the end of the world. And there may be no law left except what you make it, but if you steal my dog, you can at least expect me to come after you. If we're not loyal to the things we love, what's the point? That's like not having a memory. That's when we stop being human.

That's a kind of death, even if you keep breathing.

*

So. About that. Turns out the world didn't end with a bang. Or much of a whimper. Don't get me wrong: there were bangs, some big, some little, but that was early on, before people got the drift of what was happening.

But bangs are not really how it ended. They were symptoms, not cause.

How it ended was the Gelding, though what caused that never got sorted out, or if it did it was when it was too late to do anything about it. There were as many theories as there were suddenly childless people – a burst of cosmic rays, a chemical weapon gone astray, bio-terror, pollution (you lot did make a mess of your world), some kind of genetic mutation passed by a space virus or even angry gods in pick-your-own-flavour for those who had a religion. The "how" and the "why" slowly became less important as people got used to the "what", and realised the big final "when" was heading towards them like a storm front that not even the fastest, the richest, the cleverest or the most powerful were going to be able to outrun.

The world – the human part of it – had been gelded or maybe turned barren – perhaps both – and people just stopped having kids. That's all it took. The Lastborn generation – the Baby Bust as they called themselves, proving that irony was one of the last things to perish – they just carried on getting older and older until they died like people always had done.

And when they were all gone, that was it. No bang, no whimper even. More of a tired sigh.

It was a soft apocalypse. And though it probably felt pretty hard for those it happened to, it did happen. And now we few – we vanishingly few – are all alone, stuck here on the other side of it.

*

How can I tell you this and not be dead? I'm one of the exceptions that proves the rule. They estimated maybe 0.0001 per cent of the world population somehow escaped the Gelding. They were known as outliers. That means if there were 7,000,000,000 people before the Gelding, less than 7000 of them could have kids. One in a million. Give or take, though since it takes two to make a baby, more like one in two million.

You want to know how much of an outlier I am? You, in the old picture I have of you, are wearing a shirt with the name of an even older football club on it. You look really happy. In my whole life, I haven't met enough people to make up two teams for a game of football. The world is that empty.

Maybe if this were a proper story it would start calm and lead up to a cataclysm, and then maybe a hero or a bunch of heroes would deal with it. I've read plenty of stories like that. I like them. Especially the ones where a big group of people get together, since the idea of a big group of people is an interesting thing for me all by itself, because though I've seen a lot, I've never seen that.

But this isn't that kind of story. It's not made up. This is just me writing down the real, telling what I know, saying what actually took place. And everything that I know, even my being born, happened long, long after that apocalypse had already softly wheezed its way out.

I should start with who I am. I'm Griz. Not my real name. I have a fancier one, but it's the one I've been called for ever. They said I used to whine and grizzle when I was a baby. So I became the Little Grizzler and then as I got taller my name got shorter, and now I'm just Griz. I don't whine any more. Dad says I'm stoical, and he says it like that's a good thing.

Stoical means doesn't complain much. He says I seemed to get all my complaining out of the way before I could talk and now, though I do ask too many questions, mostly I just get on with things. Says that like it's good too. Which it is. Complaining doesn't get anything done.

And we always have plenty to do, here at the end of the world.

Here is home, and home is an island, and we are my family. My parents, my brother and sister, Ferg and Bar. And the dogs of course. My two are Jip and Jess. Jip's a long-legged terrier, brown and black, with a rough coat and eyes that miss nothing. Jess is as tall as he is but smooth-coated, narrower in the shoulders and she has a splash of white on her chest. Mongrels they are, brother and sister, same but different. Jess is a rarity, because dog litters seem to be all male nowadays. Maybe that's to do with the Gelding too. Perhaps whatever hit us, hit them too, but in a lesser way. Very few bitches are born now. Maybe that's a downside for the dogs, punishment for their loyalty, some cosmically unfair collateral damage for walking alongside us all those centuries.

We're the only people on the island, which is fine, because it's a small island and it fits the five of us, though sometimes I think it fit us better and was less claustrophobic when there were six. It's called Mingulay. That's what its name was when you were alive. It's off the Atlantic coast of what used to be Scotland. There's nothing to the west of it but ocean and then America and we're pretty sure that's gone.

To the north there's Pabbay and Sandray, low islands where we graze our sheep and pasture the horses. North of them is the larger island called Barra but we don't land there, which is a shame as it has lots of large houses and things, but we never set foot on it because something happened and it's bad land. It's a strangeness to sail past a place so big that it even has a small castle in the middle of its harbour for your whole life, and yet never walk on it. Like an itch you can't quite reach round and scratch. But Dad says if you set foot on Barra now you get something much worse than an itch, and because it's what killed his parents, we don't go. It's an unlucky island and the only things living there these days are rabbits. Even birds don't seem to like it, not even the gulls who we never see landing above the wet sand below the tideline.

North-east of us are a long low string of islands called the Uists, and Eriskay, which are luckier places, and we go there a lot, and though there are no people on them now, there's plenty of wildlife and lazy-beds for wild potatoes. Once a year we go and camp on them for a week or so while we gather the barley and the oats from the old fields on the sea lawn. And then sometimes we go there to do some viking. "Going a-viking" is what Dad calls it when we sail more than a day and sleep over on a trip, going pillaging like the really ancient seafarers in the books, with the longships and the heroic deeds. We're no heroes though; we're just scavenging to survive, looking for useful things from the old world, spares or materials we can strip out from the derelict houses. And books of course. Books turn out to be pretty durable if they're kept away from damp and rats. They can last hundreds of years, easy. Reading is another way we survive. It helps to know where we came from, how we got here. And most of all, for me, even though these low and empty islands are all I have ever known, when I open the front cover of a new book, it's like a door, and I can travel far away in place and time.

Even the wide sea and the open sky can be claustrophobic if you never get away from them.

So that's who I am, which just leaves you. In some way you know who you are, or at least, you knew who you were. Because you're dead of course, like almost every single human who ever walked the planet, and long dead too.

And why am I talking to a dead person? We'll get back to that. But first we should get on with the story. I've read enough to know that I should do the explaining as we go.

Chapter 2

The traveller

If he hadn't had red sails, I think we'd have trusted him less.

The boat was visible from a long way off, much further than white sails would have been against the pale haze to the north-west. Those red sails were a jolt of colour that caught the eye and grabbed your attention like a sudden shout breaks a long silence. They weren't the sails of someone trying to sneak up on you. They had the honest brightness of a poppy. Maybe that was why we trusted him. That and his smile, and his stories.

Never trust someone who tells good stories, not until you know why they're doing it.

I was high up on Sandray when I saw the sails. I was tired and more than a little angry. I'd spent the morning rescuing an anchor that had parted from Ferg's boat the previous week, hard work that I felt he should have done for himself, though he claimed his ears wouldn't let him dive as deep as I could, and that anchors didn't grow on trees. Having done that, I was now busy trying to rescue a ram that had fallen and wedged itself in a narrow crack in the rocks above the grazing. It wasn't badly injured but it was stubborn and ungrateful in the way of most sheep, and it wasn't letting me get a rope round it. It had butted me twice, the first time catching me under the chin sharply enough that I had chipped a tooth halfway back on the lower right-hand side. I had sworn at it and then tried again. My knuckles were badly grazed from where it had then butted my hand against the scrape of the stone, and I was standing back licking my fist and swearing at it in earnest when I saw the boat.

The suddenness of the colour stopped me in my tracks.

I was too shocked to link the taste of blood in my mouth with the redness of the sails, but then I have little of that kind of foresight, none at all really compared with my other sister Joy, who always seemed to know when people were about to return home just before they did, or be able to smell an incoming storm on a bright day. I don't much believe in that kind of thing now, though I did when I was smaller and thought less, when I ran free with her across the island, happy and without a care beyond when it would be supper time. In those days I took her seeming foresight as something as everyday and real as cold water from the spring behind the house. Later, as I grew and began to think more, I decided it was mostly just luck, and since she disappeared for ever over the black cliff at the top of the island, not reliable luck at all.

If she'd really had foresight, she would never have tried to rescue her kite and fallen out of life in that one sharp and lonely moment. If she'd had foresight, she'd have waited until we returned to the island to help her. I saw the kite where it was pinned in a cleft afterwards, and know we could have reached it with the long hoe and no harm need have come to anyone. As it was, she must have tried to reach it by herself and slipped into the gulf of air more than seven hundred feet above the place where waves that have had two thousand sea miles to build up momentum slam into the first immoveable object they've ever met: the dark cliff wall that guards the back of our home. She wouldn't have waited for us to help though. She was always impatient, a tough little thing always in a hurry to catch up with Ferg and Bar and do what they did even though she was much younger. Bar later said it was almost like she was in such a hurry because she sensed she had had less time ahead of her than the rest of us.

We never found her body. And with her gone, so was my childhood, though I was eight at the time and she only a year more. Two birthdays later, by then a year older than she would ever be, I was in my mind what I now am: fully grown. Although even now, many years after that, Bar and Ferg still call me a kid. But they are six and seven years older than us. So Joy and I were always the babies. Our mother called us that to distinguish us from the other two.

Though after Joy fell, Mum never called any of us anything ever again. Never spoke at all. We found her halfway down the hill from the cliff edge, and we nearly lost her too. Far as we could make out she must have been careering down the slope, running helter-skelter, maybe mad with grief, maybe sprinting for the dory with some desperate doomed hope that she could get it launched and all the way round the island against the tide to rescue a child who in truth could not have survived such a fall. She never spoke because she all but dashed her brains out when she stumbled forward, smacking her head into a rock as she fell, temple gashed and watery blood coming from her ears.

That was the worst day ever, though the ones that followed were barely lighter. She didn't die but she wasn't there any more, her brain too wounded or too scarred for her to get out of herself again. In the Before she'd have been taken to a hospital and they would have operated on her brain to relieve the pressure, Dad said. But this is the After, so he decided to do it himself with a hand drill: he would have done it too, if he had been able to find the drill, but it wasn't where it should have been, and then the bleeding stopped and she just slept for a long, long time and no more fluid leaked out of her ears, so maybe it was best that he didn't try and drill a hole into her skull to save her.

I hope so, because I know Ferg hid the drill. He saw me see him, but we've never, ever spoken of it. If we did, I'd tell him I admire him for doing it, because Dad would have killed Mum and then would have had to live with the horror of that on top of everything else. And, even though she's locked away inside her head, you can sit and hold her hand and sometimes she squeezes it and almost smiles, and it's a comforting thing, the tiny ghost bit of her that remains, the warmth of her hand, the skin on skin. Dad said that day was the darkest thing that ever happened to us, and that we're past it, and that now we have to get on and live, just like in a bigger way the worst thing happened to the world and it just goes on.

He holds her hand sometimes, in the dark by the fire, when he thinks none of us notice him doing it. He does it privately because he thinks we would see it as a sign of weakness, a grown man needing that moment of warmth. Maybe it is. Or maybe the weakness is hiding the need, which is something Bar said to Ferg one evening when she was upset and no one knew I was listening.

I'd had enough time to leave the ram, whistle in my dogs from their rabbit hunting and sail the narrow sea mile back home to warn the others long before the traveller came ashore. I could have taken my time, because sharp-eyed Bar had seen the red sails too and they were ready and waiting, which meant that she and Dad were at the shoreline and Ferg was nowhere to be seen. Bar was not sure it was necessary for him to be hiding and watching over us with the long gun because she thought the boat under the red sails looked like the boat the Lewismen used, and that maybe they had just found new sails. The Lewismen were a six-person family who lived five islands north, the closest people we knew, and we knew them well. Bar wore her hair in a long plait that now reached down her back and she would, in time, pair up with one of the boys. This was what she had decided, though being Bar and thus contrary in all things, said she did not see why she should be in any hurry making a choice as to which of the four it was to be. It was not as if they were going anywhere, or as if there were four other girls they might pair up with instead. They were a practical family, and we sometimes joined together to do things that needed more than four pairs of hands, but we never took up their suggestion that we move to be closer to them, and they never thought of moving south. Or if they did think of it, they did not think well of the idea. But they were our neighbours and the only other people within a hundred miles. They were just the Lewismen to us, though they had a family name which was Little. And when the red sails got closer we all saw Bar had been wrong, that it was a different boat beneath them altogether. It was bigger and the man at the tiller had hair that streamed behind him like a banner in the wind. All the Lewismen cropped their hair close to the skull for cleanliness, even Mary the mother did so, though she was in fact more mannish than woman, for all that she'd borne four boys.

The long-haired traveller proved to be the only person on the boat, though at first sight it seemed too big for one person alone to sail. He neatly drew into the shallower water in the lee of the small headland that topped our beach, showing a good eye for a sound anchorage, and hailed us as he dropped anchor. His voice was hoarse but strong, and he said he was alone and wished to come ashore if we would have him. He had things to trade and indeed had been told of our whereabouts by the Lewismen, who he had left two days before. He bore a letter from them, which he waved in the air, the paper white against the darkening sea behind him.

Dad beckoned him in, and he dropped a small dinghy over the side and rowed in to the beach. I helped him ashore, and we pulled the boat above the tideline together.

I felt Dad's hand like a warning on my shoulder, as if I'd been too enthusiastic and unguarded, but then he ruffled the short hairs on the back of my head which he only does when he's feeling kind.

I'm Abraham, said Dad, nodding at the stranger. Call me Abe. And this is my boy, Griz.

Hello, Griz, he said with an answering grin that I liked the moment it split his thick red beard in a flash of white.

And then the dogs barrelled down to surround him before I could ask his name. They barked and snarled and arrived in a great tangle of teeth and tails and then, as he knelt to greet them, the tails started thumping and the snarling turned to whines as each dog seemed to want to be patted and petted by this stranger from the sea. He had the way of dogs, and he told us he had lost his own one only weeks ago, over the side in a storm around the North Cape and he missed him like an arm. She was a half Husky cross-breed called Saga, clever like a man he said, white, black and brown with a brown eye to match her ears and a blue one to match the sky. He'd had her safely kept below in the small cabin, but when he fell and hurt himself as the boat slammed into the trough of an unusually big wave, Saga heard him cry out in pain and – being a clever dog – pawed the latch and came to help him. The next wave took her over the side and he never saw her again, not even a head bobbing on the face of the mountainous seas piling up behind the stern as the wind blew him beyond any chance of finding her. He showed us the scar on his head, and we could see in the gentle way he ruffled the fur of our dogs as he spoke that the hurt was deeper than the healed skin.

Like I said, it was a good story. And – as I found out later – some of it was even true. The dog with one brown eye and one blue being clever as a man, that was true as death itself.

Looking at a new person is not something you would have found as interesting as we do, I expect. You lived in a world full of new people all the time. If you lived in a city, they must have flowed round you like a great mackerel shoal and you'd be just one of thousands or millions, still yourself alone in your own head no doubt, but part of something much bigger too. Here, every fresh face is an event, almost a shock, every new person rare enough to seem like an entirely new species. The traveller looked like no one I had ever met. His long hair, for a start, was thick and wavy and the colour of flames. A redhead. Something I'd read about and seen in faded pictures but never met in real life. The hair was a startling colour, as alien and abrupt as the explosions of orange flowers we found on the other islands, always close to old gardens, flowers my mother called crocoz, when she still spoke. She knew all the flowers and plants. Bar told me she said crocoz weren't native to the islands, but were tough survivors, like us. And he was not just a redhead, but a redbeard too, a slab of a thing that jutted as far down in front of his face as his hair hung behind it. His skin was pale but weather-beaten and his eyes, which peered out at the world from beneath the high cliff of his forehead, were dangerous blue. I don't know why I thought the blue was dangerous, but that was the word that jumped into my head as I saw them. Maybe it was because they turned on me in the same instant and just for a moment, as he caught me looking at him, I saw them without the smile that followed, and I do know I thought it then and that this is not something I added later, after things happened: I definitely thought dangerous blue, but then I thought better and discounted it.

Maybe you, swimming in a world full of difference and choice, were better tuned to believing your gut when it came to people. I had – still have – little to compare people with. So I dismissed the dangerous blue in his eyes when he smiled at me an instant later, and decided it was just different, the blueness, only having seen brown or green eyes before. And when he smiled it was hard to think of those eyes as cold, but maybe that was part of why he was hard to keep a hold of in the mind, juggling the two things at once, the fire in his hair and the shiver of ice in his eyes. The face that was hard as a hammer when it was not smiling and the smile that seemed to warm the world when it found you.

You look like a Viking, were the first words I said to him. And he did. I had seen him, or faces like him, in history books and old pictures, men in horned hats carrying axes and plunder.

And the second words he said to me, this man who had sailed out of the north, were:

What's a Viking?

Which shows that even a question can be a lie if asked in the right way.

Chapter 3

Who are you?

It was one summer while we were a-viking ourselves that I found you. When Ferg began to tease me for wanting to write things down because who in the whole empty world was going to read it, Dad said that it was a natural result of reading so much. He said if you read a lot you start to think like a writer, the same way as if you grow up with a fiddle player in the house you start whistling and learning the tunes without thinking, like Ferg had. I read a lot. I'll get to that. Dad plays the fiddle. I told him Ferg maybe had a bit of a point, since I didn't know who I would be writing for as everyone I knew already knew my story because they're a part of it. But I wanted to maybe keep a diary sort of thing, and so he said then just write like you talk, don't be fancy, and I said but when you talk you do talk to someone, at least most of the time, and he said then just use your imagination: he said imagine a someone and keep them in mind as you write and I thought of you, the boy with my face.

So. You.

You're in a photograph I found in a house up in North

Uist one summer. This time we were looking for parts to scavenge for the windmill that gives us electricity, and Dad knew there were windmills of the same type up near where North Uist is joined to Berneray by the old causeway. We'd sailed the lugger up there and he and Ferg were gutting the turbine off an old fallen mill while I went on the scrounge through the big house on the skyline. We'd decided to camp in the house overnight. It was somewhere we had visited before, solid, stone-built with a roof that still held out most of the weather. Better than that, it had a lot of full bookshelves in it, and a thing called a snooker table.

It was one of the old buildings, a large farmhouse that had been added to over the years, so it sprawled expansively when compared with the other island houses. The walls had once been whitewashed but now little of that remained, so it was a grey house with a dark slate roof and intact glass windows that seemed to watch me approach up the old drive. A car had rotted to the axles and stood amid the long grass by the back door as if waiting to pounce. The door was not as easy to open as it had been when we visited three years before, but I was bigger now and managed to kick it open carefully enough that it would sort of close after us when we left. I left it open as I waited for the dogs to scramble ahead of me and put any waiting rats to flight.

Jip and Jess tore into the house, feet scrabbling on cracked plastic flooring as they went, whining and barking as they always did when excited, but there was no sound of rat murder close or distant, and they soon stopped their noise and trotted back to meet me, looking disappointed and a little bit hurt as is their way, as if I had promised them fun which had not quite materialised.

Something had changed in the house since we had last been there. I couldn't say what it was, and I couldn't see or smell anything that put me on edge, but there was a difference. Before, it had been like many of the houses we went into, damp and mouldering, full of things you could see as poignant or pointless according to your way of viewing the world. Dad, for example, would turn photographs of people to the wall as he passed through derelict houses. I don't know why he did that. He said it was to give the spirits rest, but then he doesn't really believe in spirits, or he says he doesn't. Bar, my sister, has the habit too, and she says it's to stop all the dead eyes watching us.

I don't think she believes that.

I think it's just to try and scare me, because she does like jokes and teasing when she's in a good mood. Apart from the books, it's little collections of things that people used to put on shelves that fascinate me in the empty houses. It's not just the photographs, a lot of which are faded so badly they just look like water-damaged paper now, unless the rooms are dark, but the little china people and the mugs and jugs and bits of glass and wood and stuff. Ornaments. Trophies. Mementoes. Things that meant something to people once, meant enough that they'd make a space for them and display them, something to see every day. We don't really have ornaments, or the time for mementoes. Everything we do is about surviving, moving forward, keeping going. No time for relics or souvenirs, Dad says when we go a-viking, only take the useful stuff. Maybe that's why I decided to write this. A souvenir I can carry in a pocket. Anyway.

The picture of you.

The picture of you was definitely a memento. You meant something to someone, even if it was just yourself. I found you under the snooker table. And the way I found you was strange and secret, and because a photo is a small thing, I took you and no one knew and now you live between the pages of the notebook I write all this in, and until someone reads this, I suppose you're still a secret.

I'd been in the snooker room before, the last time we were in the house. The room was almost filled by the table, which was covered by a dustsheet that had begun to deteriorate into rags at the corners, where maybe a hundred years of just carrying its own weight had worn holes. We'd taken the cover off and rolled the bright balls around the pale green playing surface, trying to bounce them into the pockets. Once there had been poles to hit the balls with, but now the racks that had held them were empty. I had liked the smooth motion of the balls and the healthy smack and clack as they bounced off each other. Not much runs so true in our day-to-day world, patched together as things are. There was a big wall of books to the left side, and a shuttered window at right angles to it. I'd already been through them, but now I was older I went back to see if the grown me would find books I might not have liked the look of last time.

The shutters were stuck shut, and though I could have wrenched them ajar I didn't. Light not getting into the room was helping keep the books safe, and I knew I'd break the shutters opening them which would make closing them harder. Hinges rust, and where they don't screws do, rotting out of old wood that no longer holds them. So I got out my fire steel and lit my oil lantern and used that instead. Then I dropped the fire steel and it rolled under the skirts of the snooker table.

We hadn't found you the other times we were in the house because of the boxes. Someone had stacked boxes of cork tiles under the table, filling the space. They were the same cork tiles peeling off the floor in the kitchen down the hall. What we'd missed was the fact that the boxes were arranged around the edge of the table, and that the centre of the space beneath was empty, like a square cavern, a room hidden within a room. My fire steel had rolled into the narrow crack between two boxes, and I only discovered the secret when I moved one to get at it.

Fish oil lanterns throw more smell than light, but even by the soft glow mine gave off I could see someone had once used the space as a concealed den. It was the reflection of my flame in the glass jars on the opposite side that caught my eye, jars with candle stubs in them. Old candles burn better than the ones Bar makes, so my first thought was to scavenge the stubs, and see if there were any unburned ones left too. So I crawled in, and that's how I found the chamber of secrets.

Someone had slept here, what must have been long, long ago. There was an unrolled sleeping bag and blankets and pillows, and there were books and tins and medicine packs lining the inner wall made by the boxes. A string of tiny little lights was taped all round the edge underneath the table-top, the kind of things you used to put on Christmas trees in old pictures I've seen. But of course they weren't lit and never would be again. It made me think what the hidden space must have looked like when they had been – cosy, cheerful, maybe a bit magical even. On the bottom of the table, which was slate, someone had glued a few of the cork tiles to make a decorated roof to the den, a roof and a pin-board. The board was covered in photographs and drawings.

Maybe it was because of the string of lights that would never be lit again, but I found I wanted to see what the space looked like when it was illuminated by more than my smoky fish oil lamp, which is why I lit some of the candle stubs, and why I lay back on the crinkly sleeping bag. I felt the synthetic filling crumble to dust under my weight, and that's when I saw you. You were the picture right above the pillows. You must have been the last thing whoever slept here saw before they put out the lights, and you would have been the first thing they saw when they woke in the morning. Or maybe that sleeper was you. Maybe this was your den. Either way, you were important to someone. Loved. Mourned maybe. Or celebrated. Or both.

In the picture, you're doing a star jump on the beach, and next to you is a girl who must be your sister. It's a bright sunny day. You look very alike. She's smaller. The picture has caught you both at the top of your jumps, frozen for ever between sand and sky, your arms and legs wide, laughing, eyes flashing with glee. You're looking right into the lens. She's looking at you with a wild and happy look that's so fierce it hurts me to see it. And beside you on the other side is a short-legged terrier also jumping and looking at your face, mouth wide in a smile or a bark. And just as I sometimes think you look a lot like me, the girl looks familiar too. If I squint and imagine, then she looks like Joy might have been. Maybe that's why I took the picture. Because of course I have no picture of my once bigger – but now forever little – sister. Maybe I thought it would help me remember when I get older and more memories jostle in and fill the space that used to be just the two of us. Or maybe the slight likeness is just the reason why I'm writing this to you. All I know for sure is that I've never seen a picture that made me so happy and so sad at the same time. And even without the girl – which is what the picture looks like when it's folded to fit in my notebook, it's you and your dog – like the last happy people at the end of the world, before the afterwards began.

Or maybe I'm writing my life to you because the people I could talk to about things are gone, or can't talk back to me any more. Dad says I think too much. Says I ask too many questions. Says he thinks the lack of answers always makes me unhappy. Don't know if that's true. Do know he hates the asking. As if it takes something away from him, not knowing how to reply. It's just information I'm after, not responsibility for something that is far too big to be down to him anyway. And why does he spend all the time when he's not working or playing the fiddle with his head in a book of facts if he's not looking for answers too?

And that was the other thing I took from the chamber of secrets. The books. Whoever had made the den had a line of books all along one side, and after I'd lain on my back looking at the photographs, I turned sideways and looked at them. I scanned up and down the row of spines several times, and then began picking them out at random, reading the descriptions on the covers. They weren't practical books, the histories or technical things Dad insisted we read so that important knowledge wasn't lost, something I later began to call Leibowitzing: they were fiction, made-up things. It took me a couple of minutes to work out what these ones all had in common, but when I did so it gave me another jolt, a kind of shock that was close to excitement, though I don't know why it should have thrilled me as it did. All the books were about imaginary futures in which your world, the Before, had broken down. They were all stories about my now, the After, written by people with no real knowledge of what it would be like.

I stuffed my rucksack with the book hoard and found another bag in the attic which I filled with the rest. Dad and Ferg tried to make me leave them behind, but they were in a good mood having found two working spare parts from the old windmills, and they also liked the three and a half boxes of old candles that I found under the table. I didn't tell them about the hidden chamber though, and I slid the box back in place after I came out, so if it was your secret place, it's secret still. As far as I know.

That autumn I read all those books, some of them twice (that's when I started calling Dad's obsession with technical manuals and science books "Leibowitzing", after one called *A Canticle for Leibowitz* about monks in a devastated far future trying to reconstruct your whole world from an electrical manual found in the desert). I read the books hoping to find some good ideas, but what I got was nightmares and a kind of sadness that stained my mind for weeks.

I know you can't be nostalgic for something you never actually knew, but it was that kind of longing the books often woke in me. Dad hated me reading them. Thought they were the most pointless things there could ever be, out-of-date prophecies that had turned out wrong anyway. I liked them. Still do. They may not be accurate about life after the end, but if you sort of look sideways with your mind while you read them, you find they say lots about what things were like before. They're like answers to questions you didn't know enough to ask. Though saying something like that to Dad would only make him even angrier. The past's gone. We only have the now he says, and the only answers that are useful are the ones that will help us survive into the future.

Chapter 4

Traveller's tales

The red-sailed stranger told us his name was Brand.

He had a bag with him. It was heavy enough to pull down a shoulder as he walked up the slope past the drying racks that were thick with fish. There was rain in the air, but it had not yet started to fall, and we paused and took the last of the evening sun on the bench outside the main house. He put the bag carefully at his feet as he gratefully accepted a mug of water from the burn.

Good water, he said. Clean and cold.

He looked at the cod and mackerel on the drying racks.

If you've fish to spare, I've something to trade with you, he said.

We have everything we need, said Dad.

You don't have a voltage converter for the windmill, grinned the traveller. But we'll get to that tomorrow maybe. Your friends in Lewis told me you have been having problems.

Dad looked as if the traveller had already got the better of him in a trade he hadn't even said he was interested in. But it was true enough. The windmill was eccentric in its performance, and Dad felt it was the converter and had been grumbling for a year or so about making a voyage to try and find another one.

Hmm, he said. Eat with us tonight. Trade tomorrow. We have time.

There are two questions that Dad, in my limited experience, always asks the few travellers who we meet: is there anyone else? And: are they coming? I never know if the questions are about hope or fear, though the fact we never go looking for ourselves makes me think that it might be the latter.

Before I was born, Mum and Dad did go to the mainland, way down the chain of islands and into the river called the Clyde. They went in one boat and came back in four, each piloting their own craft and towing a smaller one, all loaded with many of the things I have grown up with. My own boat in fact was the one my mum had towed. I always thought she had chosen it from the other ones because of the name, the *Sweethope*. Dad told me later it was because of all the yachts they had cannibalised in the tilted mess of the long abandoned marina it had smelled the least bad when they opened the hatch.

They had made two scavenging trips into the empty city that was once Glasgow, and then never went back. Ferg asked why, once, and Dad just said there was something there that neither could quite explain, but it sapped them and made them very low, so much so that neither could face a third trip, no matter how rich the pickings still were. One of my memories of Mum when she still spoke was her telling me about the huge library she had found there, miles of shelves and doors wide open. They'd slept there for several nights, camped out safely in a fortress of books. She closed the doors to keep the cats and foxes out when they left, and said if there was one thing that might tempt her back it was that. She loved books when she could read, especially stories, and I expect she gave that to me too.

So Dad asked his first questions, and Brand said yes but not many and seemingly less every year, and no, they weren't coming.

And then, without much prompting from us, he began to tell his story. He was a good talker. His deep voice and easy smile drew you in slowly and gently, so smoothly that you didn't know you'd been hooked until his sharp eyes caught yours, and even then it felt like he was sharing something merry with you, like a joke. It never felt like bait.

What did feel like a lure were the temptations he freely unloaded from his bag and laid out on the grass at our feet as he talked, seemingly without any other intention than getting them out of the way until he found what he was searching for at the bottom of the thing. Soon he was surrounded by a fan of interesting stuff, like knives and binoculars and first aid kits – military-looking – and a pair of hand cranked walkie-talkies as well as various tins and bottles whose contents would doubtless be revealed if we should choose to ask.

I know it's in here somewhere, he said, as he carelessly laid another treasure on the ground and rummaged his hand deeper inside the bottomless bag.

We all exchanged glances over his bowed head, but none of them betrayed anything other than interest. Dad's look contained no hint of a warning and the closest to a reservation about our new guest was the wrinkled nose Bar pantomimed at me.

I knew what she meant. He smelled different. Not bad, just not us.

When the world was full, did everyone smell the same?

Or were you all distinct from one another? I can see from the old pictures what a crowd looked like, but I don't know what it smelled like. Or sounded like even. That's something I often wonder about. Did all the voices become one big sound, the way the individual clink of pebbles on a stony beach adds up to a roar and a thump in the waves? That's what I imagine it was like, otherwise all those millions of voices being heard and distinct from one another at the same time would have run you mad. Maybe they did. Anyway. Brand eventually found what he was looking for and pulled it from the depths of the bag with a satisfied grunt. It was a long, clear glass bottle, and he handed it to Dad with a grin.

A guest-gift, he said.

But it came with a warning. We should be careful. It was strong stuff and it would make you woozy if you drank too much of it. Dad laughed and explained we knew all about alcohol since we made both heather ale and mead. But this bottle was from the Before and it was still sealed. It was clearish, like peaty water, and though the paper label was long gone there were embossed letters standing proud around the neck of the bottle that read "AKVAVIT".

An unopened bottle from the deep past is a rare thing. The Baby Bust had a lot of sorrows to drown, after all. But Brand made little of the gift. He had more, he said. He had found a military ship grounded and tilting on a tidal flat in the far north, maybe Norwegian. It had unopened crates full of tinned food – all age tainted – and medical supplies. And the Akvavit. Lots of Akvavit. It was good, he said, but tasted of a herb. Dill maybe. Unexpected but not bad once you were used to it.

We moved inside as the sky began to spit, helping him bring in the contents of his bag and laying them anew across the hearth mat. Then Dad opened the bottle as Bar and I got the supper together, making a stew from salt cod and potatoes. We all had a drink, except for Mum who just sat by the chimney as she always did. Her eyes never left the redhead's face. Understandable, because he was a new thing and she saw few enough of those, though she looked less interested than horrified. Dad explained she had injured herself a long time ago, and Brand bowed his head at her and smiled, raising his glass.

To the lady of the house, he said. *Skol*.

The alcohol made me choke. It felt like flames going down and my first thought was that Brand had poisoned us, but then he drank his glass in one gulp and grinned at me.

Firewater, he said.

That's what it felt like, warming me from the inside. I coughed and nodded.

Better than that, Dad said, looking round at us all. It's time travel.

There was a long pause. I didn't know what he meant.

We're tasting the past, said Bar.

Exactly, said Brand. That's what I always think when I drink it. This is what they liked to drink. This is what the Before tasted like.

Bitter. Harsh. And not a bit sweet, I thought, not like the honey mead we make.

But time travel was not the only magic gift he gave us the night of that uneven trade. He had another trick, which was sweeter and being so was of course the one that snared us. And as with everything Brand did, it came so well wrapped in a story that you couldn't quite see where the danger was.